TAKING A CHANCE ON LOVE

"Would you like to dance?" Steve asked. He looked at her with great intensity, a look that said more than mere words could.

Kate felt the bounce in her heart as she stood up. She twined her hand into his. Then she knew that there would be more than enough time to work through the list of things she didn't know about him.

She melted in toward him on the dance floor. He held her strongly, tightly. He moved slowly but lightly to the rhythm of the music and she felt the warmth of him, the closeness.

She relaxed her head onto his cheek and nestled into him. She felt protected and safe. He was so certain, even now as he moved to the music, leading her and yet doing so in a way that made following him as natural as leaning against the wind. And now a delicious tiredness began at last to envelop her. It wrapped her in a cotton ball of softness and she knew what she wanted now. She reached up, and her fingers found the nape of his neck.

"Take me home," she whispered in his ear.

AMERICAN ICON

Pat Booth

Kensington Books
Kensington Publishing Corp.
http://www.kensingtonbooks.com

To my darling daughter, Camellia . . .
and to Pashy, my wonderful friend

Prologue

Two roads. Two men. Kate slammed her foot on the brakes. The car skidded to a stop. She looked once again in the rearview mirror, as if for the multitude of past memories. But there was no history there, and no cars to hurry this moment. It had to be resolved. But still she didn't know what she would do, although her choice would change her life forever. It seemed the world had gone to sleep in a blanket of whiteness. Before her, the headlamps lanced through the falling snowflakes illuminating the fork in the road.

Kate, the American icon, Ms. Perfection, was copied and idolized by millions. Across the land, Kate wannabes tried to live her every fantasy. They had no idea how hard her journey had been. Ease was the illusion. Difficulty was the carefully kept secret. All her life, by acting bravely she had become brave, but now, as the road diverged in front of her, Kate's courage wavered. Left or right? Should she choose reason or emotion? Loyalty or longing? This life . . . or that one?

She took a deep breath and let it shudder away from her. She was sweating in the warmth of the car, and she wiped her hand across her moist upper lip. Kate had traveled this way a thousand times, but now the fork had meaning. She had never felt so alone and so responsible. It was all up to her, as it always had been, always would be.

Indecision, life's great agony, held her tight in its fist. Then she remembered Macbeth. Whatever had to be done should be done quickly. She banged the car into gear, let out the clutch, and pressed down on the accelerator. The wheels spun in the snow as she hurtled forward.

She reached for the indicator, and she flicked it down.

Would her right turn turn out right?

1

Kate knew she was going to be famous. She just didn't know what for. She leaned against the counter of the kitchen where the food came up and tried to contain the excitement that bubbled inside her. She felt reckless. She was dangerously alive, like a wire in the rain. So this was freedom. It had been a long time coming, but it was better for the wait. At last she was out in the open, staring no longer at that little tent of blue that prisoners called the sky. Her family had been her jail. Her school had been an institution. But all that was then. This was now.

At any moment, somewhere is the intersection of everything. In the spring of '70 that place was a steak house/concert hall/hangout joint whose regulars called it "the store." It was also known as Max's Kansas City. But Kate was not a waitress in the corn belt. She was at 213 Park Avenue South between Seventeenth and Eighteenth off Union Square. She was waiting tables in a city whose residents thought it so special they named it twice. At twenty years old, Kate was on the inside of the underground of New York, New York.

On the other side of the counter, the kitchen hummed with the controlled chaos that allowed creativity and efficiency to live together. Lenny, the chef, orchestrated it, equal parts neurosis, bravado, back-chat, and brilliance.

"Where are my ribs, Lenny?" Kate yelled out cheerfully.

He looked over his shoulder at her and smiled. "Carefully concealed, darling, from where I'm looking."

Kate laughed. She was learning fast, as she always did. A chef was either your friend or your enemy. There wasn't much in between. If he didn't like you, he could effectively put you out of business. Max's was steaks, ribs, lobster, and chickpeas, albeit the best of each. It was *not* sauté of camel's lips and sheep's eyeball terrine. The clientele liked their food quick and their beer cold as the dead. The waitresses who collected from the kitchen first got the big tips and the satisfied customers.

"Lenny! I never thought a boy like you noticed such things."

"I'm gay, sweetheart, not blind."

He clicked his fingers and Kate's ribs were produced by an assistant chef, much like a rabbit from a hat. The massive platters were plunked down in front of her, hot and steaming. In seconds, she would have another table full of happy diners.

"Thanks, Lenny," said Kate, sweeping up the tray.

By her side, Lori sneered her irritation. Kate was pretty, her wide-open Nordic features chiseled like the ice floes and fjords in which her Viking ancestors had sailed. But Lori was a beauty, if a fifties one, her Bambi face coated with a veneer of fake innocence. She curved like a ski slope and pouted with a vengeance, but her glossy-magazine looks were overshadowed by the lamplight personality that shone from Kate's face. Lenny didn't like Lori, because she wasn't bright enough to have a sense of humor. Kate didn't like Lori because Lori didn't like Kate . . . and Kate, whose self-respect was high, didn't do people who didn't like her.

"Some people always get to cut into line," whined Lori.

"Lines are for cutting into," snapped Kate. She felt the flash of temper that each day she vowed to control. There simply wasn't any point complaining in this life. Nobody wanted to know about grievances. They were simply the sound in the forest unheard, the bleating of sheeplike losers. Her childhood had been one giant excuse to moan, but she had kept the angst inside. She had stored it up in the way that a dam caged water, and she let it out bit by bit to fuel the energy that would carry her to the places she longed to go.

Bearing her tray like a trophy, she turned and made her way through the cavernous open-plan restaurant. She unloaded her ribs at a table for four amidst a shower of come-ons, fending them off goodnaturedly. At the same time she checked the glasses, remembered they were out of ketchup on the middle banquette, and took in the brilliant Pucci colors of the models at the next table. Times were changing. As she had walked to work that afternoon, past the drab buildings of the Village, it had been a stock-still black-and-white world, the blank page of a child's coloring book. But at design school that morning all the talk had been of the English artist Bridget Riley and of geometrical op-art sculptures, black, and white maybe, but *mobile*. There had been talk, too, of Peter Blake and his bright *Babe Rainbow*. Everywhere, movement and color were replacing the immobility and Eisenhower-Kennedyesque monochrome that had held the world by the throat since the war. Everything was happening at once, and it was happening here.

Her customers called out to her from every side, waving, laughing, shouting, gesticulating. Nobody was angry or impatient. Nobody cared. Everyone knew they were in the right place at the right time, and that even the losers would win in the end. To have discovered the gravitational pull of Max's was enough. To have passed the needle-eyed doorwoman; shed ties, suits, and all semblance of straightness; and avoided the upstairs Siberia was to be more than halfway to fame.

Somehow, Kate symbolized the place. It wasn't just the way she looked. Bowie, Lou Reed, and Iggy Pop, eyeing each other jealously at an up-front picture window banquette, outdid her in the big, round mascara'd-eye contest. Patti Smith, Debbie Harry, and Alice Cooper, far whiter shades of pale, effortlessly anemic, won the ghostlike makeup war. Against the scene-making glitter of the glam rock, Kate looked almost mainstream in her knee-high soft leather boots, her beltlike miniskirt and the wide, low-slung black leather band that competed with it.

But everyone could relate to the confident bounce of her walk. The take-me-as-I-am strut was instantly recognizable. Because this was Max's, the counterculture hot spot where in the words of Jimi Hendrix you could "let your freak flag fly." Here everyone was in nervous retreat from normality. All were pushing boundaries, throwing up safe, middle-class back-grounds and parentally planned futures to lose themselves in the excited panic of the here and now. Drugs and drink fueled the dangerous process that was definitely not for sissies, despite the androgynous look of the players. But the natural spontane-ity and self-confidence that Kate possessed, self-esteem that didn't come from a pill or booze bottle, was a rarity much ad-mired.

Jeff Niccora, the manager, hurried past, smiling frantically. "A zoo this evening," he muttered happily to Kate.

"Hungry animals," she agreed as she rushed on. But it wasn't so much zoo as theater. The Velvet Underground were sound-checking upstairs for the first of their two sets. Everything else was entertainment too. It was the beginning of restaurant as spectacle. This was far from the quiet, cozy places where middle-aged people ate French cuisine and had conversations. The back room, where Andy Warhol and his superstars held court at the round table, was so wild it was known to the waitresses as the punishment room. It was where you got sent to serve when you had done bad things like eat the shrimp. Actually, Kate quite enjoyed it. The night when Iggy rolled in broken glass and was taken to the hospital by Alice Cooper covered in blood was one she wouldn't forget! As if to emphasize the stage analogy, the burgundy laser beam homed in on her. Outside it ran for seven blocks in every direction, but then it arrowed in through the plate glass window and was finally refracted by a mirror into the infamous back room.

Kate turned in its red beam, stopped for a second, and surveyed her turf. Her tables were all filled, apart from the small one they called a deuce by the potted areca. Instinctively, she looked toward the door for new customers. She saw him immediately. He was good-looking . . . very. The man who was with him was not. First she noticed his suntan, which had to be from abroad because the spring had been cold and overcast in Manhattan. Then it was the deep-set blue eyes that matched her own. He wore a mauve shirt of what might have been expensive curtain material, silk something or other with bits in it. It had a small, rounded collar supporting a knotted black string tie. His pants were well cut and flared, and his jacket was sculpted to his lean frame, double-breasted, waisted, and square of shoulder.

He looked around him with interest, but not trepidation. Kate sensed he was a regular who had not been in during the three weeks she had been working there. He must have been on vacation. She wouldn't have forgotten him. Mickey Ruskin, the owner, was talking to him now, familiar, friendly. He turned and pointed to Kate's deuce. The man nodded, accepting it. Kate felt the beat of a drum somewhere inside her. It was only now that she realized that she had been hoping for this. Why? Lots of customers were cute. Usually she was too busy to think about it. But now she was thinking of what Frankie was always saying to her. It's fate, Kate. Kismet, Kate. And the guy was walking toward her.

"Hi," he said, sensing that she would be his waitress, smiling at the fact.

"Hi!" she said. "Two?"

She wondered why she'd said that. She didn't usually state the obvious.

"Yes, just two," he said. The men sat.

First impressions kept piling up. He wore a wafer-thin watch in a faded shade of gold that indicated twenty-two carat. It looked like a Vacheron. He was too quietly sure of himself to have made his money the old-fashioned way, by inheriting it. And he was an earner who had not used his hands for the process. They were smooth and brown against the white of the menu, delicate almost, sensitive anyway, his nails well manicured. His trio of words had hinted at some southern gentleman drawl, filtered through the subway grilles and air conditioner vents of the dirty city.

"I'm Kate," she said. "I'll be your waitress." Once again, Kate wanted her words back. She *never* said that. Of course she would be their waitress. What the hell did he think she was going to be? His pet Martian?

He smiled as he read her thoughts through the slight blush that had appeared on her high cheekbones.

"I'm Peter," he said. "I'll be your literary agent."

His friend laughed. Kate felt a frisson of annoyance. She didn't like to be the target of jokes.

Retaliation was as instant as Kate was immediate. "Uh-oh, I feel an agent joke coming on," she said. She was unable to stop herself. If Peter the literary agent was like her, and not a fan of humor at his expense, she might as well forget him . . . despite the blue eyes that matched hers, and the funny feeling in her stomach.

He groaned. "Can't we do Poles or attorneys?" he asked plaintively. But there was interest in his expression. He wanted to hear her joke. And it wouldn't matter if it was good or bad. She had chutzpah, and her mouth was more attractive than anything on the menu.

"How many agents have pacemakers?"

"I don't know," he intoned, holding his head in his hands as if he were in pain. "Look, what about a knock-knock joke? OK, OK. How many agents have pacemakers?"

"None," said Kate. "You have to have a heart to have a pacemaker."

He laughed openly, not at all offended. His whole face was involved. Kate took in his features. A neatly broken nose saved him from clinical perfection, and his teeth, while even, were no piano keys. There was a bit of stubble that he had missed shaving, right up by the left nostril, which offset an otherwise almost clinical cleanliness. He smelled of Eau Sauvage. Kate, who noticed everything, recognized it instantly. She was aware that things were going well. Inside her, adrenaline was marching, if liquids could march.

Then, quite suddenly and before she could react, he reached out and he seized her hand. He pulled it toward him, and her whole body had to follow. It was not done roughly. It was done insistently, and his ambush, as ambushes should, possessed the element of surprise. Kate's hand, captive, was thrust beneath his jacket. He pressed it against the exact place where his heart should be. And there it was, against her flat palm, warm and beating. She felt the flush explode on her cheeks like a firework in the dark night sky. It was so fast, so incredibly intimate, so natural. He had his revenge for her joke. It was her total confusion. He had caused her heart to beat at twice the rate of his. Then he let go of her hand, but he didn't let go of her eyes. He seemed constructed of cool. "You've touched my heart," said his eyes. "Have I touched yours?"

Kate stood up straight. She couldn't do anything about the blush. "That's the last time I tell an agent joke," she said at last.

"I was hoping you had some more," he said. The feelings crackled between them. *Feel my heart again. I liked your hand against it. I like you. I like you very, very much.*

"Can we order some drinks?" said the friend, who was out of

the emotional loop. "I'll have a Beck's. What are you having, Peter?"

"I'll have a Bud," he said. He looked at her closely and smiled.

"I'll get the food order later," said Kate, and fled.

She hurried to the bar. She felt strangely elated. Who was Peter the agent? It seemed important to know. Frankie was already at the bar, waiting for drinks.

"What's the matter?" said Frankie instantly. She knew her friend that well. "Don't tell me an artist has actually paid a check."

"Oh God, Frankie. Disaster," said Kate in a voice that sounded more triumphant than worried. "Over by the wall. The guy at the duece by the areca."

"Which one?" said Frankie, peering over Kate's shoulder.

"The *cute* one, Frankie!"

"Oh. OK. The suntan. The mauve shirt. What about him? Never seen him before."

"Darling, we've only been here three weeks."

"Who is he?"

"Some literary agent. I told an agent joke. About them having no hearts, and he grabbed my hand and stuck it on his chest to show he had one. Neat move, huh?"

"Expect you at breakfast, shall I?" said her roommate with a laugh.

"For*get* it, Franks. No way is he going to ask me out."

The bartender arrived. "A Beck's and a Bud, please," said Kate.

"Spike his drink. Loosen him up," said Frankie. "Remember the piano teacher at school."

"He passed out," said Kate.

"Yeah, well, I was in there with a chance just before he did. There was a two-minute window of opportunity there, I swear."

Frankie's forlorn expression faded into the memories. For a

second, Max's receded, the noise, the thump of the Velvets tuning up, the clatter of glass. Escape had been too recent and too
welcome for looking back. But Frankie was still here, with her,
and Kate couldn't imagine a time when she wouldn't be by her
side. It hadn't been just a boarding school. It had been more
like a concentration camp. "This is a place for girls who have
had difficulty adjusting," the headmistress had said on that
cold, grim day five years earlier when Kate's cold, grim parents
had finally washed their hands of her. She could still smell the
chill of those corridors, the forbidding dormitories, the soulless
classrooms. The private schools could neither tame her nor
break her adolescent spirit, and the parental love that would
have enabled her to be just a bit like other girls of her age had
been absent from birth.

But just when she had been at her most lost and lonely, she
had found Frankie. A friend in need had discovered the friend
she needed. Together they had fought the world of authority-for-
authority's-sake. When they couldn't beat it, which was nearly
always, they had retreated together into the fantasies that now
they were busy turning into reality. Art had been their drug. For
Frankie, it had been the dream of photography. For Kate, it was
an open-ended love of style and design, and her rare talent for
improvisation and creation that defied categorizing, and might
always. When that institutional torture had finally ended,
Frankie and Kate fled together to New York, the wicked city that
her parents and schoolteachers would have expected her to go
to. So now, waitressing in the evenings, at design school by day,
Kate was the uncaged bird she was meant to be.

"Mamacita, who's the agent at Kate's deuce by the areca?
You know him?"

Ellen, the waitress who had just arrived to pick up some
drinks, flicked her head in the right direction, as Kate emerged
from her past.

"Oh, that's Peter . . . Pete someone. Repped one of the Joan

Didion books. Used to come in here with a Pucci model, one of those starved ones, all acid colors and white lips. Looked as if she'd given her last pint of blood. Haven't seen her around for a bit. Probably died. He's kinda neat. Sorta straight. Why?"

"How old?" said Frankie, doing the legwork for her friend.

"Twenty-five, maybe more. Comes across older. Good tipper. Guy he's with is one of his authors. You fancy him?"

"Nah," said Frankie, winking at Kate.

"Drinks are getting warm," said the barman.

"Thanks, Nick," said Kate, picking up the tray. She flashed him a smile and headed back to the table. "Wish me luck," she said over her shoulder to Frankie. She left in her wake her laughter, a chuckling, gurgling sound made completely original by its out-of-control quality.

"What's up with Kate?" said Mamacita.

"Oh, nothing," said Frankie. "She's just fallen in lust."

2

Kate stumbled up the narrow stairs to the fourth-floor walk-up, balancing the brown paper bag with the half-liter mugs of coffee, and the one containing the doughnuts. She hadn't bothered to tie the laces of her sneakers, because she'd been desperate for a caffeine jump start to her day. Tripping was a distinct possibility. She had had two hours' sleep. Somehow, she just had to wake up. Being out of Folger's had been the last straw. It was her job to buy it. So she had thrown her black velvet cape over her nightie and made it to the corner deli as best she could. Frankie, the wise virgin, had got to bed early . . . two A.M. Because today, Kate had promised to model for her, and Kate was little more than a dead woman walking.

Outside, New York had been bright and sunny. Now Kate, vampire-white from last night's makeup, was actually looking forward to the Transylvanian gloom of the two-room whose view was the building's bowels. One, she had to get back to bed. Two, she had to get some coffee in. Three would look after itself. She fumbled with the keys for the several locks. The door, battered and scarred from a thousand inexpert assaults by burglars too out of it to get in, finally yielded to her.

"I'm back," she yelled.

She slammed the door behind her. For a second she leaned there in the doorway, trying to get her head straight. She had a bit of a hangover, but not much. It would be gone by lunchtime. They always were.

"Get in here," shouted Frankie from the bedroom. "I want the postmortem."

"Oh, Frankie," groaned Kate. "Coffee first."

She stumbled into her friend's room and collapsed on the bed, somehow managing to unload the drinks and the doughnuts on the bedside table. Frankie went for the doughnuts first. "Great!" she said. "You remembered my chocolate one."

Kate lay back on the pillows and closed her eyes, only opening them to steer her coffee safely to her mouth. "Oh, God, that's better," she moaned. "That is *so* much better. The moment I'm awake I'm going straight back to sleep till lunchtime." She tried it anyway, knowing that it wouldn't fly.

"Kate, you *promised* you'd do my photographs. The project is due tomorrow. You *have* to do them."

"OK, OK. I know. I'd just forgotten. Don't panic. I'll do them. You don't think you could stretch the theme to, say . . . 'Sleeping Beauty,' do you? Like, I just sleep and you just photograph. You could shift me about. . . . I mean, you'd draw the necrophiliac interest . . . and . . . and . . ."

"For*get* it, sweetheart. Live model. Moving model. Vivacious, energetic, full-of-life model, all made up and pretty and humming with . . . well, with caffeine or whatever it takes."

"All right. All right. I'm beginning to feel better. I think my day is starting. Hell, what was I *doing* all night?"

"I'm waiting for you to tell me. Like . . . did you?"

"No," said Kate. "Didn't."

"Ah," said Frankie, "serious."

Serious. It was, in a way. The tiredness lay on Kate pleasantly, like a warm, soft blanket. She snuggled her head into the pillow and sleep plucked at her. He had asked her out in the restaurant, the old what-time-do-you-get-off routine. That line was like a joke that only worked when the right person told it. He had said he was going down to the Village because Dylan was playing at a place he knew, and Joan Baez was going to be there, and it might be fun. He was intending to take extra batteries for his pacemaker and a penknife so she could change them if things turned nasty! It had all sounded so easy. He was going anyway—did she want to come along for the ride?

"We went to some dive in the Village. Dylan was playing."

"I thought you didn't like Dylan."

"I liked him last night."

"I wonder why."

"You know—this sounds really weird—but somehow I think of Peter a bit like a father I never had."

"Five years older, and he's a *father* figure?"

"It's not to do with age. It's attitude. He's so grown-up. In command. And he was protective. Like the place was semiprivate. There was a hassle at the door. I mean, there *would* have been a hassle if it had just been me and you. But they all seemed to know him, and he went out of his way for everyone to know me. It was like a father's being proud of a daughter."

Kate was intrigued by the idea. It had only just come to her. Her own father had been a reverse model of fatherhood. He had led his own life in the distance, and his boisterous child had been nothing but a distraction from his diary-ruled accountant's life. Method and Methodism had been his mannered existence, and Kate's mother had fitted into it as snugly as a tax return into a brown envelope. Kate could never understand where or how she had learned that life didn't have to be like that. Not from carbon-copy correct school, or from the slide-rule-straight family friends and their calculator-conceived children. All around her, like walls, from as early as she could remember, had been the constraints of dates, deadlines, neatness, and order. But she had known, somehow, that there were other ways to spend your life, and so she had learned the techniques of family guerrilla warfare. Every example she was set, each pointless rule she was forced to obey, became in her soul a contrary commandment. *Don't talk so much! Talk till their ears fall off. Don't laugh so loud! Deafen them. Fear God! Enjoy jokes about Him.*

But Peter had been like a father should be. He knew so much, and yet he showed by example. He knew everyone, but he didn't drop their names. He was on his way up, but the ride was fun, not deadly serious. Kate had felt so comfortable with him. She had held his hand and hugged him when he made her laugh, which was often, and he hadn't gotten the wrong idea . . . or the right idea. And when, finally, at the end of one of the happiest evenings of her life, he had leaned over to kiss her, it had been on the cheek and not on the lips. But his lips had lingered, and he had held her hand tight. He had thanked her for a wonderful time, and his breath had made her ears fizz with an excitement that no kiss could have matched. Could it? He would call her. She knew that. He hadn't even had to say that he would.

Kate looked at the telephone.

"When's the rematch?" said Frankie, in mind-reading mode.

"Whenever."

"Hmmm," said Frankie.

"What do you mean . . . 'Hmmm'?" said Kate.

"Nothing." Frankie paused. "Well, I mean, fathers . . . and you didn't . . . ," she continued hesitantly.

"He'll call," said Kate. She was certain of it. Sometimes she wondered where she had found her belief in herself. She hadn't gotten it from her tax-deadline dad, or her Sunday-school mom. They had believed in God but not in her. Prostitution, drug addiction, prison . . . whichever might be worse . . . had been their scarcely veiled predictions for her. Private-school teachers had concurred. So had the battery of counselors, educational psychologists, and ministers who had been consulted about her behavior. Frankie had been the first outside believer. Before that, Kate had been her very own congregation of one. She had learned one thing: if the person who believed in you was you, then everyone else was, in Dylan's words of last night, "blowing in the wind." Peter would call because he had the good taste to like her. If he didn't, then she had got him wrong. It would be his loss, and it would be her gain that she had discovered his lack of taste so early on.

"Jeez, Kate, can you lend me some of that arrogance? I'm clean out of it."

"It's not arrogance."

"Well, whatever it is, can you please put it to work getting ready for my photographs? From where I'm sitting you look like a ghost who's seen a ghost."

"Watch me," said Kate. Whether the caffeine had hit her or the challenge had, she was on the move. Her tiredness lifted like a sea fog as the wind of her famous energy blew through her. Frankie smiled as Kate bounded from the bed. She knew her friend so well. Veiled criticism got her going like nothing else. Perhaps that was Kate's simple secret. She had learned how to turn adversity to advantage.

In the tiny bathroom, Kate worked fast. She had this planned. Despite her apparent spontaneity, the truth was she planned most things. That much of her father had stuck with her. She had seen the power of organization and recognized that what was organized didn't have to be dull. Beneath the white makeup, her cheeks were pink. Now she highlighted them with rouge. Her beehive hair had survived the two hours of sleep, and a couple of chopsticks and some quick manipulation produced a Suzie Wong hairstyle. She did a neat little mouth, making hers smaller, and by shadowing out the Scandinavian cheekbones she soon had a rounder, more oriental face. She slipped out of the bathroom, out of Frankie's sight. In her own room, she pulled the dress she had made out of the cupboard. It had been a piece of red satin in a Chinatown store, but she had sewn it by hand into the simple sheath dress that was half Betsey Johnson, a quarter Hong Kong bar girl, and twenty-five percent Kate Branagan. She slipped on a tight bra to slim down her infrastructure to oriental proportions, and didn't bother with panties. If you wanted to seem wanton it was better to feel it. She had dyed some tights blood red to clash with, not to match, the dress, and she had painted an old pair of black leather shoes bright red with nail polish. On the front of them, in black, she had drawn a Chinese character. According to the man in the Chinatown store, it was a command to the reader to perform an anatomically impossible act. God, in Kate's anarchic life, was in the detail.

"Are you ready for me?" she shouted.

"Sort of," called Frankie from the other room. As Kate slid in, walking already in chip-chop steps to get into character, her friend's back was toward her. Frankie was fiddling with the old tungsten light she had found in an upstate garage sale. That light, and the used Pentax Spotmatic with the 28mm lens, would have to handle it. Frankie turned around, and her face filled with equal parts wonder and gratitude. There, in front of her, was the shot. In a black cellar with a box Brownie it would have been in the can. The model was picture-perfect, Macao on Fifty-third and Second. Once again, tired but happy, over the top but straight down the line, larger than life but full of it, Kate, her very best superfriend, had saved the day.

"God, Kate, you look wonderful. I have never *seen* a more believable prostitute."

"Well, darling, you know what Miss Kent used to say about my career prospects. Maybe we should send her a snap for the school notice board."

They laughed together at days that had been so deeply un-funny, times that had been made bearable by their friendship.

They were on their way, now. They were going places . . . good places, fun places, sophisticated places . . . but above all, places far, far away from where they had been. Frankie would become one of the best photographers in New York. Kate would be one of its top designers. They had no money, but chic was cheap. They had no contacts, but charm was magnetic. They had no experience, but God, were they young!

"OK, how do you want me?"

It was Frankie's turn. The big four-poster wrought-iron bed might at a stretch have been Boxer Rebellion Peking. The bare white walls of the rented room were an anonymous enough background for the blood-red harlot who now lay across it.

"OK. Chinese mother, Danish sailor dad. That's your character. There you are, on your own. This kind of life is just for now. OK? You just need a little money to turn yourself around. That's it, pout a bit, a bit more . . . that's nice, that thing you're doing with your thumb."

The click of the shutter, the heat of the harsh light, the stark iron of the bed that framed the shot, had their own harmony. Frankie directed well, but Kate acted better. She hadn't been taught, but she knew instinctively how to do it. It was like everything: nothing taught, everything learned. It was her knack. It was Kate. Sometimes it bothered her. Where was the focus? Shouldn't you have a direction, like Frankie? She wanted to be a photographer, a fashion photographer. That was a narrow ambition with a circle around it. It had boundaries and goals with names like *Harper's Bazaar* and *Vogue*. In contrast, Kate was a loose cannon of skills, a scattergun of purpose. She did everything well, and perhaps therefore would do nothing brilliantly. If she did worry, she worried about that. But for now, she was living where she liked to live best . . . in the moment. She could be a model, just, but catalogue not catwalk. So she made believe as models did, and Frankie's skills did the rest.

"Hang on," said Frankie. "Got to reload."

Which was when, with perfect timing, he called. It did not occur to Kate that it was anyone else. As if daring fate, she picked up the telephone and said before anyone had spoken, "Hi, Peter."

"How did you know it was me?"

"I'm psychic."

"You're amazing. What are you doing?"

"I'm lying on a bed dressed up as a Chinese hooker."

"I'm afraid I'm going to have to ask why."

"Why don't you come over and find out."

"I haven't got any Chinese money."

"No Chinese money, not my number-one guy," said Kate in her best chop suey Mandarin.

Somehow it was typical of him, of his sense of fun, of his efficiency, of his ingenuity, that when he arrived at her apartment an hour later, Peter had in his hand a sheaf of notes bearing a likeness of the head and smiling face of Chairman Mao.

3

Donna slammed the door. She ran across the red-carpeted hallway and took the dark, wooden steps two at a time. The tall, thin building was wrapped around her, tourniquet tight. It was stifling her. She needed to get out onto the street with its tourists and terracottas, its bells and its belfries, to the slapping sound of water lapping the sides of the gondolas. Above all, she wanted to escape from the emotional desert that was Paul and from the row they had just had. She had to baptize herself in the liquid of Venice, a place to which people were parvenus . . . and passions the only interesting things they possessed.

As she hurried downward, her heart pumped with anger. Tears of frustration welled in her eyes. Rays of light lanced in at her from windows revealing surprising roofscape vistas. It was raining. The ancient tiles wore a sheen of wetness. Clouds hung low over the city, coating it in a mood of marble gray. But Donna didn't mind. Here, the climate was a subtle kind of revelation. It was the gift Venice received from the sea, that

changeable carpet of magic to which the city was but an exotic
beach. She wanted to open herself to its unstable brilliance. She
wanted its impression stamped indelibly on the unexposed film
of her future.

A maid, white-aproned and uniformed in black, wafted across
a wide landing and was gone like a half-imagined spirit. Donna
continued her descent, beneath gloom-framed mirrors that reflected her furious sadness. God, what had she been doing all
her life? What had she been thinking? Most of all, where the hell
had all her feelings gone? She nearly missed her step as her
sneakered foot slipped on the shiny wood. She was in flight
from Paul, but it was far more than that. She was also in retreat
from herself. She was fleeing from mediocrity, from middle-
class order and the thoughtless conformity of her medical-
student life.

She slowed. She was halfway to the ground floor. She looked
up the somber stairwell, half expecting Paul to have followed
her from their room. But there was only the quiet of the old
building. Paul was not there, *The Anatomy of the Brain* in his
hand, muttering about rain and umbrellas. Paul was not there,
the reproachful look of an unwalked dog on his face, the desire
to have the argument's last word shining dully in his eyes. Paul
was not there, calling her back, summoning her to senses that
right now she wished to be rid of forever. And Donna was glad
that he was not there. Because it meant she could escape.

The realization of freedom, as it does, quieted the urgency of
her desire to be free.

She had reached the first floor. A large sitting area contained a
grand piano, heavy Florentine furniture, potted plants, and a dark
painting of the school of Bellini. A series of writing desks had
been placed along a wall long before the rude intrusion of the
telephone. Donna walked to a brown leather chair and sat down
in it. It seemed possible she was the first person in fifty years to
have done so. From downstairs the smells of breakfast . . . cof-

fee, croissants, toast, bacon . . . rose to tempt her. She realized she was hungry. But she was also angry. The argument still reverberated, but her irritation was fading. She had voted with her feet. Paul, for all his desire to be right and his certainty that he was, would have been shaken by her disappearance. Right now, he would be sitting there, waiting for her contrite knock on the door. He would probably be practicing his expression of brave politeness, the more-sinned-against-than-sinning look that he did so well.

Donna took stock of her situation. Practicality, learned over a lifetime, did not vanish in an instant. She had scooped up her bag as she left. Inside it, she had her passport, money, even her return ticket. All that was left in the room were underwear, a couple of pairs of blue jeans, makeup, etc. On their Cook's City Break week, they had not expected invitations to the gilded aristocratic palazzos of the Grand Canal. Good! Whatever she decided to do, she wouldn't have to hurry. Most important, she didn't have to go back and hammer on the door she had just slammed shut on her past.

She got up, walked downstairs, and picked her way through the tourists in the lobby, noticing the gleam of interest in the lazy Venetian eyes of one of the younger receptionists. Now that fury was fading she could see the fight in better perspective. As always, the surface argument had concealed deeper issues. Paul and she—hard-working, obsessive, dedicated to their careers in medicine—were similar people. He had been her boyfriend because she had recognized a brilliant surgeon in embryo. Paul had been, still was, a deeply predictable and reliable member of the human race. And those were qualities that Donna had been taught all her life to respect, if never quite to love.

But from the moment Donna had arrived in this city she had been invaded by its influence. In its sophisticated charm and spontaneity, its gaiety and grandeur, and even its decorous

decay, Donna had been confronted by the aspects of her character that she lacked, and didn't want to lack. Paul, in contrast,
had been somehow inoculated against the magic of Venice. He
had simply dismissed it as a "place living on its past," taking it
for granted that that was a bad thing. Maybe analytically, intel-
lectually, he was right. But now Donna no longer cared about
such things. She had been touched by the city directly, in the
gut and in the heart. Already the brain and its silly mind, the
organ she had lived by, was fast becoming an irrelevance to her.
They had fought about Venice, but what they had really been
fighting about was themselves. Donna had changed; he had not.
It was as simple as that.

Donna smiled as she realized she no longer cared. She didn't
mind anymore about Paul and his pompous opinions. She felt
sorry for his "sensible" worldliness and wall-to-wall pessimism. Now the only thing that mattered was her and the new
person she vowed to become. In that small hotel room a few
moments before, she had experienced some kind of renais-
sance. Paul's negativity may have been the midwife, but Venice
had given life to it.

Leaving the hotel, she turned left. Immediately there was a
bridge to cross, and a canal under it, narrow as an arrow to the
heart. A gondolier loitered with his vessel, as unmarked as a
London cab, beneath the bridge, and Donna paused to watch
him. The *gondolieri* had much in common, their huge hands and
lithe legs, their effortless cool, the agility and intricate paddle-
work with which every part of their bodies were employed to
prevent the collisions that threatened every moment of their day.
As their snippets of opera filled the acoustic air of the thin canals,
the gondoliers were revealed for what they were—sellers of
dreams to those wealthier but no more worthy than themselves.

Donna walked on. In the admiring eyes of the men in the
street she saw herself. Hers was an Italianate beauty, the
aquiline nose, generous mouth, eyes dark but bright, brown
hair streaked with gold, the full but flowing contour of hip. It

had been like coming home as she had climbed aboard the *vaporetto* at the tiny airport and found recognition in the eyes of the natives. She knew from psychology that people were drawn to their doppelgängers, and the feeling had been mutual. Now everything was a voyage of discovery about herself, as the city peeled away the onion skin around her, exposing her to strange new elements of herself in the same way that the years, the seasons, and the sea had worn away the surface layers of the buildings among which she walked. Stucco, concrete facings, exposed bricks, made a patchwork quilt of their facades. The hand of design seemed to be everywhere. It was all but impossible to believe that this "damage" had not been carefully planned. Green-and-black shutters, peeling paint, were the background to carefully tended window boxes whose bright flowers were the only garish colors to be seen. Shades of terracotta were endless. Hues of yellow, gradations of gray and marble, merged in secret harmonies. Some bits of buildings were held together with rusty ironwork, like people by bandages, like unhappy marriages by promises, convention, and children.

The streets were impossibly narrow, some hardly umbrella wide. But Donna was used to jostling now, the enforced intimacy that bound the bit players into the wider plot of the city.

A left, a right, a bridge, an alleyway, and the tourists had thinned out. The melange of aromas . . . espresso, expensive perfume, May methane from the stagnant canals . . . was a symphony of smell. Donna breathed it in, flaring her nostrils and closing her eyes so as to miss nothing. She felt as if she had a lifetime to make up for. In all her twenty years, she had experienced nothing but mundanity. Now it was different. She didn't mind that the soft rain was beginning to flatten her tousled hair. She welcomed it. She was feeling at last. She wanted to burst into song and let her emotions out. She hummed some bars from *La Traviata*, giggling to herself, not caring how trite it sounded.

Suddenly, she found herself alone. She had traveled a bridge too far, a turn too tight. The chatter of the crowd was finished. There were no bodies to thrust against her. The bridge ahead was deserted. Donna looked around in surprise. How could it have happened? How could this oasis of loneliness exist so close to the jostling tourists flowing through the narrow streets? Donna was strangely alarmed. She looked back. Which was the way back? The buildings stood tall over the still blue water of the deserted canal, their shutters and boathouse doors closed. There was no life in them. And then Donna felt the sense of danger.

She was alone. Again, she realized it. The metaphor was too close for comfort. If you followed your dream and ignored the prosaic dreams of others, you came to be alone. And loneliness was not for the weak. You had to be strong to choose passion. It was the timid who sought refuge in reason. Once again, Venice was playing tricks on her.

A bell sounded somewhere. A call to an early mass? The striking of the hour by some clock? Donna took a deep breath and walked on. She crossed another bridge, and then walked down a long alleyway that brought her to the water's edge where there was no bridge. She looked back, in the shadows now but facing the blue of the waterway. And then she heard the steps. Their sound was amplified, funneled toward her by the narrowness of the street. Someone was coming. The footsteps stopped, as if the unseen person had sensed her presence. There was something animal about it. Donna suddenly had the ridiculous feeling that she was being stalked. Death in Venice. Yes, the city had an easy relationship with death . . . with change, decay in all its forms. She began to retrace her steps. She had traveled from romance to fear in a hundred paces. Once the Pandora's box of emotions was opened you could not, apparently, select the ones that would be set free.

There was a corner ahead. She turned it bravely, her chin high. An old man, bent over his stick and breathing hard from the exertion of his walk, watched her closely. Donna felt the tension leave her. He nodded at her as she approached. He knew she was lost. He knew the question she would ask. He knew the answer. Lost tourists in Venice always asked the same question.

"*Scusi,*" said Donna. "*San Marco?*"

Again, he nodded. He made some gestures. Right. Left. *Una ponte.* It was simple, he said, and it was. In less than three minutes, Donna was knee-deep in the pigeons of St. Mark's Square. She breathed a sigh of relief. She made her way down through the Piazzetta to the waterfront. People teemed around her. Then, in front of the grand old Hotel Danieli, she saw the water bus station for Murano. It was a place she had wanted to visit, the island where Venetian glass had been made for hundreds of years. It was half an hour's ride by boat. Donna bought a one-way ticket.

She sat down and looked around her. The world had never appeared like this. It was as if she were looking down on herself from the heavens. She was at the heart of a great adventure, the heroine of an unscripted drama in which from now on everything was possible.

She thought again of Paul. He would not have missed the *free* breakfast. He would be eating it this moment, sensibly, so that he could save money on lunch. It was clear to Donna now that he was the last person on earth that she needed. If two people were the same, then one of them was superfluous. A group of hippies in Afghan coats and crushed velvet pants, thin and androgynous, stood near her. They would have been appalled by the comparison, but they reminded her of Paul. Hippies were dedicated followers of fashion; Paul was cast in the unbreakable mold of middle-class molasses. The trouble with both was that you could predict everything they would think, do, and say. Vietnam? The hippies would be against. Paul . . . "a necessary evil." Sex? Hippies for. Paul . . . "an unworthy pleasure in the absence of commitment." Drugs? Hippies . . . "Getting high is what it's all about, man." Paul . . . "Only a fool would experiment with . . ."

Donna's thoughts were interrupted by the thud of the *vaporetto* banging into its parking space with Venetian panache.

"Murano," shouted the man controlling the gate.

She stood in the prow of the vessel like a figurehead, with the tangled hair of Medusa, and she felt the thrill of the past as it merged with her present. Venetian galleys had set themselves against this same head wind as they had fled from Attila the Hun. Donna sensed the turmoil and excitement as the centuries telescoped away. Marco Polo had started here, and found China and the jewels and spices of Kublai Khan. She knew, now, how the great explorer must have felt . . . certainty, elation, gratitude for the chance to squeeze the fruit of life until the pips squeaked. If he could do it, she could do it. History was alive inside her. No longer was it dead passages in dull books.

Seagulls, known by the locals as the pigeons of the lagoon, soared overhead on the thermal currents. Donna's spirits flew with them. Her life was beginning and it didn't matter where it would end. In the old days, the brave mariners had wondered about sea monsters and whether they would fall off the edge of the earth when the sea ended. Then, as always, it had been the young who had been the optimists; the older, the more cautious.

From time to time the water bus was passed by the varnished motorboats of the trio of grand hotels—the Gritti Palace, the Danieli, and the Cipriani—ferrying the Louis Vuitton mariners to the airport or to personalized excursions. It would be rocked, too, by the wakes of the expensive water taxis. Donna didn't mind that she was not rich. She felt sorry for the rich in a way, because they were nearly always old and wanted to be young. But youth was the only thing they could not buy.

And so, past the private islands with their boarded-up homes, past the canal markers, away from the hazy beauty of the now distant cityscape, Donna traveled onward to Murano. At her back was her inspiration. Before her was her destiny.

4

Donna walked along the canal that cut Murano in two, past the glass shops selling the brightly colored Bambis she had owned as a child. To her right was a corridor. Above it, in faded capitals, a sign read "Fornacia di Giovanni Ferali." On a whim, she walked into the alleyway. Above her was a black-painted, metal cantilevered ceiling covered with grime-coated glass. She knew she had entered a glassblowing studio. All along one wall were brick kilns. It was dark but far from gloomy, dirty but ordered . . . a foundry rather than a fancy workplace. As she approached, Donna could see the furnaces. The corridor opened out into a large space lit by sparse neon. It smelled not unpleasantly of sulphur. It was hot, and the sources of the heat were everywhere. Small doors were open on a dozen furnaces arranged in a circle in the middle of the room.

Five or six men were hard at work. Although they concentrated on their jobs, they had time to joke and back-chat among themselves in the manner of true professionals. Each had a task. One man carried a long rod at the end of which a bright marmalade ball of glass glowed fiercely. He laid it before another, who sat at what looked like a metal desk. In a series of deft movements, this worker took the glass and began to mold it rapidly with ancient tongs that looked to Donna as if they had been designed for medieval torture.

One man in particular caught her eye. He stood out from the rest. His blond hair was tied in a ponytail. A thin film of sweat shone on his naked torso, like rain on the wet tiles of the roofs of Venice. She saw him first from the back and the side. He seemed to be burying something in a burning furnace. He wore sandals, and shorts gathered up around a tattered belt. His legs were muscular, but he was tall and therefore graceful, not merely powerful, as he extracted molten glass from the fire and twirled it in the air flamboyantly. Donna wasn't quite sure if the movement was done to cool the glass or to assert his mastery over it. She reached up to tidy the disaster area that was her hair. As he turned, she saw a sunburned face with lips parted to reveal far better teeth than an Italian should have. He had a stubble of beard, and although he was grimy he looked, somehow, not dirty. The thought that he was very good-looking seemed almost superfluous. As she watched him, he walked to a bench and laid the globule of glass on it. His concentration on his task seemed total.

Then, quite suddenly, he looked up at her and winked.

Steve had noticed her the moment she arrived. This foundry was not open to tourists, and he liked it that way. But occasionally one strayed in. Like this one—the sort that would always be welcome anywhere. A very pretty girl. He rolled the molten glass ball on the table until it was long and thin. Then, because the girl with the beautiful, interested face was frankly staring at him, he winked at her. She looked away at once. He had expected her to do that, and he smiled. The nearest worker, and Steve's friend, wrinkled his face in the smirk that Italians had invented and the Venetians perfected. He had seen it all.

Steve picked up the shears and cut the glass away from the rod to which it had been attached. She wasn't actually blushing, but across the flickering twilight of the foundry he thought that the color on her cheeks had deepened. Again he smiled at her. Again she looked away. But then she looked back, and she, too, smiled. Steve held the rod of glass by the tongs now. He waved it through the air until it was long and rounded at the top, like a thick whip bending as he manipulated it. It began to lose its straightness, then recovered it again. The girl, despite her aquiline features and straw-colored, highlighted hair, was almost certainly an American. She had that directness that Steve's countrywomen couldn't hide, a vulnerable bravery, a determination, the legacy of feminism, to give little away to a man.

She would think he was Italian, of course . . . a potential comedy of errors that would never reach the stage of reality, because he and the girl would not meet. He turned back to the job at hand. The glass waited for no one. Like a surgeon, he probed at the cooling substance with tongs, drawing it into shape, flattening it, making it narrow at the top, wider at the bottom. Then he moved toward his friend seated at the bench nearby and laid his glass like an offering before him.

"I think that one is for you," said Sergio, cracking a sad, snaggletoothed smile and emitting a tubercular laugh.

"Yours, Sergio. She has your name written all over her." Steve spoke in Italian, enjoying the joke and the closeness he shared with these workmates who had become his friends.

"It's not me she stares at," said Sergio ruefully. "Only the fat, ugly ones stare at me, and then only on Sunday in church when I have my suit on." He shook his head with mock pathos.

"But the Chianti loves you, Sergio. And the glass. Who needs women?"

He looked up, and she had gone. Steve felt a pang of sadness, the feeling of might-have-been. He was vaguely aware that that feeling was the cause of his looking at his watch; the prime

mover of the pang of hunger in his stomach; the reason he
reached the sudden decision to take his lunch break a bit earlier
than usual.

Donna sat on the wall by the *vaporetto* station, her legs dangling above the blue water. She had bought her ticket. It was
over. She felt a sweet misery that she had missed something,
someone, but it was already merging with the gratitude that once
again she could feel. She had walked the streets of Murano in a
dream, and even slipped into a small church and fantasized
about a fairy-tale marriage to a glassworker. She smiled at the
thought. At this very minute, he was only a hundred yards from
her. But Donna was wrong about that. He was less than one.

"Hi," he said.

She turned. He stood there, wearing the same shorts but with
a T-shirt, plain white. He seemed even taller.

"Hi," she said at last. It was all Donna could manage,
through the shock.

"I saw you in there," he said. He was diffident, almost shy.
He was being very polite, not wanting to irritate her. His body
language was rich in reserve. He was standing over her and yet
holding back, a willow bent by the wind.

"You're not Italian," she said.

"No. American. I've been here a few months. When in
Venice . . ."

"You looked Italian." Donna was acutely aware that she
sounded as if she was accusing him of something . . . false pre-
tenses?

He laughed. It was an extraordinarily pleasing sound. His
whole face relaxed into it.

"I'm sorry to disappoint."

"No, no, it's just . . . I mean, well, you know . . ."

"I know. Italian until proven otherwise. The tourists don't
usually work the glass. They just buy it."

Donna started to get up, then she started not to.

"Do you mind if I sit down?" he said.

She nodded helplessly. Then she felt her grip coming back. She wasn't used to losing it for long.

"You're English," he said simply. The conversation was already underground. This surface nonsense was background music.

"Yup," said Donna with a smile, tossing her hair. "A tourist who buys the glass."

"Are you here with your family?"

His attractiveness was quite scary. Was it his American accent? Donna's Americans had been mainly in movies. She had never seen one like this, whose skin glowed. She breathed in secretly, trying to capture the scent of him, like an animal might at this stage of a meeting. He had just asked her if she was single. They were at that stage already.

"No," she said, more than happy to move it along. "I came with a friend. A fellow medical student. I just had a great big row with him, actually." She laughed bravely.

"My father's a doctor in Pennsylvania," he said. "And my mother, too, only she doesn't practice."

"Goodness. And here you are blowing glass on Murano. Are they pleased about that?"

He turned his head to one side. She was very natural, forthright, and she had cut deep early. It was far too soon for that to be a fault. He really liked her smile, and the way she dangled her legs as they talked. She looked Italian too, not at all English. Her hair was a beautiful mess.

"Pleased? No. Bemused, confused, lots of soul-searching of the where-did-we-go-wrong kind. You know the kind of stuff. Parents want you to be happy, but they want you to be happy their way. I guess it's a bit of a leap to realize that there are different kinds of happiness."

"Yes," said Donna. "You know that in your head, but not in your heart. Deep down you feel that what makes you happy is what would make everyone else happy if only they were honest enough to admit it. Leads to misunderstandings."

"Like to your row?" At last he had got back to Paul. She had wondered why he had let that one go.

"Oh, that . . . him . . . ," said Donna, waving her hand in the breeze as he had waved the long, thin piece of glass.

"No offense to your parents, but doctors and would-be doctors can be very dull people, the sort of people who don't understand places like Venice."

He nodded, totally in tune with her thoughts. "Oh yes, I know the attitude. The place is old and dirty, going nowhere, all about art and dead science. All about death, period, while doctors are obsessed with fighting death, keeping things clean, mending things, shoring them up. Venice is a bit indigestible for the medical profession, I suppose. But not for you, apparently."

"I love Venice," she said, her voice quivering with intensity. "It has changed me totally. I never thought a mere place could."

There was a silence.

"Were you waiting . . . I mean *are* you waiting for the *vaporetto?*"

"Yes," she said.

"I wondered if perhaps . . . Look. Do you want lunch?"

"Sounds like the best idea I've heard all day."

5

"So you passed on Harvard. That was brave," said Donna, laughing. She would rather have given fingers than miss out on London University.

"Yeah." He smiled. "Breaking it to Dad was the hard part. He was valedictorian of his class at Harvard Med School. It was quite funny. I waited until this long lunch we were having was just about over and I told him. Then I said I had to leave in a hurry for this meeting. He asked the waiter for a couple of cognacs. I said, 'No, sorry, Dad, I really have to go.' He said, 'They're both for me!' The Rhode Island School of Design wasn't exactly Ivy League. In Pennsylvania, it didn't earn a lot of brownie points."

"So Harvard actually offered you a place and you turned it down?" Donna was impressed, among the other emotions. Lunch was going very well. "So then what?"

"Three years at Rhode Island. Then a Corning Museum of Art grant that allowed me to come here."

Donna broke off a piece of bread, ran it through the small pool of virgin olive oil on her side plate, and chewed it slowly while she watched him. His eyes met hers, questioning, exploring. He was very cool. Very laid back. Yet he wasn't boorish, or boastful. He had turned down the academic hot spot to follow a dream. He had an obsession, yet he came across as relaxed. It was an attractive combination.

"What about you? Are your parents pleased with a med student?"

"They're both dead," she said quickly. Then, wondering if that sounded callous, she softened it. "Five years ago. I'm over it now . . . mostly."

"I'm sorry," he said.

It was the traditional response, but he sounded sorry. He even looked sorry.

"It was hard, I suppose, but we had a big family. Lots of aunts and uncles, and there was quite a bit of money. So Mum and Dad never really knew I'd be a doctor, although it was always sort of assumed I would be. Dad was a solicitor. Attorney, you'd say. Mum was basically his wife. I mean, that's what she did." She laughed, determined not to let sorrow, or its remnants, spoil this great lunch.

But the spirits had been summoned. What had her parents actually been like? What had her childhood been like? It was so difficult to know, memories being so unreliable. She had been given everything on one level, little on another. Emotions had been scarce. Food, warmth, clothes, holidays plentiful. There had been clockwork mealtimes and safe discussions of small earthquakes in Chile and the state of the back-garden roses. She hadn't been a totally seen-but-not-heard child. However, her opinions, when expressed, had usually been met with tolerant smiles or glazed expressions of the you'll-grow-out-of-it variety. It had been safer to think by numbers, and she had tended to do that, even though the "numbers" had been long and complex. She had been fiercely studious, and her school reports had been read with reverence, but kissing and cuddling had been off the menu. And in her home there was never a mess . . . physical

or emotional. Messes had simply not been tolerated. The final
mess had been totally unpredicted. Her parents were killed in a
train crash on their way to visit relatives in Leeds.

"When I was leaving, I saw you talking to that man who sat
at the bench. He was saying something about me, wasn't he?" It
was a playful question, dispelling the vaguely disturbing mood
that memory had dredged up. For a second he looked marginally uncomfortable.

"I was just turning the glass," he said, grinning. He knew he
would have to be honest with her. She demanded honesty. He
really liked that.

"And?" said Donna, smiling, persistent.

"Oh, he said something about there being a beautiful girl
watching us."

"Watching you."

"Whatever." He laughed easily, as the temperature notched up.

Donna sipped her wine. The soup had been magnificent, thick
with chunks of fish and mollusks, a meal on its own. Next, there
would be cuttlefish cooked in its own ink. He had insisted she
try it. Somehow he seemed more European than she was.

"OK," said Donna, "what were you thinking when you
winked at me?"

The sapphire blue of the canal a foot below their alfresco
table sparkled up at her, engagement-ring perfect. What would
Paul be doing? Sitting in the Piazza reading a book on genetics,
sipping a cappuccino, and wondering why the hell he had come
to this tattered city. The hell with him. In terms of Donna's own
personal time, he was as ancient as Hippocrates.

Steve paused, and smiled at her question. Then he raised his
fist in the air and said, "I thought, 'Yes!'" He shook his fist to
emphasize the word, and Donna saw the quintessential nature
of his Americanness. It shone through his patina of European
sophistication like a ray of light lancing into the water of a
Canaletto. He had said earlier that he had done crew at prep

school. With his physique he could have rowed for Harvard against Yale. Like his father, she could not entirely suppress the sense of waste that he had not done so. But immediately, she recognized the thought as a vestigial remnant of the old Donna, the one she had so recently buried. She was enough of a realist to know that the limbs of that creature would be constantly creeping from the crypt.

"OK," he said. "My turn. What did you think when you first saw me?"

Donna felt the blush coming up, the same one his wink had caused. But she had started this. She couldn't back down.

"I thought—OK, I suppose I asked for this—I thought you were pretty cute-looking, if you must know. I didn't think you were American."

Now the blush rose like the thunder of a Mandalay dawn.

"Didn't think I was just some draft-dodger waiting out the war blowing glass?"

"Did *not* think that," said Donna. For the very first time, she felt him go on the defensive. Vietnam must be a big one for Americans, especially for those living in Europe. She said nothing, sensing that he would.

"I had a good number. A really good one, in the lottery. They have my address. I'd go if I had to. It's a crock, but I'd go. But I wouldn't enlist. When you want to spend your life making things, you don't want to blow things up. I think communism is wrong, but I don't think it's evil. Ho Chi Minh isn't Stalin. I for sure wouldn't want to die for the capitalist thieves who run the South. I'd rather sit right here and look at you, and wonder whether or not you're going to make up with your medical student."

With the charm of the deeply self-confident, he slipped from a conversational cul-de-sac to the emotional freeway that could be "them." They both knew the stakes; they both knew what was happening. He was twenty-three, she was twenty, and this was called falling in love.

"My things are in the room at the hotel," she said simply. She was aware that life came down to logistics in the end: Where were your things? Where should they be? How would they get there?

The waiter, as waiters did the world over, sensed the crucial moment in the conversation. He swooped down and swept away the large soup plates. *"Scusi, scusi,"* he muttered, with no hint of genuine apology.

Donna's things were left, metaphorically, in the room.

"Fritto misto," said the waiter. *"No! No! Seppie al nero."* He banged his head with his hand theatrically to emphasize his mistake.

"What about you?" she said, trying to sound as if she didn't care. "I mean, do you have a Paul equivalent?"

He laughed at her openness, approving it. "A Paul equivalent? Let me see. No. No. No male English medical students lurking in the wings! There was a girl from Sorrento who went home two months ago and sent me a postcard. Murano isn't exactly swinging London. Not until you arrived."

"God," said Donna. "I am as far from swinging London as the devil from grace. I'm a fifties girl in a sixties town."

He spoke quickly, as if the moment might pass, but he leaned forward as he spoke, and reached across the table. He touched her arm. It was the first time their skin had met, and it was already sealed in memory.

"If you don't want to go back to that hotel room," he said, "you can stay with me if you like. You get the bed, I get the couch. I can sleep standing up," he added as an afterthought.

But it was not about his sleeping that Donna was thinking.

"I call it *The Vein of Life*," he said. The piece of glass stood rectangular, green, and moumental, lit by the early afternoon light that shone through the shutters from across the canal.

It was veined like gold in a gold mine, and there was a narrow window toward its top, one that you could see through. The surface was gouged out in smooth tracks, like the sandy bottom of a recently dried river. Donna looked at the glass and then at its maker. It was difficult to tell which was the more beautiful.

He could see from her expression that she was impressed, that it had touched her. And she could see in his eyes the pleasure that her admiration gave him. Donna didn't know what to say. She allowed the beauty to sink deep inside her. Glass for her had always been, well, glasses and bowls, containers that contained things. This, however, was a sculpture. The work felt old, enriched by time, and yet it was also the most modern piece she had ever seen. The longer she stared at it, the more subtle shades of green were apparent. She could actually feel it, and she knew, then and there, that at some time in the future she would recognize that this was the moment she had fallen in love.

She splayed out her hands and laughed to convey her awe. They had walked the few hundred yards from the restaurant and crossed a bridge to the ancient house with the green-and-white-striped awning that contained his apartment. She had longed to get inside, to see revealed the secret parts of him.

The old building, hopelessly and gloriously decayed, had a door that belonged to some Byzantine tomb. A slab of marble topped it. Square columns defined it, and the damp, agreeable aroma of old wood had surrounded them on the narrow stair. He had opened the door for her, and held back to let a lady go first. There had been *The Vein of Life*. Donna had been swamped by beauty and originality, those inseparable partners that separated genuine art from utilitarian craft.

He hurried her on to the next visual feast, seemingly concerned that she would gorge herself on beauty . . . as they had on the bread and soup, leaving little room for the fish and ice cream. And there was another one—*Many Short Stories in One,* he said it was called. A thin sheet of glass in the same green as *Vein,* the aquamarine of canals caught by the sun in certain aspect, was separated from another of the same size but of opaque frosted glass color by four short metal columns. This sandwich of glass was held together by four knobs of the kind that fixed the terminals to car batteries. These were black. A square area of shimmering shades of green floated seemingly free in the body of the "sandwich."

"Oh Steve, it is *incredible,*" she had to say. "They both are." She turned to look at him, and she saw way past his smile and into his soul. Even now, in the dawn of their relationship, Donna was vaguely aware that here were the rivals. The girls from Sorrento would be postcards on the breeze. Steve was in love with glass. And glass, it seemed, loved him right back. How much love would there be left for a mere person?

"Look, would you like some coffee? I've got a proper machine."

"I'd love some."

"I'm glad you like the work," he said, out of sight, in the small kitchen.

"Who wouldn't?" she called back as she moved around deliciously. She picked up a book of Hesse's, *The Prodigy;* a leather-bound volume in French, Proust's translation of Ruskin's *Stones of Venice;* a silver-framed photograph of his parents. There was so much to know about him. He spoke French well enough to read Proust's translation of an English book! Harvard would have been so easy for this one. He was part of his times enough to be into Hesse. His parents, suited and solid, posed for the photographer in the upstanding way that they would pose for life. They looked like grown-up versions of him, like parents should, and for a single second Donna wondered if he would grow to be like them. Was his art obsession a passing whim of youth? At twenty-three, was he still in rebellion against mortgages and dinner parties, country

clubs and Phi Beta Kappa? The *Vein of Life* screamed, "No!"
So did *Many Short Stories in One.*

Paul would vote for a "phase." Donna could all but hear his
gloomy prediction: "Probably end up a stockbroker."

"Where will you go," she asked her unseen friend, "after
Murano?" How soon? How far? Where will I find you?

"Probably Paris." It would have sounded very Hemingway
but for the fluent French. "The Corning will just about stretch
to L'École des Beaux-Arts."

He was back before she had time for any more secret investi-
gations.

"Aimez-vous Proust?" she said, testing him.

He didn't fall for it. "Yes," he said, laughing. "I do speak
French. And Italian. And yes, I do like Proust. Did you know
his brother invented the prostatectomy? They called it a
Proustatectomy."

She laughed. He was very sharp . . . and neat. The tray he
carried was immaculately laid out. Two little cups were brim
full of black espresso. Two biscuits and two small macaroons
lay on a plate. With the Herman Hesse it was somehow very
Zen here in the heart of Byzantine Venice. Steve would take
himself wherever he went, to Paris, to Murano, or no . . . back
to Pennsylvania.

He put the tray on a table and flopped down into a wounded
dark brown leather couch. It seemed to swallow him whole.
"Or I could go to Berkeley and work with Lipofsky. That's really the other option."

She sat down beside him, swimming in the formidable comfort of the upholstery. The room was still revealing bits to her,
some black-and-white photographs by J. H. Lartigue—a dog
jumping, fashionable women walking in the Bois, a little boy in
an inner tube floating on a pond.

"So this is where you'd sleep?" she said. It was a statement
of claim. He had made an offer. Was it still open? "I think who-

ever gets the bed has the worst deal. This sofa is *so* comfort-able." She felt her doubt. Was she being too forward? No. It was her way, and she had to be natural, not that she could be anything else.

"Nothing is set in glass. We could swap around. Does this mean you're my houseguest?"

"I think it does," said Donna with a slow smile.

"A definite maybe?"

"Definitely." She still had the tiniest escape clause.

It seemed extraordinary. There had been, in quick succes-sion, a row, a walking out, a discovery, of herself . . . of him. Where would it all end? It was impossible to say, but with a thrill of excitement, Donna felt the beginnings of delicious speculation.

"Your work means so much to you, doesn't it?"

He lay back and stretched like a sleepy cat. "Everything, so far. My uncle had this friend who had a studio in the Hamptons. I saw him work once with glass. It was instantaneous. Love at first sight. I didn't believe it was possible."

"Neither did I."

He didn't get her double meaning. In fact, he misunder-stood it.

"You felt like that about medicine? Don't tell me your uncle took you to see someone cutting up a corpse!"

"No, no," said Donna, laughing too. He was almost childlike when he laughed. She thought for a second. Why was medicine so important to her? Although it felt good to do good, it was more than that. It was something about control, and beating the odds. Even though you had to lose against the Grim Reaper in the end, the game was fascinating and the opponent worthy. She was brilliant at dissecting, and in life you fell in love with what you were best at. So Donna dreamed of being the first woman president of the Royal College of Surgeons. It was an ambition every bit as strong as Steve's desire to make beautiful objects in glass. She would follow it anywhere, as, apparently, he would his dream. Different dreams. That was the nub of it. Would their dreams collide? Would one dream survive the collision, the other be ruined by it? Or would there be dents and dings and addresses exchanged before each drove off in separate directions. Nobody hurt. A meaningless meeting in the dreamscape, an accident on the freeway of life.

The thought needed a sip of strong espresso to go with it.

"I think it's in my blood," she said, answering his question as she sipped the delicious coffee.

"Great-grandfather, grandfather, an uncle on my mother's side. All doctors. I was doing science anyway at the time of my parents' accident, and it had always been sort of assumed that medicine was what I'd do."

Steve looked deep into Donna's eyes. It was time for American-style cutting to the chase. He had come to realize that he did not want to let her go.

"What about the medical student and your things?" he said.

"I'll go across on the *vaporetto* this afternoon and pick them both up," she said. "I'm sure you'll be very comfortable on this couch with Paul."

For half a second his eyes opened wide in alarm. Then he was laughing again and so was she . . . because this whole thing was suddenly deadly serious.

6

Donna woke to the sound of the bell. She had slept deep. Now, in the middle of the night, she didn't know where she was. Then it filtered back to her, as slowly as sand filled the hourglass of memory. She was here. She was really here, sleeping in Steve's bed. Moonlight arrowing in through the open window quivered on the bedcovers. She could hear the lapping water of the canal. The chime was finished; it was a small hour. She shifted on the soft mattress. God, it was almost unbelievable, and the excitement pricked her sleepiness. She buried her head in the pillow and breathed in. But it was no good. She couldn't find the scent of him. He had been the perfect gentleman, and part of her had liked that even as another part had longed for the perfect wolf. He had asked her if she had everything, a glass of water, enough blankets, whether she wanted the window wide open or half closed. Was she sure she was all right? He would be in the next room if she needed anything. If she needed him! It was ridiculous, wonderfully so.

She ran over the mad events of the past important day, and they all added up to magic. Everything had worked as if

planned by the hand of the Master Designer. When she had returned to her hotel in Venice, Paul had been out. She had simply
packed her few things, left him a note saying "Good-bye," and
left. The bill had been paid in advance; she owed him nothing.
He would have a single room for the price of a double, and a
place to practice his pessimism in private. Good-bye, Paul.

She looked across the moonbeams at the door. When would
it happen? It would, but when? She felt the tingling of desire.
What if she got up, and tiptoed across the room, and opened
that old door? He would be lying there, completely asleep, exhausted. And she could touch his bare shoulder. He would stir.

"I need you," she would whisper. And he would hardly wake
up. *Forget it,* she thought. The impossibility of it mocked her.
The thoughts turned in her mind, then turned again. The door
would not be locked. What was the problem? Why the hell
couldn't she do something spontaneous for a change? She
knew that he wanted her. She had seen it in his eyes. Donna
smiled in the darkness at the memory of the way he had looked
at her. And then, perversely, she thought of her parents. What
would *they* think about this brand-new Donna? They would be
horrified, of course. Or would they? Who knew? Maybe they
would be thrilled. "Thank God, Donna is finally learning to live
a bit," they might think. "She was always far too sensible for
her own good." How much of what you thought others were
thinking was the projection of your own ideas?

She swallowed. Would he sleep naked? Yes, she thought, he
would. Projection again? *Stop it, Donna! Go to sleep and
dream of your seduction.* But she looked again at the door and
was glad that she could see it in the moonlight.

Donna felt the chill run through her. She wrapped the bed-
cover around her. *Damn!* Now she was cold as well as trussed
up tight in the canvas of her moral straitjacket. She curled into
a fetal position to preserve body warmth. Why couldn't she be
like everyone else? The sexual dark ages were history. This was

just sad! Now she even had an excuse. She should stand up, wrap herself in a blanket, slip into the next room and say she was cold, did he have any extra covers? It was the straight-forward, sensible thing to do. He would want her to do that, a man like him. His parents would want her to do that. Hers would. It was no big deal. It was just two people who liked each other, two friends dealing with a problem of body temperature. Oh, *yes!* What a crass come-on it would be! A cold girl in the middle of the night. Can I jump in with you? Oh, dear *God,* how obvious it would be! And the next morning, over break-fast, he would know her for who she was . . . a romantic billiard ball on the rebound on the green baize pool table of life. So much for moral grandeur and healing the sick, lofty ideals, and being "different." She would be as significant to him as the girl who had sent the postcard.

But, in the way that life worked, she got up nonetheless. She wrapped the blanket tight about her and made her way like a sleepwalker toward the door. She was past thought. It didn't matter. This had to be done, apparently. Control was remote. Autopilot was on. It was with the fascination of a completely detached observer that Donna walked toward the door and opened it. She didn't know if he was awake.

"I'm cold," she said into the darkness.

"Come here," he said, his voice husky.

7

Spring 1970
The Hamptons

"There! Stop!" yelled Kate.

Peter stomped on the brakes, and the '65 convertible Mustang squealed to a stop in the country lane. The leafy trees arched over them, their branches meeting overhead. Birds sang in the sudden silence. Kate pointed excitedly to a gate. It was painted white and framed by a hedge, as the trees had bordered their road less traveled. Through the gate's chipped, wobbly woodwork a patch of white could be seen. It was the Hamptons in late spring, and Kate had never been there before.

"What are we looking at?" asked Peter indulgently. At twenty-five, he had never thought of himself as world-weary. But seeing life through Kate's champagne-bubble eyes made him seem so by comparison. Everywhere she looked, she saw magic—invented it, perhaps. All was new when he was with her. It was like being a foreigner in a strange country. It was like seeing through the eyes of a child. Any old artist could find beauty in a sunset; it took Kate to find it in a loaf of stale bread.

That was why being with her was so special. That was why his feelings were teetering dangerously toward that thing called love.

"Here! Come on! Let's explore it. It looks deserted." She grabbed his hand and pulled him out of the car, not minding that it was blocking the lane. If someone came up behind they could toot. Nothing was a big deal. And if they banged into the back of the Mustang . . . well, bridges should be crossed when you came to them.

Kate opened the gate that hung by a thread to its post. The path to the cottage was overgrown. Wildflowers grew everywhere. To the right were the remains of a greenhouse, hardly a pane of glass uncracked. There were uncountable shades of green, patches of sunflowers, a rusting bicycle abandoned among them.

"I would die, *die*, to live here," said Kate. "Can you imagine it? Can't you just feel it!"

The sun beat down on their backs now, out in the open, warm but not hot. The birds were deafening.

"Look. I see a gravel path, with frames and roses over the top . . . or honeysuckle . . . no, that lavender-colored stuff, what's it called? Quick! Quick!" She snapped her fingers at him for the answer, she wanted it so badly. Peter laughed. She was so impetuous. He was far from slow, yet slow as a tortoise relative to her.

"Wisteria?" he tried.

"Absolutely! Wisteria! And great wooden barrels, black against the white of the fence. Real barrels, ones that have been used for beer. Impatiens, pansies, ivy cascading down them like foaming ale!"

She turned toward him. She seemed to have blossomed with enthusiasm, as the flowers she imagined would grow some perfect spring. She wore a big, floppy straw hat, and the house and its quiet clapboard, the sparrows nesting in its eaves, the long grass, had all been constructed by God as her backdrop. She wore no makeup, but her eyes were still big, and her mouth was somehow wider, her teeth whiter, as she dreamed her contagious dreams.

She ran up to the front door and Peter trailed behind her, amused, slightly worried that they were trespassing.

She peered in at the windows. "It's empty. No furniture. God, look at that fireplace! That floor! Oh, it's heaven. Imagine it polished. Imagine a fire burning in winter. Why isn't there anybody *here?* It's a crime."

"Hey, Kate, slow down."

But she wasn't slowing down. She was trying the front door, and, of course, it was unlocked. The hallway, small but perfectly formed, showed a miniature grand staircase. The wood, old and scratched, was mahogany. Even Peter could see that it would sand into a dream of shining magnificence. But Kate had liftoff. She ran from room to room like a child in FAO Schwarz, but the words that ran from her mouth in a torrent were far from childish. Peter had already acquired the habit of listening carefully to Kate. He did so now.

"Stippling. That's what to do with the walls. Old yellows, and eggshell colors copied from real eggs. Browns, and greens, warm yellows and terracotta. This room would have rough-stippled walls, the paint laid on with carpet tacked on a piece of wood. Then the windows . . . paisley blinds, and the color of the blinds picked out on the same material lining the corners of the room. We'd find a beautiful turn-of-the-century fireplace, very simple, and then above it, oh, something modern. And then you mix old and new. We could have one of those great Barcelona tables, all square and chrome, and an Eames chair sitting on an old Persian rug. It would be so fabulous, so different. Can't you see it, Peter?"

Peter didn't even laugh, because he *could* see it. He could actually see what she was talking about. It was 1970, and the times really were changing. Music had led the way. Design was way behind. But as Kate spoke, he could see the way forward. The only thing that was dead was convention. The only thing to be thrown away was the rule book. It was at that moment, as the sun streamed into that empty living room, that Peter Haywood began to realize that Kate was not just a fascinating, beautiful, infinitely charismatic twenty-year-old. She might easily be the most interesting person he had ever met.

"Do you think it's for sale?" said Kate.

She noticed the way he was looking at her.

"What are you staring at?" She laughed. She wore her thoughts on her tongue.

"At you," he said. It was catching.

She lowered her head and looked up at him from beneath her bangs. "What are you thinking?"

"I'm thinking . . . I'm thinking . . . I'm not sure that I dare say what I'm thinking."

"Are you *ashamed* of what you're thinking?" She cocked her head to one side and hooked a thumb in her belt. She stuck out one bell-bottom-jeaned leg, well aware that she was being flirtatious. Her hat tilted deliciously.

Peter swallowed. She was impossibly, dangerously attractive.

It was an invitation, of course. He walked the few feet toward her. She waited for him, smiling.

She stood her ground, not moving. He reached forward and tilted up her chin and she didn't resist. But her smile was changing. Her lips had opened a little, and he could see that her breathing was more shallow, quicker. Her eyes softened but were still alive with the humor that would soon turn into something else. He held her cheek with his left hand and her chin with his right as, very gently, he moved his lips toward hers. He felt the rush of her breath on his cheek, and their lips touched, dry, soft, neither moving, neither kissing, just both being there at the beginning of everything.

"Kate, you have such style. Where did you learn it?" he whispered, perversely. His lips moved against hers as he spoke.

"By looking. Too many ideas. Not enough time." She spoke fast so that the kiss would not be delayed. But, in a way, it had already started because you had to move your lips to speak, and his lips and hers were already against each other. So they tasted first each other's breath, each other's words, each other's thoughts.

And then he kissed her, so softly, his mouth moving to enclose hers, but not invading, not pressing. It was warm and without wetness. There was no distraction of desire's moisture, no hint of the hunger that so soon would come. He moved his hands from her chin and cheek. He passed them to her shoulders, and then around her waist, drawing her in so carefully, as if by roughness she would be lost.

She kissed him back, parting her lips just a little to show what she had in store for him. She brushed his lips with a film of wetness, the promise of it; then she withdrew. She nuzzled in again, running her now open mouth over the surface of his and down his chin, but still dry, still tender. She looked away in the almost-kiss. But as her eyes slid from him, paradoxically she moved closer to him with her body. She pushed in toward him until he could feel the length of her against him, her belt buckle at his stomach, her legs hard against his.

"You could write a book all about your design ideas," he murmured into her open mouth, "and I could sell it for you."

"And would you make me a star, Peter?" she drawled dreamily, playing the role he had capriciously cast for her, mentee to his mentor, success to his Svengali.

"You *are* a star," he said softly, hardly able to speak because of the increasing insistence of her lips.

Her tongue darted at him, silencing him. It slipped into his mouth and the drought was over. He joined with her then in the drawing room of the ruined house that one day he would buy for her. He could feel the old cottage springing to life as his desire for her came alive. And they swayed together in what he prayed would be a kiss without end in a life of togetherness. In this magic house in this leafy lane, Peter had found what he had been looking for.

Had Kate?

8

Donna and Steve were walking hand in hand in the quiet square when the wedding erupted from the basilica like champagne from a bottle. Children flowed down the steps, shouting their relief from the seriousness of ceremony. They wore white party frocks, clean now but soon to be dirty, and their faces were filled with fun and mischief. In the middle, trying not to trip over the children, the bride and groom laughed and smiled their relief that the hard part was over. It was the end of the beginning. The bride held a bouquet of white and yellow, and the groom, neat in his black shiny suit with its red carnation boutonniere, guided her carefully down the steps. He was protecting her already, as he would forever. The promise to do so was still loud in his heart.

They had been about to enter the church at the moment of this unexpected exit. Now they stood back, amused, intrigued, as the wedding party exploded into a square that was already springing into action like the set of a musical. A cluster of gondolas, moored at the edge of the canal in the protection of the bridge, hardly noticed before, were now revealed as part of the party. The couple would leave for the reception, Venetian-style, by water. An accordionist began to play, and a tall, thin boat-man sang "O Sole Mio" in a foie gras baritone that seemed to require a rounder, shorter singer. To this welcome, the remainder of the guests came blinking into the brightness. Parents called excitedly to their children, trying to reassert dwindling control. The maid of honor smiled shyly at nonchalant young men. A crinkled grandmother, dressed in black, cried noisily into a sheetlike handkerchief. There were twenty or thirty wedding guests in all . . . those nearer to birth, those closer to death . . . and in between, the married couple, stars of the wedding day they would remember forever.

Tears and laughter, shouted parental orders, the oily lubricant of "O Sole Mio" were the background music to the chaos of the scene. A maid of honor whispered the secrets of friendship into the ear of the bride. A laconic man, standing a little apart, lit a casual cigarette to signal his discomfort perhaps at others being the center of attention. A mother adjusted the bow in her child's hair. Now the groom tried to take control. He gesticulated and shouted above the noise.

"What's he saying?" asked Donna.

"He wants them all to pose for a photograph outside the church," said Steve. "Dream on," he added with a laugh.

A sallow photographer, holding a camera that looked as if it should have been in a museum, materialized seemingly from nowhere. Steve's prediction was accurate. The wedding group was not easily held together. The children danced around it, hungry for attention. Here a mother rushed off to grab a running daughter; there a father knelt to straighten a son's tie. The grandmother, her tears ignored, wanted to sit down because she was feeling faint. The young men eyed the gondolas longingly, thinking of the food and rich red wine that waited for them at the reception. The girls, each with her bouquet, were already dancing in the eyes of their minds, swirling, singing, making life and love as they dreamed and planned marriages of their own. All had been weighed down by the solemnity of the church. Now they wanted the freedom the photographer threatened to delay.

In tune with the secret wishes of the guests, the accordionist changed his tempo. The snakelike singer, bending and uncoiling in turn, unleashed a song of cheerful rebellion against authority. But the photographer and the groom persevered. With difficulty the exuberant group was brought to order. One couple remained in anarchy. Clearly sweethearts, they danced close across the cobblestones of the square, their cheeks touching, their bodies swaying cunningly to the currents of the music. Some clapped for them, and a boisterous girl, plump and happy, threw her bouquet at them. It struck one dancer on her shoulder and she turned, laughing and smiling at the missile thrower. But then they too returned to the fold for the photograph. The photographer looked up to heaven in exasperation; then he bent to the viewfinder to capture the elusive moment. He held up one hand into the shouted jollity. *"Prego. Prego,"* he barked. One. Two. Three. It was done.

For a moment, before the dissolution of the group and the rush to the boats, there was an aura of stillness. It was as if the enforced togetherness of the photograph had fathered a sudden reluctance to part. There was solidarity in that moment. The family was gathered together for the scrapbook that would hold the memories. When might they all be so close again? Who would be lost to them? Who gained?

Donna sensed that family moment. She looked at the bride, whose face was alive with love. What would become of it? She stole a quick glance at Steve. For three weeks they had lived together, and already she could not imagine her life without him. For now, he was hers. But to have was one thing, to hold another. This marriage was an attempt to assuage the fear of losing love. Would it succeed?

"She's so pretty," Donna whispered. But the bride was not really pretty. Her face was plump and round, and her arms were meaty where they fled from the encircling lace. Even her frock was plain, but it would reign in honor in a tall dark cupboard for the rest of her long life. Then one day she, too, would be a bent old crone, faint and weeping at a grandchild's wedding in some far-off time in this selfsame square. Donna smiled at the thought. Happiness had made this girl beautiful. Had happiness made her beautiful, too?

As Donna watched the bride, so Steve's eyes were on the groom. He felt the bond strongly. He knew the meaning of the shining eyes, the back straightened by pride. He understood about the heart stretched on the rack of passion, about desire placed so briefly on hold by the formalities of ceremony. Steve knew the care with which the groom had that morning shined the cracked leather of his shoes; tied the knot of his unfashionable tie; combed his black, brilliantined hair until nature could no longer be improved upon. The groom caught Steve's eye then, man to man, stranger to stranger, and he smiled proprietorially. In the moment he was no longer the baker, the souvenir seller, the driver of some water taxi. He was king. He was emperor. He was the doge of the republic. For the first time in his life, Steve envied another man. Neither money nor art, goodness nor determination, could bring happiness like this. Only love could. He had not known that before. Now, twenty-one days after he had met Donna, he did.

The stillness of the photograph was transformed suddenly into feverish activity. The party was readying itself to board the gondolas. The married couple went first, and suddenly the air was full of flying flowers as the girls threw their bouquets to bedeck the boat. Several missed the target and floated serenely around it on the waters of the canal. Others, more accurately thrown, formed a blanket of flowers against the silken seats. The older people boarded stiffly, threatening to overturn the slim vessels. But these were Venetians, who had lived for a thousand years on the waters of the lagoon. They did not fall in. Their genes forbade it.

And then they were gone. Boat by boat, the wedding party cast off from the bank to float beneath the old bridge. They took their music with them, and romantic again now, it slid back across the aquamarine canal, until the last gondola disappeared from view.

Donna and Steve were alone.

Donna turned to Steve, laughing happily. "I feel I've known them all my life," she said.

"Me, too," he agreed. "Let's go and see inside." He had wanted badly to visit this church with her. When he had first arrived in Murano, its beauty had amazed him.

They walked inside, and the dark, but not the gloom, descended. Somehow, Donna expected the gaiety of the wedding party to have lingered here, but all was peace. It was the other world, of which, of course, it was the symbol. Beauty did not take away Donna's breath. It was like a feeling, inflating within her, blowing her up with astonishment and a sense at once of awe and of escape from self. It was like a room, not a church. The pews, polished and simple, seemed to have been added by afterthought. The high altar tore at her eyes as the rich incense, lingering still, seeped into her consciousness. Flanked by Cabianca sculptures, surrounded by fourteenth-century frescoes of the gospel writers and topped by the Virgin herself in a golden vault, the altar contained the urn of a saint. Donna knew that from the guidebook she had read the night before, but it was far more than mere art history that moved her. Never before had she seen so many colors merge in such perfect harmony—the terracotta marble of the steps, the white Carrara of the columns and altar base, gray-veined stone merging with dark gray, the golden fire of the sarcophagus of Saint Donato. Yellows and golds, the red background against which a white dove sailed . . . the greens, the blacks, and the blue of the Virgin's dress. Together, Donna and Steve walked in a daze around the church, knowing somehow that this was an ante-room to heaven, a taste on earth of what God's home had in store. Neither of them was a Catholic, but this was a house that belonged to another world.

The spirit poured down on Donna from the rich oils of Bastiani and Letterini, from the Roman arches, and up from the griffins, crickets, and eagles of the mosaic floor. A priest prayed in a corner. A tourist lingered lighting a candle. The lights played on the colors, and the colors sang back to them in the silence. How had a wedding happened here? How that noisy wedding that still filled Donna's mind? The church had already returned to timelessness, retreated from the world in the mere moments it had taken for the humans to leave it.

By some unspoken agreement, both were ready to go. Outside, Steve said nothing. There was a garden nearby, formal, surrounded by ornate brickwork and guarded by a statue of a saint. He had seen it before and thought how peaceful it looked. Now he walked toward it. On the cobbles of the square, a bouquet of white flowers had been left behind in the rush. He bent and picked it up, holding it thoughtfully, twisting it in his hands.

"Where to?" said Donna, threading her hand into his.

He didn't answer. But he led her to the garden. It was a little overgrown, the grass long. White daisies grew in it.

"Come here," he said.

She smiled at him indulgently. What was he up to? He was going to show her something secret. It was that kind of moment.

And he did. He dropped suddenly to his knees in front of her. With that same shy smile she had come to love, he handed her the bouquet of flowers.

"Donna," he said. "Will you marry me?"

She took the flowers, held them to her chest, and looked down at him. Then the tears came, hard and sudden as rain from the lagoon.

"Marry you!" she said. "Marry you?"

She spoke as if he were mad, but her tears said that she was caught up in his madness. There were two Donnas now, where there had been one. His words had divided her down the middle. His eyes reached into her for the answer that he wanted, but she did not know which part of her should respond. The old Donna had not died in Venice as she had thought. The old Donna lived on and had resurfaced at this the most important moment of her life so far. Three weeks. Three weeks. Three weeks. Three times the words repeated themselves. It was crazy; it made no sense. She couldn't marry a stranger, however much she loved him. It wasn't logical. It wasn't right. The voice of her parents spoke in unison: "Don't be a damned fool, Donna. Get qualified first. Don't go overboard for a holiday romance." There must be time to discuss this. He must give her time. She must demand it. On the one hand this? Debits and credits. Carefully laid plans. She saw the determination in his eyes.

He rose and stood close to her, taking her gently in his arms. He knew what she was thinking. He knew about the old Donna. But he had fallen in love with the new one, with the one he had helped create. He spoke to her gently now, not arguing, not persuading.

"What does your heart say, Donna? Not your head. What does your heart say?"

"It says yes, but . . ."

She couldn't stop the tears. She was awash with emotion, but still her brain barked out its orders. Time. She needed time. She looked down at the crushed bouquet in her hands. She felt the stillness of the church. She remembered the joy on the face of the girl who would one day exist only as a faded photograph. And then she made her decision. She listened not to the old Donna but to the new. She listened to her heart, and she obeyed it.

"Yes," she said. "Yes, I will marry you."

9

Summer 1973
The Hamptons

The candles flickered low, their light fingering the polished wood of the floor, reaching down the table, angling up to light the animated faces of the diners. Indian music moaned its sitar chic as background to the curry dinner Kate had spent three days preparing. There were earthenware bowls of carefully spiced chicken masala marinated in yogurt, the color of the saffron robes of Buddhist monks, bright as the pilaf that partnered it. The poppadums were crisp and warm. The nan bread, baked specially that afternoon, was doughy soft. And the chutney, too, was homemade from the fruit in the orchard.

Kate loved to cook, but cooking alone was not enough. She liked her dinner parties to have a theme in which all the separate elements blended. The Ravi Shankar sitar music, the candles filling the air with the aroma of India, the silk cushions on which they sat . . . all contributed to the magical atmosphere that was far more than the sum of its parts. For most people, to have discovered the recipe for the dinner in some dusty book on an Afghan war in the library on Main Street would have been more than enough. Not for Kate.

Teddy Winner, bearded and serious, tried to put into words what everyone was thinking.

"Look, Kate and Peter," he said, as if addressing one of the literary conventions at which he often spoke, "I'm not a connoisseur of food, let alone Indian food. It's pretty much fuel to me, but I have to say that this is one incredible meal."

There was a chorus of approval, some of it wholehearted, a certain portion tinged with the reserve of jealousy.

"Did you really make it all yourself, Kate? I think that is awfully clever of you. You're so lucky to have the time."

Veronica Winner couldn't help herself. Her own cooking, when the cook was away, had never produced a speech like that from her husband. Come to think of it, nothing that she had ever done had been the occasion for such a statement. By her remark she had managed to insinuate that Kate had had the whole meal sent down, vacuum packed, from some restaurant in the city and had simply warmed it up in the microwave. It wasn't that she didn't like Kate. She did. It was impossible not to.

Frankie flew to her friend's defense. "I watched her do it. And it did take an age, but the thing about Kate is she does about ten things at once. While she was steaming the chicken, she was cutting up some old Indian skirts she found in a thrift and making it into the cushions you're sitting on." She turned to her friend. "Really, Kate, you are quite amazing. One day somebody is simply going to bottle you!"

Kate laughed. "Don't tell anyone," she said to everyone, "but a lot of it is smoke and mirrors. We can't afford a proper table yet so we're sitting at orange crates with a bit of plywood on top. And the tablecloth is a double sheet."

"Darling," said Peter, "with your talent who needs tables?" He stared down the table adoringly at the woman who had transformed his life.

Kate, in a simple dark green velvet dress she had made from curtain material, smiled back at him. She wore a black velvet band around her neck, and her bodice was cut low to show off her young, perfect breasts. As he watched her, she raised her glass to him, sipping the Beaujolais and smiling, always happy, unfazed by veiled criticism and cunning cut-downs. She was too busy for it all. She was lost in the play-store of life, plundering its treasures, obvious and subtle. She was gorging herself on delights that others, and especially the old, didn't even know existed. Déjà vu and jaundiced eyes, the deadening lessons of education and experience, had washed past her, not touching her, leaving her gloriously unpolluted. What was there not to love?

Peter, too, raised his glass. "To my brilliant Kate. Thank you for this food. Thank you for this house . . . no, this home . . . thank you for . . . for giving me the kiss of life," said Peter.

All his heart went into the words. It had been a transformation. That first kiss had put the color back into his existence. They had found this house—Kate had found it—and it had become a symbol of everything. Peter had never been a great believer in destiny, but Kate had converted him. The house had been for sale of course. It had been owned by an elderly couple who had decided to move to a condo in Florida and who had allowed it to deteriorate. It had needed a ton of work, and the owners had seemed genuinely surprised that anyone would be prepared to take it on. They bought it for next to nothing, but it had been enough to leave Peter very short on cash for the improvements. They had decided to do as much work as possible themselves, and so Kate had taken over. The house had become hers, not in deed, but in fact.

As their relationship had deepened, they camped out in the leaky old house from Friday nights to early Monday mornings. Peter had tried to draw the line at plumbing, wiring, and mending the roof, but Kate's energy and initiative had simply swamped him. So he had discovered the glory of self-sufficiency. There were books that told you how to do everything. Carpenters, painters, and bricklayers were not, as Kate was fond of pointing out, brain surgeons. He smiled at the thought. She would have a go at that, too, if the occasion arose! He could imagine her talking about it afterward. "I used *Gray's Anatomy.* It seemed quite a straightforward job once I'd found the tumor on the X ray. The trick is to hold the drill steady once you've anesthetised them with the bottle of vodka. . . ."

They had painted and nailed, stuck and plastered, until they had dropped. They had dropped together, dirty and tired, and they had made love on the floor and in wet attics, in damp cellars, and up against a wall on which the paint that Kate had mixed personally had not quite dried. Slowly, it had begun to come together, and every corner of the house was filled with body memory, every eave thick with love. And so, inexorable as evolution, their future had begun to take shape like a picture on the horizon of time. There had been so much to do, and so much scarce money to spend. Kate had suggested that she spend a couple of nights there a week, and then three. Next, she had given up her part-time job at Max's Kansas City, and soon she decided to save her design school money and learn instead in the most effective academy of all, the school of experience.

On Fridays, when Peter arrived from the city, the house would be a triumphal welcome for him. There would be fresh bread baking in the Aga that Kate had cleaned out herself; Kate's own mixture of coffee beans filling the air with its seductive smell; wild, and now not so wild, flowers from the garden and greenhouse that Kate was restoring pane by pane with hands that never seemed to roughen with manual labor.

And so, the cottage had become a home. Their home. Despite being born in one, living with parents in one, she felt, perhaps like Peter, that she had never had a home before. She had given him the kiss of life, had she? It was a funny thing for him to say, but it was sweet, and she thought she understood what he meant. He had been an old soul. And he always would be. In many ways it was what she most loved about him. He felt she had made him younger. In turn he had helped her to grow up, to move away from mere rebellion to a world where she could build something lasting on the firm foundation he provided. Kate, the guerrilla warrior, with the undirected energy of a firecracker, was metamorphosing with his support into Kate the architect, Kate the interior designer, Kate the chef.

She had taught herself everything. It was amazing how much information there was just waiting to be found if you had the energy to look for it and to act on it. She had taught herself how to cook by preparing every one of Julia Child's recipes in *Mastering the Art of French Cooking.* If at first she couldn't make them work, she played around with them until she did. If she couldn't afford caviar, she used lumpfish and added a bit more seasoning. All was innovation. Everything was built on the basic experience of the pathfinders who had gone before. Art was in the subtlety of the variation on the art of others. History was a gold mine longing to be excavated, like this age-old curry from a Rudyard Kipling frontier war. The trouble was that nobody could be bothered. Nobody had the time, the initiative, the inclination; opportunity was there for the grasping by those with fists that could clench. French cooking had been there before Julia Child had found it, as was America before Columbus, and the sunflowers before van Gogh had noticed them.

But if she could read books, she could write them. She would take a bit from here, a piece from there, blend, mix, and serve in a new and different way. Writing was there in her future, like this house, like Peter. He had discovered her in Max's not Schwab's, and she knew that all he wanted to do was guide her toward the greatness that both knew could be hers. So she smiled her gratitude down the table at him, and there was something else in her smile, too. There was the knowledge of the secret she was bursting to let out.

"Look, darling," said Ellen, a friend of the Winners', "you'll probably think me quite, quite mad, but would there be any chance of your rustling up a curry like this for one of my dinner parties? We live in Southampton, and my cook has three meals she can do and that's it. My friends are bored to *death* by them. I heard one of them saying the other evening, 'It's the chicken chasseur again, Arch.' For God's sake, say if it would be a bore. It's just that you're so good at it and I wondered . . ."

"Of course I could do it. I'd love to do it," said Kate. "I do Thai, too, you know. And I've got some recipes for old Apache things that I *guarantee* your friends won't have tasted before!"

Ellen's eyes sparkled as she dared to imagine the post-mortem at the Meadows Club.

"Kate's not inexpensive," said Peter from his end of the table, winking at Kate.

"Peter! Don't be crazy. I'd do it for nothing . . . just the cost."

"Nonsense, darling," said Ellen. "Think of a number and triple it. That's what everyone else does. I've reached the stage in life where I can't afford to have my faith in human nature restored. I've spent most of my life in bed with a trust fund. If I can't spread my money around, all that time will have been wasted."

Her plutocratic husband laughed gamely at the joke, having had a certain amount of practice.

Kate laughed too. She'd been asked to do this kind of thing before. The people who owned the house across the fields had been intrigued with the way she had organized the greenhouse. Could they buy some advice? The Upper Crust Bakery in East Hampton had taken some of her mince pies, sold out, ordered more, and asked if she did anything else. Now she had a dinner party to cater. And Ellen Dillon's dinner party, no less. Twelve people would eat it, maybe more. The grapevine had many branches. And it was all so easy. *Kate Branagan's Frontier Cook Book,* published by Knopf. Sold by trendy young agent Peter

Haywood. *A House to a Home, Cooking up Dreams, Zen and the Art of Baking.* The titles fell over themselves in her mind.

"Peter, we're nearly out of wine," she said waving her empty glass at him.

He stood up and made for the kitchen.

Teddy Winner stood up too. "I'll come and help," he said.

The kitchen was stripped down like a ship of the line in Nelson's time, scrubbed and bare, ready for battle. One day it would be resplendent with color, draped and decorated. Now it was strictly necessities. The Beaujolais, several bottles of it, was stacked by the open window to keep it *frais* but not chilled.

Teddy laid his hand on Peter's shoulder. "She's quite a girl, your Kate, isn't she?"

Peter was aware that Teddy's visit to the kitchen was with a conversation like this in mind, as much as to "help." Helping had been what Teddy had done so often in Peter's career. He was a very senior editor at an old, established house, and when Peter had been squeezed out of his own editor's job in one of the consolidations that were beginning to be a feature of the publishing industry, Teddy had eased his passage into agenting. He had pointed promising young authors Peter's way, and had always listened with an attentive ear when Peter pitched a book. So there was something of the protector about Teddy, and the protégé about Peter, although now Peter was off and running on his own.

"What do you think of her, Teddy?"

Peter drew the cork from a bottle of wine as he spoke. Winner was wise. Judges of books could judge people, too.

"Original. Talented. Wouldn't know what laziness was. Ambitious, I expect." There was a hint of warning, there. Just a hint.

"I think it's the ambition I like most, I mean apart from, well . . ."

They both laughed, as men were allowed to.

"It's serious, isn't it? I mean *marriage* serious."

"I don't think she'd have somebody like me."

"Oh, she would. She would," said Teddy, nodding in a way that was not totally reassuring. "She loves you. In her way. I think she loves you as much as she can love."

"What do you mean, Teddy?" Peter started on a second bottle with the opener.

"I think she lives in the moment. All young people do to a certain extent. But I think she does more than most. I remember your telling me about her unhappy childhood. Miserable parents. Some sort of institution as a school. She's busy forgetting her past, I feel. Busy making up for lost time, maybe. One of those people who run just to be on the run, because to stop means listening to the feelings, and that might be painful."

"Jeez, Teddy, I thought you gave up that shrink three years ago."

"I'm sorry. I'm sorry," said Teddy, holding up his hands in mock surrender. "Never give advice about a woman a man loves. Rule number one in friendship."

"No, no, I'm not saying that," said Peter, well aware that he was. "It's just that . . . well . . . I know all that about her. She will change. And I'll change with her. People do. People must."

Teddy turned his head to one side, as if considering the advisability of carrying on with this conversation. He decided in favor. "You know what I think, I think that one day she's going to be pretty famous. I don't know how, or for what. And I think that she wants that very badly. Maybe she doesn't even know it. Maybe she does. But she knows you're going to help her, and you are. That's what I think, for what it's worth."

"Why am I wondering whether this is the good or the bad news?" said Peter, laughing.

"Listen," said Teddy. "All news is good when you're in love. Let's get back in there and get stuck into that wine."

They walked back into the candlelight together.

"At last!" said Kate. "We thought you two had left."

"Kate has a toast," said Frankie.

"A toast?" said Peter, circling the table and filling glasses.

"Yes," said Kate. "A very special toast."

A silence descended. It was something in the way she said it, in the animated look on her face. She waited for Peter to sit down; then she stood. She held her glass high.

"I would like to drink," she said, "to the three of us."

Peter looked at her closely. He had never seen her more beautiful, but he had to wonder whether she had had too much wine. Whom was she drinking to? Frankie? Herself? Him? It seemed a little rude to leave everyone else out. Frankie, too, did not get it. She looked frankly surprised, and was clearly about to say something to that effect. Her mouth opened in question.

"In case anyone is confused," said Kate, "I'm pregnant."

10

"Aaaaaaaaagh!"

Kate let out the despair. This wasn't pain. There was no simple garden-variety agony here. It was out there in a different realm, where words meant nothing. Only sounds of the kind she had just made came close to describing what she felt. She was full of panic. It had started. There was no turning back. The only way out was to go forward along a path, a canal, that was simply too small, too narrow to travel through. She tried to tell herself the nonsense that this had been done before. The nurse, in a wicked, stupid irrelevance, urged her to do something called "push." But Kate could only concentrate on desperation. Hope had gone. Camels could not pass through the biblical eye of the needle. Babies could not pass through the space that God in His infinite stupidity had so inefficiently designed for the purpose.

Kate's head thrashed from side to side. In her pain and fear she noticed that the obstetrician looked cucumber calm. The nurse was actually smiling. A medical student seemed disinterestedly interested. But the fact that they thought all was "under control" didn't help. Nothing helped, because she wanted to faint and she couldn't faint. She promised that she would never, ever do this again.

She was aware of the door opening. For the third time, Peter, looking like she felt, stuck his head around it.

"In or out, please, Peter," said the obstetrician cheerfully. "But not both."

Doctor and nurse exchanged glances. "Out" would be better. He looked like a fainter, and it was so easy to trip over husbands during delivery. The doctor had even been sued by one who had fractured his skull in a fall.

"Darling, are you all right?" said Peter from the door. His face was gray.

Kate simply stared at him. It was as if a Martian had arrived and asked for directions in a dialect of Mars-speak that even Martians had difficulty understanding. She didn't blame him for this horror. He was her husband, and she loved him. It was just that a huge chasm had opened between the two versions of the species. On the one hand stood women. On the other, men. It seemed unbelievable that the two genders had ever got together to make this hell possible.

"Push. Push," said the nurse.

"Oh, shut up!" said Kate weakly. She didn't know if she was or wasn't pushing. Prenatal classes were another part of a weird world that had faded into nothingness. There was no preparation. There had been no warning. All there had been was a conspiracy of silence to hide the truth. That this was the pit. Here was what Hades would be like. Compared to this, burning in eternal flames was the equivalent of sunning oneself on the beach. If there was punishment for wickedness in this world, here it was.

She was sweating swimming pools. Her eyes rolled in her head like marbles. Why women? Why her? What could a man ever know about suffering? They should be made to lay a grapefruit . . . no, a watermelon, a steel one, with spikes on, with knobs on, and then a year later they should be forced to do it again, and again, and again. Only then would the sexes at last be equal. Only then would they begin to understand one another.

"Not long now, Kate. Here's the head. Hang in there. You're doing just fine."

Oh thank you, sir, for your kind, reassuring words. I'm doing just fine. There's the head. What about the shoulders? What about the rest of it? She prayed it would be a girl. Then, one day, she would know the pain she had caused.

"Ooooh," she moaned. But the only effect was to turn poor Peter a grayer shade of pale as he hovered at the door, neither in nor out, another fatuous question loitering around his lips. Kate tried to identify it. Where was the pain? Did it have a place? Was it worse here than there? Then she realized what it was. She felt as if she were being ripped apart, torn asunder from the inside out. The racks of the Spanish Inquisition might have been a little like this. It was as if her skin were magnetic and she were surrounded by a mighty magnet that was sucking every bit of her in different directions.

Peter took a deep breath, one step backward, and closed the door. He had never lived on a farm. His parents had led sheltered lives in the literary Groves of Academe. He had avoided science wherever he had come across it, and when science had been biology he had broken into a run. Now he was running in his mind, and beads of sweat were running down his nose. He had never felt so helpless, never so useless. Words couldn't hack it. Feelings of solidarity were grossly insufficient. All he could do was be there, and yet he knew he was in the way. Were men really necessary? You had to ask that at a time like this. All they could provide was a sperm with its warped little Y chromosome, a deformed thing, he had once read, compared to the

X variety. One day, probably in his lifetime, there would be cloning and incubators and this whole barbaric business would be history. He shook his head as he paced the corridor, his thoughts punctuated occasionally by the cries of his wife through the swing doors.

It was all right. He knew that. People survived this. A baby being born was no big deal. Any moment now he would be a father and Kate would be a model mother. Obviously it was uncomfortable. It was well known to be. They said there was no pain like it, and they were probably right. They usually were. He sat down and scooped up a copy of the *New York Times*. Oh! Great! One of his authors was being reviewed. He hadn't realized it was due out so soon. With only the mildest twist of guilt, he was soon deep in the article.

"Waaaah!"

It wasn't her sound. It was over. It had started. Never in her whole life had Kate felt such a sudden change. The pain stopped. What had seemed so real it could never end, had finished and left not a trace behind. She didn't ache, she didn't hurt. She had been delivered from horror. And then, as if closer to the light in a near-death experience, she began to focus on the child that the doctor held up for her. There it was. Life. The miracle. The moment of ultimate truth, when she realized that God existed and she was merged with nature. A nurse was mopping at the baby as she handed it to Kate, who reached up to take what someone said was a daughter into her arms.

The feeling of transcendence wrapped her. She felt at one with all the women through all of time. It was a sisterhood of souls. This birth through pain was the entrance fee to a club so mystical that it could never, by divine law, be joined by those who had not lived through this experience. She had traveled from the depths to the heights in the moment of passage. From hell to this heaven. From ordinariness to motherhood. Seconds ago, she had vowed with the breath she had wanted to use for screaming that she would never go near a man again. Now, this second, she wanted once more to be pregnant. Say the word, and it would be done. "More" had replaced "never" in a seamless progression that was beyond mere understanding.

"Peter! Peter!" she yelled at the top of her voice, and out there in the corridor, in the middle of some well-turned critic's phrase, he heard her. He jumped up and threw down the paper and ran like a rabbit toward the baby they had both decided—boy or girl—would be called Sam.

11

1974
London

"I'm sorry."

The pregnant girl who sat on the edge of the examination couch was twenty-three. She looked not so much sorry as desperate. The reasons for her sorrow were the sixteen-month-old baby she dangled from her ample lap and the toddler, snotty-nosed and filthy, who roamed around her ankles with dangerous energy. It was only a matter of time before this one set off around the tiny cubicle on a mission of search and destroy.

"I had to bring them. There's no one home," she added.

"That's fine, Mrs. O'Grady," said Donna. "It's no problem at all. All antenatal clinics should have children. As a warning of what to expect, if nothing else."

They both laughed at the ridiculousness of it all. The whole business of pregnancy, the discomfort, the inconvenience, and the expense, was all about the production of children, who apart from being a joy were also potent sources of discomfort, inconvenience, and expense.

Donna sat down on a metal chair and opened the notes on the wooden flap that let down from the wall and served as a desk. Mary O'Grady was an unmarried mother living in a council flat. Her young one was called Tony; the toddler was Liam. Immediately, Donna felt a pang of guilt. Liam had been born the month before her Daniel, and right now Daniel, unlike Liam, was not with his mother. Instead, he was at home in the womblike comfort of the sky blue Laura Ashley nursery with the babysitter. Unlike Mrs. O'Grady, Donna did not have the opportunity, the necessity, or the inclination to bring him with her to the antenatal clinic.

"I've got one just like Liam at home," said Donna.

"Oh," said Mary O'Grady, her expression brightening. Then she said, "I suppose you've got someone to look after him." She smoothed a wisp of dank, lifeless hair from her eyes and looked suddenly a little ashamed. Her remark might have sounded like an accusation. She didn't know that Donna was a senior medical student and not yet a fully qualified doctor. In Mary O'Grady's book, doctors, even National Health Service ones, were rich.

"Yes, I do. I'm lucky, I suppose," said Donna. But as she spoke she didn't feel lucky. She felt deprived, as deprived in a way as the worn-out girl who sat before her eight months pregnant, with two kids to look after already and way out at the end of her tether. The truth was Donna missed Daniel terribly. Right this minute he would be smiling for someone else. As she sat there, so briskly efficient and asking all the right questions, Daniel would be gurgling for another. His gratitude would be to Janice for the fun and companionship she would be providing. Who was the real surrogate mother? Janice, the babysitter who had the hands-on job? Or Donna, caring for her patients, for the "bleeding crowd," but not for the magical child that Steve and she had produced? It was impossible, of course. She had wanted a baby. And she had wanted to be a doctor. There was no way on earth, despite the optimism of women's magazine articles, that both jobs could be done well. In this life, you could only concentrate fully on one thing at a time. Anyone who told you otherwise was a liar.

Donna's stethoscope, with its bright red plastic tubing, lay next to the notes. Liam, the mobile child, lunged at it. "What this?" he said, dragging it into his orbit.

"Leave it *alone,* Liam," snapped Mary O'Grady, leaning forward with an effort to retrieve it. She pulled at her child, pried the instrument from his grasp, and handed it to Donna.

"I hope it don't 'ave to be sterilized," she said hopefully.

Considering Liam's "hygienic" state, it was not entirely a pointless hope.

"Oh no," said Donna, with a laugh that suggested she was totally at home with the full-time demands of toddlers. "It's fine."

"He's a nightmare sometimes," said Mary.

"How are you coping?"

Donna could hear the frustration in the young girl's voice, the life-wasn't-supposed-to-be-like-this feeling. Donna was good at picking up on things like that. One of her biggest surprises at medical school was how few doctors were. Sometimes she wondered where her interest in other people, in their emotions, not just the functioning of their bodies, came from. Probably from her parents' apparent *lack* of interest in her. As long as she had been clean, polite, hardworking, and presentable, they had always been approving, but in a distant, unemotional way. Donna had learned a paradoxical lesson from their comfortable upper-middle-class detachment. She had learned that valuable people were those who valued other people. Would her cold parents in their cold graves be pleased they had taught her that? Not really. Being pleased had never been their specialty.

"Well, it kicks all the time an' wakes me up. An' I 'ave to sleep on my back now. An' then I 'ave to go to the toilet every ten minutes. Constipated. Tired. The usual, I suppose. I done it before." She waved a hand at the two she had already produced.

"I really meant psychologically, dealing with everything. Is Harry helping at all?"

" 'E done a runner three weeks ago, didn't he? 'E went to Preston, up north, I heard down the pub. Got a job welding."

She spoke with the deadpan lack of emotion of her working-class origins. Economy was everywhere. Economy in shopping, in heating her home. Economy in words, economy in feelings. Again, Donna felt guilt . . . for the valuable freehold house she had inherited and the little bit of money that went with it. She had been left financial security and a work ethic of epic proportions. What a paradox it was. Mary O'Grady had been left neither, but she, in a way, was the real woman, with a child in her belly and children at her feet to prove it. But then again, Mary O'Grady did not have a husband and Donna had Steve. She stopped short at the thought of him. Somehow, other people's problems were safer territory.

"Any chance of him coming back?" Donna didn't want to probe, but she sensed that Mary O'Grady would be too busy with the children to have much time for friends. She probably needed to talk even if she wasn't much good at it.

"What, to this?" said Mary with a bitter laugh. She touched her abdomen to emphasize her point. "I'm surprised 'e stopped at Preston and didn't go off to bleedin' Timbuktu. Sorry about the language," she added as an afterthought.

"Yes, husbands and babies aren't always peaches-and-cream, are they?" said Donna. There was something about her tone that brought a thoughtful expression to Mary O'Grady's face.

"Is your old man good with your one?"

It was the beginning of a conversation. Hierarchical relationships were breaking down.

"Sort of . . . I suppose," said Donna, acutely aware that her trumpet was sounding an uncertain note. In her mind, the Pandora's box that was Steve flew open. It was amazing how much things had changed between them since marriage and the misty magic of Venice. What was difficult to pinpoint was *what* exactly had changed and why. The more she thought about it, the more it seemed that it was the moment they had met that had been the aberration, the mad exhilaration of a strange and mystical place at a weird and wonderful time. It had been all about passion, lust, sex, and the seductive frontiers of brave new worlds. They hadn't thought it through, and then, slowly but surely, reality had begun to strangle the dream that both had dreamed.

Daniel had been the starting point. Steve had adored him at first sight. Donna had not expected that, and it had been both a surprise and a relief. Her wild, heroic artist husband, seemingly so free and obsessed with the glassy sea of his creations, had taken to bottle sterilization and bottom polishing like a model dad. But with the revelation of this domestic side to his personality had come a less welcome attitude toward Donna's style of mothering. His schedule was far more flexible than hers, and gradually he had begun to show his disapproval of her absentee motherhood in a hundred subtle ways. Donna had begun to learn the secret language of marriage. An eye averted spoke volumes, the absence of a kiss good-bye, the joke that had to be accompanied by an unconvincing laugh to show that it was indeed a joke and not a criticism. "Off to heal the sick babies?" he had said once when Donna had been leaving the house and Daniel had been starting a cold. The list grew longer in memory. They made love less often now, and they laughed less, and there was less time together. Notes on the fridge door, meals uncooked, frozen food, a lessening of interest in each other's days. He tried to explain to her the things he was trying to achieve with his glass at the Royal College of Art, but she was trying to hold the biochemical reactions of the Krebs cycle in her mind and the distribution of the nerves in the brachial plexus. She still worshiped him, adored him even, but he was a god no more, and no more was she his goddess.

Donna forced herself back to the business at hand. Mary

O'Grady had asked if Steve was a good father. "At least he hasn't gone off to Preston. Yet!" she said, laughing to lighten things up.

But of course it wouldn't be to Preston that Steve would go, if, God forbid, he ever went. It would be to America. He had never really acclimatized to London. It was extraordinary how the shared language persuaded one that the differences between the two cultures were small. Steve could not understand the English love of sarcasm and irony, nor the endless puns of the newspaper headlines, nor the world-weary pessimism. He wasn't intrigued by cross-dressing, or the Royal Family, and he had never got into the habit of replying in a downbeat way when someone asked him how he was. "Mustn't complain" or "Struggling on" were as alien to Steve as Americans' relentless optimism and belief in experts were to the British among whom he now lived.

"What does he feel about you working?"

"Not over the moon about it."

"Rather 'ave you back at 'ome so's he knows where you are."

It was funny how simple people could make things simple. But was it true that Steve wanted that? Did he want her to be a wife and mother and not a doctor? Did he want her to be like his own mother, the cornerstone of a family against which he had rebelled but perhaps for which he had a subterranean respect? Those were the messages Donna seemed to be receiving from him now. But they were not messages that would ever have come from the Steve she thought she was marrying three years ago. Then, he had wanted her to do what she wanted, to fulfill her dreams, as he had to fulfill his. He had married a strong, independent woman. They would drink the same liquid but from different cups, play the same song but on different instruments. It had all been about freedom of expression, following your dream, being blissfully together but wonderfully apart. But Daniel was reality, and the two beautiful dreamers had had to hire Nanny to bring him up.

That was where sweet harmony had first become discord.
Nanny Holmes had *not* been Mary Poppins. To Nanny Holmes,
Mary Poppins would have been a dangerous, half-witted dishonor
to her profession. At sixty, Nanny was from a school older than the
"old" one. Donna was called "Mummy." Steve, to his horror, was
"Daddy," never even "Dad." Daniel had been potty-trained almost
before Nanny had unpacked, and the cheerful chaos of his nursery
and his clothes had been banished before she had slept the first
night in the house. Nanny had only wanted half a day off a week,
and was as dependable as the clockwork clock she had brought
with her, a clock that was soon ruling not only hers but Daniel's,
Donna's, and Steve's days and nights. Donna, a Virgoan, had been
brought up by a similar benevolent despot. She didn't mind, was in
fact rather drawn to the petty rules and regulations of Nanny's
tough love regime.

Nanny did not like Mummy and Daddy to visit her domain unscheduled and unannounced. She liked to issue formal invitations
to nursery tea—scones and clotted cream, Marmite-covered toast
"soldiers" and soft boiled eggs, McVitie's digestive biscuits covered with milk chocolate. Steve had not liked Nanny, and Donna
smiled as she enjoyed the understatement of the thought. Aquarius had rebelled, even as Virgo had acquiesced. And so they had
found Janice, nineteen, with her good heart, thick legs, and resting
pulse rate IQ. Steve had OK'd her . . . just . . . although he had
clearly envisioned a more American personality, with a quick line
in backchat and a whiff of anarchy, which was far more than poor
Janice could manage.

With an effort, Donna dragged herself back to the present.
Luckily Mary O'Grady was the last patient of the afternoon.
Still, she had to get down to the business at hand.

"Gosh," said Donna, looking at her watch. "We'd better get
on with it." It was half past five. She would be staying in the
hospital overnight in case any of her assigned patients on the
obstetrics ward, those with complicated pregnancies, went into

labor. When she had checked them on the ward round that afternoon none of them had looked ready, but you never knew. Her previous post had been the emergency room. She had loved it, and made some good friends among the nurses and doctors. When this clinic was over she was intending to go down to casualty and spend the evening there, helping out when there was action and hanging out in the long gaps between incidents. She had a beeper; if obstetrics needed her, she was right there in the hospital.

She managed to separate Mary O'Grady from her children and get her over to the examination couch. She tested the urine sample already provided for the sugar that would signify diabetes brought on by pregnancy. She took Mary's blood pressure quickly, and then listened to mother's and baby's hearts. She pressed down on the skin of Mary's ankles; there was no swelling there, or in her hands. The in-depth preliminary examination had already been done by the registrar. The vaginal wouldn't be done till the thirty-sixth week. There was nothing else to do but weigh her. She had put on the regular couple of pounds since the last visit. Everything was proceeding normally.

"You're fine, Mary. Right as rain. Not that I have to tell you that. You're the expert."

"Thanks," said Mary. "I bleedin' better be by now."

Donna couldn't resist scooping up Liam for a cuddle. He didn't resist. He sucked happily at his huge pacifier and pulled at her nose. She tickled him in the way that Danny liked, and he gurgled as Danny did. "He's adorable. Got his mother's eyes."

"An' 'is father's habits. Won't go to sleep, up all hours, bloody nightmare. Is yours like that?"

"Actually, he's quite good," said Donna. Again, there was the shot of guilt. Nanny, and now Janice, had had that problem to deal with. It was only the hospital that was allowed to keep Donna awake . . . only other people's babies, not her own.

"Well, nice talkin' to you," said Mary, straightening her

clothes and gathering up her brood for the journey home. "Not
a lot of them talk, do they?" she said with a laugh. It was
halfway between a criticism of the medical profession and a
compliment to Donna.

"The men aren't really in tune with the problem, and they're
mostly men."

"Yeah, let them try 'aving a baby. They'd cry blue murder.
Drama queens the lot of them, if you ask me," said Mary. Her
tone signaled the resigned bitterness of one who had been left
holding not one, but three babies.

Donna laughed. Suddenly, she felt better. Steve was a million miles from a drama queen, and he was not a leaver either.
They might have their problems, but then every married couple
had problems. It was part of a continual adjustment from the
first thrill of enthusiasm to the deep and enduring friendship
and mutual dependence that would, one distant day, be old age.
Nothing stayed the same. Change was the nursery of music,
joy, life, and eternity, as the poet had said. So what if they
fought about nannies. Who cared that he was perhaps a little
jealous of her career. They would get over the fact that she had
to be an absentee mum. For every con there was a pro. Daniel
might not have a hands-on mother like Mary, but he would
have security and education, and warmth. There would always
be two parents to love him and be there for him in moments of
crisis. He could count on two role models, good, worthy, creative, and hardworking people who would show him the way
forward and help him make his own brilliant and individual
life.

Mary and her progeny were just about to depart. Donna felt
sorry for them. On an impulse she reached out and gave her patient a hug.

"Good luck, Mary," she said. "God bless you."

But she could have no idea that it was she who was going to
need the blessing.

12

Little Daniel was red with rage. His tiny mouth formed a perfect *O* and his scream was precise and penetrating. Janice wouldn't have been too concerned, but he had been deep in his tantrum nonstop for an hour. The problem was simple: Daniel wanted to go out in the garden and play, and it was cold in the garden and warm in the nursery. Janice didn't want to go outside, and Daniel wasn't allowed out on his own. What gave a greater than usual urgency to the whole situation was that Kathy McGowan was about to interview Mick Jagger on "Top of the Pops."

"You're not going out," said Janice definitely, "so you'd best stop crying and find something else to do." She was quite used to Daniel's temper, but today it was getting on her nerves. She felt just a bit like slapping him, but she wasn't allowed to. Janice liked this job. She particularly liked Donna, who left precise instructions and was always calling to check on things. And Steve, well, he was American and a bit intimidating, but good-looking enough to have been in the movies. Then there was little Daniel. He was a sweet child, but he had this temper, and when he started howling it was difficult to get him to stop.

On the TV, sassy Kathy McGowan, queen of the mods, toothy and tireless, flicked her bangs from her eyes. Janice liked to imitate that gesture, but always ended up looking as if she were trying to frighten away a wasp at a picnic. Kathy, smiling with all the fake, naive enthusiasm that had made her a star, waved the microphone at Mick.

In turn, Mick flashed his trademark the cynical leer that merged with a scowling pout, giving his india-rubber lips a serious workout in the process.

Janice reached forward and turned up the sound. Daniel moved closer, his whole body rigid with rage and frustration. In this state he was beyond explaining what he wanted, so he wanted Janice to be fully exposed to his screams.

The telephone rang loudly, competing with Daniel's howls and the Kathy-Mick TV dialogue. *Oh, damn it!* thought Janice, and picked up the phone.

"It's Donna. How's everything? Why is he crying?"

"Oh, hello, Donna. I don't know. I think he's just cross about something."

There was a pause at the other end of the line. Janice was aware that she had given a less than adequate explanation. But then she didn't want to be ordered to bundle him up and play with him in the garden.

"Is he hot?" said Donna. "I mean, I suppose he might have an infection. Do you know how to take his temperature?"

"Oh yes, I do," said Janice quickly. "But he doesn't feel hot." She was getting a little flustered. She liked this job, and she wanted to keep it. She was aware that she was on probation. "I'm sure he'll calm down in a little while. He usually does."

"Is Steve back yet?" said Donna hopefully.

"Not yet. He called about an hour ago to say he'd be late."

Janice sneaked a look at the TV. Mick was in those crushed blue velvet trousers with the bell-bottoms that she really liked.

He looked fab. He always looked fab. *Damn!* She really wanted to catch the interview.

"Did he eat his tea?" said Donna. She was making an effort not to sound abrupt. She wasn't quite succeeding. A mother's worry was coming down the line loud and clear. Janice looked at her Mickey Mouse watch. Her friend Teresa had brought it for her from Disneyland the year before. "He had an egg and some toast and honey," she said.

"Have you played with him?" said Donna, getting close.

"We played with his Legos; then he threw them all over the place and started carrying on," said Janice. Still no mention of the garden.

"Maybe it's that damned TV. I can hear it from here. Can't you turn it down a bit?"

"Don't worry, Donna. It's OK. It's all under control. Kids cry sometimes. He'll be fine in a minute."

"OK. Sorry, Janice. Sorry I was snappy. You know how it is. It's been a long day, and they've just called to tell us to expect a traffic accident. Tell Steve to give me a call when he gets in, will you? Good luck."

She rang off.

Janice felt a little leap of excitement.

"Tell me about Marianne Faithfull," said Kathy McGowan. Her toothy grin managed to insinuate that there was a terrific story to be told. "That song you wrote for her . . . 'As Tears Go By.' There's a lot of stuff about children in it. Any chance of children on the horizon anytime soon?"

Mick smiled enigmatically. His extraordinary lips were curling anacondalike around some sort of reply. Janice strained to hear it through the barrage of Danny's screams.

"Yeah, well . . . ," said Mick in the traditional beginning to an early 'seventies-style speech. "It's like . . . well . . . pretty much of a . . ."

He tossed his head to give his hair an outing, and he stuck out a skinny leg. His Dandie Fashions pants flared at his ankles.

Janice felt the funny feeling inside. She really fancied Mick Jagger. Her teenage dreams were thick with him. Only last week she had read an article in *New Musical Express* about Mick's possible marriage to Marianne. Here it was, straight from the exotic mouth that would put any horse to shame.

"Well, people read a lot of things into songs," said Mick. "an' I don't want to fuel rumors an' that, but . . ."

Daniel's mouth, round at her ear, fought for Janice's airwaves. "Oh, do shush!" she said, feeling a burst of irritation. Immediately, she felt guilty. He was only a kid. But she had to hear this. Once again, she reached forward to turn up the volume on the TV.

But Daniel didn't shush. He sucked in a lungful of air, took a step closer to Janice, and let her have it right in the ear.

Janice could almost hear something snap inside her. She jumped up as if she had been shot and reached out and grabbed Daniel by the arm. In surprise, he actually stopped crying, but he started again as she dragged him out of the nursery and down the stairs.

"All right!" she yelled. "You want to go in the garden? You damn well go in the garden. OK? OK?"

Daniel wasn't sure if it was OK. He was going down to where the garden was, that much seemed clear. It was possible he had got his own way.

He downshifted his crying. Janice opened the door to the garden, shoved Daniel outside, and closed it behind him. There. That was that. He'd got what he wanted. He was in the damned garden, and if she ran like the wind she could catch the end of the Mick interview. She hurried up the stairs. It would only take a minute or two, then she'd come down and get him, even play with him for a few minutes. She just needed to hear about Mick and Marianne and take a miniholiday from the screams.

Daniel looked around him warily. Never before had he been alone in the garden. Over by the wall the big oak tree beckoned. The ladder was against the wall. The ladder was fun. Dad held

him on it, showed him how to go up. Up. He walked to it. Up.
Yes. He was going up. He giggled. Fun. Up. More. He giggled
again. The world looked different. Up. Oh! *Big* up. Ladder finish. Sky! Up. Up . . . Down!

The ladder slipped sideways under his weight. Like a cata-
pult, it cast Daniel away from it, and he flew through the air in
an arc of perfect geometry. His little hands reached out, and his
face wore an expression of toddler surprise as the sharp edge of
the garden table prepared for his arrival. His whole weight was
behind his head as it collided with the pointed wooden corner.
Then he rolled over on the old flagstones and lay still against
the low wall that separated the terrace from the rose bushes.

Donna kicked off her operating room clogs, flopped down
on the dirty couch, and wiggled her toes. The adrenaline still
coursed through her. The road traffic accident had been a big
one—a stove-in chest with a punctured lung, a head wound
with intracranial bleeding, a straightforward fractured femur
that had needed a cast. Then there had been the wall-to-wall
psychiatry for the shock and worry of the relatives and friends.
It had all gone well and she had been in the thick of it. The excitement had been intense. Split-second decisions. Getting the
neuros, the orthopods, the ORs mobilized. There had been
X rays, collapsed veins, and intravenous infusions. Now it was
over, the ER quiet once again. The injured had been distrib-
uted around the hospital to where they could best be looked
after.

The team was relaxing now. They did so in the way that all
medical people relaxed, by drinking strong coffee to prepare
themselves for the next trial and by making bad jokes to let off
steam.

The surgical registrar was lying on the floor in an exaggerated posture of tiredness.

"I think he's angling for some CPR from Donna," said the senior house officer, who had a bit of a crush on her.

"With my luck she'd do the compression, you'd do the mouth-to-mouth," came the resigned comment from the floor.

There was general laughter, in which Donna joined. She loved this. She hadn't panicked. She had known what to do at every step of the way, and she had seen the professionals recognize it. She was part of the team, one of the boys, as she had always wanted to be, and one day in the not too distant future she would be better than all of them. It wasn't just being good at the job. It was the whole thing: the difficulty, the overcoming of it, stretching yourself, getting out to the edge and seeing if you could hang in there. From the doctors there was admiration. From the patients there was gratitude. All the time she had been praying that obstetrics wouldn't beep her, and her prayers had been answered.

"Thank you, luv, for all you've done, and for being so kind," one granny had said. "You don't look old enough to be a doctor like you are, but you're kind, luv. You got time when there ain't none." She had squeezed Donna's arm and pushed a liquorice Allsort at her as a small token of her esteem. It had meant as much to Donna as the duty neurosurgeon's complimenting her on anticipating the need for the IV mannitol to reduce the swelling of the head injury's brain. At times like this, Donna knew she had made all the right choices. The doubts had receded at last.

The door opened into the atmosphere of relieved hilarity. An orderly stood there.

"We've got a toddler," he said. "Head injury. Age three. He's having a seizure. Babysitter says he's been having it for the last half hour."

They all jumped up. Head injury plus seizure equaled a bleeding brain. A seizure for more than ten minutes equaled status epilepticus. The child was probably as good as dead.

Donna was first through the door. In the corridor outside
stood Janice.

"I couldn't help it. He fell in the garden," she said, and the
tears streamed down her face.

With a crash, the gurney came through the swing doors. On
the green sheets was her son. And across that distance of several feet, Donna could see that Daniel was dying.

The music washed over the tiny coffin like waves in a burial
at sea. Donna had chosen the hymn because she loved it, and
love was what she wanted to give little Daniel for his journey.
Her tears would not stop. She felt they never would, because
they would never be able to clean away the terrible sorrow that
was consuming a part of her soul.

Steve was beside Donna at this funeral, but he was not near
her. He stood straight, in a suit that was not as black as the darkness in his heart, and he did not cry, because he was past tears.

The choir sang so beautifully. They were boys of ten and
twelve. Daniel would have become like them, but now he was
an angel, taken by God before his time. Donna wanted to go
forward to him and lay her hands on his coffin. She needed so
badly to be closer to him for the last time. Soon he would be
gone, although of course he was gone already. But she would
have to leave him, and she didn't want to. She tried to picture
his perfect face, asleep in the darkness with Edward Bear. He
had been so afraid of the dark, and now she was so desperately
sorry she had made him sleep on his own in the nursery. There
was so much regret. Nothing inside but emptiness. She had lost
her son, her life, her most precious part, and she would never
recover, not ever, all her long, lonely miserable life.

He had his "blanklet" with him, and dear sweet Teddy, for
his journey to paradise. How he had loved them, as much as her
perhaps, as much as Steve. Teddy and Blanky had always been

there, through the terrors and the tantrums and in the dark of the frightening night, ever ready with their warmth and comfort. They had not worked late, had other priorities, been preoccupied when a small child had wanted to play childish games.

Flowers covered the altar and the coffin, and Donna would never again look at a garden with peace in her heart. His silver christening mug from which he had drunk his "mink" would stand forever in the solitary cupboard at Cunningham Place. "To our beloved son, at his christening. Twenty-Second September, 1971. From his loving parents."

But where had love been when it was needed? Wasted on the bleeding crowd in the casualty department; on outpatients, on the generic sick rather than her own child in need. He had wanted to climb the old oak tree in the garden. That was all little Daniel had wanted that day. He had wanted to show Teddy the view. Had he wanted to be like Spiderman, and do whatever a spider can? How could she have trusted a silly, selfish teenage stranger with her precious son? He must have been so surprised as he fell, so frightened. Had he hurt? Had he been in terror there at the end of a life that should have been just beginning? Donna sobbed out loud and reached for Steve, to touch his arm and feel the solidarity of his pain, but he drew away from her. She was alone, as Daniel was alone just feet away from her, when he should have been alive and giggling in her arms.

The hymn was over and an intense feeling of unreality wrapped tight around Donna. She recognized the defense mechanism as her mind tried to escape this intolerable suffering. The pastor was climbing the steps to the pulpit, his shoulders sagging with the weight of the meaningless words he would speak.

"There is nothing so sad as the death of a child," he began.

Yet again, Donna looked at the tiny coffin, tearing away the wood, ripping it apart to gaze in lingering love at what she had lost. He was dressed in the Spiderman costume he had loved so much, Teddy in his arms, blanklet beneath him. His big blue eyes, so full of wonder at life, were closed now in his endless sleep. Inspector Gadget, He-Man, Master of the Universe, and Man-at-Arms were the spirits watching over him. And she wept openly as she remembered the missed bedtimes, the stories unread, the dear back unstroked by an absentee mother who had never dreamed that time was so short and so precious.

"It is not given to us to know the mystery of God's purpose. But faith comforts us, because faith . . ."

Steve felt the numbness of death. He had no faith in God's purpose. Anger rose up within him as he stared at the coffin. Inside it was his life. Daniel was the son who had lit the bright ring of fairy lights around his heart. Melancholy, seriousness, obsession, the cold, strong emotions that held him in their grip, had melted like fog in sunlight when Daniel had been in his arms. Daniel had made him laugh, taught him how to feel warm and protective, lightened his life.

Beside him, their backs straight and their lips stiff, sat his parents. Their presence, their very demeanor, was a reproach to him. *They* had never farmed him out to an au pair. His mother had given up her career in medicine to raise him. He had rebelled against their self-sacrificial decency and chosen a different path. It had ended in this tragedy. He remembered his father's shocked silence when he had told him on the telephone three years ago of his plans for a sudden wedding. That silence had somehow predicted this ending. Donna had been many wonderful things, but she had not been a traditional mother to Daniel. She had put her career first, and despite his attempts to rationalize it, Steve had always resented that. He had read the bedtime stories. He had roughhoused with Daniel on the nursery floor. He had been there at bath times while the nanny that Steve loathed and Donna relied on had tut-tutted her disapproval at his presence.

He turned to look at Donna, whose beautiful face was crumpled by grief. He knew at that moment that he must leave her. There was no room for forgiveness in his heart. It was brimming over with blame. Daniel had died because of Donna . . . and his love for her had died with the child. He felt the choking feeling at the back of his throat. "Dada!"—never again would he hear that blessed sound, never run his fingers through that soft hair, never feel the clasp of those dear hands on his forehead as his son rode high and proud on his shoulders.

He would leave little Daniel behind in the cold earth of England, a country he had never learned to love. There would be a stone of gray in that bleak churchyard:

DANIEL GARDINER

1971–1974

Safe in the arms of Jesus

And it would be a memorial, too, to the part of Steve that would sleep forever beside his son, his sunlight.

He would go home now, to America, to the land that believed in children. And he would bury himself in the work that had always been his salvation. Maybe these times would fade with the years like the photographs of Murano and the memories of the Royal College of Art, where he had learned so much, and of life with Donna, whom he had loved so well but not wisely. They had not known who they were. He had been a traditional father all along. And Donna had been the earnest, ambitious doctor who had traveled to Venice with a medical student called Paul . . . a boy who had terrified Donna by being more like her than she had cared to believe.

It was the last hymn. "The day thou gavest, Lord, is ended. The sun sets on another day."

Dragging his heavy heart up with him, Steve stood. By his side, the panic of the parting roaring inside her, Donna climbed to her feet. The pallbearers, like the bleak clouds of their future, were gathering. Out there in the drizzle of the London autumn would be a small, fresh grave.

And so, somehow, together they went there. The wind plucked at their dark shapes as Daniel led them along the path, borne by but two men, all that were needed for so small a burden. Donna looked up at the hurried clouds as they sailed on a grim sky. Where would Daniel say his good-bye? Could she hear his "Mummy" on the restless breeze? She buried her head in her hands as she walked with no hand to support her. *Spiderman, Spiderman, goes wherever a spider can. Da, da, da, da, Inspector Gadget.* "Oh, Daniel," she whispered. "Oh, Daniel, I love you so much."

They gathered there, bleak and bowed, as he was lowered into the ground. She fought back the desire to go to him. Down, down, away from her the best part of her went. A baby's tiny fingers wrapped around her thumb, those staggered steps, the first sweet words . . . only memories. She had only those inadequate traces of her dead child with which to face her future.

13

Kate stood still. She closed her eyes and took a deep breath. Coffee from the Rift Valley in Kenya, three quarters, to a quarter of a Colombian brew that blew your brains out; the comforting smell of the Cornish pasties browning in the oven; scents from a melange of herbs hanging in carefully tied bunches next to the gleaming copper pots and pans that doubled as works of art and cooking utensils. She opened her eyes again. It was 7:30 A.M. Both her Cartier Santos watch, a Christmas present from Peter, and her even more accurate biological clock told her the time. Her day, as always, was on strict schedule. All across America, other households were in chaos now as grumpy children, sleep dust in their eyes, rooted in the fridge on search-and-destroy missions. Frazzled mothers searched for lost shoes and tried to clean marks off school clothes which would hardly do for another day. But in Kate's kitchen, order ruled. The table was laid for Sam's breakfast. There were yellow pansies on the scrubbed pine. A choice of cereal, a hopeful bran and an outsider muesli competed with the favorite Frosted Flakes. The plain earthenware bowl of fresh fruit contained mangoes, dew-dripped from their night in the Sub-Zero, cherries, and big fat gooseberries, as well as the more standard apples, oranges, and bananas. A linen napkin was placed with geometrical precision next to the place setting.

It wasn't extravagant but it *was* well organized. The secret was time. Time and the cunning use of it was what separated Kate from the herd. She had been up with the sunlight, because she didn't need more than five hours' sleep. She felt the rhythm of the day unfold. This was her favorite part—waking Sam.

As she walked up the stairs to the attic bedroom, she straightened pictures on the way, noted buildups of dust, a new mark on the otherwise spotless carpet. She ran her finger along the gleaming banisters; counted the minutes in her mind before the pasties would be done; calculated the time they would have to leave the house to get to Hobbes's, drop off the pasties, and still get Sam to school. She knocked on the door. She always did that. If you were polite to children they learned to be polite to you.

The room, dark and warm, smelled of sleep. But Sam was already stirring. All was tidy. Sam's clothes were laid out neatly across the chair, clean and pressed, her shoes side by side beneath it. Kate flopped down on the bed and knelt in to nuzzle her daughter. It was an old game. Sam would pretend to be asleep; Kate would kiss her awake. "I love you, darling," she whispered against the warmth of her daughter's six-year-old neck. "It's seven-thirty and it's Friday. What happens on Friday?"

"Daddy comes home," said the voice from beneath the covers, buried deep in the pillows. Daddy coming home easily beat "No more school."

"Yes, he does, my darling," said Kate, her voice full of the love she felt for her family. On Friday nights they were always together, and on Mondays too, if they were lucky. Peter had taken to spending only three nights a week in the city. It was one of the many advantages of all the extra money she was bringing home.

Sam sat up in bed. At six she was already beautiful, and totally unbratlike. She tried to focus big blue bleary eyes on her mother.

"Mom, you did your hair in a piggy tail. You were going to show me how to do it."

"I know I was, darling. I'm so sorry. I'll show you next time. It's just that I have a day from hell, and so I did it when I got up. And I didn't want to wake you because . . ."

"I need my sleep," Sam finished for her. "Anyway, it looks real pretty, Mommy." She flopped forward against Kate. "I love you, Mommy," she said.

"I love you too, darling," said Kate with feeling. The terrible twos had never materialized. Were the horrors being stored up for adolescence? At six Kate had been "impossible," according to her parents and all their grown-up friends. But perhaps "impossible" was in the eye of the beholder. Maybe one person's high spirits and love of life were another person's diagnosis of delinquency or hyperactivity. It was difficult to get an accurate picture of just exactly what *had* happened in your childhood.

Kate stood up with a feeling of regret. The day speeded up from here. Fast forward had been pressed. Homework and packed lunch, pencils and books somehow flew together and disappeared into the schoolbag. Fresh milk, cold from the fridge, made its way via a silver mug into a wide-awake Sam, who had metamorphosed into a neat schoolkid from the Rip van Winkle of moments before. The pasties, neatly arranged on silver paper on a vast wooden tray, were carried carefully across the crunchy gravel to the back compartment of the bottle-green Range Rover. Kate had washed the car at dawn, before bathing and expertly juggling the roles of hairdresser, baker, cook, laundress, cleaner, housewife, and mother. She let out the clutch and off they went; then she bent forward and pushed the tape into the player.

"Bonjour," said a cheerful Frenchwoman. *"Ça va bien? Quelle heure est-il?"*

"Il est huit heures moins le quart," said Kate firmly.

"Sept something," said Sam, stealing a glance at her watch. They had about six-and-a-half minutes to drop off the pasties. Even if Sam wasn't learning much French, Kate was.

As she drove along Main Street, with Sam in the back of the car for safety, Kate polished the dashboard with a kleenex and answered the Frenchwoman's questions. There was still room in her mind to rehearse the sales pitch to John Hobbes re the Cornish pasties. Not that she needed to sell anything anymore. As far as East Hampton's Kitchen Art store was concerned, Kate could do no wrong. She had been cooking and baking for them for nearly five years, and they had never been disappointed. Kate reversed neatly into the parking spot outside the village's premier delicatessen. John Hobbes, the owner, seemed to have been waiting for her. Kate smiled. He usually was. He hurried onto the sidewalk. Kate's window whirred down.

"Hi, John."

"Good morning, Kate. 'Morning, Samantha. Beautiful morning it is, too. It was misty earlier, but a breeze came in from the east."

"You and I are the earliest risers on Long Island, John," said Kate with a laugh.

"Best time of the day. No people around." He laughed too.

Kate felt the warmth of her life. She loved this place and its village atmosphere. It was so deeply civilized. There was time for a discussion of the weather. . . . There seemed to be time for everything, although that was partly an illusion. John was always in haste, but never in a hurry. She knew that. She herself had three minutes before taking off again. And yet there was room for manners. For the make-believe, or perhaps the reality, that the beautiful day was as important as any of the hustling and bustling that would take part during it.

"They're in the back," said Kate. "And they are delicious. Sell them with English ale, or better, the cider they drink in the West Country of England. And fruity cheddar cheese to go with it. Real tickle-the-gums stuff. Maybe a crisp green Granny Smith. Some rough, crusty bread. They're the Cornish equivalent of what the English call a ploughman's lunch—cheddar cheese, bread, and pickled onions so big you can hardly get them into your mouth. Give them some blarney, John, and they'll run out of the store."

"Your baking runs out on its own. Doesn't need any rubbish from me," said John in admiration. "Oh, I had Mrs. Van Holland on the telephone yesterday, going on about you and your cooking, saying how marvelous it was."

"I'm seeing her later. I think she wants me to do a big dinner or something."

"Good luck," he said, and rolled his eyes upward. Suki Van Holland was married to perhaps the richest man in the Hamptons. With the tenacity of someone who never quite knew what she wanted, she made it her mission in life to confuse everyone else. Kate rather liked her. The secret to getting on with her was not to need her. That was true of most people and things.

"You have a good day at school, young lady," said Mr. Hobbes to Samantha, as he took the pasties out of the back of the car.

"I will, Mr. Hobbes. Daddy's coming home this evening."

"Well, you tell him I've got those caramel candies that he ordered. The Callard and Bowsers. Jeff Daniels, the dentist, gives me a commission every time they take out a filling!"

They were all laughing as Kate drove off. East Hampton was a family. She waved at Mrs. Schmidt, the librarian who dug out the old recipe books for her; avoided running over the spotted dog that belonged to Buzz Chew from the garage; and narrowly missed Fran Allport, who came out of a parking space without looking. School was reached with one-and-a-half minutes to spare. *"Le jardin est très joli,"* said madame on the tape deck.

"Good-bye, darling. See you at three," said Kate.

"Bye, Mommy," said Sam.

Her car phone rang as she pulled away from the sidewalk, and Kate answered it as she watched in the rearview mirror as Sam joined a bunch of her friends.

"Darling, it's me."

"Hello, husband," she said brightly. She was pleased that he had called. Today felt very good. Clockwork good. Peter calling was the icing on the cake. "Don't say you're not coming this evening." She had a sudden premonition.

"No. no. I just wanted to call you and tell you ... apart from the fact that I love you . . . not to forget Suki Van Holland."

"I'm going there right now. It was in my book. Since when do I forget things, Peter? My problem is that I *remember* things. Like you saying you were going to give up those candies that rot your teeth! There, got you." She giggled delightedly as she drove.

"I did give them up," said Peter brazenly.

"Liar, liar, pants on fire!" squealed Kate. "John Hobbes just told me you ordered some more."

Peter laughed. Why would he ever doubt Kate? He'd bumped into Bill Van Holland at a deadly drinks party a few nights before and pitched his wife as the ultimate domestic troubleshooter in the Hamptons. Van Holland had said that his wife, Suki, played too much tennis to be on top of the household. He had added that he had some Japanese bankers flying in for the weekend to put together the deal of the decade, and he would pass Peter's message on. He had remembered to do so. Suki already knew Kate a little, and had friends who swore by her. Hence the meeting today.

"It would be good to get in with the Van Hollands," said Peter as the laughter subsided.

"I can't charge them more just because they're rich," said Kate.

Peter laughed. "My darling wife. Don't change. Stay just the way you are."

"If I did get them to give me a whole lot of money would you come and live with us all the time and be a kept man?" said Kate.

"The way you're going, I'm almost a kept man already." He could laugh about it, because it wasn't true. Quite yet . . . He was still the number-one breadwinner and he liked it that way. Kate was his brilliant creation. His magnificent find. Everybody she knew now, she had met originally through him. From then on, she had made her own contacts, but, still today, she was more his wife than he was her husband. He longed to see her. Three days was almost too much to bear. He loved to bask in the force field of her energy, her amazing, infectious enthusiasm. To Kate, life was a game, a sandbox of pleasure and fun where nothing was work and everything was exciting.

"What are you wearing?"

"Oh, nothing. I mean denim stuff. Not really *nothing!*"

"What's for dinner tonight?"

"Secret. Something that will blow your mind."

"Tempt me!"

"Oooh! These jeans are too tight. I just have to undo the top button and, ah, that's better."

"Kate!"

"You said 'tempt me.' "

"Oh, God! Look, maybe we should skip dinner!"

"I could pick you up at the station in that black miniskirt you like and . . ."

"Good-bye, Kate," he said in desperation.

"I love you," she whispered, her voice husky with the desire that was suddenly crackling through her. She shifted against the leather of the seat and tried to remember exactly where the Van

Hollands lived. Was it the first or the second left turn off Georgica Road? Kate stopped briefly, consulted her pregnant loose-leaf file and the inch-to-the mile map, then took the second left on Briar Patch. The driveway to the Van Hollands' announced itself on the left by big white gates and a shingled gatehouse that was larger than Kate's home. She wove along the twisting drive, its unnecessary curves attempting to give an impression of length and consequent grandeur. Oak trees formed a tunnel, and beyond them, a tall white picket fence ringed a paddock in which yew trees and maples stood around with the odd horse. The hint of a lilac mist lingered. The sun shone weakly in shafts filtered by the trunks of the trees.

The house finally revealed itself, sprawling, vast. It had been added to but never subtracted from, as the succession of plutocrats who had owned it through the years had grown wealthier, never poorer. Like the other houses around Georgica Pond, the side facing the salt water had a different ecosystem from the aspect pointing inland. The lawns, formal gardens, walled orchards, and kitchen gardens of the estate radiated out from the graveled forecourt where Kate now parked. She noted that the lawns, while well maintained, were dotted with clover. The clipped topiaries that flanked the front door in old urns showed the telltale yellow leaves of manganese deficiency. Money couldn't buy God, love, or detail.

A black-uniformed maid in a white apron opened the door to her. Apparently, she was expected. Kate was ushered across pickled oak floors to what looked like a Mark Hampton library . . . a room that was more Manhattan than Long Island. Its leather books didn't look as if they liked the salt air any more than the Dutch oils that dotted cherry red walls. Kate flopped down on a chintz couch. As she did so, Suki Van Holland came rushing in from an adjoining room.

"There you are," she said, consulting her watch. She was neat and muscled, in white tennis clothes. She insinuated that

Kate was late. Kate wasn't. She was never late. She just wasn't early.

"Hi, Suki," said Kate, not getting up. "We did say eight-thirty, didn't we?"

"Whatever," said Suki, conceding defeat. Kate was not a person to be browbeaten. Suki Van Holland now slid effortlessly into another mode: charm.

"I've got a lesson at the Maidstone at nine. I've simply *got* to do something about my backhand." She raised both arms in the air and clenched her fists, shaking them. She managed to convey both the life-and-death matter of her tennis game and the peculiar impossibility of the world in general. She smiled as she portrayed an all-purpose neurosis. Kate had been exposed to the gossip. Bill Van Holland didn't give a damn about his wife's games, tennis or otherwise, as long as she ran the house like clockwork. The business guests expected it. If a man's house didn't work, it was possible that his companies wouldn't either.

Suki sank into a couch opposite Kate. "Coffee, darling? It'll probably be instant, in the present state of the kitchen."

"Nope. All caffeined out," said Kate brightly.

She looked around the room. The patterned carpets in geo-metrical designs were now signature Mark Hampton, although David Hicks had used them first. The carpet, indeed the room, was out of synch with the pickled floor of the hallway. Kate would have gone more D'Urso, less Buatta; more Donghia, less Saladino, for such big rooms so near something as elemental as the sea.

"What do you think of the room?" said Suki, who never missed a trick.

"Beautiful. Very traditional. I love it."

"Bullshit. It's Park Avenue B.S. I know it and you know it. Frankly, I just didn't have the time." Again, Suki waved her hands in the air. Time was the enemy. She managed to imply that everyone and everything was. She looked like an award-winning ad for the fact that money didn't buy happiness. Kate got the message strongly. There was hardness around Suki's eyes that spoke of inner insecurities, although she was pretty in a brittle, worked-out way. Had the hardness appealed to a hard man like Bill Van Holland? Had it been the cause of his attraction to her, or was it the result of being married to a multimillion-dollar emotional cripple?

"Now, everybody tells me *your* house is beautiful. They say it's a home," said Suki. There was a sadness in the way she delivered the compliment. Kate knew in that instant that Suki would trade everything for the peace and tranquillity of a genuine family. She was the third wife. A son was in and out of rehab like a yo-yo. The pro at the Maidstone would have more than her backhand to sort out.

"Home, sweet home," said Kate. Payne's cottage, in which he had written the song "Home, Sweet Home" was only a mile or two away.

Suki took a deep breath of the cutting-to-the-chase variety. "Anyway, here's the problem. We have a load of Japanese flying in this evening on a private plane, and Bill wants everything to be perfect for them. They're buying something or selling something—God knows what—and the bottom line is that if they don't buy . . . or sell . . . it's going to end up being my bloody fault. The soufflé will be to blame, or the flowers, or . . . or . . ." Suki looked around to find other things that would be held responsible. Drawing a blank, she said, "So you've got to get the cook straightened out, because she's having one of her endless nervous breakdowns."

"You want me to do dinner *tonight*?" said Kate.

"Everything, darling. The whole damned weekend. Breakfast, lunch . . . I think it's twelve meals in all, but frankly I've lost count. Whatever a Japanese thinks he ought to get, that's what I want." She looked at her watch. "So can I just leave it all up to you?"

"I can't possibly do it. Peter's coming down, and my daughter . . . and I promised to do Sunday lunch for the Jeffersons. Then John Hobbes wants a whole load of things . . ."

"No, no," said Suki. "You don't understand. I need you. I need you for the whole weekend." Creeping around the edge of her words was an unmistakable message. Money was talking.

"It's completely impossible," said Kate definitely.

Money had been silenced.

"But what . . . I mean, why would you want to fiddle about with Hobbes and the Jeffersons? If you do my weekend you'd be here in one place, and surely it would make much more business sense. Whatever your normal rates are, I'd be happy to pay a substantial premium . . ." Suki, faced with disaster, was beginning to babble. If you couldn't rely on cash, what could you rely on?

"I gave my word," said Kate. "I've been working for John for five years. The Jeffersons use me all the time. They're friends." "This is the first time you've asked me to do anything" hung unspoken in the air. Kate felt her power, and a strong sense of righteousness. It was great to be wanted, but it was still better not to be controlled—by desire for money, for success, for anything. Kate was making her way on her own terms. Family came first. Friends, second. Business, way, way third. But still, she couldn't help wondering just how much of a premium Suki Van Holland would pay to please Bill and his Japanese. If a huge deal really depended on it, it might be a serious amount of money. Five thousand bucks for an unsinkable soufflé that wouldn't scuttle a billion-dollar deal? The attorneys would charge more for their handshakes. She fought back the impulse to ask what sort of money they were talking about.

"But I need you *more* than they need you," said Suki. There was something touching about her despair. It wasn't put on. There was a thin film of tears in the tough eyes. She didn't know how to do the weekend properly. She didn't know who to hire to do it. In life you had to know the second if you didn't know the first. If you knew neither, you were lost on the slippery slopes of the nouveaux rich whose money bought nothing but laughter and ridicule.

Put like that, the Van Holland request appeared far more reasonable to Kate. She was the one who was needed, and was acknowledged to be so. With the resources of the Van Holland kitchen, Kate's recipes would cook themselves. The flowers could be done in a couple of hours with the army of help that would be available. She could envisage a gigantic mass of sunflowers in the hall, and irises, lilies, tulips, an all-white Beaton-esque theme for the other floral arrangements. It would be a subtle appeal to Japanese minimalism, phrased in terms of North American excess. The cook's "breakdown" would have been caused by the uncertain sound of Suki Van Holland's trumpet. Dithering on that grand scale was highly contagious. It would take only a minute or two of hand-holding to get the cook back on track.

Kate thought quickly. She wouldn't have to be there in person the whole weekend. It would be a question of setting it up, restoring the morale of the troops, and then keeping everyone on their toes with lightning visits. Today she could organize the house. She could do the menus; get the vital Evian and digestive biscuits for the guest rooms; the little wicker baskets full of colognes, shampoos, needles and thread, Maalox, and all the other good things like Godiva chocolates that would make a Japanese heart sing. The gardeners would have to trim the topiaries and cut out the yellow leaves one by one, and the gravel of the drive needed raking. Each room would need potpourri. The house simply didn't smell delicious, and houses must. There would be shopping to be done. She remembered that the crown of lamb had looked good at Dreesen's; John had some well-aged Aberdeen Angus beef; and her own larder was stuffed with a bewildering array of rough pâtés, cornichons, olives, and all sorts of other fruits and vegetables she had pickled herself.

Kate made the decision. It could be done, and without compromising promises.

"OK, Suki. I'll do it. I can't be here all the time, but I guarantee your Japanese will have a weekend they won't forget."

Suki jumped up and clapped her hands in relief. "Oh, Kate, that's wonderful. Now, what do I have to do? Do I . . ."

"You have to improve your backhand," said Kate with a laugh, "and you have to introduce me to the butler, the head gardener, and the cook, and tell them I'm boss for the weekend." And she laughed, because she was beginning to realize that being boss was what she liked.

The cook was on the verge of tears. "She keeps changing her mind. 'The veal Milanese, no, the sole boone femme. What about the sea bass?' I don't know what I'm doing anymore. I can't take much more of this."

"Listen, it's OK," said Kate, with a cheerful laugh. "She's stressed out. Mr. Van Holland's been on her. You know how it is. Pressure. Wanting everything to be perfect, worrying that it will be, and then messing everything up as a result. All we have to do is keep calm and the whole thing will go like clockwork."

An outsize table dominated the old-fashioned kitchen. A couple of kitchen maids smirked in corners, with the perverse satisfaction of those who lacked responsibility when things were going wrong. Kate sat and sipped her tea. The English were right about the drink, it was good for nerves. The cook, fifty, plump, and plain, was regaining her poise by the minute. Kate could tell by the neatness of the room that she would be more than competent, if a little less than creative. She would follow instructions well when they were given accurately and simply.

Kate reached in her tote bag for her notepad. "OK, let's start at the beginning, with English tea."

She talked fast, jotting notes as she did so, the carbon creating a separate copy for herself. The sandwiches must be moist and delicate. The cucumber should be put in the refrigerator only for an hour before serving. Any longer than an hour and it would go brown and watery. There should be plain, buttered toast (white bread) and also toast with Gentleman's Relish—on which the British Empire had been built. Kate would provide the blended teas, the chocolate cake, the orange cake with the white icing that was her speciality. Dinner that evening would go for novelty. Each of the twelve guests would be served a different type of terrine . . . rabbit, duck, chicken, sausage. . . . This would be an ice-breaker. Each diner would be encouraged to try what another had. Which was best? Who won? Originality would be separated from cuteness by the seriousness of the wine, a mighty Le Montrachet, a collector's item, from the huge cellar. The Japanese knew the prices of their wines.

Next would come something that the cook and the Japanese would never have experienced before: Cornish pasties, made of light, flaky dough, full of meat and potatoes for the men; carrots, leeks, onions, for the women. Kate explained how the pastry was folded and nipped by hand to produce a bundle that a workman could carry and eat without implements, using the frill at the pastry's edge as a handle. Once again, for this all-important getting-to-know-you dinner, the food would serve as a conversation piece. Suki would gain brownie points all over the place as she discoursed on "the first fast food." Bill Van Holland would beam down the table at his trophy wife. In turn, the Japanese would nod and smile as they concluded that they were dealing with an honorable man of substance, a man who had not neglected to sweeten the delights of this "workman's fare" with a mind-melting Pétrus 1961.

The weekend roared on, through breakfast on Saturday morning—smoked salmon and scrambled eggs; kedgeree; bacon, eggs, and tomatoes under silver—as the camaraderie of professionals kicked in. Agnes, the cook, was now confident that her melange of homemade sorbets could rise to the occasion of dessert on the first night, and Kate suggested an Yquem to go with it. Agnes chipped in with her own ideas, and soon the whole process was what it was meant by God to be: fun. The moment it became that, it would be great food, too. The broken woman of twenty minutes before had been stuck together with Super Glue by the time Kate got up to go.

By midmorning, as the house hummed with activity, they were all on her side. She had explained to the gardener how to get clover out of the lawn and color out of the flower beds for the formal white, green, and just a touch of lavender-blue effect that was so stylish. Color was for the cut flowers from the walled garden, for the inside of the house, not for out, although on this occasion the theme was white. An undergardener was lavishing attention on the topiaries with what looked like nail scissors. All was calm, all was busy. There was focus and purpose at last. The army had a general. The day was saved.

It was not until the following Monday afternoon that Kate realized just how thoroughly saved it had been. The envelope was delivered by special messenger. Kate tore it open in the hall. The personalized writing paper of Suki Van Holland contained a message that said it all: "Miracle worker! The Japanese bought . . . or was it sold. Anyway deal went through. Bill thrilled. Backhand mended. Love you. Suki."

"Yes!" said Kate, giving herself a high five of congratulation.

As she walked to the kitchen to throw away the envelope, she noticed another piece of paper inside. It was a check drawn on Citibank in New York and made out to Kate in the amount of ten thousand dollars.

14

Peter opened his eyes. The birds were tuning up in the orchard. Dim light was probing the drapes. But the other part of the triad of certainty was absent. Kate's eyes were still closed. She had actually missed a dawn. He smiled in the semi darkness. He was pleased he'd beaten her at something, even if it was only early morning waking. It was odd that he was so competitive with someone he loved so much.

There was another reason he was pleased to have a start on her this particular morning. He had some very good news, news so good he had wanted to deliver it in the freshness of a Saturday morning so that they could savor it together. Kate's breasts rose and fell beside him. Her hair, like new-mown hay, was scattered over the pillow. He turned in bed carefully, trying not to wake her. She turned too, throwing out an arm and making a little noise of satisfaction. He hadn't won the waking race by more than a minute or two. Her biological clock was ticking toward its briefly delayed alarm.

She was never more beautiful—blond and tan, white-toothed and rosy-lipped—and she smelled like a warm puppy that had

just had a bath. He moved closer to her in the bed, his naked leg
touching hers. Once again she moved but did not wake. He felt
the thrill of pride as he looked at her. From the moment he had
seen her, he had recognized her promise. In those days they
hadn't known where she was going, and in a way they still
didn't, but Peter had always known that she was going somewhere. All along the road so far, she had forged ahead. But
from behind he had gently guided her, steering her away from
the craters, pulling her back from potential disaster, smoothing
her way. She was the energy, the raw, original talent, but she
could go nowhere without him. That made him feel safe, important, and deeply secure. The key to it all was that she recognized his contribution, and in a sense everything she did was
for him, to impress him, to make him feel that she was clever.
They were partners in life, and he loved her very, very much.

And then her leg moved very gently against his.

"You woke up first," she whispered, her voice cloaked in
sleep.

"I beat you," he said, smiling, giving voice to his earlier
thought. He twined his fingers in a lock of her hair and propped
up his chin with his arm and fist as he watched her.

"Beat you at staying asleep," she said, yawning hugely and
stretching.

"After that Van Holland thing, you're more or less beating
me at making money. You star," he said. He collapsed onto the
pillow and nuzzled his face close to hers, breathing in the delicious smell of her.

She tweaked his nose playfully. "But who was the guy
pulling the strings behind the scenes, making things happen,
dropping names in the right ears? I can't see Suki Van Holland
laying ten big ones on me if I took an ad as a caterer in the local
paper." She gave his nose a final twist. Then, with the hand that
had twisted, she touched his stomach and giggled.

"What's so funny?"

"I was going to ask how long you'd been up."

"Kate!" He laughed. He liked it when she got crude. There was something of the naughty child in her, the desire to shock the adults. And of course he was the adult, even though he was only five years older than her. Adult was attitude, not age. Everything was attitude, come to that. Kate's attitude was perfect. She seemed to know intuitively what he wanted, what he needed. He had been fishing with the Van Holland remark. It was a tiny bit threatening that she was doing so well, and there was more of that to come when he told her the secret he had been holding on to for three days. She had sensed his frisson of insecurity, perhaps unconsciously, and she had defused it by acknowledging his role in her success. *He* knew that he had got her the Van Holland job. The important thing was that *she* knew it. To be a silent partner was to suffer the world's lack of recognition. To have Kate's more than made up for it.

"We're a good team, aren't we?" said Kate, again in tune with his thought. "You rope 'em in. I nail 'em down." She sighed. "I'm so happy," she said. "I just feel there's nothing that can go wrong." Her hand moved on his stomach. "I love you," she whispered, and her voice sunk low, to where his feelings were. He put his arms around her and turned fully to face her, and she moaned her satisfaction at the fact that life could get even better than this.

Neither of them were ready for Sam's arrival, but that was Sam's plan. She ran across the room and launched herself like a missile, landing on top of them in a flurry of limbs. "Couldn't sleep," she shouted breathlessly. At precisely the same moment, the telephone rang.

"Oh, great!" said Peter. "A daughter is one thing this early in the morning, but who the *hell* is on the phone?"

Kate laughed as she picked it up to find out.

"Look, Kate, darling, it's me, Suki. I'm so sorry to ring, but I remember you saying you were always up at this time . . . and I'm desperate . . ."

"Hi, Suki. No, it's fine. Peter and I were wide awake." She

tried to kick him under the covers, but Sam had set up a road-block between them.

"Well, I'm just getting organized to go to a tennis camp in Montana, and Bill's got this think-tank seminar . . . you know, an all-male, all-bore, golfing, drinking, Fortune Five Hundred thing . . . or is it Forbes Four Hundred . . . I don't know. Anyway, he says I can go to Montana if I can get you to make it all go smoothly. If I can't get you, he says I have to stay. I mean, can you *believe* the boredom . . . all that money talk, jock stuff, taxes, and the politicians they bought or sold. I mean, I'm just too *old* for it . . . or too young, I don't know. The bottom line is, you have to do it. Same deal as last time. Bill hasn't stopped raving about those Cornish pasties. There's a head of some Japanese bank who eats them all day long now, after the famous weekend. Anyway, you will do it. Save my life."

"Of course I will," said Kate, laughing. "When did you say? Thursday through Saturday evening? No problem. Yes, the gar-den. No sweat. Yes, flowers. The butler. He's a sweetheart. Yes, I do mean it. You just have to tell him he's terrific. No, you don't have to call. You just practice that killer serve. Are you going alone? Oh, Joe from the club. No, never met him. Somebody said he looked like Valentino. Better? Really? Well, that should be *lots* of fun. No, don't worry about a thing. I'll even get them go-go dancers if they want. OK. OK, Suki, hold the go-gos. Only joking. Talk to you next week. 'Bye."

Kate slammed down the phone. "A boys' weekend for Bill Van Holland and his cronies. I can't believe it, Peter. Agnes is a superb cook, the butler is a real pro, yet she wants to spend ten thousand bucks on me because she can't handle them."

"There you have it," said Peter. "It's all in the handling. People are a people game. The help can't handle Suki. She can't handle them. But everyone can relate to you. Lots of trou-bled waters in this life. Not enough oil."

"Oh, you wise one," said Kate, punching out at him in happiness.

"*I'm* a wise one," said Sam, squealing as Peter tickled her.

"Attention, attention," he said, laughing and loving her. "How come I'm not cross when an insomniac daughter comes crashing into my bedroom in the middle of the night?"

"An in-what-ack?" asked Sam.

"Do you want to make a dollar, darling?" said Kate.

"Oooh, yes, please."

"Two cups of tea. Like you usually make it. No mess in the kitchen."

"Two dollars if you take ten minutes," said Peter.

"Is ten minutes enough?" giggled Kate. "It never used to be."

Sam scampered across the room, kitchen-bound.

They laughed together when they were alone. There wasn't time of course, but there was time for Peter's news. It was the perfect moment for it.

"Do you want the good news, or the bad news?" said Peter, setting her up for it.

"There's *more* good news? Better than the Van Hollands?"

"About . . . well, let's see, about, say, ten times as good."

She went silent.

"You know I took those notes up to Manhattan for that idea for a book. *Lifestyles.*"

"Yeees."

"Well, I had them typed up into proposal form. I fiddled around with it a bit and came up with a concept . . . you know, 'you don't have to be rich to be stylish,' cheap chic, along the lines we discussed."

"And?" Her head was to one side. Half of her knew about half of what was coming.

"I took it to Brad Feinstein at Prestige, and pitched him the idea."

"Oh, Peter!"

"He loved it. *Loved* it. I got us fifty in advance, best-seller clauses, a guaranteed thirty thousand first printing. But the real news is he's sold on the idea. He's right behind it, and he's the number one guy there. They *make* best-sellers. Fifteen-city author tour, point of sale, trade and magazine advertising. They're going to put you *out* there, Kate, where everyone can fall in love with you, not just me."

Her mouth dropped open, and her eyes shone with a wild joy. Peter felt his heart opening wide. This was it, the best moment of his life so far. Telling her was better than selling the book. He had never quite realized before how quietly ambitious he was. It was Svengali business. He liked to pull the strings and watch Kate take curtain calls. He was the star-maker and only the star knew it. It was like a secret obsession . . . winning through his wife. That way he was never on the line himself, never at risk. It was ignoble in one way, perhaps selfless in another. Like so much of life, it was difficult to say if it was good or bad, easier to say that it was true.

Now she would melt in his arms. If there was not time to make love, there would be time for a long, lingering kiss and for the all the warmth and closeness that he treasured so much. But she didn't lean in to kiss him. Instead, she jumped from the bed, naked and breathtakingly lovely as she scooped up a terry cloth robe from the chair over which it had been draped.

"That is wonderful, Peter. That is deeply, incredibly *wonderful!*"

"Where are you going, Kate? What are you doing?"

"What do you mean, what am I doing? I've go to get down to the office. I've got to get those notes out. I've got to get to work on the book you've just sold."

"Don't you want to hear more about it?" he tried.

She laughed at his expression of incredulity. "You just told me. Fifty thousand, a bestseller, Feinstein loves it. What else is there to tell? Now I've got to write the thing."

She saw the disappointment in his face, but for the very first time she didn't seem to understand it. She ran back to him, tying the robe's cord around her waist. She leaned down and gave him a peck on the cheek. "Darling, you are so brilliant. You sold my book. You are *so, so* clever." And with a little squeal of delight, she was gone.

Peter put his hands behind his head and wondered what had happened. Her words, for the first time, had sounded strangely empty. He was alone. The warmth and closeness had gone, as if the sun had slid behind a cloud. A chill had descended. The fullest moment in his life had turned almost immediately into the emptiest. As if to highlight the fundamental nature of the change that had so suddenly and inexplicably occurred, Samantha came into the room struggling with a beautifully laid out tray, as befitted breakfast-in-bed by the daughter of Kate.

"What's happened to Mummy? She rushed past me on the stairs and nearly knocked me over," said Sam.

"I don't know," Peter answered, and he truly didn't. But what he had wanted to say, had nearly said, was "I think she's left us."

15

Donna Gardiner stripped off the green tunic and flung it into the bin. It was wet with her sweat, and her bare skin glistened beneath the neon light of the washroom. She was alone. The ordeal was over for another day, the glorious, terrifying challenge that left her dripping and drained. She undid her bra, and shook her head, freeing her bunched-up hair, which had been crammed all afternoon in the hideous green cap. She slipped out of her panties and stood there in the cool for a moment, savoring the relief of the coming shower. She caught sight of herself in the mirror. Her body looked very good, fit and lean, and it needed to be. She had been standing for four uninterrupted hours beneath the hot lights of the London Hospital operating room, bent over, both hands sunk to the elbows in the abdomen of a man who had turned obesity into an art form. They had brought him to the emergency room in the upper abdominal agony that could only be gallstones in the common bile duct. The cholecystectomy in which Donna had removed his gall

bladder had been uphill all the way. Chalk from the inside of
the latex gloves was clumped with sweat on her hands, little
beads of white that would soon be washed away with the tension of her tired shoulders and the stiffness of her aching neck.
Talk about manual labor! Dockers didn't come close. In
surgery there were no breaks, no lapses of concentration, no
coasting along on muscle power alone.

She walked into the shower and turned it on, cold only. She
shuddered as the water hit her, and let out a small shout of
mixed pleasure and pain. She closed her eyes tight and tried to
shut out everything but the tingling physical sensation. It didn't
work. The operation flashed back . . . high speed action replay
complete with the standard droll jokes of the anesthetist: "That
little area's got a good blood supply," when Donna, as all surgeons did from time to time, sliced through a slightly larger
than normal artery. Then there were the traditional house surgeon's witticisms: "Do you want this next stitch cut too long or
too short, ma'am?" She relived the panic that came at some
point in nearly every operation when there was neither room to
maneuver nor the space to stitch amidst vital organs that threatened on every side. The BP of the hypertensive patient had
forced her to hurry, even as the obesity that caused it had
slowed her down. But she had got there, as she always did.
There had been the usual thrill of triumph. And there had been
the added reward of admiration in the eyes of the house surgeon, the medical students, and the operating room nurses, who
knew that God in his strange wisdom divided surgeons into
good and bad like he did people into rich and poor.

Donna felt her adrenaline high begin to wind down. Now the
least favorite part of her day loomed—evening. She looked at
her watch, wiping water from her eyes with her right hand. Six-
thirty! *Damn!* It had been knife to skin at two and she should
have been closed and bandaged by five. Bob was coming at
eight-thirty. She wouldn't have time to relax before dinner. She

stepped out of the shower, grabbed a towel from the pile, rubbed herself briskly.

The door opened. It was Rosie Frances, the woman in charge of the OR, who had been assisting Donna that afternoon. The two were old friends.

"That was hardly surgery," said the Irish woman. "It was more like mining. Great job, Donna. I wouldn't have liked Rogers to have drawn that one." She looked around the room, feigning guilt, as she bad-mouthed Donna's colleague. Rogers had the unhappy knack of making the easy look difficult and the difficult impossible whenever he operated.

"Oh, Johnny would have got there in the end. It's just that he adores drama. He should have spent his life on the stage, not in the theater." Donna walked across the room to her locker, un-selfconscious in her nakedness. She fiddled with the combination lock and started to pull out exercise clothes: a track suit, sneakers, big white socks.

"Fun evening lined up?"

"Oh, *superb,*" said Donna with mock sarcasm. "Dinner with someone called Bob. Middle manager at an oil company. Picked me up swimming at the RAC. Divorced. Forty-something. Dinner will be somewhere safe, like a Wheeler's. He'll look brave when I turn down the invitation to come up for coffee."

"You never know with men," said Rosie. "Maybe he'll sweep you off your feet and you'll end up eating breakfast in Paris."

Or Venice, thought Donna. The old memories plucked at her. "And maybe," she said with a laugh, "your Mike will give up Guinness and you'll never be pregnant again. Anyway, I've been swept off my feet once before in my life, and I didn't like it at all."

"Ah," said Rosie, Irish eyes smiling, "there's your little problem, Donna Gardiner. You never got over your husband. Kept his name all these years, and all the Bobs in the world are guilty until proven innocent. Pity the pair of you weren't Catholics. You'd be happily married today with a houseful of kids to prove it. If God had meant us to divorce He'd have the Pope permit it."

"That sounds almost unbelievably Irish, Rosie," said Donna. But Rosie had a point. Even after all this time Donna still thought a lot about her husband. What would Steve have thought? Would he have approved of this, hated that? God, he'd have been proud of me today! Oh Lord, I'm glad he can't see me now! Never to this day had she met a man she admired so much, nor one so difficult to live with. They had fought over nannies and toothpaste, décor, day care, and Dostoievsky, and an argument with him was still better by light-years than the evening of fawning flattery and suspect self-promotion she would soon be enduring with "Bob." Where was the only real love of her life now? What was he doing? Who the hell was he seeing? Was there a "Sue" to her "Bob"? Probably not. He would be in his great, hot studio molding, carving, and blowing glass as if his life depended on it, which of course it did, and always had . . . as hers had depended on her damned scalpel, needles, and catgut.

She felt the sudden ache in her heart. She wanted to see him now, this minute, even though, in her tracksuit and parka, she looked like a leftover from the Rotary Club bicycle tour. He would frown at her with that great, beautiful furrowed brow and grunt something at her. She would complain about something and then they would be in each other's arms. After that, nothing would matter as the world went away and a magic joy exploded into the purest pleasure she had ever known. And then, inseparable from thoughts of Steve, were the memories of little Daniel. But they were too dangerous to indulge, and Donna blocked them out as, at long last, she had learned to do.

"Irish or not, it's true," said Rosie. And the faraway look in Donna's eyes was evidence that the truth had been spoken.

* * *

The big old house had about it a peace and tranquillity that Donna loved. She walked the bicycle through the gate and chained it to the black-painted railings. The Nash terrace stretched away along the street, secure and stately. Inside the black-painted door with its big brass knocker, thick floorboards creaked reassuringly beneath the Kirman Persian rugs in the hallway. Her grandfather clock ticked comfortingly while her ancestors stared down from magnolia-colored walls in kindly mockery at the triviality of latter-day life's pursuits. They weren't very grand relations, but the family tree went back to John Wood, innkeeper of Bolton, born in 1610.

Donna poured herself a whiskey and soda. She flicked on the answering machine. The fax had already spewed out reams of information from Jane, her superefficient secretary, from her private consulting room. There were several messages: a couple of general practitioners with referrals; two persistent and marginally famous patients who had managed to discover her private line; and one from "Bob," the evening's man, warning her that he was running ten minutes late. His worried tone sounded as if he were signaling the end of the world. Donna's heart sank. He sounded a bit obsessional. The self-confidence that had drawn her to him when they had met seemed to have wilted during the course of his day. She sipped at the Famous Grouse as she wandered out into the garden, which in the heart of London was an oasis of different shades of green. Such color as there was, was strictly white: hydrangeas, iceberg roses, daisies in weatherworn pots. She lay down on the wooden chaise and set the whiskey beside her. She looked back at the house. There was a conservatory on the second floor, and a vine crept up the wall from the garden to fill it with leaves and the most delicious hothouse grapes. Creeper and clematis snaked up the ancient London brick. A fat gray squirrel munched a nut from the big oriental plane tree that shadowed one corner of the garden. A pigeon, one of a much loved pair, was so fat it was

16

Kate came into the hotel room on the run. The scheduled limo hadn't picked her up at Dulles airport, and she had had to take a cab. Her anger had built on the long drive into Washington. In vain she tried to tell herself that these things happened. An author tour was a military campaign constructed of split-second timing. In times of war things went wrong. Planes were late. Weather conditions were unpredictable. But this was human error. That meant someone was to blame. She scooped up the telephone and dragged her schedule, thick as a telephone book, from her tote bag. She found the number of the author tour guide who was to meet her.

A voice came on the line before she even dialed the number: "Ms. Haywood?"

"Yes," said Kate, surprised. It was the hotel operator.

"I have a call for you."

Kate waited, hoping it was Peter. It would be good to let off some steam at him. She had been traveling now for three weeks, on the kind of book tour that Jimmy Carter had said was worse than a presidential campaign. She was exhausted. She wanted to be home. She had overdosed on people, questions, adulation, the adrenaline high of TV and radio fame.

"Kate? It's Barbara."

Kate switched gears for the hundredth time that day. Barbara ran the catering operation in the Hamptons on which the huge success of the books was ultimately based.

"Look, I'm sorry to bother you, Kate. But we have a problem. You know those Italian megabuck people, the Volpis—the count with the house on the lake at—"

"Yes, I know them, Barbara . . . " Kate looked at her watch. A big radio station in Chicago was due to do a phone-in interview in half an hour. Her mind was scrambled eggs. She didn't need biographies of Southampton's itinerant Eurotrash.

"Well, I'm afraid their catered dinner for two hundred last night went rather wrong."

"Rather wrong?"

"The tent blew over, but that was a freak storm and it was late in the evening. The real trouble is that several of the guests got salmonella from the *gambas al ajillo*. One of them is in the hospital. He's OK, but he's very sick. I've just had a call from the Volpis' attorney."

"Where the hell did you get the prawns?" snapped Kate. The Chicago radio interview would take an hour. Then there was a print interview with the *Post* and another with the *Times*. That gave her about an hour to get ready for Larry King, but now she couldn't rely on the Washington transport people.

"Bemerman's."

"We don't use Bemerman's," said Kate. Her voice had gone icy cold. "They sell bad prawns, Barbara. Don't you remember, last year, at the Bernstein's? Bad prawns. Bemerman's. Bad prawns. It's why we don't use them anymore. Remember?"

She spoke slowly, distinctly, her voice dripping with sarcasm, as if to a small and stupid child. She could hardly believe what she was hearing. It was a mighty screw-up. Could she be saved? Thank God the Volpis were Europeans. Litigation horror hadn't filtered through to the Old World yet. Frederico Volpi, an ancient Venetian aristocrat, could probably be sweet-talked out of attorneys. But not by Barbara, the imbecile who had actually bought prawns a second time from Bemerman's.

"I'd forgotten, and they looked so good and fresh. I just thought—"

"Barbara," said Kate, "you are a moron. A great big stupid moron. I'm on live radio to everyone in Chicago in twenty minutes trying to sell my goddamned cookbook, which *includes* the recipe for prawns in garlic. Now you tell me you've put someone in the hospital for eating them. Can't you do anything right? Must I do everything?"

'I'm sorry, Kate, I . . . I—"

"Who did you use for the tent?" Kate cut through the self-indulgent sorrow.

"Peterson."

"We don't *use* Peterson. He's overpriced and he's inefficient. We use Hulett. Or we use Brown's."

"They were both booked out that evening."

Kate sat down on the bed. The doorbell rang. It was her luggage. "Come in!" she yelled. Hell! He'd want a tip. She dug in her bag for change, but there were only twenties. Her mind whirred. The Volpis would have to be pacified. She'd have to call them herself. Her usual tent people would have done her a personal favor if she'd begged them to, but Barbara wouldn't have known how to plead, cajole, subtly threaten, call in IOU's. So the tent had fallen down on the Volpi party as the guests began puking on the bad prawns. Great! Word of mouth would be just terrific! She'd be the laughingstock of the Hamptons. Fifteen minutes to Chicago. And this one to sort out first.

"Give me the Volpis' number." She wrote it down.

"Don't screw up again, Barbara. Do you hear me? Do you hear what I'm saying? I don't need this. I'm working my ass off here, and you're messing it up there. You're undermining me. Do you understand? Who the hell is going to buy the books if the catering operation is chaos? Journalists hear about these things."

She slammed down the phone and tried to stay calm. Did she have time for Volpi damage control? Why did she have to do everything herself? Where was Peter? Why couldn't he take some of the pressure off her? She'd made a million bucks this year and it had gone into their joint account. He had pulled in maybe $125,000. If he took half the cash, why couldn't he take half the heat? Her anger was free-floating. It needed someone to rest on. The telephone rang again.

"Kate. It's Don. Just checking in to see how things are going. How is our nation's capital?"

Kate's heart sank. Anger wouldn't hack it with this call. *Lifestyles* was in its sixth reprint. It had sold 275,000 hardbacks at thirty-five dollars a pop, and it was still motoring. *Kate's Cookbook,* which she was promoting now, looked like it would do as well, if not better. *Kate's Garden,* in development, promised to be another winner. There were videos planned, talk of a TV show, several endorsement deals in the works. Each promised to put upward pressure on book sales. So now Don, the chairman of Prestige Books, had taken to calling her two or three times a week to make sure she was a happy camper and that she wasn't losing it in the pressure cooker of fame and success.

Once again, Kate was forced to change mental direction. "Washington's fine. I'm doing the McCarthy call-in from Chicago in a few minutes," said Kate, trying desperately to sound up.

"And you've got Larry King tonight. That should be a lot of fun. I hear he has an eye for a pretty woman." Don chuckled. He would be sitting in that big office at Prestige, surrounded by wall-to-wall secretaries who took care of every aspect of his life. He'd have had a leisurely lunch at the Four Seasons with Mort Janklow or some other publishing heavy hitter, and he'd actually be a little envious that she was going to do a *Larry King*. Men thrived on this kind of thing. They'd been bred for it—the battlefield, the hunting ground. And Kate enjoyed it too, if she could just focus, if she could just be freed from the distractions. If she could simply have a holiday from all these goddamned *people* who seemed to have taken over her life . . . people who didn't care the way she cared, who let the details slip, who brought prawns from Bemermans, hired tents from Peterson, forgot to send the limo to the airport to pick her up.

She thrust a twenty at the hovering bellboy, furious that she didn't have any change. Hiding her irritation from Don was harder work than letting it out on Barbara.

"Well, Kate, the *Cookbook* is jumping off the shelves. Big sale to England. Even the French have bought it, and they never buy anything, let alone cookbooks. You're our star, Kate. You have a new family with us here at Prestige."

"Thanks, Don. I appreciate the support." Ten to Chicago. The Volpis would have to wait. Would the dress be creased? The cab's trunk had been as small and humid as the black hole of Calcutta. Usually she carried the garment bags in the back of the limos with her. But of course there had been no limo.

"There was just one thing I wanted to raise," said Don, clearing his throat in the way that people prepared others for discouraging words. "There was a review of *Cookbook* in the *New York Times*. Did you catch it?"

"No," said Kate.

"Not the greatest, but who cares? You win some, you lose some."

Why bring it up then? thought Kate, but she was beginning to concentrate on the conversation.

"Nelligan tried a few of the recipes, apparently. She said that two or three of them didn't work. The quantities were wrong, or something, a couple of steps were missing. I don't know anything about it. My wife won't let me near the kitchen or the cook." He sounded definitely charming. Not at all worried. But he had raised it. Just before *Larry King*.

Kate felt the frisson of fear. She had tried out most of the recipes in *Cookbook,* but there were one or two that she had lifted straight from dusty tomes that were long out of print, and, she hoped, out of sight and mind. Now, their ghosts were back to haunt her. She didn't blink.

"I don't know what she's talking about. I tried everything in my own kitchen. Every recipe has been used in the catering operation. It was all tested, all found to be delicious. Nelligan is just a jealous journalist who wishes she'd done a book a quarter as successful as mine. She's probably trolling for publishers right this minute trying to sell one."

"That's what I thought," said Don. "Hope you don't mind my mentioning it. Listen, I'll let you get on. Enjoy, Kate. These are the good old days. You've earned your success."

He hung up. *Shit!* Kate jumped up. Where could she get a copy of the *New York Times?* She scooped up the phone and asked the concierge to send one up. The reviews had mostly been raves. But the *Times,* and Buffy Nelligan! That was a disaster. Everyone would pick up on it. Larry King's researchers wouldn't have missed it. Neither would the guy in Chicago, most likely. She had to know which were the suspect recipes. In five minutes she would be on the air. She felt panic build inside her. Success had been so sudden and so complete that she couldn't help feeling it was all some giant mistake. Money and instant fame hadn't brought peace, they had brought fear. She felt like an impostor. She had attended no prestigious cooking schools. She was no Cordon Bleu chef with stars in the Michelin to prove her worth. She was out there winging it, doing her best, and succeeding. She wasn't consciously fooling anyone. If they wanted to throw money at her, and buy her books like hotcakes, who was she to stop them? It was a free world. But all the time, she was watching the horizon for the storm clouds to gather. That frightened her, and the anxiety made her angry. Then her anger had to find an outlet.

She jumped up. She had to check the dresser. If they were a disaster the Drake might be able to sort them out in time for the evening. But the telephone rang yet again.

"Hi, darling," said Peter. "It's me. Look, we've got a problem."

"Well, hello, darling. Yes, I'm fine, thanks. Well, actually I'm not at all fine, but thanks for asking anyway."

"I'm sorry," said Peter quickly. "What's up, Kate?"

"Oh, nothing much. I have a live radio any second. Barbara has just called to say we're being sued by the Volpis for poisoning their guests. Don's just called to say the *New York Times* says my recipes don't work and the whole book is a con job. Nobody picked me up from the airport. I'm tired and I'm lonely and I'm losing it. Oh, and you've just called up and not asked me how I am, and said you've got some other problem to unload on me. That's it for right now. But then the day is young."

"Shit. I didn't see the *Times* piece."

"Well, what do you do in that office all day? I mean, aren't you supposed to be an agent? Don't you read book reviews, especially your wife's?"

Peter took a deep breath. This was par for the course these days. Kate had changed. Success had changed her, or something had. Her life had got more and more complex. She was stretched thinner and thinner by the demands on her time. In the old days it had been the two of them against the world. They had had time for friends, and somehow their work had been leisure, too. But now there were zeros on income figures that were as long as telephone numbers. With that came an army of people, each with an agenda and vested interest, each having to be handled, manipulated. There were underlings and overlings. Decisions had to be delegated, and with delegation came loss of control. Things went wrong because employees never cared as much as you cared. It made for frustration, and Kate was not good at bottling things up. It was one of the traits he had always loved about her—she blew, she got rid of angst. Then, after the thunderstorm, there would be blue skies again, rather than the constantly somber heavens of a partly cloudy personality. The trouble was that he had become the whipping boy. He, and the army of staff who were beginning to see Kate as a bit of a bitch rather than as a winner who had to pay the price of winning: constant vigilance, insistence on maintenance of the highest standards, the verbal punishment of those who through ineffi- ciency or stupidity put success at risk.

"Anyway," said Kate. "What is it? I have to talk to Chicago. I can't spend all day talking to you."

"It's Sam," said Peter. He was unwilling to lay this one on Kate right now. He hadn't realized what a bad moment it was. There wasn't any going back, however.

"Oh God, not Sam," said Kate. She felt herself deflate. It was like being kicked in the womb. There was business—impossi- ble, time-consuming, full of conflicting demands—and then there was being a mother.

Guilt bubbled up into the mixture of anger, frustration, and anxiety that gripped her. Last week she had been away on the West Coast, touring and had missed the school play, in which Sam had had a big speaking part. Somehow she had known that her spirited daughter would not let that pass. Over the last three years, since *Lifestyles* had taken off, Sam had been living on the back burner. The house had hummed from dawn to dusk with activity, but Sam, who liked attention, had not been the center of it, even when Kate was home. And Kate had not always been at home. For the first time in Sam's life Kate had been away for long periods at a time, like this one, building the career whose trajectory was parabolic.

"There's apparently been a problem at school. Sam stole a tape recorder that belonged to one of the other girls, then lied to the headmistress. Her grades are way down, and they want to refer her to the school counselor, or some child shrink. . . . I don't know."

"Peter, I can't deal with this." Kate felt the tears well up in her eyes. "Don't lay this one on me. Not now. I can't handle it."

Sam was her weak spot. For the first seven years of her life Kate had been the perfect mother, the perfect wife, the perfect manager of the perfect cottage industry. But now she was a cottage industry no longer. Something had had to give, and it had been "wife," and more important, "mother," that had given.

"You don't have to do a thing, darling," said Peter. "I'll talk to the principal. I'll go straighten things out. Sam's fine. It's just one of those things that girls do. I'm sorry I brought it up. Forget it, OK? Just concentrate on what you're doing."

"Oh yeah, great, 'have fun,' like Don says. Barbara, and poisoned guests. Don, and recipes that don't work. You, and our thief-daughter. All I need is brain cancer and then I can get right on and 'concentrate on what I'm doing.' Well, listen to me, Peter. I'll tell you what I'm going to concentrate on. I'm going to concentrate on the contents of the minibar. Right? I'm going to start with the champagne, and the wine, then work through the whiskey, the gin, and the vodka and whatever else they have in there, and if he wants to see me, Larry King is going to have to get the hell over here and hold my head while I vomit. Understand? Are you reading me? Do you hear me out there? I made a million bucks this year, and you picked up a hundred and a quarter nannying that bunch of incompetent clients who call themselves writers. Nobody holds *my* hand when I get writer's block. I don't even *get* writer's block. I'm the one that unblocks the bloody plumbing. Now get the hell off the line so that I can tell the idiot in Chicago that I can't do his show because I'm going to get pissed instead."

She slammed down the telephone and burst into a flood of tears.

17

Peter sat on the plane to Washington, looked at his watch for the hundredth time, and wondered how the hell he could have been so insensitive. These days, handling Kate was eggshell-walking. He had done the equivalent of dancing a jig on her in football cleats. He tried to analyze it. Part of him had not adjusted to the changed circumstances. He still saw Kate as the sweet, competent amateur. She was still somehow his adoring wife, who found time for everything . . . for Sam, for him, for being a superhousewife and, at the same time, pulling in a whole load of money on the side. He had wanted more for her—well, actually for them—and had helped to propel her into the business stratosphere where she was now. He had gloried in the role of back-seat mentor, pushing the buttons and pulling the strings as Kate took on more and more. But with success had come the businessmen, publishers, PR people, accountants, attorneys. Slowly but surely, his vital role in the process had become diluted.

"Anything to drink, sir?" He looked up. The flight attendant was smiling, pretty, uncomplicated. She looked fresh and young.

"No, thanks," he said, distracted. The girl reminded him of how Kate had been. She didn't look at all as if she would need "handling." But then she wasn't earning a million bucks a year. He remembered what Kate had said about that, the reference to his pulling in a tenth of what she made. That hurt, because he had given her her start. If he hadn't sold to Prestige, Kate would still be deadheading the roses and Sam wouldn't be stealing tape recorders. But then they wouldn't be rich. He wouldn't be "Mr. Kate Haywood"; invited to a better class of party; his name on the lips of players who hadn't heard of him a few years ago; his house full of weekend guests whose names were in heavy print in the gossip columns. Next month they were invited to a State dinner at the White House. The First Lady was a Kate wannabe. It blew his mind, but somehow it was neither good nor bad. God, in His mysterious wisdom, took with one hand what he gave with the other.

Peter shook his head, trying to clear away the ambivalence. Hell, he had had to ditch one of his most important authors to make this unscheduled trip. What would he find in Washington? Had Kate been winding him up? Would she really be drunk when he got there? Surely not. Kate never got drunk. Kate, especially the new Kate, loathed being out of control. But then she didn't deal in idle threats either. He tried to assess what the impact of a failure to appear on *Larry King* might be. It was something the publishers wouldn't forget, and the media might pick up on it too. More frightening than that by far was the whole alien concept of Kate's, in her own words, "losing it." He had never expected to hear that from her. Kate was still Superwoman, but maybe she had been exposed to kryptonite in the process of becoming famous. With great difficulty, Peter tried to come to terms with the fact that his wife might actually be human.

Landing, getting the taxi, and the long ride in from the airport yielded few definite conclusions. All Peter knew was that fame had changed Kate; that the change was not for the better;

that he was less important in her life than he had been, and a whole lot wealthier. Now the question was . . . what would he find in the hotel room?

He had not found Kate there. He had knocked on the door but there had been no answer. He had managed to prove that he was her husband, and eventually was let into the room. Had she been lying unconscious on the bed as she had promised? No. The minibar, which he had checked first, was intact. On the bedside table, by the telephone, were some neat notes that looked like questions she had been asked by the listeners of the Chicago radio show. A schedule of her author tour, sitting on the desk, showed ticks against a couple of print interviews scheduled for that afternoon. She was supposed to be at the *Larry King* studio in twenty minutes. There was an address. Peter let out a sigh of frustrated relief. His trip had been in vain, but at least the catastrophe he had hurried to prevent had not occurred.

He thought quickly. He could go back to Manhattan and pretend he had never come. Or he could go on to *Larry King* and gain brownie points by giving moral support, by his overt display of how much he cared. The latter seemed the better plan. So he hurried downstairs, crossed town in a taxi, and talked his way into the green room of the *Larry King Show*. Once again he used the open sesame of "Kate Haywood's husband" to gain entry.

Kate was alone, sitting in a corner, thumbing through a magazine. A huge television monitor was playing a CNN program, the sound turned down. She looked up as he entered, and smiled briefly. Then her smile disappeared. Her initial reaction had been pleasure and surprise at seeing him. But a thought had wiped those feelings away. In a plain white dress with a single row of pearls, she looked simple, yet immaculate, like the million dollars she earned. Whatever she felt or did not feel, she hadn't been anywhere near a drink.

"Well, hello," she said.

There was a mild defensiveness in her manner. He knew her so well. But then, she knew him, too.

"Worried that I would dent the carefully prepared image?" she said.

"Worried, period," said Peter.

"Well, you can relax. I did Chicago. I did the prints. I'm doing the *Larry King*. Your trip was wasted." Her tone was bitter, but not very bitter. He could sense that she felt guilty about creating a scene, and about dragging him all the way from New York. Peter was a man, and men had this thing about exploiting women's weakness when it grossly inconvenienced them. Whichever way you looked at it, he was owed an apology.

"So I see," he said. His tone, too, contained bitterness. "I had to cancel lunch with Ordonez. He's late with his book, and he needed my help." Almost immediately, he regretted the way he had put it. He had given Kate the opening she needed.

"Oh," she crowed in exaggerated understanding, "he needed your help, did he? He's late with his book. Oh my God, how awful! He's late with his pathetic, boring, self-indulgent, crappy book that's going to be read by three hundred people if he ever gets around to finishing it, and which pays us five thousand miserable dollars or less. What about me, and the help *I* need? You don't warn me about bad reviews. Hell, you don't even know about them when they come out. I've answered a hundred questions about that Nelligan review already today. Luckily, *I* got to read it first. *I* was able to refute it point by point. And all you are is number six or seven in a list of disasters to be dealt with. You're not the answer anymore, Peter. You're coming to be part of the bloody problem."

Peter felt the anger well up inside him.

"So your daughter is six or seven on the list is she?" he said, his voice cold. "I just thought you ought to know what is going on in her life. You used to care. It would help if you'd call her from time to time. You should be able to fit her into your sched-

ule somehow. You handle most of the other things." He knew
he had aimed low. The fury had made him do it.

Kate jumped up and threw the magazine across the room.
"Don't you dare throw Sam in my face like that! Don't you
dare!" Her face had gone instantly red beneath the TV makeup.

He knew he shouldn't be doing this before a live TV show,
but he couldn't help it. "I'm just saying call her," said Peter. He
was backtracking.

"Do you have any idea, *any* idea, what I go through?"
screamed Kate. "Every second of my day is spoken for, and a
whole lot of seconds that I haven't got. I have to look good,
sound good, create, manage, delegate. I mean . . . I mean . . ."
She clenched her fists with frustration and waved them by her
sides. Nobody could understand. Peter hadn't a clue. It was too
much for a mere mortal.

"Look, Kate," said Peter, trying to inject a note of sweet reason into the argument but succeeding only in sounding sarcas-
tic. "It's not brain surgery what you do. There are a whole lot of
other successful women out there who are getting through days
just like yours, and aren't making such a fuss about it. Oprah.
Sherry Lansing. Jane Pauley. I'm not saying it's easy. I'm just
saying cool it."

"You lazy, incompetent, arrogant, *asshole!*" screamed Kate.
"Where's Oprah's child? And where's my help? Sherry Lansing
has more assistants than God has angels, and Jane Pauley has researchers and producers and a little operation called NBC behind
her. I have to do everything myself, and it's a different everything.
I'm a one-woman industry, and I even have to carry a half-witted
husband along as a passenger. What I damn well need is a *wife!*"

The assistant producer chose that moment to check that Kate
had everything she wanted and to tell her she would be on live
in ten. Larry liked the guests to come on cold. He said hello to
them only a minute before air time.

"Hi, Kate," the woman began. She didn't finish. Kate carried
on as if nobody were there.

Peter stood still, his face white. He had started something he couldn't finish, and he wished like hell he hadn't. The insulted part of him was furious. The reasonable side of him admitted that his wife had a point. She needed an assistant, a personal assistant who would travel with her and smooth the way and field her calls. She needed the people that stars of her caliber had. Eddie Murphy didn't answer the telephone. His "people" did. They made the statements. Spokespeople said this and that. The famous were shielded from the lesser mortals, and the lesser mortals expected, even demanded it. If you were available to speak to anyone, then you probably weren't important enough to speak to.

"Look, I'm sorry, Kate—," he tried.

"No, it's *me* that's sorry," yelled Kate. "You are just the most insensitive, unsupportive, inefficient idiot I have ever met. You sit on your ass basking in my reflected glory and spending the money I make, and then you have the gall to tell me what *I* do isn't brain surgery. Well, let me tell you this: brain surgery isn't brain surgery. I'd like to see the neurosurgeon that could handle my day. He's learned how to do his thing and he does it. He doesn't have to make it up as he goes along, every day, every minute. The average brain surgeon would probably be paralyzed with fear at the thought of doing *Larry King*. And he for sure wouldn't have to be a mother, because men have got that particular area of general respect pretty much sewn up. That's what you men do, isn't it? You get the glory, and we do the heavy lifting, out of sight, out of mind. The only time you get off your goddamn butts is when you think that the poor little woman is falling apart, and then your own precious little life will take a hit. Let me tell you this, Peter Haywood. I'm the breadwinner in this family. Me. Not you. You're the small change. So maybe you should start treating me with a little respect. It isn't you they want at the White House next month, it's me."

"Look, maybe I should . . . You're on in two," said the producer, and fled.

Peter tried to distance himself from his wife's words. Men could do this. The rational side of his brain was taking over from the less developed emotional one. How could Kate be brought down from this fury in five minutes? In this state, she would go into the studio and tear Larry King's suspenders off the moment he asked a difficult question.

The knock on the door was tentative. The producer poked her head around it like a soldier in the trenches searching unenthusiastically for snipers.

"Are you ready, Kate?"

Kate took a deep breath, closed her eyes and quite suddenly she was "ready." She smiled sweetly and walked from the room without looking at Peter.

He slumped in the chair, and turned the sound up on the TV. Larry King was doing his lead-in to the show: "The woman that many women in America want to be . . . arbiter of style and taste . . . best-selling author and TV personality . . ."

It was almost impossible to believe that Kate would not appear looking fried and flustered. Peter was still quivering like jelly from the arguement. He couldn't have told someone the time of day in this state. He waited in trepidation. Then, there she was, cool as iced tea in summer. Her face was wide open in a broad smile, and Larry King was leaning forward in the way that he did, but somehow with a greater degree of enthusiasm than usual.

"Kate," he began, "what we all want to know is how you do it. How do you find the time in the day to do all the things you do? How do you stay calm?"

"Well, for a start, I'm blessed with a wonderful family," said Kate brightly, the sincerity smiling through. "My daughter Sam and my husband Peter are there for me, and I'm there for them. When you have that in life, you can do just about anything."

Peter's mouth dropped open. It was impossible not to believe what she was saying. But then what about the fight that still reverberated in the air of the green room? Could the things that Kate had said then be true if the ones she was saying now on TV were also? It defied the laws of logic. Or did it? You could change your mind about people or situations. It happened all the time. But in two minutes? From one extreme to the other?

It was at that moment that Peter began to realize that he no longer understood Kate, and that she no longer understood him. A gulf had opened between them and he no longer knew how to bridge it. Once again, he searched for practical solutions as men did. She definitely needed an assistant. He remembered the enthusiastic, strangely charismatic girl whom Kate and he had interviewed once for the job. Kate had, for some reason that he had failed to understand, mistrusted her. She had said something about having "bad feelings" about her, and Peter remembered thinking how unlike Kate it was to be paranoid. Ruth somebody or other. She had written two or three times since, because he had told her that they had still not quite decided whether or not to take on an assistant. They had been clever letters, not badgering, not pleading, but firm in their admiration for Kate and for what she had achieved. He must have them on file somewhere.

"Your husband is an agent, isn't he?" said Larry King.

"Yes, he's a wonderful agent. And of course he was the one who encouraged me to do my book *Lifestyle*. That was where it all started," said Kate. "He's the most loyal person I know."

They were discussing him, Peter Haywood, on *Larry King*. Peter Haywood, the wonderful agent, the loyal husband. They would be watching this on Madison Avenue. The other agents would see it, the publishers, the authors. And suddenly it felt very good to be Kate's husband, whereas only minutes before it had felt very bad.

Perhaps they were not so different after all.

18

1993
East Hampton

"Hell, Kate, you for sure throw one heck of a party."

Jimmy Longstreet was the kind of man who knew what a good party was. Yet, beneath the bonhomie and the loud Hawaiian shirt that was the concession to the Caribbean theme of the evening, behind the red, round face, his mind was that of a shrewd strategist and tactician. He hadn't invented Magnum Inc. He had worked his way up through the ranks of it. When he had reached the top, the company had gone into orbit. Everybody knew he was responsible for that. As a result, nobody questioned his decisions anymore. And nobody was right.

Kate looked around. Her shrewd, professional eye took in both the broad picture and the details all at once. The delicate pink hibiscus flowers that were the table centerpieces had been flown in from Palm Beach that afternoon, having opened with the sun that morning. In four hours they would be wilted. Tablecloths were the garish colors of the islands. The reggae band had a couple of survivors from Bob Marley's outfit, and the "No Woman, No Cry," was pinpoint authentic. Beef patties, corn, the rum-punch bar, a bewildering array of hot sauces from all over the Caribbean, were the details that mattered. It was perfect, that clever mix of luxury and down-market that titillated the jaded palates of the Hamptons' haves. What Longstreet could not know, would not know and would not *want* to know, was that Kate had had nothing to do with it. Ruth, the brilliant assistant that Peter had hired, had handled everything. Kate remembered the telephone call when she had set the whole thing in motion.

"Caribbean or Mexican," Kate had said. "You choose, Ruth." That had been it, and this was the result. Sometimes Kate wondered how she had ever lived without the extraordinary girl who had sat there at her original interview and told Kate to her face that she admired her so much, she sometimes dreamed of *being* her. For some reason, Kate hadn't liked her then. She did now. She was as attached to Ruth as she was to her own right hand.

"I have had a certain amount of practice," said Kate in reply to Longstreet's compliment. Not for one second did she feel guilty about taking the credit for Ruth's efforts. Longstreet would do it without a second thought. In a male business world, you had to play the game the male way if you were playing to win . . . and with this Magnum deal—which this party was celebrating—Kate had won, and won big.

"We should have had some cameras here. Would have made a great scene for the TV show," said Longstreet, swallowing hard on his planter's punch.

"Did it this afternoon just after the flowers arrived," said Kate. "It's much easier to do cameras before a party. I had some friends over and put them where they looked best. It comes across much more spontaneous that way." She laughed the full-throated giggle that Jimmy Longstreet had been attracted to from the beginning. There were not many people at Magnum who were overjoyed about the huge investment they were about to make in Kate Haywood. It had been Longstreet's personal call. When Kate first sat across the vast desk in his office, he would have given odds of a hundred to one against his doing a deal with her. He had hardly heard of her. But his wife had. It was Mrs. Longstreet, a shrewd and hard-nosed corporate wife, who had given Kate Haywood the good press. For that reason alone, he had agreed to meet her.

Then, as Kate had unleashed her grandiose schemes at him, her personality had forced him to use both ears to listen. That was something he seldom did these days. Longstreet had always subscribed to the back-the-person view of investment, but halfway through Kate's sales pitch he had seen the attractiveness of the actual deal she was offering Magnum. Her books had made a fortune for Prestige, and Magnum's own publishing imprint, Millennium, wanted her badly. Then there was the Kate Haywood magazine prototype that embodied the back-to-simplicity/pleasure-of-country-living theme the periodical division had been playing with for so long. The cable interests could capitalize on the publicity from the books and magazine. Hungry for low-cost programming, what could make more sense for them than the cooking, gardening, and decorating shows that Kate had outlined? It was synergy and symbiosis rolled into one.

Now the deal memorandum had been signed, and for the first time in her life Kate was very close to being seriously rich. But not quite yet. Magnum had an "out" clause, a carefully written formula that allowed Magnum to withdraw from the deal if various profit objectives were not met. There was one remaining problem, and Jimmy Longstreet intended to bring it up with Kate this very evening.

"Listen," said Longstreet with an appreciative laugh, "spontaneity is almost as difficult to organize as sincerity. The people who know how to do it go far."

He looked fondly at his asset. Kate had not come cheap, but his finely tuned gut told him she was going to pay off big. There was just this one hurdle to be jumped. How high would it be? It was a question of choosing the approach, getting the timing right. He looked over his shoulder to the dance floor. Peter Haywood looked more prep than Caribbean in his lime-green linen trousers and Cole-Haan loafers. His beautiful daughter, with whom he was dancing, had decided Palm Beach was about as near to the islands as she was prepared to go. She was dressed in a bright Lily Pulitzer shift, her blond hair drawn back from her face, a large white hibiscus flower twined into it. Father and daughter were laughing, happy, as they gyrated in-expertly to the band. Each time a speeding of the music seemed to demand that they split apart, they hurried back together again at the first opportunity. They looked close. Two-thirds of a happy family. Longstreet felt a sliver of doubt.

"Kate, what about a dance? I'm sure you've got a book in you called *Dancing*."

She stood up, smiling. "I've got a book in me called *Dying* if you think it would sell." Again she laughed, that deep-throated giggling business that he just loved to hear. She was a man's woman. Hell, she would be a man's man if she wasn't so damned good-looking. Longstreet liked her cynicism. She wasn't afraid of talking bottom line, there was no hypocrisy. The most impor-tant thing in business was to get along with your partners. Talking straight saved the time that was money, the paranoia, the BS, the misunderstandings that undid the most promising deals.

The floor of the tent, carefully sprung, was bouncing. Mag-num executives were everywhere. They were the ones who had dressed for the theme. The Hamptons regulars hadn't bothered. Notwithstanding their loud attire, the corporate people danced with decorum, ever aware of the presence of superiors and infe-riors. The preppie crowd, in contrast, dressed, drank and danced like the upper classes: with careless abandon, zero sense of rhythm, and extravagant narcissism. Unlike the busi-nessmen, they had no one to impress but themselves.

The music slowed as Longstreet and Kate approached the floor. It was going to be a slow dance. As he took her in his arms, Longstreet had a moment of doubt as to who would actually lead. Kate let him do it, but in a subtle communication of body language, this was signaled as a concession.

"Look," said Longstreet, deciding to go straight to it. "There was something I needed to talk to you about. I thought this was as good a time as any. Do you mind doing a bit of business?"

Kate looked at him and smiled. What the hell did he think this party was for? Fun? But she managed a small "must we?" expression that would enable her to run for cover if Longstreet had discouraging words.

"I know I can be blunt with you, Kate. It's one of the reasons Magnum wanted you in the first place. No pussyfooting, no secrets."

"Right," said Kate. She tried to relax in this man's arms. Tension might cost her.

"We had a big meeting today on the structure of the new company. No problems really. Everyone agreed on everything. Except one thing, that is." He paused. She simply stared at him, poker-faced, giving nothing away. She was good. Very good. He had to plough on.

"The consensus is that Peter can't be a part of the decision-making process in this new venture. I mean, obviously he can advise you, and you're a big shareholder. But he can't be an active member of the board. It's nothing personal, but the boys are right: he's an agent. He's a real nice, real bright literary guy, but this is the big time. The major leagues. At Magnum, we pride ourselves on being pros, not amateurs. We're a Big Board company. We have Wall Street breathing down our necks—analysts, bankers, shareholder meetings. Image is everything. I know how important Peter is to you personally, and I know what a big part he has played in making your career come together like this. But things change. What works in one situation doesn't cut it in another. I don't know what you feel about it. I'd like to hear what you have to say."

Kate suppressed the feeling of relief that flooded through her. She had imagined much worse. What did she think? It was a totally new idea. She had always imagined that Peter's position in the business would be toned down somewhat by the deal she had done, but she hadn't envisaged it being totally abolished. Would he mind? She wasn't quite sure. A bit, probably. But then it might be a relief. And there was the money cushion. They were going to be seriously wealthy. In a way, it would be the best of both worlds. His advice would be permanently available to her, yet he wouldn't be coming back moaning about Magnum from various board meetings; poisoning her attitude against her new partners; winding her up to mistrust them. In fact, it sounded like a pretty damned good idea.

"Peter will be devastated," she said instinctively.

"But can *you* live with it?" The Longstreet question insinuated that Peter's being put out to grass was nonnegotiable. Kate knew better. Everything was *always* negotiable.

She flew away from him on the wings of some change in the rhythm of the music. It was purposefully symbolic. "Watch out," her gesture seemed to say, "I can flit away like a butterfly." She twirled, sending her long white skirt billowing out, feminine, capricious, a deadly dealer.

Longstreet waited. He wondered, irrationally, if she would ever return . . . if his remarks about her beloved husband had alienated her forever. And then she was back in his arms.

"I think I could persuade Peter. I don't know how. Maybe, if I built him a big office wing on the new house, you know, with state-of-the-art computers, the billiard room he's always longed for. That would be something. Something to soften the blow."

"Sounds like a hundred and fifty grand to me," said Longstreet.

"More like a quarter of a million," said Kate, her face only just straight.

Jimmy Longstreet laughed out loud, and moved in close. He couldn't remember when he'd had so much fun spending two hundred fifty thousand dollars.

"Isn't it great?" said Kate. She clicked her fingers in the air. "A quarter of a million. Just like that. Ten seconds. Less. Can you believe it?"

On the couch, slumped against the chintz, surrounded by embroidered cushions, Peter looked as if he did not believe it. Further, he looked as if he did not *want* to believe it.

"Why?" he asked simply. The music wafted in through the windows. The party was firing on all cylinders.

"What do you mean, 'Why'?" said Kate. Impatience was in her voice already. She had convinced herself that she had brought glad tidings, and that was how they should be received.

"Why," said Peter slowly, "should I be phased out like some superannuated old fool, when I know more about your business than anyone? When I helped *create* it. When my contribution to its future has to be as important as anybody's."

Kate took a deep breath. "The people at Magnum are professionals, Peter. This is a whole new ball game. It's the big time. It's not just you and me making things up as we go. That's what happens. Businesses grow. Big things need to be handled differently from small things."

"Those idiots don't know a thing about what we do. About what we want to do. They're a corporation, Kate. They don't understand this operation. The fact that they want to get rid of me proves it."

"Hey, wait a minute," said Kate. "This is *my* business they're buying into, not yours. Me. Kate. Frankly, Peter, I think they're right. I know you helped get me started. You helped up to a point, and that was great. But you got half the profits, too. We've always had joint accounts. You're going to make a whole load of money from this deal, *and* I just got you two years' salary as play dough. Don't stand in my way on this. They want you out of the decision-making loop. It's not negotiable. I've agreed to it."

"Then you had no damn *right* to agree!" Peter shouted suddenly, the anger welling up inside him. He was aware of how rarely he raised his voice to Kate. But there was a sense in which it wasn't Kate he was talking to. The old Kate wouldn't have thought like this, let alone talk like this. They had always been a team. That was what they had. It was what they were. They had stood side by side covered in paint and plaster and fallen dog-tired into bed at the end of hard, happy days. They had sat up nights and pored over layouts and dreamed up ideas, sparking off each other until their batteries were flat. Yet there had always been time to make love. There seldom was now.

"Right? Right? I have the right to agree to any damned thing I want. I have the legal right and the moral right. Who the hell do you think they're buying here? You? *Forget* it, Peter. They don't even want you near the board. They don't want you on the writing paper. They're even prepared to pay a quarter of a million to make you go away. What you get is what I give you, because it's me they're paying the megabucks. Me. Me. *Me!*"

Peter lay back on the couch and stared at the stranger that had been his Kate. He had never seen her like this. Oh, she had changed, acquired a temper, been dismissive of him, intolerant. But this was something else entirely. It was almost as if she were ill. When next he spoke, he did so quietly, trying to reason with her, although he could see that she was too angry for reason.

"Kate, Kate, listen to me. Listen to me."

"I don't want to listen to you! Don't screw up my party. Why do you have to spoil everything, just at the moment when everything is perfect? You're jealous of me. That's the problem, isn't it, Peter? I've made it and you haven't . . . and you can't bear it. You always patronized me. You always felt superior to me, and that was how you liked it. My clever little wife! Look what she does! Look how well she does it! Then the money started coming in and you liked that, too. You loved it. This great big house, the place in Manhattan, Montana. But still you wanted to think that you were the one who had made it all happen. I let you think that. I went along with it. But it wasn't true, Peter. You were the passenger, I was the locomotive. Because you were my husband and I loved you, I let you live in your fantasy world. But now it's different. It's payoff time. We all have to wake up and stop pretending."

"Yeah, it seems there's been a lot of pretending," said Peter bitterly. "I notice you say 'loved' in the past tense."

"Don't pick on that. Don't pick out one damn thing I say like some pedantic lawyer. 'Love,' 'loved,' who cares? You're my husband, you're Sam's father, and we're a family. What the hell's love got to do with it? I'm talking about business here."

He shook his head. It was pointless to go on with this. They were looking at the same past through different eyes, and they saw different things. Peter couldn't imagine not being part of every aspect of Kate's life, and he had always believed that she had wanted that too. When he looked back he saw them as inseparable, up ladders, digging ditches, their bodies twined together in passion. In his mind they were one. They had always been one. So it was impossible to say who had done this, which had been responsible for that. Yes, she had been the front woman, he the back-room boy . . . but they had been a unit. It was that fundamental truth that Kate was now denying, and it was turning his whole life upside down.

Kate stared at him, her eyes open wide in anger and exasperation. He had wanted this from the very beginning. This was what they had worked for. It was the dream come true. She was somebody at last. She had suffered through all those early years of neglect, the lack of comprehension on the faces of her parents, their total abject failure to realize that she was special. This was the payoff for that. She had proved everyone wrong, the dismal teachers at the hideous institution, the reports, the dire predictions, the shaking heads. She had thought that Peter was different. She had imagined that he had wanted her success as much as she had. But all the time he had been ruled by male pride. He had wanted her to be his creature, his plaything, his prize possession to show off and put back on the kitchen shelf. Here was the proof of it. At the summit of her life so far, he was raining on her parade. She had made him millions, and he was trying to make her feel guilty. Well, she wasn't going to feel guilty. Not now, not ever. She was going right back to the party and she was going to have a good time. Peter could damn well apologize in the morning.

19

The models came out fast to the reggae beat, jiggling, swaying in carnival mode. They snaked through the tables, laying their hands on the shoulders of the guests, titillating, tantalizing, hurrying on. It was another of Ruth's ideas, and Kate's bad mood vaporized as she saw the effect the fashion show was having. It was a neat touch. Kate had come out with a line of bath wear in bright knock-your-socks-off colors . . . big bath towels, terry-cloth robes . . . to complement her line of "Kate" cosmetics. She was in the process of negotiating a deal to sell them exclusively through Bloomingdale's, and it was a contract that Magnum was interested in buying into. So now, the models were wearing the towels in any number of provocative combinations—as long saris brushing down to the ankles; bunched up as short dresses; as turbans. The multicolored effect and the African-American models fitted in perfectly with the Caribbean theme, while at the same time putting Kate's wares on display to the Magnum executives and their wives. Kate's eau de cologne, Islands, was getting an outing, too. Several of the girls carried it, spraying it lavishly, scenting the air with the fragrance of night-flowering jasmine, citrus blossom, and the heady aroma of gardenias.

Kate sat down at a table of employees from her own company amidst a chorus of compliments. Her eyes sparkled. All around the room they were applauding the fashion show. She saw Jimmy Longstreet huddled with his wife, smiling, talking intently. He caught her eye and his smile broadened. He gave her the thumbs-up sign across the crowded room, and his wife waved enthusiastically. The campers were happy. The whole thing was a superb example of what Warhol had liked to call "business art." Everyone was having a great time. Everything was in the best of taste. But it was all about making money.

"Anybody seen Ruth?" said Kate. "I mean she has *really* done it tonight." There was a chorus of agreement from the people who knew. Everybody had seen Ruth at some time or another, moving like a ghost in the machinery of the party, smoothing rough edges, oiling squeaky bits, making it go faster, slowing it down. Nobody had seen her recently.

Kate felt the sharp tap on her shoulder. Samantha stood there, color high on her cheeks.

"What the hell have you done to Dad?" she said, not caring who heard. Employees were family.

"Hello, darling," said Kate, half turning in her chair. She could tell there was going to be unpleasantness. Her cheery welcome was a forlorn attempt to head it off. Samantha was looking very beautiful tonight, Grace Kelly cool, somehow untouchable, cold, and yet as explosive as the film star princess. Kate flashed back to all the ugly stages . . . the braces, the plump phase, the time when Sam had refused to bathe or clean her teeth. Samantha had always been difficult, attention-seeking, demanding, but Kate loved her. It was just that she had so little time for her now. Luckily, Sam was grown up, off at Brown. But as she stood there, the childish spite that Kate remembered so well sparked in her eyes.

"What have you done to Dad?" Sam repeated, ignoring her mother's friendly welcome.

"What do you mean, what have I done to Dad? I haven't done anything to Dad. You make him sound like a child some bully has beat up in the school yard." Kate laughed, still trying to pass it off. There were nervous titters from the employees.

The color on Sam's cheeks deepened. Escalation was in progress. "He says he's out of the company. That Magnum wants it that way. That you agreed with them. Do they? Did you?" Sam's tone was that of a heavy-handed policeman.

Kate felt the bile rising. She didn't need to be talked to like this. She had never needed it from Sam. Nor from anyone else, for that matter. Hell, this was her big evening. She had made the family a fortune, and all she was getting from everyone was grief and pain. The only people who seemed to understand what was really going down were the suits in their Hawaiian shirts. Kate was aware of the inadvisability of letting this row continue in front of people who worked for her, but her temper couldn't be controlled once it was let loose. She wished she were one of those cunning people who could use their temper rather than lose it, but she wasn't. She took a very deep breath.

"Listen, Sam, you're not stupid. Just listen to me. This is the deal of a lifetime. Magnum is paying a fortune for a share of the business. They're brilliant businesspeople. Professionals. In exchange for their money they want some control. They want their managers, their people. I understand that. I respect it. They think it would be better if Dad wasn't involved. They might even be right. The bottom line is that it's nonnegotiable. I'm not going to jeopardize the entire deal because Dad's feelings have been hurt. He's getting millions as damages for hurt feelings. Nobody pays me a red cent for my hurt feelings. Like now. Like when your father accused me of selling him out this evening."

Sam paused. She had a quick mind, and she had already developed an interest in the material things in life. She might be a daddy's girl, but she had always respected and admired her mother. Kate knew Sam well enough to know that there was a war going on inside her daughter. Emotion versus reason. The age-old enemies.

"You never take account of Dad's feelings, do you? You expect people not to have feelings, like you. You run over him like a steamroller. You abuse him, and you give him no affection. All he wants is for you to love him. Can't you see that everything he does, he does for your approval? He doesn't have any friends anymore. He doesn't have a life. You and the business are his life. Now you're taking the business, and you're gone most of the time, too. Sometimes I don't understand you, Mom. I don't know where you learned to be so tough. Are millions all that matter? Didn't someone say once, money doesn't buy happiness? Or fame, or success, or all this . . .?" Sam held out her hands in exasperation to include the whole party and what it meant.

"Well, *thank* you, Samantha," said Kate, her voice getting louder. "You and Daddy again, against me, is it? You don't get it, do you? He spoiled you rotten as a child. He was always the good guy. He gave in to you over everything. I had to be the disciplinarian. I handed out the tough love. Somebody had to do it, or you'd have been a nightmare by now. And don't blame me for your father's feelings. They're his. He chose me; he married me; he knew who I was. He loved the success and the money as much as I did. He pushed me, put me up there. He didn't want a housewife with extras. He wanted a full-blown corporation, and he got one. And when you get what you want in this life, you can't go bleating and whining because your prayers have been answered and you don't like it. Know this, Samantha: if you want success, you can't be too sensitive. I don't see you being particularly sensitive, giving me all this crap in front of everyone on my big night."

The employees didn't know where to look. Kate's rows were getting to be famous. There was a collective sense of relief that nobody at the table was on the receiving end of the boss's irritation.

Sam paused. Her mother's words had reached her. There was some truth in them. Being megarich was far from unattractive. It was just that she adored her father and couldn't bear to see him miserable. One thing she felt with absolute certainty: whatever happened to her in this life, her dad would always be there for her. He was her rock, the foundation on which she could build. That was the basis of her loyalty and love for him. He would never desert her. Never.

"Well," she said, "I'm sorry I'm not being sensitive, but as you are now so very successful and therefore, according to your dictum, not too sensitive, presumably my words haven't upset you at all on your 'big night.'" With a supercilious smile at having the last word, Sam turned and walked away.

"I'm sorry," said Ruth. She stood in the doorway of the living room in an attitude of indecision. Her body language said that she hadn't expected anybody to be there.

Peter, slumped on the couch, his head in his hands, looked up as she spoke. "Oh, hello, Ruth," he said.

"Not out there enjoying the party?" she said with a half smile.

"No. No. I mean, it is a great party, Ruth. You've done a fantastic job. Everyone thinks so. I was just having a rest." He waved his hand in the air in a halfhearted gesture that was meant to signify tiredness.

"Well, thanks a lot, Peter. If *you* think the job has been well done then for sure it has been."

Her smile was warmer now. She advanced into the room. Peter watched her. What an extraordinary person she was. In one sense she looked ordinary. She was barely pretty, her hair cut in a severe bob, her suits always Armani stylish, in dark, slightly forbidding colors. But somehow the quietness of her clothes, the bare minimum of makeup, the shoes that were always sensible rather than daring, seemed like a disguise. She was nearly, but not quite, short. Her breasts, however, were large and well-formed but hidden by flattening bras. It was another example of a woman in hiding, camouflaged against the world for some mysterious purpose. Most of all, it seemed, Ruth gloried in keeping a low profile. Perhaps that, even more than her competence and flair, was her cleverest attribute of all. Around Kate, it had survival value.

"Everything under control out there?" he asked. It was an effort to talk. Black despair was settling over him like a cloud. He had been put out to grass, but somehow it was more than that. He had lost contact with Kate. It had been a long time going. The relationship had eroded over the years, sometimes in bursts, sometimes slowly, like a beach washed away by the sea. Kate had moved further and further away from him into her own private/public world where constant action protected her against the dangers of thought and reflection.

But there was always a moment of truth when some line was passed; when the elderly relative with Alzheimer's didn't recognize you for the first time; when the credit check at the car dealership came back negative; when the doctor said "I'm afraid we've found a bit of a problem on the MRI." That moment had been a few minutes ago. It had not so much been Kate's betrayal of him. It had been her failure to *understand* that it was a betrayal. Her failure to know him well enough. Her ultimate failure to care.

"Is anything the matter, Peter?" said Ruth. She came nearer. He had the strong sense that she wanted to sit down but would not do so unless asked.

"Sit down for a minute," he said. "If you can spare the time."

"Oh, yes," she said, smiling again. "The evening achieved critical mass ages ago. The thing now is to let it go by itself. The details only really matter in the beginning. Then the party spirit takes over." Ruth sat down.

"What do you think of it all?" he said. "I mean the Magnum deal. The big time."

"It will be different," she said. "Good and bad, I suppose. What about you?"

"It doesn't matter what I think. I'm out of it. I won't have anything to do with the new company. Kate just told me. Magnum insisted my departure was part of the deal." He laughed bitterly. "Usually the other way around, isn't it? The deal dependent on some key person staying, not leaving."

"I can't believe that," said Ruth. But she said it in a way that insinuated that somehow she could believe it, perhaps had even known about it. It was possible. Ruth had become Kate's eyes and ears. This had probably been discussed before this evening.

"Why not? I'm redundant. I'm not a professional. Kate is the talent. I'm just the unsuccessful husband." He was a little ashamed of his fishing expedition, but he was gratified by the fish he caught.

"That is such *nonsense,* Peter." Ruth leaned forward in her chair to give emphasis to her words. "You started this whole thing. You sold *Lifestyles.* Your contacts started the catering business. You bought Mill Cottage and paid to do it up. Without all that there wouldn't be a business." "Wouldn't be a Kate" was left carefully unsaid.

"Tell that to my wife," said Peter, his laugh a little more cheerful now.

"I'd rather not, if you don't mind." Ruth looked down into her lap with a demure smile. She was diplomatic as well as everything else. Peter and Kate had had a row, but rows blew over. Perhaps, when calm returned, this conversation would be reported.

"I know in one way it seems crazy to care. All the money, everything, it *is* a wonderful deal . . . on paper . . ."

"It's about gratitude, though, isn't it? And recognition. You know how hard you work in this life, and you want others to know it as well. Especially those close to you. People who are close ought to know how you feel and mind if you feel bad," said Ruth.

He looked up. That was it. She'd got it exactly. It was almost as if she could read his thoughts. Yet once again Ruth had surprised him. She was a mind reader, too. Or was it just that she was in the same position as him? Doing all the work for Kate and getting no credit. OK, yes, she was paid, and paid well. But money was beside nearly every point, as long as you had a bit of it. Self-esteem was hard enough to find. It didn't help if others gave you no respect.

"The good old days are always the early days, aren't they?" said Ruth. "The old cliché about the journey and not the destination being important."

"Yes," agreed Peter, laughing, feeling a little better as he talked to someone who apparently understood. "Life is so weird. You have dreams and you struggle to attain them. Then you find they were a mirage in the desert. The struggle was the fun. The dream was just the motivating force, nothing more."

"So," said Ruth. "It's easy, isn't it? You just dream more dreams."

"Why does that sound easier said than done?" said Peter.

In answer, Ruth stood up. She walked across to him and knelt down next to his chair. She reached out and put her hand on his knee.

"I can help you to dream," she said, and she smiled at him.

20

1997
New York

It was a new beginning. Kate knew it. She threaded through the tables and the applause toward the microphone and the small dais. She wasn't nervous—speeches, like most other things, were easy for her—but she was eager. She wanted to say a lot of things to a lot of people. This award ceremony was a God-given opportunity. She wore a long indigo-blue silk Versace dress, one shoulder bare, that accentuated the feminine curves of her figure.

They reached out to touch her as she hurried by them: the waiflike editors of the fashion glossies; publishing panjandrums; the shelter magazine crowd; and the more obscure party people without whom a Manhattan night was not really a night at all. The fact that they had made her Woman of the Year had touched her in a deep and hidden place that money, fame, and the adoration of the Kate wannabes had not visited. She felt different. Tonight the hard-nosed, take-no-prisoners Kate that had hacked success out of stone with her bare hands had gone. She felt soft, female. She felt warm and forgiving. Was this, at long last, the peace that was supposed to arrive by magic at the pinnacle of achievement? Kate didn't know. All she knew was that the time was right, and she was going to take her time. For once platitudes wouldn't cut it. She was going to speak from that dusty, half-forgotten organ that had been silent too long. Her heart.

She had rehearsed her speech but not written it down. It was scattered about in her mind, and there would be surprises. She reached the platform and looked out across the room. The applause was increasing. She smiled, and then laughed openly, the sound of her happiness submerged in the noise of the acclamation. It actually sounded genuine, and Kate briefly experienced the "you really love me" feeling before her intellect squashed it. This was business politics as usual. She had won this award because she had won, period, and some of the people who were clapping loudest were those she had personally beaten. But that truth didn't spoil anything. She wanted to talk to the real people in her life tonight: to Frankie, to Ruth, to Sam, and most of all to Peter. He had put up with so much, but he had stayed the course and now he was about to be rewarded. How had he lived with her temper, her obsessive perfectionism, her unblinking focus on her career? Well, he had. That was what mattered. Kate felt the old love, warm once again in her heart.

She raised her hand to call for a silence she didn't quite want yet. They obliged her with another minute of applause, clapping not just for her but for her books; her magazine, *Kate Haywood's Life;* the television shows; the mighty enterprise she had built.

"Thank you . . . thank you so much . . . please . . ." She laughed and swung her hair from side to side, glowing with the luminous, soft-focus, see-through-gauze smile that America loved. She was a woman now, no longer a girl, but she had never lost the aura of naïveté. It sold well, even to this hard-

bitten audience, who could see beneath the surrogate innocence.

At last there was quiet.

"Thank you from the bottom of my heart. Thank you for this
incredible honor, which of course I don't deserve." She held up
the small glass statue of Aphrodite and waved it to emphasize
her point. "I'm not the woman of this year or any other year.
Out there, across America, hundreds of thousands of women
deserve this more than I do. So I dedicate it to them." She could
see the TV cameras. She looked straight at the one with the red
light on top. This was going out live on her cable show. She
might be speaking from the heart this evening, but she would
also be speaking to the heartland. Her voice, soft, reassuring,
quietly authoritarian, conveyed the message.

"I know how hard you women out there have to work to
make your homes beautiful, your meals wonderful, and your
gardens productive. I know what you sacrifice, and how many
of you aren't appreciated. And I know that despite all sorts of
difficulties, so many of you aim for the stars, to make your lives
and your families' lives more stylish, beautiful, and rewarding.
This is for you. You're all women of the year tonight."

Again she waved the statuette. On cue, the audience clapped
some more. She had them in her grip now. They, too, were
aware of America peering in at them, eyeing their Armanis,
criticizing their Gaultiers, envying their Valentinos. But Kate
had a little more for them. She had some hard news, that even
this well-gossiped gathering of glitterati would not have heard
yet.

"I want to start by telling you something. Most of you will
have heard that our wonderful partnership with Magnum is
drawing to a close. Well, this afternoon it actually ended. I can
let you know that at five o'clock this evening I bought back
Kate Haywood Enterprises from Magnum. It's my business
again. All mine. Ain't that grand?'

There was a chorus of stunned "ah"s, sporadic clapping, and a buzz of animated conversation.

"I just want to say how proud I am to have been associated with Jimmy Longstreet and Magnum. We were a wonderful, beautiful team, and I have nothing but respect, admiration, and gratitude for the way they have behaved to me in all this. Needless to say, we will continue to collaborate in all sorts of areas. But many of you know me well. I have strong views, and when a general has strong views, she likes to be commander in chief. From now on, that is what I will be. I am only sorry that Jimmy couldn't be here tonight." Nor anybody else from Magnum, thought the more beady-eyed of the media-savvy crowd.

Kate gazed over at the Haywood family table. This was the part she was looking forward to. Business was out of the way. It was time to say some very private things in public. She looked at Peter. He sat still and straight, smiling quietly. His tuxedo fitted him perfectly as always. He looked far younger than his fifty-one years, and Kate flew back through time, to Max's Kansas City, when she had first seen him.

"Peter, wonderful husband, mentor, counselor, very best friend, this next bit is for you." Again, she held up the award. "This is your award, darling. Everything I have ever won or achieved or created is in large part to do with you. You saw the point of me before anyone else did . . . before *I* did. You encouraged me. You put up with my moods and my temper. You held the fort when I was away, and you kept the home fires burning, always. No woman could have had a better, and more long-suffering, husband than I have. So I want to do two things tonight, before my friends and colleagues, and before you viewers out there in your homes. I want to thank you, darling Peter, from the bottom of my heart. And I want to apologize to you for all the trouble I've been. I might be Woman of the Year, but I am for sure not Wife of the Year. No way. No way." She shook her head to emphasize her point, and bit her lip as the clapping started again. Her eyes were misty. Peter was smiling his support across the room. She could have sworn there was a film over his eyes, too.

"I'm sorry, darling," she added. "I love you. I . . ." She was choking up.

Somebody shouted from the back, "Bravo, Kate!" and somebody else, "You're the greatest, Kate."

Kate took a deep breath. She hadn't intended to let go this far. But she had had a premonition that this might happen. Somehow, this evening was a watershed. The deal with Magnum was undone at last. The way was clear to begin again, to wipe the slate clean, to atone for past mistakes.

"And I just want everyone to know that Peter will be back on board in the new company, at my right hand, as he always has been. I'm going to need you more than ever, darling. It'll be a new me, I promise you. This is a public pledge, before witnesses."

She was aware that she was pushing the limits into personal areas, but her sense of her audience told her it was OK. This was catharsis, public confession, a show of genuine emotion before both the wider and the smaller Kate Haywood families. American icons were not perfect, even when they sold perfection. They had to be human, to be able to show their humanity. She was not doing this cynically. It was what she felt from the bottom of her heart. But it *was* a professional judgment call not to suppress it. You could be far more than two people at the same time. Being human was a complex business, full of contradictions, layers, and ambivalence.

Now she turned toward Sam. "And my daughter Samantha . . . she's the drop-dead beautiful one next to Peter, for those who don't know Sam. Sam, what can I say? I'm Woman of the Year, but not Wife of the Year, and *certainly* not Mother of the Year. Oh dear, no. You have turned into a wonderful woman, Sam, and a brilliant editor, and we have to thank Peter for that, and you yourself. So, hell, maybe I didn't do such a bad job after all! As I never tire of saying, sometimes you have to hand things over to the experts!"

Sam smiled back happily at her. Would the millions make up for the long absences, the missed sports days, the precious "quality time" that was gone forever? There was no expression of reproach on Sam's face. Kate felt the relief. Heck, what was she worrying about? Sam hadn't been a tenth as neglected as Kate had been as a child, and Kate turned out Woman of the Year.

Who had she left out? Frankie? Mmm. She didn't want to bore this audience, especially the television one. Frankie was now one of New York's most successful fashion photographers. Through all the years, she had been Kate's closest friend and supporter. How odd life was. The two misfits had become the women that other people wanted to be.

She thought fast. The pause was getting longer. Oh God, Ruth! She had nearly forgotten mousy Ruth, who was as easy to forget as she was invaluable.

"And a very special thank-you to my personal assistant, Ruth, who is so much more than that. Ruth, sometimes I think you *are* me. It's like having a doppelgänger, a stand-in, a double. Thank you, Ruth, for all your patience and understanding. If it wasn't for Peter, I'd have to say you were my better half!"

They all smiled at that, and they appreciated Kate's largesse in giving credit to a lowly assistant. It wasn't something she had a reputation for. Kate felt good inside. A new leaf was definitely being turned. She felt the power of her new personality. Across the room, she watched Ruth, demurely dressed in a black dress with a Peter Pan collar, look over at Peter as if apologizing for earning the description of Kate's better half.

Good, thought Kate. *Great. I've done it. A few more less personal thank-yous: to the money people at Dillon, Read; to*

Mariel, the editor of the magazine; to the Bloomingdale's guys, and then I can relax and have some champagne. Tonight I'll sleep better than I have in months.

But even as she had that thought, another one lingered around its edges. A tiny voice, ridiculous and silly, was speaking to her. It wasn't in her brain. It was in her gut. For some odd reason she remembered the first line of Dickens's *Tale of Two Cities:* "It was the best of times, it was the worst of times."

And then, somehow, Kate knew that on this night, the high point of her life, something terrible was going to happen.

21

Kate slumped down on the couch and kicked off her satin pumps. She let out a sigh of relief. It had been wonderful, but she was glad it was over. She could relax at last with the only two people in the world with whom she didn't have to try. Peter was by the couch table, pouring himself a whiskey from the flat-bottomed ship's decanter.

"Well, darling. That couldn't have gone off much better," she said.

"Great success," he said turning around. "Woman of the Year. You deserve it, Kate."

He seemed strangely serious. He wasn't smiling. He held the whiskey in his hand stiffly, not sipping it.

"Well, thank you, sir. You sound a bit like a schoolteacher congratulating a student on exam results." She laughed to lighten him up. He smiled, but without a great deal of enthusiasm. Kate noticed that behind his head the Stubbs of the Derby winner was on a very slight tilt.

"Where's Sam?" he said.

"In her bedroom, I guess," said Kate. She felt so happy. The feeling lingered, and she looked around the beautiful apartment and wondered at the magnificence of her life. East Hampton, Manhattan, the ranch in Montana . . . they had all made *Architectural Digest*. Success didn't get much more magnificent that this.

"Peter, I feel like some more champagne. Can you open some for me? I know I shouldn't, but I feel like it."

"Of course," he said. He walked across the room to the door slowly, deliberately, as if all his movements were carefully planned. That was the second moment that Kate felt the alarm tremor in the pit of her stomach. Something was wrong. Something was very wrong with Peter.

"Are you all right, darling?" she said quickly.

He stopped and turned. He looked drawn, suddenly pale. He took a sip of his drink that was more of a gulp.

Kate jumped to her feet. The adrenaline rushed through her. Oh God, he was fifty-one. He was going to have a heart attack! "Darling!" she said. Both her voice and her face registered her alarm.

But he held up a hand and waved it, dismissing her concern with the strangest expression Kate had ever seen on his face. What on earth was going on?

"I'm leaving you," he said.

"What do you mean?" said Kate. Quite literally, she hadn't a clue what he meant.

"I want a divorce," he said. He spat out the words like grape pips. "It's over. I can't live with you anymore. I'm leaving."

He had turned around now, and stood facing her.

Kate sank very slowly to the couch from which she had just jumped up. There was a numbness now. It crept down from her head, climbed up from her toes. She sat quite still.

"You're *what?*" she said softly.

His fists were clenched. The one that held the glass was tight and white around it. He wasn't joking. She had never seen her husband more deadly serious in her life.

"I'm in love with someone else," he said. "I haven't loved you for years. Sometimes I wonder if I ever loved you." The way he said it was brutal. If words were daggers Kate would be bleeding.

"Peter! Peter?" The second time, it was a question. She was pleading with him not to do this, to reveal that it was all some ghastly, perverse joke.

He took another gulp from his drink. Dutch courage? There was more. But surely there couldn't be any more.

"Sam!" said Kate. "What about Sam?" Her thoughts tumbled over one another. Peter adored Sam. Sam was their daughter. What about Sam?

"Sam's grown," he said. "It's not Sam's life; it's mine."

Sense of sorts was returning to Kate's mind. Her brain was still scrambled by shock but it was beginning to work again. "In love with someone else?" she managed.

"With Ruth," he said simply.

"Ruth! Ruth?" Kate felt as if she was going to be sick. She shook her head, denying it. Once again, reality seemed to fade away from her. This was a game she didn't understand. Try as she might, she simply couldn't grasp the punch line of the hideous joke.

"Ruth loves me. I love her. After the divorce, we're going to be married." He didn't look happy. He looked somehow wary, as if there was a part of him that questioned the wisdom of what he was doing.

"What the *fuck* are you talking about?" said Kate. She spoke loudly. Anger had arrived. "You've been having an affair with Ruth? You've been fucking my assistant? You're leaving me for *her?*"

"I love her very much, Kate."

"You can't love Ruth! Ruth's Ruth. You can't love Ruth. She's a mouse, she's a nobody. She's my assistant, damn it. She's an employee!"

She jumped up and took a step toward Peter. He took a step

back from her. He put the drink down on a side table. There was red on his cheeks now. He hadn't liked what she'd said about Ruth.

"She might be your employee, Kate, but she's a real woman and she's been doing all the creative work for ages. She has all the talent you once had, all the energy, all the freshness, all the charm. You've turned into a monster, Kate. You've lost all sense of balance. You haven't treated me like a husband in years. You've treated me like a servant. What did you honestly think I was going to do? You live in your own world, Kate, and it's not mine anymore. I don't want it to be. You can say what you like about me, but don't ever insult Ruth in my presence again." He spoke slowly, deliberately. The pain and the anger in his voice were palpable. Spite and hostility had been festering inside him for years.

The Chinese vase was Ming. It was genuine. It should have been in a museum, really. But it would do the job quite well. Kate scooped it up, drew back her arm, and hurled the vase at her husband. It hit him on the shoulder, quite hard, bounced off, and crashed to the floor where Persian rug met Carrara marble. There, it exploded into a thousand fragments.

He smiled then, as if relieved by what she had done. He rubbed his shoulder, and his small, tight smile tightened further.

Kate stared at him. Her mouth was open. She was breathing fast. She remembered the look that Ruth and Peter had exchanged at the dinner. There was a different explanation for it now. Peter had always been Ruth's champion, hadn't he? On the very few occasions Ruth had screwed up, Peter had stuck up for her. Kate hadn't thought twice about it, or about the interest that Peter had always taken in picking Ruth's birthday present. She did now.

"Thank you for making this a little easier for me," he said.

"Get out!" screamed Kate. "Get the hell out of this apartment. Get the hell out of my life. You bastard. You *bastard!*"

Her fists flailed ineffectually at her sides, and already she was dissolving into tears. She backed away from him as her eyes filled, blurred, then overflowed with the advent of her dreadful grief and humiliation. She was vaguely aware of him, walking away from her backward, facing her still, as if fearing some new assault. And then he was through the door and into the hallway, and she heard the front door of the apartment close behind him. He'd gone.

Kate sat down again. How could a life change so fast? How, in such a ridiculously short time, could the good be made bad, the beautiful, ugly? There was no sense to be made of it. A minute . . . two minutes . . . before, her life had been a dream. Now it was a nightmare. Humiliation. Rejection. Lies. Betrayal. Peter was not the same. All the memories were rubbish. Her whole life had been built on a foundation of shifting sand. Never loved her . . . he had never loved her. And he was leaving her for Ruth. She sobbed out her frustration, but it grew and grew inside.

"What the hell is going on? Where's Daddy? What happened to the vase?" Samantha rushed into the room. Her voice was full of accusation as she stood over her mother. "Where's Daddy?" she said again.

"He's gone," said Kate, turning a tearstained face toward her daughter.

"What do you mean, he's gone? What did you say to him, Mom? What the hell did you do this time? He's not your servant, you know. He's a man. And you treat him like shit. You know that. And you always have. You're just so *intolerant* of him. Not everyone wants to rule the stupid world. Some people just want to enjoy life, not to die the richest and the most famous in the damn graveyard."

"He wants a divorce," said Kate simply. "He's in love with Ruth. He's going to marry Ruth."

"He's going to do *what!?*" said Sam.

22

Kate was awake, but she didn't open her eyes. She curled up in a fetal ball and closed them tighter. Sleep had always been like a safe death in which she could escape into dreams. But now Kate knew that, like Macbeth, she would sleep no more. Soon another day would be dawning. She would have to get through it somehow, despite the constant lump in her throat; the panic in her gut; the sad, hopeless thoughts that caused her voice to break and the mist to form in her eyes.

There was a word for it—depression. The Prozac had dulled her misery for a bit, but it had dulled her, too. She had wandered through her days like a zombie, the undead walking the earth, hardly caring, hardly functioning. So, without telling anyone, she had stopped taking the tablets. Peter had not called, and somehow she had expected him to. He had disappeared, with Ruth, and he had sucked the life from Kate like a bee sucks nectar from a flower. And now she was withered inside. The fountain of her energy and creativity had been turned off. She was simply a shell of the Kate Haywood she had once been.

She steeled herself and opened her eyes. Darkness filled the room, but as she stared into it, there was the tiniest band of light around the edges of the drapes. Dread crept into the back of her throat. She had to get up. She had to make some tea. She wanted to call Frankie, as she had on many such a bitter dawn. She wanted to walk down the hallway to Sam's room and fall sobbing onto her daughter's bed. Kate fought both impulses.

She managed to get up, and switched on the light. She wandered downstairs, her mind fuzzy with sadness and the melatonin that she was trying for her sleeplessness. Everything was an effort. All was pointless. What did her body need tea for? Or the cereal and piece of fruit that she would force into herself to try to hang on to the weight she hadn't already lost. What the hell was today anyway? Was it the weekend still? Or Monday now? God! The thought hit her. It was the board meeting. It was the day she had to be in Manhattan. She'd promised everyone. They had all seemed so determined that she be there. Oh, no! She couldn't handle it. She'd call in sick. It was her company, nobody could make her do anything. In the kitchen, she walked to the fridge. A message was stuck to the door on a pink Post-it. Sam's writing said "Board Meeting—noon—don't forget. Love you. Sam."

Kate groaned. She had neglected business over the last months. In the days before the black cloud had completely engulfed her, she had struggled on. She had tried to produce the ideas that were her trademark . . . a thousand interesting ways to brighten and beautify your life, your house, your garden . . . but it had been like swimming through molasses. Somehow, the instincts she had always relied on had deserted her. Certainty, her mainstay, had vanished. She was constantly second-guessing herself. Before, she had known in her gut what women everywhere wanted. Now she didn't. What was worse, there was a part of her that didn't care. When she spoke on the telephone to Mariel, the editor of the magazine, and Mariel questioned a decision, Kate would bark down the phone at her, "Just do it!" Then, the moment the conversation was over, she would be full of doubts and fears.

She made the tea on automatic pilot, selecting a special blend of Japanese and Indian. Then she added a touch of ginseng, although she had quite forgotten what good things it was supposed to do for you. And all the time she was thinking, "How can I handle this meeting? Everyone will be there. Not just the girls, but the financial officer, the chairman, and Mariel . . ." She heard a noise behind her, and turned. It was Sam, wiping sleep dust from her eyes, in a bathrobe.

Kate tried to smile. "Hello, darling. Got your note. Thanks for remembering."

"Couldn't sleep again?" asked Sam.

She was worried sick about her mother. Sam came to the Hamptons from Manhattan every weekend and sometimes for a night during the week, too. Her father's desertion had been an earthquake in Sam's life, and now nothing was as it had once appeared to be. He had been the foundation on which she had built everything. His love had seemed the one constant in her life. So his leaving, especially with Ruth, had been a betrayal that she could never forget. Paradoxically, the closeness she had thought they shared made it infinitely unforgivable. With the devaluation of her father had come a reevaluation of her mother. Now Sam could see how much Kate had done for the family, what she had achieved in life against all odds, and how much Sam had always loved her. With the benefit of hindsight, Kate's treatment of Peter had been not so much insensitive and inconsiderate as frankly indulgent. So she had decided to stop blaming her mother for her own insecurities and help make it up to her by pulling her through this crisis.

"Sleep is hell," said Kate.

"Doesn't seem as if those pills are working," said Sam. She sat down at the kitchen table. The kettle began to whistle. Kate didn't appear to notice.

"Are you organized for the meeting?" said Sam gently.

Kate let out a long, shuddering sigh. On one level she was

organized. The car had been ordered. There were clothes to wear. But she hadn't gone through the briefing files. It was hard to concentrate on anything. She'd had to read each of the articles in the most recent edition of her magazine several times. Even then, the information hadn't really sunk in.

"Not really," said Kate.

"Well, in that case I'm coming with you," said Sam.

Kate felt the relief rush through her. It was just what she needed, Sam by her side. There was a surge of unaccustomed warmth in her damaged heart.

23

They all stood up when Kate and Sam entered the board-room, the women as well as the men. Kate was acutely aware that she had not stormed into the room in her normal fashion, shooting from the hip, throwing everyone just a little off balance to keep them on their toes. She looked around, not for victims but for danger. She saw Mariel, the magazine's editor. God, she looked so together in a Dolce and Gabbana tweed trouser suit.

"I'm sorry I'm a little late," Kate said, looking at her watch apologetically and wondering who the hell this mouse was and why she was making this silly speech. In one sense it was her. But she didn't feel like "her" anymore. "You'll all know Sam. I brought Sam, my daughter . . ." Kate paused. She was vaguely aware that her words were stilted and awkward, and that everyone must be noticing. "I wanted her to see what a board meeting was like." It seemed like a mile across the green carpet to the mahogany table. She could see her empty seat. Out of the corner of her eye, she noticed a fast-thinking assistant getting Sam a chair.

Sam threaded her hand into her mother's. "Hi, everyone," she said brightly. "This was my idea. I bullied Mom into it." There was relieved laughter and a general murmur approving Sam's presence.

"So, Kate, shall we start?" said the chairman. He was so good at this, a distinguished professional politician turned businessman. He looked as if he could play God in a biblical movie.

Kate nodded.

"I think the best method of approach is the usual one," he said. "It usually is," he added with a little laugh, and then a small cough as he realized the poverty of his joke. "So let's run through the divisions one by one. Mariel, if you could start off with the magazine."

Kate Haywood's Life was the starship of the enterprise. It had been a costly launch, but now it had liftoff and was beginning to enter the nation's psyche to the extent that they were making jokes about it on Jay Leno's show. In the days when laughter had been possible, Kate had found them funny even when the jokes had been at her expense. Name recognition was the name of the game when you were trying to turn your name into a brand. Mariel was a careful magazine professional, with a Condé Nast background, whose job it was to oversee the nuts and bolts of production, advertising, and distribution. Kate controlled the editorial content. The tight expression on Mariel's face hinted that she was the bearer of bad news.

"Well, circulation hit a high in July. As you know we started at two hundred twenty-five thousand. In July, we were at two million and change. Advertising is holding up well, but we have two problems. The first may mean nothing. There are no straight lines in business, after all. But I have to point out that there has been slippage in circulation over the last three months." She paused. Nobody said anything. Kate looked down at the table. Everyone else appeared preoccupied. They were looking at files, at the ceiling, at their glasses of water.

Nobody was looking at Kate. The exception was Sam, who turned to her mother and smiled her support. Kate tried to smile back. She knew precisely why circulation had fallen. The editorial content of the last three editions of the magazine had been overseen by a person on Prozac. Her brain had been barely ticking. Her creativity had croaked.

"How much slippage?" said the chairman.

"One hundred thousand in each of the last three months," said Mariel. "We're at one point seven million now."

Kate gazed out through the big picture window at Central Park. It was bleak out there. Fall had all but surrendered to winter. The trees stuck up like bones from the gray ground. Tiny figures no longer meandered but hurried, bundled against the cold, as they rushed toward their destinations. Kate envied them and their anonymous lives. They possessed purpose, the precious thing she had once had. Purpose had been something she had taken for granted, but now she was adrift, at the rudder no more, lost and without a compass. And the circulation was drifting with her. It would, wouldn't it. It went where she went. And she was going down . . .

"Any clues? Seasonal trends? Competitors? Anything changed that might account for it?" said the chairman. They were the right questions.

"It's difficult to say," said Mariel carefully. She did not say "It's difficult to know."

"I think it's been my fault," said Kate into the long silence. "I think editorial content has . . . has . . . lacked its usual energy. It's been a difficult time . . . for me . . . and for Sam . . ." She petered out. All around the table were murmurs of sympathy. Eye contact was coming back. Hope was returning. She struggled on. "I will do better," she said. Her voice sounded hollow. Could she do better? Hell, could she do anything at all?

"Well, there it all is," said the chairman. "A blip on the radar screen. Time the great healer, et cetera. I don't think we need worry too much about circulation. What was the other problem you mentioned?"

"In a word, costs," said Mariel. "Despite the overall increase in circulation since launch, we're running an annual operating loss of a million five, maybe two million factoring in the circulation drop in the last three months." She looked at Kate directly. "The trouble is at the margin, Kate. We could be out of the red and into the black if we could keep a tighter grip on expenses."

Kate took a deep breath. She tried hard to concentrate on the discouraging words she knew she was hearing. The magazine should be throwing out a profit by now. The trouble had been her single-minded pursuit of excellence, or at least the old Kate's pursuit of it. When the shelter magazines decided to do a piece on tablecloths, they would send a lowly researcher around to the tablecloth manufacturers. She would grab some likely samples, throw a set together in the corner of a studio, snap them, end of story. That had not been Kate's way. Tablecloths would be specially designed for the piece, lace ones found in out-of-the-way sales, bought and paid for. Agonizing meetings, long on woman-hours, would stretch on as the tablecloth selection process was made. Finally, perfect houses would be rented for the photography so that the tablecloths would look "at home." As a result, an expensive photographer would have to travel far from his studio together with his equipment, assistants, and other paraphernalia. To Kate perfection made all the difference. Unfortunately, it made a difference to the accounts, too—the vital difference between profit and loss.

There was silence. They were waiting for her to say something.

"If we cut back on quality, I suppose circulation might fall back . . . more," she said at last. She felt drained by the effort. She looked down at the table.

'Maybe," said Mariel. "Maybe not. But if we go on this way, we go on losing money."

Kate felt Sam watching her. Her mind was blank. Her energy was gone. There had been arguments about costs before, and Kate had always won them effortlessly. Now she felt out-gunned by the competent Mariel.

In the end it was Sam who spoke. She knew what her mother wanted to say. "Look, surely the thing to do is to hold the quality and simply wait for the circulation to climb to break-even point and higher. After all, it's come up from two hundred thousand."

"But how long can we wait?"

Again, silence descended. Everyone was thinking the same thing. The answer to Mariel's question was "not long."

"Perhaps we should move on," said the chairman. "Books. Stella?"

"Are going well, going well . . . ," said Stella slowly. Somehow, her need to repeat herself seemed to contradict what she had just said. "The Kate books are holding up nicely. Of course, the problem is . . ."

Kate braced herself. "The problem is the non-Kate books. Of course, it's only a matter of time before we break even here, but we have major launch expenses. We have to pay top dollar to entice people away from the more established art imprints. And the sales force is Kate oriented. They have to develop skills at selling non-Kate art books that don't come naturally to them. It's a marketing problem that we can overcome, but it will take a bit of time, and then we'll see great things. I'm sure starting the art-book imprint was the correct thing to do, and we went into it with our eyes wide open. No regrets, but we're at the heavy pounding stage right now."

Another division, the one Sam worked in, needed time, thought Kate. That made two out of two so far, and they were major divisions of her company.

"Television?" said the chairman. He seemed to have shed some of the aura of optimism that had previously surrounded him.

"Syndication is holding steady," said Steve, who ran Kate's cable channels. "The heartland is buying, and the south, but we're sticky in the coast markets. Again, it's bound to get better. Five hundred channels is still a dream, but one day it'll come true. The BTTV station group in the Seattle area took the cooking channel, but they felt home decorating was too elitist. Overall, television is down a bit from last year." He coughed. "Down quite a bit," he added.

"And where are we doing well?" said the chairman with a short laugh.

"The paint is a big success at Bloomingdale's," said somebody way down the table, "but the wallpaper is sticking."

There was nervous laughter at the unintentional double meaning.

"Good for the wallpaper!" said the chairman brightly.

Kate felt the dread well up inside her. New dread was climbing up the wall of the old. Any minute now somebody was going to sum this up, and the tidings would be anything but glad. Kate Haywood Enterprises was slowing down. The business was in trouble. It wasn't just her, but her own troubles had coincided with problems in the various marketplaces.

"Perhaps we should hear from Margaret," said the chairman. Margaret Court was the chief financial officer. The bottom line was near.

"What I want to talk about is the debt," said Margaret briskly, in a tone of voice that said she was cutting to the chase. "I'm afraid we're in trouble. As of today, total borrowings are thirty million dollars, and interest costs are not being met out of cash flow. The debt is nearly all short-term. We've talked to the banks about longer term financing, but they are not too eager. We promised them we'd be doing better than this by now.

Frankly, they're worried. When current loans mature we're going to have problems refinancing, even short term. The bankers simply can't see what we can see, now knowing the business as we do. It begins to look as if we should try to sell an equity interest. I know Kate wants to keep total control, and we've only just got that back from Magnum. But anyone who is prepared to buy an equity stake will want input, too. That's been my experience, especially in areas such as this. Frankly, the sort of investor who wants to buy into us is a player with ideas of his own how this thing should go. So it would be a question of finding somebody that Kate . . . that we . . . can work with."

"And what if we just soldier on?" said Kate. She sounded so weary. She *felt* so weary.

"It may well be that the ammunition runs out. By ammunition, I mean money." Margaret Court's tone was firm. She wanted everyone to be clear about the seriousness of the situation. "When that happens, we would have a house-of-cards situation," she continued. "We can't let it get to that stage. The moment we start downsizing, buying fewer books, laying off staff, slowing payments, the word is out. Advertisers back away, TV stations don't buy, and pretty soon the value of an equity stake is worth half what it is today, then a quarter, and then . . ." Margaret spoke with feeling. She, like the others at the table, had a personal interest in the business. Kate had sold shares to these executives as part of an incentive plan. The more of the company they owned, the harder they worked. Together, the directors owned 20 percent, and for many, perhaps most, it was by far their largest investment. Some of them had even borrowed money on their houses to invest in the "sure thing" that had been Kate Haywood Enterprises to date.

Kate knew what they were thinking. They were thinking about their significant others, husbands, wives, children and their school fees, mortgage payments and the homes they loved. They were thinking about their self-respect, the jobs they could expect, if any, after this one, if it came to that. They were kicking themselves for thinking they had found security with Kate Haywood and her great big company. They were discovering firsthand what so many Americans had discovered over the last few years—that security was the biggest myth of all. And they were hoping, too. They were hoping that Kate's pride, her legendary desire to control everything, would not stand in the way of her finding an investor to replace Magnum and inject capital into the company. The more farsighted among them would also be wondering if they would survive such a dilution of control. Because any new investor would have people of his own, loyalties to trusted staff, IOUs that could not be torn up.

These people had trusted her. These people, now beginning surreptitiously to look at each other, were wondering who would survive, who would not. Many of these people lived near the brink. Pushed on by wives, they owned houses too large and too grand for themselves, each mortgage payment paid for in psychic blood, each fee demand from a private school a sickening kick in the stomach. Did these people lie to their spouses about their financial predicament? Had they been lying to themselves? Was it their fault that they had believed in the endless upward mobility of the American dream, led on by Reagan-esque false gods, by the treacherous cult of the equity, by the fairy-tale mongers of Madison Avenue?

Guilt gnawed at Kate. These people had hitched themselves to her wagon, and so far she had paved their private worlds with gold, their public ones with prestige. But now the gold might well turn into the fool's variety. She tried hard to pull herself together. There was more at stake here than her misery. This situation had not happened overnight. The warning signs had been there to see for those with eyes to see them. But Kate hadn't wanted to confront her business's problems, and, as with all unconfronted problems, they had worsened. Now the crisis was on the verge of becoming a catastrophe.

"Of course I have had discussions, informal discussions, with different people. I have made explorations . . . with regard to taking on partners, Condé Nast, Time Warner, Bertelsmann. There have been approaches . . ." She trailed off. It was useless to pretend that she had seriously considered taking on a partner. It would have involved Kate's giving up control of her business, and after Magnum, she was simply not prepared to do that again. Even now, in her debilitated state. Even now, when her own company was stumbling.

The chairman cleared his throat. "It may be that we shall have to pursue the possibility of raising outside capital with, ah, rather more aggression," he said.

"We haven't got long, Kate," said Margaret.

"Are you saying that the company is near to failing?" said Kate softly. She needed everything to be simple. Yes or no. Her mind wasn't working fast enough to keep pace with the conversation. She tried to envisage what it might mean if the company went down. Failure. The end of her dream. All the years of struggle wasted. But, strangely, she didn't care as she once had. When Peter had gone, the music had died. Unlike the others at this table, she would be financially insulated from the company's bankruptcy. Kate owned 80 percent of it, having bought out Peter's 10 percent when he left her. But, quite apart from her controlling interest in the company, she owned her houses, and there were stocks, mutual funds, insurance policies, paintings. She would have the option of becoming a recluse and retreating into the simple life.

"Yes," said Margaret in answer to Kate's earlier question. "I would be failing in my fiduciary duty as a director of this company if I didn't emphasize to the board that I think we are close to chapter eleven, as things stand right now." She paused, looked down at the table, looked up again. "And you do remember, don't you, Kate, that the bank loans are backed by your personal guarantee?"

"What!" said Sam.

"Oh," said Kate. "No, I don't think so." Her words sounded as strangely empty as her mind. Yes, she had signed a personal guarantee in the beginning, but only as an interim measure to speed up the separation deal from Magnum. It had always been intended that the new company would take over the guarantees. In her chaotic frame of mind, she assumed it had been done. But she hadn't checked to make sure.

"It was never revoked," said Margaret simply. She flicked through the file in front of her with surgical precision, and pulled out a document.

Kate stared at her. She was aware that all eyes were on her. Nobody was avoiding her now. They were watching with the detached fascination of those seeing a traffic accident unfold.

"Mom?" said Sam.

"But that was just an interim measure," said Kate slowly, "I mean, when the Magnum de-merger was finalized, then the company was going to guarantee the loans. The company's assets . . ." Surely not. It couldn't have happened. Something like that couldn't have been overlooked. Not by Kate Haywood, who could pick out a loose thread on a tapestry pillow at twenty paces.

"I was never instructed to renegotiate the terms of the loans," said Margaret.

The silence was deafening.

"So," said Kate putting the obvious into words. "If the company were to fail, everything I own would be . . . would be . . ." She fought for some appropriate word, but she couldn't think of one. "Would be needed," she said at last.

The feeling of unreality was strong now, the faces around her blurred and distorted like the images in a fairground fun house. One of her hands on the mahogany table seemed twice as large as the other, and in her mind the thoughts sounded strangely like voices. "You lost your husband," they said. "And you cared so much about that, you practically lost your mind. Now, you're about to lose everything else."

24

The two lawyers sat across the gleaming table, smiling and offering Kate coffee, tea, or a soft drink. They were so charming, so well dressed, so ordered in their suave simplicity. Their lives were UNDER CONTROL in capital letters, and from Kate's new perspective that seemed a rare and wonderful thing. Phil Seeley had been there from the start. Rob Evans was the firm's back-room boy on living trusts. Seeley was one of the partners who pulled in the business. Evans was one of those who sorted it out. Phil was outgoing and personable, good at small talk. Rob was highly articulate but spent words like a cheapskate spent money. In order to disguise the realities, Phil was eager to show that he knew a lot, while Rob was anxious to prove he was not psycho-toxic.

"So, Kate. This seems quite straightforward. You want to make over half your holding—that's forty percent—in Kate Haywood Enterprises to Samantha. And you want to set up an irrevocable trust to receive the stock, with myself as trustee," said Seeley.

"That's right." said Kate.

"Any problems that you can think of, Rob?"

"Not really. Mrs. Haywood will have no control over the trust. That way it avoids inheritance tax." He coughed. This was a slightly tricky bit. As if on cue Phil took over the conversation.

"Might I ask the purpose of this gift? It makes it easier to go over all the angles and ensure that your objectives are met."

Kate stared at him blankly. For some reason he looked as if he came from another planet, with his gray-and-white-striped Brooks Brothers suit, his black glasses, and his clipped Boston accent. Yet she had known him for many years. He had come to dinner and was a friend of sorts. She knew it was her problem, of course. Her mind was going. *She* was going. It was all going. That was why she wanted to make something over to Sam before it all went. There didn't seem to be any way of putting that into words.

"Oh, I just thought it was time," she said. She waved a hand in the air in a way that she hoped signified the unimportance of it all.

"We will have to have some sort of valuation of the shares," said Rob.

"The accountants, Margaret Court the financial officer . . ." Kate felt so tired.

"Yes, of course, you leave that with us. It's a private company, so we can more or less choose our own figure, within reason."

Kate took a deep breath. There was the next bit.

"And I want the trust to be the owner of an insurance policy on my life that I have recently taken out."

The two lawyers looked at each other.

"And how much is that policy to be worth? Is it a term policy?"

"Ten million dollars. Twenty years."

The lawyers exchanged glances again.

"That would be outside my estate, wouldn't it? No inheritance taxes?"

"Yes," said Rob, "a new policy is outside your estate if it is to an irrevocable trust and if someone else, in this case Samantha, or rather Samantha's trust, is the owner. But the trust has to own the policy from the start. Otherwise you have to live for three years from the date you change the ownership of the policy."

"Not a problem in your case," laughed Phil. He was acutely aware that the conversation was lacking that efficient bonhomie that ought technically to characterize such conferences.

"It's a new policy. It hasn't been issued yet," said Kate.

"With?"

"TransAmerica."

"Good. I mean, they're a good company for such a large policy," said Phil.

"Look, I have to rush," said Kate. She stood up, managing somehow to give the impression that she was about to fall down.

The lawyers jumped up too.

"OK, so we'll draw up the trust deed—at least Rob will— and we'll send it over for you to have a look at. Then you can pop in any time and sign it and have it witnessed. You want me as the sole trustee, right?"

"Yes, Phil. You know Sam. You've known her forever. And me. Yes, please, that would be great if you could do it."

"No, that's no problem. It would be an honor."

They showed her to the door and handed her her coat. Kate had a bit of a problem putting it on.

The moment the door had closed behind her, Phil said, "What did you think? She didn't look well."

"I thought she looked depressed," said Rob.

"Depression and a ten-million-dollar insurance policy," said Phil. He tapped his pen on the blotter.

Rob was silent for a moment. "It's not our business," he said at last. Then he paused. Human emotions were not his field. "But do you think, I mean really, that she . . .?"

"Kate? Suicide? No way," said Phil. "She's one of the strongest women I know."

25

The warm womb of the Racquet Club turkish bath and steam rooms was the perfect retreat from the world. Peter stepped over the threshold into the white marbled heaven of dry heat. He felt the tension slide from shoulders that were already brushed with sweat from the furious game of squash he had just played with Teddy. He adjusted the rough white towel around his waist and let out a sigh of relief. Teddy Winner, his oldest friend, was ten years his senior but he made up in court experience for his shortness in wind. As always, the game had been close.

Teddy was already there, reading a copy of the *Times,* stretched out on a chaise longue covered with a crisp white sheet.

"I had you today, Peter. Nothing you could do, was there?"

"It was three games to two, Teddy. Hardly a landslide!"

He flopped down into a deck chair next to his friend. There were things on his mind. This weekly meeting with Teddy Winner was a hell of a lot better, and less expensive, than a shrink. Anyway, Teddy rather enjoyed handing down his considerable wisdom like tablets from the mountain.

"No, you weren't your usual self today, Peter. Ruth been taking it out of you?" Teddy chuckled.

Peter smiled ruefully. It was an invitation, the one he had wanted. "Not in the bedroom, if that's what you mean."

"Wasn't really what I did mean," said Teddy, putting down the newspaper.

"She's changed, Teddy. She's different somehow. I don't know. It's everything and nothing. If you ask me to give you examples, they'll all sound meaningless. But when you add them up, it amounts to something." He waved a hand to signify the difficulty of summing it up.

"Not so supportive? Not so understanding? Not so warm?"

Peter stared at his friend in surprise. It was a bull's-eye. Three of them. There was a new distance between him and Ruth, a coldness, an impatience in conversations.

"Exactly. I mean, at the beginning she was so supportive. She seemed to adore me. She seemed to really understand my feelings, like she knew what I was thinking. Everything. She was just like Kate, like the old Kate, sweet, buzzing with energy and enthusiasm, brilliant . . . and then, bit by bit . . . " Peter trailed off.

"She's turning into the Kate you left." Teddy finished Peter's thought for him.

"Maybe it's my fault. Maybe I wanted to escape, but I couldn't escape, because I had to take me with me. Does that make any sense?"

"I remember a conversation, a long time ago—you've probably forgotten it—in the kitchen at Mill Cottage. Kate had done this incredible Indian dinner. I told you then she was ambitious. I don't think you liked it much. But that's the problem. You're drawn to clever, ambitious women, and you push them onward and upward. They feed off you, and then one day you wake up and find out you've become a superfluous Frankenstein, and there's a monster on the loose."

Peter shook his head at the seeming inevitability of it all. Teddy was right. Partly. He was drawn to powerful, upwardly mobile, talented women, but they never seemed to be like that when he met them. Kate had been an adorable, bubbly inno-cent. Ruth, much quieter, but so devoted and adoring, hell, so *dependent* on his wisdom and support. There was a pattern, it was obvious. That meant he was responsible as much as Kate and Ruth. He was to blame.

"I'd have thought that Ruth would be riding pretty high right now. Everyone knows about the trouble at Kate's company. Any minute somebody is going to pick up on your projects. Nothing puts an ambitious woman in a better mood than success. The moment you deliver the goods, things will get better . . . for a while."

"Yeah, for a while. And *if* we can sell the book projects and the prototype for the magazine."

Peter tried to analyze his feelings as well as Ruth's. Emotions were a two-way street. The almost unbearable truth was that Ruth was not Kate. She had seemed like the old Kate. And now it appeared that she was turning into the Kate he had walked out on. He could hardly admit the brutal truth. The fact was that Ruth was a pale imitation of the former, and was showing early signs of becoming a caricature of the latter.

"I thought you were thrilled with the magazine prototype," said Teddy.

"I am. I am," said Peter, as if trying to convince himself. "It's incredibly good. It's a winner. It's just . . . oh, I don't know . . . when Ruth is pitching it, there's just something missing. From her, not the prototype. Kate would have sold it ten times over to Condé Nast last week. But they passed. They didn't even know *why* they passed. Of course, Ruth blamed me. That's another thing. Nothing, but *nothing,* can ever be her fault. She said it was because I got it printed in Hong Kong and not Italy, that I advised her against the bit on ethnic desserts . . . you name it."

"You think it's her fault; she thinks it's yours," said Teddy.

"Come on," said Peter. "Let's do some serious steam and see if we can shrink my brain even more than you've shrunk it already."

Teddy stood up with an effort and a laugh. He enjoyed helping people with their problems, but he was worried about Peter. Life with Kate had been a million miles from perfect, but the marriage had been built on the firm foundation of years of happy memories and a beautiful daughter. The loss of Sam had caused Peter so much misery, and he had taken no pleasure at all from Kate's psychological downfall as the result of his leaving. There was guilt all over the place. Now, with this personality change in Ruth, Peter must be feeling as if he had made a big mistake.

They walked along the corridor and turned left into the steam room, squinting their eyes to accustom themselves to the foggy heat. They sat down on the hot marble slab. Peter grabbed the green hose and played the water over his head. He breathed through his mouth. The dripping air was almost too hot for his nostrils. He handed the hose to Teddy.

Teddy was right. Ruth and he were playing the blame game. They had invested a fortune in the prototype; more in the vast co-op that Ruth had wanted them to buy; and then the Far Eastern stocks had gone south while everyone else was tripling their money in Coca-Cola. The pressure to succeed in their joint business project was intense, and pressure had had two effects: it had uncovered the cracks in their relationship, and it had transmitted itself subtly to the minds of potential investors. Nobody wanted to give anything to people who *needed*. They only wanted to shower money on people who didn't give a damn.

"Have you tried Joe Somers yet?" said Teddy, playing the hose over his neck and shoulders. "He has to be your best bet, if Condé Nast has said no."

"Going to see him tomorrow," said Peter. He took a deep, hot breath. Joe Somers was not only their best bet, he was possibly their last chance.

* * *

Joseph Somers's office doubled as a gallery for the private collection of avant garde art that he was fond of saying he didn't like. It was the greatest private collection in the world. Everyone agreed on that. To profess dislike for what had cost him a half-billion dollars was to demonstrate a singular eccentricity. The point was that Somers liked to be thought perverse.

Ruth sat before him. By her side, Peter looked no less urbane and sophisticated than the billionaire. The two men eyed each other jealously. Each wondered if he dared give away negotiating points by asking for the name of the other's tailor.

Ruth had talked up a storm in her intense, concentrated way, and there was no doubt that she was making an impression. Their objective was within reach. Peter could sense it. In front of him, on a Chippendale partners' desk of great elegance, lay the prototype for the new magazine. Its working title was *New Style*.

Somers thumbed through it. But all the time his eyes wandered back to Ruth. He was hardly looking at the gorgeous, glossy photographs of food and furnishings that had cost Peter and Ruth several hundred thousand dollars to produce.

Since leaving Kate's company, Ruth had become skilled at looking neat and buttoned-up yet at the same time hinting that beneath the mildly threatening exterior was a soft, sensual center. Her silk shirt was open just that one button too many. In contrast, her Armani suit was strictly conservative, her makeup subtle, her haircut severe. But then again, she smelled deliciously of Chanel Number 5, and her lipstick was fiery.

"I think it has attack. I know it has attack. It's modern without being threatening, new without being gratuitously trendy," she said, leaning forward to emphasize the enthusiasm in her voice.

Peter smiled. So far, he had had to do very little. But he was ready to jump in, if and when Ruth ran out of steam. It was something she tended to do at the most awkward times. Just when you thought she was on a conversational roll, she would dry up as if the auto-cue had been turned off. It was one of the many surprising things about her he was learning every day.

"It is impressive," said Somers. "It's very impressive, actually. I'd go so far as to say that it impresses me."

Ruth smiled. Somers smiled back. Peter smiled. They were close all right. And they were not talking to the office boy. This was publishing's equivalent of the ultimate green light. Joe Somers did not have to consult inferiors, or even pretend to. He had the authority to say yes, and the guts, the cash, and the ego to do so. But he did not run the most powerful group of magazine and book publishers in America by saying yes too often. In business, "no" was the word that made the most money, because it saved it.

"Of course, this magazine will be in direct competition with Kate's. The pair of you will be head to head with her. Your former wife is not going to like it, is she?" He cocked an eye at Peter. "Or your former employer." He turned his sly eyes toward Ruth. Somers had managed to make all sorts of implications: Peter was a cad who had left his wife for an inferior. Now he was trying to wreck her business to add insult to injury. Ruth was a parvenue opportunist who had been disloyal to her boss and then stolen her husband, to pile injury on insult. Somers gave a little laugh to soften the insinuations, but somehow that made them worse.

Ruth's color heightened. She didn't mind innuendo. What she minded was the glittering prize slipping just one millimeter from her grasp.

Somers watched the psychic damage caused by the landing of his smart bomb. As with all successful men, little was said or done by chance. There was method in his sanity. Here was the deal: His company did not have a Kate Haywood niche. Right now, there was only one of those, and possibly there was not room for more. It all depended on one thing: the slippage in circulation that might turn into a free fall for *Kate Haywood's*

Life. This was common knowledge in an industry that ate gossip, not corn flakes, for breakfast. Kate had apparently fallen apart when Peter left her for the hired help. The magazine's content had become downright dreary. A few more months of this and the game would be over. On the other hand, and there was always the other hand in business, Kate might mount a comeback. If she did, then Ruth's effort, so competent and fresh on his desk, would be buried without ceremony after a summary business execution. The key was Kate, and you never knew what was going on in the minds of others; you hardly knew what was going on in your own.

"I can put this simply," Somers said. "This idea flies if Kate crashes. If she doesn't, if she gets her edge back, then this," and he picked up the prototype, "is bathroom tissue."

He watched Peter. He peered at Ruth. She was leaning forward, with a hint of cleavage. There was something about her, something very appealing. She looked like a Tiffany tart. It was quite clear what Peter had seen in her. And she had talent. In buckets. Certainly, on this day, she was better than Kate. But then on a good day Kate was better than anybody. Could Kate mount a comeback? It was far from certain, because in commerce absolutely nothing lasted forever. The business books that ignored that fact ended at chapter eleven.

"I'm not sure I agree with you," said Peter.

"Oh?" said Somers.

"I think there is room for both Kate and Ruth. The market is big enough for the two of them. You know, McDonald's and Burger King; Planet Hollywood and the Hard Rock Cafés. The more entrants into the market, the more the market niche is stimulated. People get addicted to hamburgers. People get in the habit of going to theme restaurants. The more there are, the merrier. They'll all be spending money advertising the basic concept. Way down the line the smaller fry will get deep-fried, but we'll be one of the leaders."

"So, you're saying the opposite of what I'm saying. That it would be a bad thing if Kate fails."

"Yes. If she goes down, the niche takes a knock. The advertisers go somewhere else, like to the interior design magazines. There are enough of those, and most are making money. You should know about that."

"It's a point of view . . . I suppose," said Somers. The "suppose" part insinuated that Somers didn't think much of it. "What do you think, Ruth?"

"I agree with you, Mr. Somers," said Ruth. "I think we should go head on against Kate. Hit her while she's down. Never let her get up. Steal her covers. Raid her advertisers. Negative advertising. Go for the jugular."

Her lips were parted sensually. She seemed to be aware of what she must look like. An icy calm descended to camouflage the brief exposé of what lay inside. But her words lingered.

Peter was shocked, not so much by Ruth's sentiment but by her vehemence. He had never realized before this moment that Ruth hated Kate. He had always believed that she had fallen in love with him by mistake, and that Ruth wished Kate nothing but good. That had always been Ruth's PR. OK, so the ideas she had just expressed were business ones, and all was fair on that front. But it had sounded strictly personal. Somers was obviously thinking the same thing. A knowing half smile played around his cunning old mouth.

"Hit her. Steal from her. Go for the jugular. My word, Ruth, still waters run deepest."

Ruth tried to laugh it off. "I was only talking strategy. I imagine that's what Kate's advisers will tell her when this magazine hits the streets."

"If," corrected Somers.

"When," repeated Ruth.

"This reminds me of *The Godfather*," said Somers. "Your team seems to be talking with forked tongue. Here's Peter, who takes the 'let 'em all come' view, and then there's you, with 'it's Kate or us.' Maybe you two ought to have a bit of a talk, to get your story straight, as it were." "Before I make any decisions" was the implication.

Peter cursed inwardly. *Damn!* They had made an elementary mistake. They should never have disagreed in front of a potential investor. They had been so close to a deal, it had seemed as good as done. And he was the one who had blown it. Ruth had done the right thing. She had agreed with the man with the money and the ego. She hadn't even had to compromise principles to do so. Nobody was arguing about the content of the prototype. Everyone agreed that it was impressive. Instead, they had managed to fall out on market strategy, on advertising, on a whole gray area that would probably be revised endlessly anyway. They had disagreed on the small print before the ink was dry on the paper. In short, they had given Somers the excuse to say the easy "no" when he had been on the verge of saying the far more difficult and expensive "yes." Peter had taken his eye off the ball, and the ball was the recouping of the vast up-front expenses of producing a prototype magazine, and the launching of a business that could one day be bigger and better than Kate Haywood Enterprises.

Had he blown it because of the feelings he still had for Kate? It would be easy for Ruth to accuse him of that. And somehow, somewhere down deep, there was a sense in which it might even be true. Oh, he was deeply involved with Ruth, and he still resented Kate for the casual way she had chosen Magnum over him. But that fell far short of wanting to do anything unpleasant to her. Kate was suffering enough, it was rumored, both in psyche and circulation, the two for her intimately intertwined. But she was also suffering from what he had done to her. She had taken him for granted, but he had withdrawn the grant. He was always fond of saying that in any divorce the blame was fifty-fifty. However, there was an uncomfortable part of him that felt he was more than half guilty. He had never confronted the problems of their marriage. He hadn't communicated. He had allowed his wife to drift on in her false security, because he had been secretly seduced by Ruth. Without Ruth, he would not have had the energy, even the courage, to move out. Without Ruth, he and Kate might still be together. And he would still have a daughter. . . .

Somers stood up. "I think we should meet again. I'll talk to my people. You two obviously have things to discuss. What I always say is, if all is not sweet harmony at the start, it will be bloody discord at the end."

Peter stood too, and Ruth. She looked stricken and furious at the same time. But she held on to her cool.

Somers shook her hand. "You're a very talented lady," he said. He turned to Peter. "And you're a lucky man." He eyed the suit again. British tailoring, definitely. Huntsman? Anderson and Sheppard? No, it was more Doug Hayward. Cutting-edge style rather than Prince Charles safety. "I'll slip out this way," he said, and he disappeared through a door at the side of his office.

He probably kept a bed in there for entertaining the secretaries, thought Peter. He turned toward Ruth.

"I'm sorry—"

"I thought you were supposed to be the business brains." She cut into his apology. Sarcasm dripped from her words. He had never seen her so angry.

"It's still a—"

"Of course it is. A possibility. But no thanks to you. And it was far more than that before you sabotaged the whole thing. He was about to say yes. Couldn't you feel it? All you had to do was agree with him, for God's sake." She spat out the words.

When a personal assistant entered a few moments later to show them out, Ruth had pulled herself together again. "How wonderful to work among all this marvelous art," she said graciously as they walked out through the anteroom, hung with Stellas, Twomblys, and Jasper Johnses.

The assistant's British accent was globally dismissive. "Oh, the pictures, you mean. Oh gosh, yes, they're rather fun, aren't they? Some of them are quite valuable, apparently."

"I expect they are," said Ruth, her chin set. There was money all around, but none of it was hers, and she wanted it. A few minutes before, she had been so close, and then Peter had blown it. The idiot who was supposed to have been her ticket to ride had just thrown her off the gravy train. If she climbed back on board, it would be no thanks to him. She took a deep breath. Life was hard but it was also simple. If you had to rely on anybody, let it be yourself.

26

"How are you feeling?

"Fine . . . so far." The young man let out a nervous laugh as Donna assessed his mood. Gerald Templer was a drinker, a city type used to liquid lunches and boozy weekends in the country. His tolerance for intravenous Valium would be high. And he seemed anxious. The five milligrams she had infiltrated so far through the butterfly drip into the vein in the back of his hand might not be enough. On the other hand, too much and he wouldn't be able to cooperate in swallowing the camera on a snake that was in effect the endoscope. Without the swallowing motion, despite lubrication, he would end up with a very sore throat. Yet if he panicked, as people sometimes did, he might gag on the tube. It was usually better to give more rather than less Valium when in doubt. She had tried to interest him in the color TV monitor that would soon be showing internal pictures of his esophagus and stomach. She hadn't entirely succeeded.

"Fascinating," he had managed to comment, without much conviction.

"Drowsy yet?" she asked.

"Oh, whoa," he said in reply, signaling the beginnings of the effect.

"Like a dry martini on an empty stomach, no?" said Donna.

"Just like that, mmm," he said. There was a slight slur to his speech. Donna eased off on the Valium. The drip was open. She could always add more later.

"Just relax for a minute or two." She took his notes from the nurse. He was thirty-eight. He had a wife; two kids; a mortgage, doubtless, on the house in a fashionable part of Chelsea. She guessed there would be a company BMW, possibly a Volvo for the wife and kids. Holidays would be in Switzerland and Spain. Stress at the bank was probably responsible for the ulcer. He ran derivatives trading at the London branch of a big German bank. She rather liked him. He was a little fat, and somehow vulnerable beneath the rather forced, hearty exterior. Especially so now, when he was about to undergo an unpleasant and claustrophobic experience. Although he could breathe through his nose, there was always the sensation of suffocating when a tube was stuck down your throat. And there was the possibility of something more serious than an ulcer. Stomach cancer was a long shot at his age, but not impossible, and it killed you quickly and unpleasantly. Donna ran through the rest of the notes. It was second nature to her. The GP's letter was informative. So was the patient's history and physical exam she had done herself. Thoroughness was her thing.

The only remotely significant medical fact recorded in the notes was a successfully treated incidence of subacute bacterial endocarditis five years previously. The potentially dangerous infection of the heart valve had been successfully treated with penicillin. The conscientious GP had followed up with regular cardiograms, X rays, and blood cultures, which had all been normal. Anyway, that was nothing to do with the stomach symptoms Donna was about to investigate. Still, she would have liked those X rays up on the light box on the wall, and she would like to have seen the barium films rather than merely the radiologist's report that had pronounced them "normal." She handed the notes back to the nurse with a vague but unmistakeable sense of unease. Was there something she was forgetting? Donna banished the thought from her mind. This was a simple intubation. The patient was conscious. There wasn't even any cutting, and Valium was safe as gin.

"Open wide. I'm going to spray some anesthetic solution at the back of your throat. You don't have to swallow it."

Donna liked to keep things light. The chap was a little pale, clearly nervous. His hair was curly. His wife was in the waiting room with a child of five who had Templer's sandy coloring. Suddenly, Donna envied him. He had got it all. OK, selling cocoa beans your bank didn't own so you could, hopefully, buy them back cheaper at some specified date in the future wasn't as morally grand as saving lives. But the rest of his life was fuller than hers, perhaps simpler than hers, with more love and perhaps even less stress despite the ulcer.

She and Templer were more or less the same age. Some sort of life was in front of them both: the old age that was not for the faint of heart; retirement; grandchildren; and, in the interim, more rungs of their respective career ladders to be climbed. Would Donna be the first chairperson of the Royal College of Surgeons? There were those who thought it possible. That would mean the feminine equivalent of a knighthood from the Queen. Dame Donna Gardiner. Wouldn't her husband have been proud!

Gerald Templer opened his mouth a little too wide and said "Aaaaah," which she hadn't asked him to do. That indicated he was apprehensive. Maybe she should have given him more Valium. He appeared wide awake. "Are you all right, Gerald?" she asked, using his first name on purpose, to make him feel more comfortable. As a rule, and as an attractive woman in a male world, she preferred to be rather formal with patients.

"Yes, thanks, Donna," he said. That was a surprise. She hadn't realized he knew her name. Gerald and Donna were locked in a minor surgical procedure. Quite suddenly they were merely people at last, no longer in the hierarchical relationship of doctor and patient.

Out of the corner of her eye, Donna caught sight of the notes on a table by the window. Once again, the feeling of unease gripped her. What was it? Something in the notes? No, there had been nothing suspicious. She picked up the endoscope and adjusted the monitor for focus. Then she lubricated the tube, adjusted the angle of Gerald's head and began to lower it into his mouth.

"Now I want you to swallow, Gerald. Breathe through your nose and relax, but keep swallowing. OK, OK, that's good. That's just fine."

He began to gulp away on cue as the black snake with its camera head disappeared into the back of his throat. This was a tricky moment. It was the time when the patient wanted to gag.

"Keep swallowing. That's it. You're doing fine. There, Gerald. That's what your tonsils look like. I can see you never lost those as a kid."

Gerald turned his head toward the image of the red, tentacle-like collections of lymph tissue that guarded the entrance to his throat against bugs. He tried to appear interested despite the sensation that at any second he was going to choke, vomit, or both.

Donna leaned forward, feeding in the black tube and watching the monitor. The esophagus looked apple-pie fine, pink and unscarred. There was nothing abnormal, not that she had expected anything. The pathology would be much lower down. She pushed on downward through the normal pink mucous membrane; clean as a whistle. And then there was a bump, and a lump in the wall of the esophagus came up on the camera like the bow of an overhead destroyer on the periscope of a hunted submarine. There was no stopping for it. By the time she saw it, she was into it, and by the time she was into it, the screen on the monitor had turned a deep, dark, blood red.

Donna froze. Her hands, which had been feeding the fiber-optic cable into her patient, were suddenly as still as the hands of a corpse. Then the thoughts began to come: She knew what the lump in the side of Gerald's esophagus was. She knew now what her sub-conscious mind had recognized in the notes. She knew it with the twenty-twenty clarity of hindsight that was always correct. The lump into which she had just plunged the point of the endoscope was a "bulge," an aneurism, in Gerald Templer's aorta. And the aorta, as everyone knew, especially Fellows of the Royal College of Surgeons, was the largest and most vital artery in a person's body. The rest of it fell into place in slow motion.

But the medical facts were already mixed with other memories, other feelings, other horrors. The bacteria that had caused this patient's SBE had eaten their way through the wall of his aorta before the penicillin had killed them. They had left him with a paper-thin, pulsating bulge in his artery wall and, over time, it had nearly eroded the wall of his esophagus. Into this onionskin union of tissues, Donna had just plunged the endoscope. It might just as well have been a dagger. In the terrified eye of her mind, she could see Gerald's son in the next room, see his wife, mildly worried, flicking through a magazine. She could see the house in Chelsea—it would have window boxes—she could see the blood on the monitor.

There was nothing she could do. It was all too late. Way, way too late. So she just said, "Now, Gerald, you're going to feel a little faint for a moment . . ." And she pulled the endoscope from his aorta, unleashing the torrent of pulsing blood. Within milliseconds, as she had known he would be, Gerald Templer was dead. She had killed him.

27

Donna sat at the polished mahogany table. Across from her, the members of the General Medical Council Disciplinary Committee were almost finished deliberating. She was exhausted. It wouldn't be long now before the verdict was in and this last and most humiliating hurdle would have been jumped. The coroner's inquest had absolved her of legal responsibility for Gerald's death, but her colleagues could still find her guilty of negligence, incompetence, or malpractice. The list of punishments they could hand down would range from a mild verbal slap on the wrist to striking her from the Medical Register. The viability of Gerald's family's lawsuit against her would depend on the conclusion of these doctors.

All morning, the intellectual battle had raged like a tennis match between two top seeds. Slowly but surely, Donna's view had prevailed, and her Medical Defence Union counsel and her own lawyer were beginning to relax at her side. It looked as if it would be a mere reprimand, and a relatively mild one at that. But Donna's victory was bitter. The truth of the matter was that she had killed her patient and left his wife without a husband

and his children fatherless. An overwhelming sadness welled up inside her. Throughout her career she had saved lives. Her career had been everything to her because she meant everything to her patients. She had survived on the love, respect, and gratitude in their eyes. It had been her food, her drink, her warmth. Since her husband and little Daniel, there had been no greater love. She had been brilliant, but she had struggled to be even better, more skilled, more efficient.

And now this. Was she guilty? Maybe not in the eyes of the law or of this committee. But the verdict was "guilty" where it mattered most . . . in her heart. She hated the one committee member who had been particularly critical, but he was right. *Damn it.* He was *right.* She should have examined the barium X rays. She shouldn't have relied on the opinion of an overworked and underpaid GP, or the radiologist, who had said in his report that the pictures were normal. Everyone had been looking for ulcers; nobody had been looking for aneurisms. And in life you never saw until you looked. But in medicine, in surgery, it was your responsibility, *her* responsibility, to cover all the angles to ensure that tragedies like this didn't happen. She tried to imagine herself on the committee that now sat in judgment on her. What would she be saying, feeling? "There but for the grace of God go I?" Bullshit! She would be far less forgiving than these doctors. She would have been the avenging angel of the man who had died because of a surgeon's incompetence.

"I would like to say something," she said, her voice seeming to come from miles away. Her Queen's Counsel put out a hand and touched her arm in a gesture that meant "Be careful."

"I would like voluntarily to remove my name from the Medical Register. Whatever this committee decides, I have made my own decision. I myself feel that I am guilty of professional misconduct, and that is all that matters."

The Medical Defence Union lawyer leaped to his feet. "My

client would like to withdraw that statement and consult with her lawyers."

But Donna stood up, and there were tears in her eyes. They were tears not for herself but for Gerald Templer, who would be alive today but for her. She didn't know what she would do now. She had no idea where she would go. The future didn't exist. There was only the terrible agony of the present.

"I'm sorry," she said, her voice faint. She stood up, turned her back on them all, and walked in a daze from the room.

The cloudy sky on Hallam Street outside the suitably austere building that housed the General Medical Council mirrored perfectly Donna's mood. She felt numb, but around the edges of numbness there were the beginnings of shock and fear. Beside her, like pallbearers, stood her two lawyers. The Queen's Counsel was no stranger to the irrational behavior of clients. He simply shook his head, a sad expression on his face. *Doubtless,* thought Donna, *he's glad this was not a public courtroom.* Lawyers, like professional athletes, were judged on their wins and losses.

The Medical Defence Union lawyer was not so reticent. "I must say, by your extraordinary and unnecessary behavior you have not only done yourself a great disservice, you have cost the Union millions in the upcoming lawsuit. They were going for a reprimand, a short suspension at the very most. I could see it in their eyes. You've cut off your own head. God knows why." He stared about petulantly for a taxi.

"Good," said Donna. "I don't give a shit about the millions you have to pay to Gerald's family. I want them to have it. They deserve it. It was my fault. I know that only a couple of those people up there would have asked to see the barium studies. But I am not them. I was never them. I had higher standards. I was better. I took the credit for my successes, and I'm going to damn well take the blame for my failings."

A taxi came into view, its yellow light on. The QC waved his umbrella at it. "I'm sorry," he said simply. There was admiration in his voice. He would not have done what Donna had done. He recognized the sacrifice, the principles she had failed so magnificently to compromise. God, she was fine-looking. Brave, talented, and true to herself, that brand of truth that Shakespeare believed could make her false to no man. Just for a second he wondered about telephoning her later, for lunch, to commiserate, and then perhaps, maybe . . . but he was married, and a woman like Donna would not tolerate such sneakiness, whatever disguise it wore.

The taxi drew up beside the trio. "Your taxi," said the QC to Donna.

"No, you two take it. I want to walk for a bit."

"Law Courts any good to you?" said the QC to his colleague.

"Yes, actually they're on my way. I'll ride with you and then take it on."

They gave their instructions to the driver and said their good-byes to Donna—the one warm, the other stiff. Then the loneliness closed in on her, and the long road of life loomed before her. And she began to walk away from the disaster for which she had not shirked responsibility.

It was not a long way, and Donna loved walking the streets of London. Samuel Johnson had put it best: when a woman tired of London, she tired of life. She half smiled to herself. London was not to blame, she was. On every side, the city's new vibrancy mocked her despair. It was swinging London once again. The style of its street people, revealed its renewed energy. Restaurants and pubs spilled their customers onto the sidewalks. Everyone was drinking, talking, and laughing, caught up in dreams, schemes, and creativity. There was no sign of the dour survivalism that seemed to have plagued the cities of the West for so long. The town had become the capital of Europe's young. It was thick with Scandinavians; long-legged flaxen-haired Germans; French and Italians free of parents perhaps for the first time, and milking the moment of every opportunity.

Donna cut through the Georgian squares north of Oxford Street and soon she was in the rougher streets parallel to the Edgware Road. Her guts were churning. Was she a doctor still? How long would the bureaucracy take to expunge her from the list of medical practitioners? She had the insane desire to walk into a chemist and write a prescription as a test. Would the Indian pharmacist say, "I'm sorry, Ms. Gardiner, but our computer indicates that you are no longer on the Medical Register"? There was no doubt in her mind that she had done the right thing. That was all there was to be glad about. But now she faced . . . what? The "far, far better thing" that she had done had been rewarded by the guillotine blade descending on her career. But she did not have the consolation of a far, far better place to go. She tried to make sense of the future, but she could only think of her past. She had killed a man. Had it not been for her incompetence, Gerald Templer would be alive today.

On St. John's Wood Road she was nearly home. She walked past Lord's, the home of English cricket. Sometimes, in her garden, she could hear the muted roar when a wicket fell. Now, a match was in progress. Portly old men, some trailing sons and grandsons, were making their way toward the Grace Gate from Warwick Square tube station. They wore straw hats with MCC bands and the orange-and-yellow-striped ties of the Marylebone Cricket Club. They carried vast, striped club umbrellas and picnic boxes filled, doubtless, with pork pies, Scotch eggs, and thermoses of cold Pimms Number One. The scene's contrast to Donna's emotions was so stark as to be all but unbearable. Life was going on. These innocent people were anticipating their innocent pleasure. They were looking forward to a quiet day in the sun with the sound of leather on willow, the friendship of peers with a shared interest, a pint or two of draft ale at the lunch break.

But Donna was full of self-doubt, and the equally unwelcome emotion of self-hatred. More than ever before in her life, she realized the inseparable link between self-respect and contentedness. In the absence of self-esteem, happiness was impossible. As she turned the corner into Cunningham Place, the nice cleaner from l'Unique waved to her. He owed her some shirts and a couple of frocks, but she wouldn't face him now. Dominic, her gardener, was watering the daisies and ivy in the black window boxes as she approached her house. He said hello, but he knew from her body language not to question her today. She closed the door behind her, and peace of sorts descended. "I can heal you," this house that she loved seemed to be saying to her. "I am your friend. In winter and summer, in spring and fall. I leak and I creak and I let you down sometimes, as all friends do, but we'll always be together."

She wandered into the garden and then back up to the second-floor conservatory, where the grapes were already beginning to blacken. Soon they would be ready for eating, but the thought of eating made her feel nauseated. So she meandered from room to room, looking for comfort she knew she would not find. What next? Where to now? Her ancestors stared down at her. Granny Green, her great-great aunt, wore a prim bonnet and an enigmatic Mona Lisa smile. Her great-great uncle, the Royal Academician, whose water colors of turn-of-the-century China covered her walls, stared straight at her. His austere half-finished self-portrait had eyes that followed you wherever you went, like Lord Kitchener's finger in the famous "Your Country Needs You" poster. There was some comfort there. These old people, dead people, dozens of them, had shared her genes, but their ancient worries were as meaningless now as the wind that blew, the waves that broke on the shores of any sea. Time went on. It healed wounds, she tried to tell herself. And then death healed everything. But there was still a gap to be filled. The gap between now and the time when all worries at last were gone.

She picked up the old silver christening mug given to her

great-uncle John in 1874. He had died at twelve, poor little thing, of TB probably, or of simple pneumonia in the days before antibiotics. Had he drunk his milk from this cup in the nursery with nanny? Had he been frightened at the last? Was he looking down on Donna now? Did he know? She put down the cup. This was morbid. Could it be the beginning of some affective illness? No! She wasn't the type. But she had seen many succumb to depression who were not "the type" . . . soldiers with Military Crosses; nuns; people with perfect lives and marriages struck down by the sick grief that Churchill called the Black Dog, the illness that could tear like a hurricane from nowhere into your life and rip it apart.

She walked up to the bedroom and lay down on the outsize bed. Its faded pink damask cover had been on her own mother's bed. A Victorian bath sat in the middle of the room. She had stuck it there twenty years before shabby chic was in, and now, of course, it looked as if the room had been designed by the decorator-of-the-millisecond only weeks before. It would rent in a heartbeat, this house. And it was at that precise moment that Donna realized she was going away.

Beside her bed were the photographs of Steve and Daniel. She leaned over and picked up one of Steve, her eyes drawn as always to the shock of blond hair, the deep, brooding eyes, his strong, broad shoulders. He looked more like a farm laborer than an artist, and Donna had loved that contrast about him— the lack of effeteness, of preciousness, the dread indulgence in sensitivity that seemed to demand that so many artists adopt a feminine persona. As always, in times of joy and sorrow, and in between, she thought of him now. What would he have to say about all this? Would he feel that she had done right after the wrong? Yes. She knew that with absolute certainty. Would he have told her not to blame herself for what had happened? No, he wouldn't have been kind for the sake of kindness. In all her life she had never met a man who set himself, and others, such high standards. They had shared that. It had drawn them to each other. And it had propelled them away because a part of him blamed her for Daniel's tragic death. But he still had his career. It was going from success to success. Hers was in ruins. Or, rather, it had ceased to be.

Donna sat up on the bed. There was one thing that had to be done first. She had to visit Gerald Templer's family . . . if they would see her. She had to give them another chance to unload their grief onto her, face to face. Part of her recoiled from this final confrontation; part of her needed it, the hair shirt, the self-flagellation that could be some atonement for the crime. And was there not part of her, too, that hoped against hope for forgiveness, a kind word, a smile, a squeeze of the hand, that she could take away as absolution? Quite suddenly she wished she were able to believe in God. She needed Him now. Her intellectual arrogance had always stood in the way of belief, but if she could not live a believer's life, she could at least live a good life. That would be some recompense.

Out there, somewhere, everywhere perhaps, people needed her. In Zaire, Rwanda, and Burundi, with the genocide; in Somalia, in Ethiopia, with the famines; and in places where suffering was so common and so mundane that the newspapers didn't even bother to mention them. She could go there, anywhere, and bandage wounds, hold the hands of the dying, and they wouldn't care if her name was or was not on the principal list of physicians of the United Kingdom and Northern Ireland.

So she picked up the telephone, dialed 192 for directory assistance, and simply asked for the number of Oxfam. Later, she would call Chestertons, and soon some American banker would be enjoying the home she loved so much for two thousand pounds a week.

Because Donna was not just going away. Donna Gardiner was going to disappear.

28

New York

The wind howled down Fifty-seventh Street, and Kate strode purposefully into the face of it. The currents of air plucked at her cashmere shawl. She looked business–New York in her black felt hat, black stockings, and high-heeled shoes, and her dark glasses gave her an aura of mystery that turned heads on the busy street. This was somebody, the expressions of the passersby seemed to say. And for the first time in months Kate felt like somebody. But one thing was completely certain: she was no longer the same person she had once been.

Depression had dismantled her, as a child's castle of blocks is knocked over by a careless foot. In putting herself back together again, she had had to learn everything anew, and she had been humbled by the experience. Now she was almost glad that she had experienced the horror. Only when you were on your knees in pain, stretched out on the rack of fear, praying for elusive peace, could you start again. She had hit bottom, and there at the bedrock of life she had at last seen herself as others must have seen her. In the ugly struggle for fame and success she had

lost all humility and dignity. She had lost sight of all the little
things, the beauty of a crisp New York morning, the sunshine
gleaming from the glass of the buildings, the awe in the eyes of
the tourists as they walked the streets of the city. Most of all,
she had destroyed her own marriage, thoughtlessly, needlessly.
The bitter regret of that still lingered. She would never forget
the betrayal, but she had learned both to forgive and to understand it. Peter had given her his life, and she had lost sight of
the treasure he had been. She had showed him only the hostility
that had sprung from fear of losing her material world. But
slowly, imperceptibly, she had found genuine pleasure again . . .
in the flowering of her orchids, in a lilac dawn, in the flapping
sound of a duck's wings. With it had come gratitude and
thanks. Depression had a use: its function had been to cleanse
her as fire cleans. She prayed only that she would never forget
the lesson she had learned.

A few minutes later, Kate was striding through the offices of
the publishing division, her eyes and mind on maximum alert.
All around, the office buzzed, and she could feel the pent-up
energy inside herself, too. Kate had almost forgotten what it
was like to be human. Now she was back. The cloud had lifted.
In the open-plan office, girls sat at desks poring over mountain-
ous manuscripts, trying to edit amidst the telephone fury. There
were stacks of books everywhere, on floors, on window ledges,
piled on top of the coffee machine. There were layouts on tables, and through a glass partition drifted the sounds of voices
shouting cover blurbs at each other.

Kate caught sight of Sam, talking animatedly into a telephone while scribbling notes. Her desk had a corner to itself, as
befitted her recent promotion to number two to Gale, the art
book division's editor. It had nothing to do with nepotism or to
the large holding in the company that Sam's trust now owned.
It had everything to do with her competence, drive, and initiative. As Kate approached, Sam raised her hand in welcome and
mouthed a soundless "Hi."

Kate perched on the edge of the desk and signaled that Sam should take her time with the call. She was fielding some persistent and wordy agent with charm, but with firmness. Kate gazed down at her fondly. It was funny how strong the love was. Children could never understand it until they had their own. Her own mother had been fond of telling Kate that. "You wait, dear. I long for you to have children. Then you'll know what it's like." Kate had always laughed it off—"Oh, mom!"—but now she understood. To say that she would die for Sam was irrelevant. Even to consider Sam's dying, being hurt, being unhappy, was to experience a churning wrench in the gut. Every line of Sam's face was so dear, each blemish, each hair of her head was precious. Love flowed out of Kate, unconditional, overwhelming, from the vast bank of memories. She could see Sam's Eeyore in the eye of her mind; tattered Teddy, who had never been out of eyesight during Sam's childhood; Mr. Soldier, the dark blue marine who had been painted onto the furniture in her nursery. The fact that she was grown up now, sensible, hardworking, talented, made very little difference to the feelings. They were stuck somewhere in midchildhood as Sam cried out in pain from a wasp sting; as she hovered nervously at the door of a children's party; as she hid her milk teeth in excitement beneath the pillow for the tooth fairy.

Kate peered around appreciatively. "It's picking up, isn't it? Not just this division. The whole company is going again. You can sense it in the cafeteria. Even the meat loaf tastes better."

"*You* ate in the cafeteria?" said Sam, looking up and smiling at her mother. "God, I bet they sold some Pepto-Bismol *that* day."

"What on earth do you mean, darling?" said Kate with one of her famous giggles. "Are you trying to insinuate that people are frightened of me in this business? That's nonsense. We're all just one big happy family."

"Yeah, right," said Sam, rolling her eyes to the ceiling in mock sarcasm. Nobody had quite got used to the change in Kate's personality. Even Sam. And those employees with good memories were still wary of her.

"I was with Margaret this morning. The news is good across the board. All the divisions have turned around, not just this one. The fans out there are buying again. Morale is just great. You could superimpose my mood chart on the profits graph and nobody would be able to tell which was which."

Sam reached out and touched her mother's hand. "You did great, Mom. You'll never again have to fight a battle that hard. That was the big one."

Kate could actually laugh about it. That was how far away she felt from the bad dream from which she had at last awoken. But it had taken an age. She had had to drag herself back from the abyss using fingernails and what was left of her old determination that the depression had so weakened. Other factors had helped—the antidepressants, Frankie's endless support—but most of all, it had been Sam's strength, presence, and loyalty. Being needed at last by her powerful mother, being no longer merely the dependent daughter, had enabled Sam to get close to her. They could talk about everything now, as friends . . . even about the highly charged emotional issues of Peter's leaving and Ruth's Machiavellian scheming.

"Look, darling. The reason I came by was to see if you wanted lunch."

"Lunch. God, Mom. I thought you were booked up till next year . . . triple-booked. Starters with those on the way up. Entrées with the stars. Dessert with the also-rans." Sam laughed. In the old days, it wouldn't have been a joke.

"I canceled all three, actually four. The fourth group simply eats while I sit drinking coffee." Kate laughed too, sending up the whole idea of the late nineties cult of busy-ness.

Sam looked helplessly at her cluttered desk. She didn't have time for lunch, her expression said. But she wanted to talk to her mother. Talking, for both of them, had become therapeutic.

Kate saw the hesitation. "Don't even think about it. I order you as your ultimate boss to have lunch with me."

"Well, if you put it that way, I accept," said Sam, standing up. "Where to, Trattoria dell'Arte?"

"Absolutely," said Kate. She watched as Sam emerged from behind the desk. Kate noticed everything. Sam had been working hard, yet she looked cucumber cool in a black Armani trouser suit and plain white T-shirt. Her hair had just been cut by Frederick Fekkai. Her nails were beautifully manicured. If you could get it together to look like that *and* be the toast of the department, you were on your way. It felt very good to have an heir, better to have an heiress.

Kate's earlier brisk entry into the office had taken the employees by surprise. On the way out they all managed to catch her eye, smiling, saying their "hi"s, surreptitiously checking out the woman who was so vital to their lives. They noted the new luster in her formerly lank hair, the spring in her previously listless step, the sparkle in eyes that had been dull for far too long. Kate radiated confidence. It all made sense; everything pointed in the same direction. Kate Haywood Enterprises was back, and the future looked great.

There was deference from the receptionists in the entrance foyer as mother and daughter collected their coats and hurried across the marble floors to the bank of elevators. There were several people in the elevator when it stopped, and they flattened themselves against the walls as they slipped into celebrity-recognition mode, leaving Sam and Kate standing alone in the middle of a ring of self-styled lesser mortals.

In the lobby of the building on Fifty-seventh where the Kate Haywood offices were, Kate's fame unfurled before her across the white-and-black-checkered marble floor beneath the Léger tapestries, the gray-uniformed doormen nodding obsequious hellos as she passed. After a short walk past the Russian Tea Room and Carnegie Hall, Kate and Sam were deep in the noisy fun of the Italian restaurant. From their seats at one of the best tables in the back of the room, they made immediately for the antipasto bar.

"You're allowed seven, but the olives, anchovies, and sun-dried tomatoes don't count. You can usually get away with eight by appearing to add the last as an afterthought," said Sam. Like her mother, she liked to get value for her money.

"Would you like me to choose the antipasto for you, ladies?" asked the good-looking Italian man behind the bar. There were vegetables, but vegetables with a difference: mushrooms from Sorrento, tiny new potatoes brushed with mint, spinach dripping with garlic . . . "No," mother and daughter chorused in unison as they began their own selection process.

At last they were settled, with Chardonnay, antipasto, and San Pellegrino.

"I hear the dynamic duo made another pass at Condé Nast last week, according to Si," said Kate. She hadn't changed so completely that she didn't get a grim satisfaction from Peter and Ruth's abortive plans to set up a rival business to hers.

"Hah!" Sam spat out her exasperation. "They never give up, do they? They must know they're beaten by now. Who is going to back them against you? Dad must know that, even if the mouse that roared doesn't. He may have behaved like a complete idiot, but presumably the business part of his brain is still ticking."

"Yes," said Kate. "They must know it's over. They came close in the beginning, with Somers. They were as near as this." She held her hands together as if in prayer to signify how close that was. "Another month or two and he'd have backed them. Luckily for us, he waited to see if I'd survive." Kate sipped her wine. "You know, Sam, I couldn't have done it without you. You were really there for me. Somehow I didn't think I had the right to expect that. When Peter left, I kinda felt you'd go with him. You and he being so close and everything."

"Thanks, Mom," said Sam, putting out her hand across the table and touching her mother's. "But all that 'closeness' was a sham, wasn't it?" she continued. "That was just Dad's PR. The 'I'll always be there for you from the cradle to the grave' rubbish. I can't tell you how much I had invested in him emotionally. It was like all my eggs were in this one basket, and he just stamped on them, crushed them. He didn't even tell me his plans. He didn't ask me; he never explained things to me; he just went right ahead and deserted the ship and damned near sank it." She shook her head in disbelief. "Jeez! I mean *that* is something. If he'd been distant, or a bit absent, I might have forgiven him. Now? Never! He's history. It's like I don't *have* a father."

Kate's smile was grim. It gave her no pleasure to see her daughter's anger and frustration. Peter had left a gaping hole in both their lives, and they were still busy trying to fill it. It would take time.

"Actually, until you were about seven, I was one helluva mother. Textbook, really. So good I once thought of doing a book called *Motherhood*. I think I did *Finger Foods* instead!"

They laughed together, lightening up for a moment.

"I know. I remember a lot of those times," said Sam. "You used to drive me around on your errands. You remember that place in the village that's now the bookshop?"

"Kitchen Art. John Hobbes's place. They loved my fudge brownies. He was a sweet guy."

"He used to talk to me as if I were a grown-up. I liked that. You know, you're right. It was later, in the tens and twelves, when you were away a lot. They say the child's mind is set by five. The whole 'daddy' thing was basically the smoke and mirrors of the teenage years, I guess." She paused. "You know, I've never really said this, and I should have . . . but, sorry, Mom. I'm really sorry for being the bitch I was."

Kate felt the emotion wash over her. "You weren't a bitch, darling. You just didn't understand the pressure I was under.

How could you have? I was getting this whole goddamned thing together, and you were a child. Now you know the problems—your desk looks like it's stuffed with them."

"Tell me about it," said Sam. "If I had a child right now, I would have forgotten her name and what she looked like, and I'm just an editor."

"Associate publisher," said Kate.

"Yeah, I *am* doing pretty well, I guess," said Sam.

"And don't it feel *good?"* said Kate. Sam was far more like her than she had ever dreamed she would be.

"Do you think Ruth will leave him, now that it seems he can't turn her into you?" said Sam suddenly, as if relishing the idea.

"Possibly," said Kate, trying to keep her thoughts charitable, and not entirely succeeding.

"Well, if she ever wants a job here, the cleaning lady has got the flu," said Sam, a speculative tone creeping into her voice.

"I hope for your father's sake she doesn't leave him," said Kate.

"I don't have a father, remember?" said Sam.

Sam didn't have a father. Kate didn't have a husband. She still didn't quite know how she felt about it. At first there had been the mind-numbing shock, and then her illness had surged into the vacuum left by Peter's departure and changed the nature of everything. Now there was numbness where he had been, but it was no longer the paralysis of despair. Someday, sometime, there would be someone to replace him. In the meantime, like a healing balm, there had been the blissful return of her ability to work. Kate had thrown herself into it with the enthusiasm of the drowning person reaching for a lifeline.

"So what's the big news this month on the work front?" said Sam. Since joining the firm in which she had such a vested interest, Sam had become fascinated by every aspect of the business.

"In a word, spirituality, but with a New Age spin. The next magazine is on the theme of 'Aquarius revisited.' Chopra is always calling up and saying that the new intelligence is female. He wants me to do a consciousness channel with him on cable. I spoke to Malone about it. He was pretty interested."

"That makes a lot of sense," said Sam slowly. "I guess Chopra is to the soul what you are to lifestyles. The two cry out to be combined. The millennium is coming up. You just have to be politically correct and avoid specific religions like Buddhism or Christianity. Stick to higher beings. They're safer."

"Goodness, darling, are you being pragmatic or cynical? I usually know the difference. Either way, you're getting frighteningly wise for my little girl."

"I'm my mom's girl; sometimes I think I'm turning into you," said Sam with an affectionate laugh. "So what's in Aquarius revisited?"

"Oh, all sorts of good things. Signs of the zodiac compacts, a scent called Kate's Spirit, a piece on Donna Karan and Kelly Klein's Wellness Center in the Hamptons. I went in there the other day and there was this cute young guy lying on the floor, feet in the air. He had a middle-aged woman sitting in the lotus position four feet off the ground, balancing on his toes. I said 'hi' and he actually said 'peace.' Then Kelly said, 'You haven't wiped your feet properly, Kate. You're leaving marks all over the carpet.' I guess she hasn't quite made it to full enlightenment yet."

"Should be a smash," said Sam.

"What about you?" said Kate.

Sam answered her with a question. "What do you think about London right now?"

"I think it's hot. Shrager is looking for hotels. All the big designers are buying up space on Sloane Street. The bands are big again, restaurants are good. But it seems to be a global sort of thing. Difficult to pin down to actual people. If you're thinking artists, maybe you should look for some American with an English connection."

"That was exactly what I was thinking about," said Sam. "There's this guy who has a big show at the Tate coming up. He works with glass. *Great* stuff. Very big reputation, has work in the Met, MOMA, everywhere. There are some photographs of his work in this month's *Artforum.* He'd be great for a book. He's never done one before."

"I know exactly who you mean," said Kate. "He's the guy who lives in East Hampton, isn't he? The recluse. Lives in that big house behind the wall at the edge of the village. Isn't he supposed to be rather frightening? What's his name? . . . God, what *is* his name? He's lived there for years."

"He's called Steve Gardiner," said Sam. "From his photographs, he's rather good-looking, in a menacing sort of way."

29

Steve strode across the field to the barn. Lilac mist lapped at his ankles, and the sky above was pink with the East Hampton dawn. He had awakened early, as always, and in the precious moments between sleep and wakefulness, he had already planned the rough details of the first and most vital moments of the day's work. From then on, God willing, the river of inspiration would flow, wiping away the trivialities of life's worries, and above all, the loneliness. He was happy yet nervous here at the beginning of another day. Would it go well? Would there be beauty? Would there be the satisfaction that he both craved and demanded?

Jim Sinnecock threw open the door of the barn to greet his friend and employer. He had seen Steve approaching as he always did, head bowed, deep in thought, his mind wrestling already with anticipated problems. There was coffee brewing, but Steve would already have breakfasted, for he seldom lunched. He wore what he always wore: tattered corduroy trousers; a faded, worn jacket of old leather; and brown brogues, cracked yet soft with age. Steve's face needed to be read like the weather.

From Steve's expression Jim could tell that today would be a good day but a hard one, like those freezing but bracing winter days when the sun shone bright, giving warmth to the mind but not the body. Steve smiled a wintry smile of "good morning." Not for the first time Jim wondered at the extraordinary combination of features that made Steve's face unique. He was blond, but somehow the structure of his face, deep-set eyes, the furrowed brow, the forceful chin, seemed to demand darker hair . . . the Nordic melancholy merging with some more Italianate mystery. To a man like Jim Sinnecock who said little but knew much, it seemed that the years had been kinder to Steve's appearance than to his heart.

"Morning, Jim," he said, as Jim stood back to let him pass. "Furnace OK?" It was a needless question. The inside of the barn was like the inferno of Dante, the edges of the cavernous building darkly lit by the dancing light of hell's fire. Monolithic glass sculptures stood guard at the perimeter of the studio, several packed, some in various stages of packing, the cases marked TATE GALLERY in paint. One towered over the rest, a huge conical structure of stained sheet glass, frosted gray on a black cast-iron base. In the dead center of the room was a conical structure from which heat radiated as if from the devil's heart. It was over 2,000 degrees in the midst of the burning, fiery furnace, and throughout the night, while Steve dreamed of art, Jim had toiled to feed the hungry flames greedy for coal.

"I thought we'd lost a pot, 'bout two this morning, but she sealed, thank heaven."

"Ah," said Steve, unwinding the tartan scarf from his neck and throwing off his jacket. Beneath it, he wore a plaid shirt of soft wool and an old, English-style cardigan. "But we're all right for pots?"

"Oh, sure."

The melting pots, handmade of fire clay from the English

town of Stourbridge, could withstand 2,600 degrees of heat for thirty-six hours or more.

"How long have we been molten?" said Steve. He approached the furnace, peeling off his cardigan and rolling up his sleeves to reveal strong, muscled forearms.

"We did thirty hours molten before we went bubble free. The rubbish is skimmed, and we've been cooling for several hours. I know you wanted it on the tacky side. She's ready to go now, in my opinion."

"Looks pretty pure," said Steve. It did. The gel shone with a light blue translucent glow, white-hot no longer.

He wasn't judging it by its appearance alone. Steve had yesterday's memories to rely on. The fine white sand had been as pure as flour before it was carefully combed by magnets to remove the tiniest impurities. Wearing protective face mask and clothing, Steve had supervised the process, including the vital measuring of the bases—potash, lead oxide, carbonate of soda—and the addition to the silica of cobalt, zinc, and nickel, to produce the precise shade of blue he wanted. Neither the mechanical nor the technical had been overlooked. When finally his art was unleashed, nothing would stand in its way.

Steve felt the excitement build. This was his life . . . his work. And it *did* love him back. Each piece of glass he created was his family. It was scattered now, throughout America and the world, in great private collections, in grand museums, but the memories of his acts of creation were always there to give him strength in moments of weakness. Sometimes he felt that he had cheated by escaping life and becoming a virtual recluse. At other times he rationalized it. Were monks and nuns less worthy than those who struggled in quiet desperation to endure their material worlds? The reasons for his escape came now, like old friends or familiar enemies, to try him. But he had practiced this too often. He had learned how to shut them out by closing the opaque door of his work upon them.

But, through the glass darkly, he could see them still. Donna, and little Daniel, who had taken away the pieces of his heart that Donna had broken. Their divorce had been so sensible. They had taken nothing from each other but the memories, parting in sorrow not in anger. They had been too strong for each other, too similar. Both had discovered that their number-one loves would be their careers. He had never forgotten her, nor the tragedy that neither had totally survived. He was remembering her now, trying not to, in the heat of the barn, across the years. He had heard that she was an eminent surgeon. By mutual, unspoken agreement they had never seen each other again since the day of Daniel's funeral. Perhaps both feared the chemistry that would cause fire a second time.

With an effort, Steve cleared his mind of her image, so soft and appealing. He must get to work. Steve employed six people: "gatherers," "servitors," "gaffers," and "sticker ups," each able to do the other's job, all artists, all student apprentices working to learn and maintain the standards of an art form that had been effectively dead since before most of them were born. In the village, they respected Steve Gardiner. He was not like Duchamps, Léger, Dalí . . . other transient artists who, briefly, had made this part of the world their home. He was a local. He had been there for twenty years. And yet he was a man apart.

"Well," said Steve, "what are we waiting for?"

Together he and Jim manipulated the pot and its contents to a steel bench. Steve walked to the table with the green baize cover and picked up the long thin pipe. He twirled it in his hands, getting the feel of it, like a tennis champion a favorite racket. He put the thinner end to his lips, holding the brass tube at the area insulated by twine, and blew through the hollow tube a few times. From the moment he started, the action would be continuous. The glass would be cooling rapidly, becoming less malleable by the minute. Mistakes could not be rectified. And there would be nobody but himself to blame.

Now he dipped the thicker end of the blowpipe into the molten mass and extracted from it a bulb of semiliquid glass about the size of a baseball. He lowered it quickly into a wooden mold known as the block, which had been moistened with water against the intense heat. Then Steve began to blow, like some mysterious figure from mythology playing the pipe of Pan in the Stygian gloom.

He blew with the delicacy of a musician, fingering the pipe as if it were a musical instrument, and the shape that began to appear had the excitement and harmony of the most beautiful symphony. He twisted the pipe this way and that, his head moving like a dancer's, his whole body involved in the process. The glass grew. Charmed like a snake, it slipped into life, blue and brilliant. A second before, there had been nothing but the primordial mass. Now beauty was born. Steve moved backward, drawing the glass from the block. With his right hand he touched its bottom with a flat paddle known as a battledore. He took his lips from the pipe, and said, "Reheat."

Jim maneuverd the glass back into the glory hole. Nobody spoke. Suddenly, one of the gaffers was at his shoulder. Jim turned toward him, a frown on his face. The man was about to say something, but at moments like this silence was more precious than gold, as precious almost as glass.

The man, however, would not be restrained. "There's a young lady to see you, Mr. Gardiner. Says it's about your exhibition in London. Samantha Haywood."

Steve tried to turn his head from side to side in a negative without disrupting the intensely delicate moment as the glass literally grew from the end of his pipe.

But it was too late. "I'm sorry to burst in on you at such a delicate moment," said Sam. She was not a waiter at doors, in lobbies, or in hallways. She'd inherited that trait, and a few others, from her mother. "Don't mind me," she said, her voice open and friendly. "If it's all right, I'll just watch until you're finished."

Steve looked at her in horror, pipe still to lips. Then the horror began to fade, because this girl had such a lovely, warm smile, and because she clearly hadn't a clue what an awful blunder she had made.

30

Steve thrust his head down as he walked, and inhaled the salt air. To his left the grassy dunes stretched away past wooden fences to the sprawling million-dollar mansions, open now but soon to be closed and shuttered against the bleak loneliness of the Long Island winter. A late summer wind blew from the east, flicking fine spray from the gilded crests of the waves. A single fisherman cast long, optimistic lines into the surf. Otherwise there was nobody about to disturb the gulls that picked and scurried amidst the patches of seaweed and the little pools that the capricious sea had left behind on the beach. Later in the day, the summer people would be back, moaning about the roughness and untypical coldness of the sea. For the tourists, it had been a season from hell, six inches of rain in July, more than twice the usual amount. And the winds had left a chill in the waters that lingered still. At White's Pharmacy in East Hampton the self-tanning gels had dwarfed the sales of the sunscreen.

"Do you often walk out here in the early morning?" said Sam. She was bundled up against the cold in jeans and a big sweater. She chose her words carefully. She was stalking her prey for the book project. In fact, Steve Gardiner did resemble a wild animal in a way. He was beautiful, yet unpredictable. He probably wouldn't bite, but he might if you mishandled him. There was an element of danger. A stupid remark would not be forgiven.

"I usually come in the late evening," he said, shooting a quick, sidelong glance at her. "Nobody around, then. Or now."

"You like that?" said Sam, probing just a bit. "No people," she added unnecessarily. It was a safe bet. The only thing that was known about Steve Gardiner, except for his international reputation as an artist, was that he wasn't interested in people. The next question, of course, would be "why."

"Nothing the matter with people," said Steve with a quick laugh that sounded almost friendly. "Perhaps there's something the matter with me."

"I don't think there's anything the matter with you," said Sam. She found him strangely attractive in an objective sort of way. He was old enough to be her father, as they said. He was very much the sort of person, in fact, her mother would be drawn to, although the mixture might be explosive. She shook her head in the wind, letting her blond hair fly about in the breeze. He didn't reply to her "nothing the matter with you" remark.

"Why did you ask me out here?" she said, upping the ante.

"I wanted to see if you could get out of bed at six in the morning," he said. He gave her a sly look and smiled. It was a good question, one that he hadn't quite answered himself. He was drawn to her energy, enthusiasm, and initiative. He didn't meet many young people like her. Daniel would have been about her age by now. Somehow, he wanted to give her a chance.

"At my age I can even *go* to bed at six in the morning," said Sam with a gentle smile. He did not miss her point.

"Touché," he said.

They both laughed.

"Are you a swimmer?" he said. It was a pleasantry, neutral ground after the badinage. He walked fast, forcing her to keep up with him. He was rather enjoying this. It was weird. Small talk was usually less attractive to him than root canal work. He stole another look at her. Her bejeaned legs were long, and her Top-Siders pleasantly old. She wore no socks. She must be twenty-five, maybe a year or two older. The big sweater didn't hide the fact that she had a good figure, yet she had chosen, modestly, not to show it off. Her face was tanned and a little freckled, typically American, open and pretty, if just a tad too bland to be beautiful. If she modeled, it would be for an L.L. Bean catalogue, not *Vogue*. Her voice was lovely. That was the odd word that best described it. It bubbled.

"I don't swim much in the ocean," said Sam. "I prefer pools."

"Too cold. Too rough. The windsurfers have had a lousy year."

"And the crash. The Eight Hundred. I've never liked the idea of swimming in a sea in which so many died . . . and, like . . . so close. I found a Styrofoam cup with 'TWA' on it once. That was pretty creepy."

"Yes. Twenty miles. Not far," he said, "But burial at sea. And so sudden. Worse ways to go."

There was a melancholy about him. He was a big man, but there was a sadness, a loneliness. Sam felt strongly that he was no great fan of life. To that extent, or at least to the extent that he was prepared to let it show, he was less American than European.

"You know, you're quite a celebrity around here. A sort of private Mr. Rattiner. I feel rather privileged to have been tested at dawn, as it were." There was the slightest hint of mockery in Sam's voice. Rattiner was the white-haired Hamptons sage, a large man, a notorious talker with a theory on everything.

"Do you want to know my favorite limerick?" he asked. He stopped unexpectedly. A white gull flew low over his head, as if investigating the Gardiner stoppage. "I wish I loved the human race. I wish I loved its silly face. And each time I encountered one, I wish I thought 'What jolly fun!'"

"Jeez!" said Sam with a laugh. "I think I get the point."

"It wasn't always like that," he said. "When I was your age, I bubbled with enthusiasm just like you. Then life happens to you . . . I suppose what I mean," he said, walking on, "is that people are hard work for me now. They want things from you that maybe you don't want to give. They demand, they intrude, they prevent, they even excite . . . and then they withdraw their excitement."

"They do?" said Sam. She felt she understood him. She took a deep breath. "Was there a woman who excited and then withdrew her excitement? Or is that rude to ask? A person intruding?"

"Yes, there was a woman. A wife, actually. In London. Around the time you were born, I imagine, although I have no way of knowing when that was."

"Seventy-four."

He snapped his fingers. "There you are. A talent of mine. I am good at ages. Haven't tried it on the young recently, though."

"The rumor is you were married and divorced. Quite quickly." Sam felt it was best to be up front. She was the sort of professional to have done her homework.

"Well, good for the rumor. It's right. I married a doctor. A very fine, very talented surgeon. And she married an artist. A very committed, very obsessional—"

"Very talented artist," Sam finished for him. It wasn't just that she wanted his book. It was true, he was a very, very good artist, with a show coming up at the Tate in London soon. She remembered how he had stood in his foundry, and how he had made this thing of beauty, this conical shape of violet blue. He had been so irritated when she had burst in on him, and his work hadn't been affected one iota by his irritation.

"And we loved each other very much. Very, very much. I don't think I have ever met a woman less stupid, more admirable, as beautiful, more . . . impossible. Of course, it was a disaster from the start, but we parted friends." Steve walked on in silence. He hadn't mentioned Daniel, but he could not remember being more open with anyone. "I haven't a clue why I'm talking to you like this," he said.

"I'm glad you are," said Sam.

She looked at him quickly. He had been getting married in the year of her birth. For some reason she was drawn to him. She wanted to do the book more than ever. How should she play it? The gently rolling ocean, the orange sun, the caramel sand, had never been more in focus. The salt air was like ambrosia to her nostrils. The world seemed amplified. Her senses were on maximum alert.

There was a long silence. They walked on. A stray dog rushed toward them as if it thought they were its owners. Each stopped to pat it. It wagged its tail in pleasure, throwing off a fine spray of wet sand.

"Do you eat breakfast?" he said suddenly.

"Yes," said Sam.

"Good," said Steve. "We shall go and eat breakfast at Bean's. We will discuss this book business and bump into all your friends, and nobody will know me from Adam."

"Nonsense," said Sam. "Everyone will say, 'There's Steve Gardiner, the famous recluse.' And in the corner J. D. Salinger will be having a bagel with Elvis. And everything will be really, really quiet. Then some guy who was third banana in the fruit scene of some Hollywood movie will walk in, and the whole place will erupt into a frenzy of celebrity recognition."

"Yes," said Steve, "it's a wonderful thing to know that one is living in a nation whose heart is so spectacularly in the right place."

Sam could feel the book in her clutches. She was nearly there. *It's a wonderful thing to be living,* she thought.

31

Burundi

Donna knelt on the dirt floor of the tin shack and wiped the flies from the eyes of the children. It was a pointless exercise, but it was something she had to do. There was precious little else that could be done. There was no medicine. There hadn't been any since the coup, and all around there were the open sores of yaws, and the hacking coughs of the old and young alike. For the thousandth time she cursed the world's inability or unwillingness to put this madness right. She thought back to the days when she had practiced medicine in London, seemingly light-years away. She had felt she was doing good, and she had never bothered to thank God for such simple things as antibiotics. They had been taken for granted, like bandages and antiseptic, food and uncontaminated water. Her old life had, with hindsight's benefit, been a sick joke of complacency amidst plenty. She smiled grimly as she remembered all the concern about Mr. Jones's stupid hernia or Mrs. White's irrelevant piles. Even Gerald Templer's death, the one that had brought her to this hell on earth, had acquired some perspective now. He had been in his early thirties. Nobody in this room would reach that august age. Even without the war, the genocide, the danger on every side, forty in Burundi was a ripe old age.

She stood up. The British doctor by her side stood too. "What a mess," he said.

"There's a sucking chest wound over there. But the guy's skin and bone and nothing's sterile. Is there any point in having a go at it?"

"Something to do, I suppose," said the doctor. His chirpy British pessimism served him well, thought Donna. The American doctors took it worst of all. They had a hard time shedding their congenital optimism.

The clack-clack-clack of a helicopter drowned further conversation. Donna walked to the door of the hut and looked out. A gunship flew low overhead, ripping holes with its airstream in the sparse foliage that surrounded the hut. A straggling line of emaciated people snaked away from the doorway where she stood. These were candidates for the "hospital" in which she "worked." Many looked worse than those inside. But it was all hopeless. The helicopter was heading north to Tshiangano, where smoke was already rising and the thump of mortar fire could be heard. Rumor, that stuff of war, said that the rebels were attacking the eastern outskirts of Bujumbura. If so, the struggle was nearing some sort of resolution.

Donna sighed. All around her there was death. It was life and health that were the abnormality. She, Donna, was the thing that was wrong with the picture. Although she had lost thirty percent of her body weight, she was well and she was whole. She was nothing that a month or two in the Hotel du Cap at Antibes wouldn't put right. Why did they go on and on killing? Why didn't somebody call "enough"? Julius Nyerere, Tanzania's former president and the international mediator on Burundi, had said it all: "I believe both the army and the armed groups should now say 'We have killed enough people. Let's sit down and talk.' " That was the definition of a pious hope. Because this was genocide, the genocide of two tribes—the tall, proud Tutsis and the short, angry Hutus—and neither would rest until everyone was dead.

"If the Hutus take Bujumbura, we ought not to be around, you know," said the British doctor. He had red hair and freckles, and he was very young and very brave, and he had given up general practice in Barnes to be here. Donna admired him enormously. He had done this out of genuine goodness. He was not trying to atone for some private sin to assuage personal pride.

"You think the Hutus would kill us?"

"This is an army 'hospital.' That means it's technically a Tutsi institution, even if it's a sick joke. People have been killed for less. Like for being alive!"

"I don't think I could leave," said Donna.

"I heard there was a plane at the airport in Bujumbura. An American military transport. It's not allowed to leave because of the sanctions. The Tanzanians won't let it fly over their air space."

"It won't be held up for long," said Donna. "These days you don't thumb your nose at the world's only superpower and get away with it."

"If we drove out there, I bet they'd find a seat for us."

They both fell silent. The Tutsi coup that had started this particular chapter of regional genocide had resulted in the neighboring country's imposition of stringent economic and transport sanctions. Road and air links out of Burundi had been severed. Fuel, food, and precious medicine were not entering. Their old Renault had half a tank of gas. It would get them to Bujumbura, but tomorrow it might be stolen, shot to pieces by a trigger-happy gunship pilot, or sabotaged by anyone in the general atmosphere of hate and mistrust. Her colleague had a point. They were in serious danger. This might be the last chance to get out.

"Rwanda and Uganda won't let it overfly either," said Donna

at last. She was afraid, and talk of leaving somehow emphasized the feeling. It was funny, she hadn't thought of herself for
ages. She had buried herself willingly in suffering so dense and
all-encompassing that it made thought of self almost a crime
against humanity. But now, at the moment when the danger was
at its greatest, and escape a possibility, she felt, paradoxically,
the icy fingers of fear.

"Not yesterday, not the day before. But I bet you a fiver to a fart
that that American plane will be in Kenya before the end of the
week. Probably before tomorrow night." He laughed. "Otherwise
they'll get a cruise missile up their arses like poor old Saddam
Hussein."

Donna smiled, just. He had a North Country accent, and he
had hung on to his sense of humor throughout the whole time
she had known him.

"Look, Brian, I don't think I can leave these people . . . like
this." She looked around. The dirt on the floor seemed cleaner
than the sick and the dying who lay on it, many amidst their
own waste. It was the silence that was the most eerie thing of
all. They lay there in pain, but their eyes were wide open with
resignation and indifference. The line between life and death
had become so thin as to cease to exist. The question wasn't
would you die, it was when, how, where, at whose hands. And
death could not be worse than these people's lives. Death where
was thy sting, grave thy victory? The only significant sound
was outside, the gunfire from the hills around the Bujumbura
suburbs. The Reaper had not yet been assuaged. The vicious
circle of blood and more blood was spinning round and round.

"Donna, luv. Let's face it, we're doing bugger-all here. You
can't fight bacteria with bare hands. You can't operate in filth
like this. If you stay here, you'll likely die here with these people. And believe it or not, there's a life out there. Listen, you've
done your share. I've done mine. The only use you'll be if you
stay is to become a square meal for the bloody flies."

Donna knew in her gut he was right. In the anarchy that would follow a victory by the Hutu Forces for the Defense of Democracy, there would be a crescendo of killing. A white "doctor" would probably rate a rape first. It wasn't merely death that was on the menu, it might easily be a death of the most gruesome kind.

Then Donna saw the eyes of a child looking up at her, silently pleading. She reached down and picked up the four-year-old, holding its tiny emaciated, naked body in her arms. She thought as she so often did in times of crisis, of Steve. What would you do now, Steve? she wondered. Would you be talking Brian's sense to me? What would *you* do if *you* were here? Would you do the sensible thing and run for cover? Suddenly, her mind was made up.

"Brian, you go. It's the right thing to do. But I'm going to stay, OK? Take the car. Don't try to persuade me. Please. It's something I have to do for me."

She saw the doubt in his eyes.

"I'll let everyone know where you are," he said at last. "Maybe Buyoya can hold this together. If not . . ." He paused, then swallowed. "And if things get . . . impossible, you know where the IV potassium is? Four hundred milligrams does the job."

Donna knew. They had always known it could come to this. And they didn't run to strychnine in false teeth, the stuff of cloak and dagger novels and Nuremberg criminals. One long, hard dose of colorless intravenous potassium would stop the heart in seconds. It was what the anorexia nervosa girls so often died of. As the fabric of their bodies wasted away, serum potassium levels rose inexorably until, quite suddenly, the fear of fatness had become fatal.

"All my faith is in Major Pierre Buyoya," said Donna with a brave smile.

"Well, I'll go get my toothbrush," said Brian. He looked

deeply worried but he did not look guilty. He knew he was doing the right thing. He was saving himself so that he could fight against sickness another day. He did not want to be another death in Africa, uncounted, unknown, not even a statistic, because there had to be someone around to record those. "Estimates of deaths in the Burundi genocide range from one to four hundred thousand people," the Western newspapers would report. One . . . or four? In a sense there wasn't much difference . . . except to the three hundred thousand in between.

Later, he came and kissed her good-bye and hugged her, a warm and affectionate hug. There were tears in his eyes when he drew back from her, but this was British emotion. He ended up sticking out his hand and shaking hers and saying, "I'm proud to have known you." And her lip quivered then, because it was a very difficult sort of thing for an Englishman to say.

The thought came to her quite suddenly. "Listen, Brian, can I ask you to do something for me?"

"Of course," he said. There was a break in his voice.

"If I don't sort of, well . . . if anything bad happens, could you telephone somebody and just tell him . . ." She took a deep breath. "Tell him I've always loved him." She pulled a piece of paper from her pocket and scribbled down the number she had in her heart.

"Will do," he said, the mist in his eyes thickening. He took the piece of paper and put it carefully into his wallet. Then he turned and walked down the hill. Donna watched as he got into the little green car, and soon it was chugging down the dirt road. As it did so, it passed the banana-less banana trees, and the lines of peasants that shuffled hopelessly, with vacant faces and empty hearts, toward the "hospital" that Donna Gardiner now ran alone.

32

The warmth and security were almost tangible. Children were running around the Christmas tree; wet dogs were steaming gently before the crackling fire. The scent of pine rose from the cones in the grate, carols played softly, and snow fluttered against the windows of the ancient New England farmhouse. But, somehow, peace was missing. Kate wore a white angora sweater on which a scene of angels around a Christmas tree had been embroidered in green. She twirled the frame of a wreath in her hand and her fingers deftly wound the wire . . . 25-gauge was best—around a bunch of laburnum. There would be diagrams of how to do this in the Christmas edition of *Kate Haywood's Life*. It was a simple act of creation, a wreath anyone could make. The only thing you needed was time.

Kate sighed as she worked. She tried to understand what had happened to her, what was happening to her. Marriage had exploded in her face. Her business had returned from the brink of disaster. She had come out of that terrible depression at last. But now she faced another dilemma, the one that forever plagued her age group. What did she want from life now, as the millen-

nium approached? Meaning and purpose, that was the answer. A
success that felt like success from the inside, rather than merely
appearing so from the outside. Women wanted to return to the
optimism of their youth without abandoning the wisdom of their
years. They wanted their energy back, their enthusiasm for life,
and they would search for those fading commodities with a re-
lentlessness that no other generation ever experienced. And yet,
seemingly paradoxically, they also wanted peace, a simpler life,
joy and happiness but of a quieter kind. Kate was dragged back
into the moment by someone saying, "Kate, are you ready for
the gingerbread segue?"

Kate turned toward the voice. Reality cut into her thoughts.
Gingerbread. Right! Was she ready? Of course, she was ready.
Kate Haywood had turned being ready into a fine-art form. "I
was waiting for you," said Kate. She smiled to soften the mild
rebuke.

"Oh," said the woman with the harassed expression and the
clipboard. "Sorry."

Kate trod gently as she stepped across the wires, threading
her way through the hot arc lights, the boom microphones, and
the other paraphernalia of a TV shoot. She reached the corner of
the hallway that had been transformed into the gingerbread set.
Her mind was occupied now, by tough, tangible things. This
was the old Kate in action, delivering the old goods. She rehearsed her lines silently. "Is there anything more definitive of
Christmas than the smell of gingerbread?" Definitive? No. It
sounded bossy and pedantic. Kate had to guard against that. It
came too easily to her. "Nothing reminds me more of Christmas
than the smell of gingerbread." Better, but still not quite right. It
had a pretentious ring. She reached the place where the Scotch
tape *X* had been fixed to the carpet, and turned toward the camera. Beyond the lens, she could see into the living room with its
chintzes and children, its holly, mistletoe and crêpe streamers,
the exquisitely decorated tree. Was the scene real or fake? Could

it be both? It would be *like* this . . . a *bit* like this . . . without the TV cameras. But the truth remained: This was a shoot for the "Kate Haywood Christmas Special," and the show, not Christ's birthday, was the main event.

Kate felt a pang of guilt. It was a metaphor for her whole life, really. She sold the myth of the domesticated superwoman. She was the person who had it all, all the decent, homely, competent virtues that millions of housewives aspired to. But it remained a myth. The sudden angst welled up inside. Gingerbread! The hell with gingerbread and its magical smell! She felt lonely and unloved; the fun had gone, and she was getting old. Kate remembered the words of a Dylan song, which summed up her feelings. She was no longer busy being born; she was busy dying.

The gingerbread house she was supposed to have made sat on the table in front of her. It had taken two days to build, and Kate hardly had two minutes to spare in her frantic day. It would have been impossible for her to indulge in such a time-consuming labor of love. Instead, her genius had been to find the baker to make it, and have a smart assistant suck the salient secrets from him. The end result would be a tiny TV slot. Research had shown that attention-deficient couch potatoes couldn't handle much more than four minutes all at once. So, tips on how to stick the house together with royal icing ("confectioner's sugar, egg white, and lemon juice for taste") and dressmaker's pins ("remove with pliers before serving"); how to make the windows from caramelized brown sugar; how to construct the roof from Necco wafers (don't forget to leave a hole at the back so you can feed in fairy lights to make your house a home!") would be sandwiched between ads for dog food and Japanese cars.

Kate ran her hand through her hair. The make-up girl darted forward and dabbed a glistening area on her forehead. Sound check, one, two, three . . . and "Don't you just love the smell of gingerbread in the morning?" said Kate, her voice bubbling with enthusiasm, a conspiratorial smile playing around her full mouth as she drew America into her private world. "When I was a child some of my happiest moments were spent making houses like this, and later my daughter became a master builder. . . ."

Behind the camera, Samantha watched her mother, fascinated as always by her public persona. She would say anything that suited her image. It was brilliant, of course. There was the implication of a long line of gingerbread house architects stretching back to the Revolutionary War. Her words called up images of happy families, sweet as sugar, spending quality time together, light-years before the invention of faxes, Internet private rooms, and cellular phones. But her mother's vision was also an untruth—a little one, maybe, but a lie nonetheless. As always, Samantha tried to decide how much it mattered. The reality was that neither she nor her mother had ever sullied their hands with gingerbread house construction. Sam, like her friends, had been baby-sat by the Mitsubishi. Meals, as often as not in the last years had been pizzas not family suppers, the greasy meal wolfed down during telephone marathons to creatively challenged X-generational friends. Her later childhood had been a million miles from the myth that her mother was now so effortlessly conjuring up. But Samantha was part of the business that sold the dream. She was a co-conspirator, and had freely chosen to be one.

She noticed her mother catch sight of her in the darkness behind the bright lights. There was only a tiny pause in the lava flow of creamy, caring, competent words. "Use pastry bags for the piping . . . ask for the smaller ones for the delicate work. I used to spend hours doing this."

Sam was amazed that her mother could make it so believable. President Reagan was supposed to have believed that he, like the Gipper, had actually played football for Notre Dame. Was this one of those false memories that *Time* magazine was always going on about? What strange thought process enabled her mother to invent these things, and yet so obviously feel them. Once again, she asked herself the question. Did it matter? Was all fair, including bending the truth, in building an empire out of housewives' dreams?

"How's she doing?" whispered the voice at Sam's shoulder.

"Mother Earth, Joan of Arc, Julia Child . . . she's giving every woman in America an inferiority complex." There was a tiny touch of sarcasm, but more of admiration in Sam's voice.

"She's giving them something to live up to," Frankie corrected her.

Sam smiled indulgently. Most relationships had a pattern. This exchange defined hers with Frankie, her mother's closest friend. Sam would sometimes poke gentle fun at her mother's fierce efficiency, but Frankie would stick up for Kate come what may.

"Remember all those gingerbread houses when I was young?" whispered Sam. "I had calluses on my hands from all that Necco wafer roofwork."

"Listen, darling, you don't think the models look anything like my photographs, do you? When they crawl in in the morning it's like they've crawled straight from the crypt."

"But she's telling *lies,* Frankie. On TV."

"Oh God!" said Frankie theatrically. "Not on *television.* That's worse than church, isn't it? Any minute now she'll be telling fibs on *computer.* The mind positively *boggles.* Listen, darling, when you're a legend in your own lunchtime, *everything* is PR. Haven't you worked that out yet?"

"Oh, Frankie, you're such a cynic." Sam smiled. She liked Frankie. She deferred to no one, not even Kate. Yet, despite being the metaphorical leader of her mother's fan club, at all times she preserved her acid tongue.

"Anyway," added Frankie, "Kate isn't telling lies. They're terminological inexactitudes. They're surreal versions of the truth, words used loosely to summon up moods. And I'm sure she made at least one gingerbread house with you."

"If she did, I don't remember it." Sam laughed.

In front of the camera, it was clear that Kate had heard the sound. A look of annoyance flitted across her face. It was instantly banished, a cloud moving fast from left to right across her smile. Kate had seen Frankie join Samantha. She could just imagine the conversation.

"So there it is," said Kate, her voice full of love, "a gingerbread house for the center of the dining table. What a conversation piece, and how beautiful. In our home we save it until the day the houseguests leave, and then we eat it. And the moment the last crumb is gone, I'm already looking forward to next Christmas." She smiled graciously and glazed down at the exhibit. A camera would be zooming in on it, and out there in living-room land they would be thinking how clever, how creative, how cozy. *They* would make a gingerbread house like Kate's. Oh yes, they would, when they had the money for the pastry bags, when they could find time to get to the store for dressmaker's pins and confectioner's sugar.

"It's a wrap. In the can. Great, Kate. You're a star."

The producer gushed her relief. It was so easy working with a pro. The camera worshiped Kate. She seemed so fiercely competent. Nobody would be told off for not paying attention. And yet, and yet, there was a subtle command not to slack in terms of concentration. There was something incredibly mature about her, but although she was formidably grownup, she was saved from being middle-aged by her smile and her giggle. To hear it was to know another side of Kate. It was her sense of humor that rescued her from the austerity of perfection.

Now she walked toward the camera, to Samantha and Frankie. "What's the joke?" she asked. She spoke with a half smile. Her rebuke was intended to be a little one.

"Oh nothing, Mom. I was just laughing at the thought of me as the gingerbread master glazier."

"Didn't you do that, darling? I must have been thinking of someone else."

"*You* didn't make those things, Mom, let alone me."

"Must have been two other people," said Frankie, threading her arm around her friend's waist and laughing.

"Well, we should have. Would have if we'd thought of it. It's the thought that counts." Kate giggled. Her whole expression melted into the wonderful sound. It was quite impossible not to laugh with her, and Frankie and Samantha did. "How was I?" she asked at last, straightening up.

"You were great, darling. Magnificent karma. Can't you feel the love tonight! Spirit of Christmas. Do you remember when Peter got one of the beastly dressmaker pins caught in his throat? We were three hours in the hospital fishing the damned thing out."

An icy silence descended. Peter's ghost stalked the ginger-bread feast. Around them, the bustle of the set dismantling, the moving of the cameras, were an ineffectual distraction. The spirit of Peter had been summoned from the deep. It would have to be addressed.

"You know," said Sam slowly, "when that happened, I was really angry with you, Mom. I felt it was your fault. I remember half wondering if you'd tried to kill him. But now, now . . . I just wish he'd swallowed a dozen."

Frankie watched Kate, saying nothing. There were twin spots of red high on her friend's cheeks.

"I'm sure none of us would wish Peter harm," Kate said at last. The resentment had faded. Sometimes it seemed to disappear completely in odd moments when she seemed almost to want him back. She loathed betrayal, but the breakdown of their marriage was not his fault alone. She knew she was an intolerant person, who had not been understanding of Peter's frailties, eccentricities, and inadequacies. He, in turn, had tired of her ceaseless upward mobility, her concentration on business, her willingness to count on the undemanding support of a family that she seemed sometimes to treat as an also-ran to her career. There was nothing particularly unusual about it. Most marriages ended in divorce. It was a fact of life.

"Well, in a way I'm glad he's gone," said Samantha.

"And I'm free to do what I want. Any old time." Kate sang the last bit. The moment had lightened. It was true. It was a fact that once again she was a creature of possibility. The future was out there, and it was no longer predictable. She could make it up as she went along. She could even allow someone else to make it up for her. She was free, something that so few were in the land of freedom. She did not suffer the tyranny of poverty, or the authoritarian rule of responsibility. Sam was grown up and Peter was gone. Life was her party and she could cry if she wanted to. Hell, if she liked, she could even laugh.

"OK, Kate. Family carols by the Christmas tree are next. Can you gather the clan?" The producer scribbled on her clipboard as she spoke. In the living room the arc lights were now clustered around the tree. Children that Kate had borrowed, choristers at the village church, were being rounded up by production assistants. Cries of dissent could already be heard. An up-market karaoke device was being wheeled into place off camera. The Herald Angels would come with full orchestral backing.

"I thought that you might do a bit of decorating the tree, and then have the children sort of drift together, like a spur-of-the moment thing, and start singing carols."

"Absolutely," said Kate with a brisk laugh. "Nothing like highly organized spontaneity."

"Unless it's fake sincerity," said Sam, quite unable to resist.

'Won't everyone wonder where the music is coming from? I mean, how do you get background music if everyone has decided to sing carols on a whim?" Frankie raised the objection, not sure that it was her place to do so. Kate and the TV producer simply looked at her. Didn't she understand anything? When Kate sang, music *happened*. When Kate baked, the cookies were always golden brown and ready no matter how short the segment. All was sweet harmony in the Kate Haywood world. The viewers expected it, and it was the genius of TV to give people what they expected. Luckily, in La-Z-Boy land, expectations were not great.

While the children were marshaled, rehearsed, bribed, and threatened, there was time to relax. "I hear you've been asked to do the White House tree again this year again," said the producer. "What's that like?"

"Yes, I love doing it. You know, the First Lady is quite a friend of mine, and she has a big thing about the White House being 'our house.' But the White House Christmas decorations are a shambles. I have to bring my own, can you believe it?"

"There ought to be some commissioned," said Frankie. "You know, designed and donated to the nation by contemporary artists. Something like that."

"Frankie, that is a *great* idea," said Kate. "That is a wonderful idea. I'm going to suggest it. An American tree decorated by famous American artists of the day. It could become a tradition. A White House collection of the most amazing Christmas decorations."

"I think we're ready," said one of the assistants. A loose knot of children were gathered around her. It looked unstable, as though it wouldn't stick together for long. Any minute it would explode, casting children off to the far corners of the house, never to return "spontaneously" for carols. Kate moved forward fast to seize the moment.

"Is there any part of Christmas more fun than decorating the tree?" Her concentration appeared total as she addressed the camera, but inside she was thinking of what Frankie had said. Who on earth could she approach to design the decorations once she had persuaded the First Lady to commission them? "I make many of the decorations myself," Kate whispered to the camera.

The caressing words slipped from her lips as she conjured up the friendly ghosts of Christmas past. Metallic ornaments had danced on the candlelit trees of Victorian Christmases. Now you too, in the Twin Cities, could clamp your embosser ("available in most stationery stores") into decorator's foil ("thirty-eight-gauge, sold by the foot") and hang your very own stars and medallions on the tree. The purists could achieve the tarnished effect by rubbing them with steel wool and applying a tarnishing agent. There were icicles made by wrapping tinsel around paint-brush handles, and bunches of gilded walnuts drilled through with a dremel drill and attached to each other by metal thread. ("Where's the dremel drill, Ross?" "Where's the what?!") Victorian paper cornucopias laden with candy disputed for space with round ornaments made from paper-clay ("art supply shops") stamped with wooden molds ("check out the cooking catalogue in gourmet stores"). It was effortless. It was balm for troubled souls. It was occupational therapy of the most harmless kind.

A child wandered in from off camera left. "Can we sing some carols, Kate?"

"Yes, darling of course we can. But where's Maria?"

"Here I am, Kate."

Samantha and Frankie joined the trio at the tree, as the other children were fed into the group at strategic intervals. The music from nowhere began to play softly. "Carols around the tree," said Kate, as if giving a benediction. And so they began to sing. Kate's voice was firm, the children's shrill and strident, Frankie's surprisingly deep, Samantha's young and accurate. There were no men. This was not a man's show. It was about women who could feel, indeed who reveled in their right and their ability to express their feelings. There was emotion everywhere. There was love in spades.

No men. Kate was on cruise control. It was nearly over. Another triumphant Christmas special was almost completed.

Another baked-in-the-Christmas-pudding ratings spike was achieved. The wall-to-wall children warbled around her. Glory to the newborn King. Peace on earth and mercy mild. She could relax . . . when she had learned how to. No men. The sadness was suddenly alive inside her. Where was her man? She took a deep breath and turned it into God and sinners reconciled. Beside her, Sam looked at her with a smile that was not just for the cameras. Kate smiled back.

On auto-pilot in the depths of the familiar carol, Kate wondered again what exactly it was she wanted. It was peace, the calm that this surrogate scene was creating in the minds of her viewers, but not in her own. It was with a sense of shock that she realized a part of her wanted to be just like them, soothed by carols, caramelized sugar, and gingerbread. It was because she understood their needs so well that she was able to satisfy them.

Then it was over, and Kate saw the producer smiling her pleasure, walled off mercifully from the treasonous discourse in Kate's mind. As the group broke apart, Sam took her mother's arm.

"Mom, you know that great idea Frankie had about getting artists to do ornaments for the White House tree? Well I think Steve Gardiner would be just *perfect* for it. And I think you'd really like him. He's quite impressive."

"Even though he didn't do your book in the end?" said Kate.

"I haven't given up on it," said Sam with a smile.

"That's a good idea," said Kate. "I'll go see him. He's supposed to be a bit frightening, but he won't scare me." She laughed.

"He didn't frighten me one bit," said Sam.

33

Kate hurried across the field to the barn. She shivered, even though she was bundled up warm in the clothes she loved, a tentlike sweater, blue jeans, and green Wellington boots. Snow crunched beneath her feet, and around her the Canada geese hurried away but did not take flight. East Hampton was beginning to feel a very great deal like Christmas. She practiced her speech. She had never met Steve Gardiner, but in the small village his reputation preceded him, and it was a good one. Kate smiled. It was unlike her to be apprehensive, and it was rather a pleasant experience. Still, she came bearing good tidings. A White House commission, no less, for the man who had glass in the Met.

She knocked on the door of the barn as she looked up at the bleak, gray sky. Icicles dangled like daggers from the gutters, and squirrels skidded on the snowy road searching in vain for food. The door was opened by a man in a leather apron, his face ruddy. He looked like a Santa Claus who'd got the dates wrong and forgotten to dress. He was not Steve Gardiner. Kate was certain of that.

"Oh, hi, I'm Kate Haywood." She paused for name recognition. There didn't appear to be any. Or was it just Long Island cool? Whatever. "I wondered if Steve Gardiner was here," she said.

"He may be." The accent was English. The "He may not be" was unspoken. It would depend on what she wanted.

"I have a request for Mr. Gardiner from the President of the United States," said Kate. It wasn't quite true, but it sounded good. In fact, it had been the First Lady who had given the go-ahead for a Gardiner commission.

"I'll see if I can find him," said the Englishman slowly. Like the rest of his countrymen, he specialized in being unimpressed. But there was a wary look in his eye as he turned back into the barn.

"Do I have to stand out here in the cold?" said Kate with a pleasant smile.

"No, come in. Sorry," said the man in the apron.

Inside was hot, and Kate could see that the furnace was the reason. The room looked like an engineer's workshop. It was dirty and dusty, very far from what Kate imagined a famous artist's studio might look like. It was all rather strange. A butterfly took flight in her stomach.

There were two or three people working in the room. They hurried about their business. Despite the flames, and the fires, and the shadows the atmosphere was not dark. Along the walls huge sculptures in glass and metal, some wrapped as if being readied for packing, emphasized the dynamism and at once the transience of the artistic process at work here.

"And what is Kate Haywood doing at my humble abode?" said the voice at her shoulder. It was deep and melodious, with a friendly, gently mocking quality.

She turned and there he was, tall but slim and solid, very strong. That was the first feeling that could be put into words, but it wasn't Kate's first feeling. *That* was a physical thing, a

subtle shift of hormones that language could not properly describe. His face was flushed, from the furnace, she imagined.
He had bushy eyebrows, deep-set eyes that were rather frightening, and a square, intimidating jawline. His hair was blond
and untidy. There was a bead of sweat on his brow, and another
on his neck.

"I hope I haven't disturbed you. I came the other girl . . . I
mean the other *day* . . . and spoke to a girl, an Italian girl, who
seemed to be working here. Perhaps she mentioned . . ."

"She told me you came." He looked at her quizzically. His
face was relaxing into a smile that showed the whiteness of his
teeth.

Kate had the strong impression he was enjoying her discomfort. She looked around her frantically. This was quite ridiculous. Embarrassment was an alien emotion to her. She wanted
somewhere to sit, to be offered tea and biscuits, coffee, some
sort of Kate Haywood safe zone where she could get back to
being in control of things. But he didn't help her out. In this
room, sitting looked like it might be dangerous. A woman could
be burned and mangled here in an industrial accident that
would be a rude interruption to the ordered chaos the barn was
used to.

"We're neighbors," he said at last.

"I never see you in the village," she said, blushing for a reason that totally escaped her.

"I'm not often in the village." That seemed to explain why
Kate had not seen him there. One thing was already obvious.
Steve Gardiner was not easy to talk to. Despite that, she liked
him. Paradoxes abounded. Kate felt like Alice slipping through
the looking glass.

"You're always here, working, then?"

"Yes, working."

"Well, I'm a great admirer of your work." Kate tried to sound
brisk.

"Which?"

"Which what?" Kate was totally thrown.

"Which work?" He was patient, but he was teasing her. Why on earth was he making her so nervous?

"That conical thing," said Kate. She shot out her hand and pointed a finger at a vast sculpture. "For instance," she added lamely.

He was staring at her hard, almost too hard for politeness. But for a man who worked all the time and never got out to the village, perhaps lapses in manners could be forgiven. Kate felt her neck redden under his gaze.

"Listen," she said. "I can see how busy you are, and I'm busy too, so perhaps I should just say what I came here to say and then you can get back to your . . . your . . . blowing."

He threw back his head and laughed. "You make it sound like blowing in the wind," he said.

She could either laugh or take offense. She hadn't been quite sure of the correct terminology. Was it "glassblowing?" Kate liked to get things right. Suddenly she felt embarrassed and confused, unusual for her. However, she found his laugh attractive, and infectious. She smiled, smiled wider, and in seconds she was laughing too. As the laughter subsided, something else was replacing mirth. It was mutual interest. Both knew the other felt it. Quite suddenly, Kate sensed that she knew this man and that she had seen a side of him that few people did. The tension of excitement was in the air.

"What's all this about a message from the President of the United States of America? That sounds like powerful stuff to me." There was a hint of mockery in his remark. It was as if he had been drawn to her against his will and therefore had to drag himself away.

Suddenly, Kate was far from sure that the message she brought was an appropriate one. Maybe he would feel that blowing Christmas balls for the White House tree was beneath his dignity. The thought had never occurred to her. Now, staring into his intense eyes, it did. But she went on to deliver her message anyway, stuttering as she spoke. "The President . . . the F-F-irst Lady actually, but she'd discussed it with the President . . . w-w-ondered if you might be prepared to be commissioned by the nation to . . . to . . ."

Steve nodded his encouragement. He was listening to what she said, but he was thinking about what she looked like, and who she was, and what she felt, and of course he had met her daughter, and there was the book project that he had eventually turned down. Did Kate know about that?

"To make some very fine decorations for the White House Christmas tree . . ."

It took a second or two for her remark to sink into his mind. His forehead tightened, and he made a strange grinding motion with his jaw that was rather threatening.

"Say again?" he said quickly. He'd heard. He simply wanted to hear it twice.

"Christmas tree decorations," said Kate in a small voice. "Very fine."

Like the sun rising in the east, a look of incredulity climbed Steve Gardiner's face. It reached his eyes, opening them wide. Then, once again, he laughed. But this time it was a different laugh, a laugh so different a new word was needed to describe it. It was full of shock, horror, dark humor. It was shot through with ridicule and disappointment. And it stopped as abruptly as it started. "Do you know what I said when Annabella told me that Kate Haywood had called?" It was a rhetorical question. "I said, 'I bet she wants me to make some decorations for one of her bloody awful Christmas trees.'"

Kate simply turned around and walked away from him. Anger at his rudeness was already replacing the other emotions. All, that is, except one. As she stalked toward the door of the barn, telling herself that Steve Gardiner was the rudest, most arrogant, self-regarding, elitist, boorish prig . . . she was also frighteningly aware that he was one of the most attractive men she had ever met in her life.

34

Kate and Frankie sat on the huge white linen-covered couch beneath the Fragonard drawings from the *Orlando Furioso* series. Kate sipped her coffee as she flipped through the new Kate Haywood-at-Bloomingdale's paint color chart.

"I can't stand this Pepto-Bismol pink, can you, Franks?"

Frankie took a casual look. "Ugh, no. Come to think of it, why do they make Pepto-Bismol that color? It's enough to make you throw up just looking at it."

Kate cast the chart away from her. She was in a foul mood, and had been since yesterday. What was irritating her most was the fact that Steve Gardiner, who simply had no importance whatever in her world, seemed to have the power to play with her emotions.

"I can't get over that Steve Gardiner," she said out loud. "I wish you'd been there, Frankie. You'd have thought of something to say. I was just so surprised—"

"If I had a buck for the times you have mentioned that man's name . . ."

"Well, it's just that he was so incredibly pompous. I hate that in people. I mean, who has the right to feel superior? Nobody.

There he is, some glassblower, or sculptor or whatever he is, and he had the *nerve* to scoff at a commission from his nation's president. He should *be* so lucky! I mean after a presidential commission, everybody would know about him, not just a handful of elitist bicoastal art snobs. He was so incredibly, unbelievably rude, Frankie."

"Boy, has he got you rattled," said Frankie, smiling. "And all because you asked him to make some Christmas decorations."

"All right, all right, I admit that a great slab of glass like the ones he has lying around everywhere would have been better. But at the end of the day, what's the matter with Christmas decorations? You'd have to be some incredible artistic *snob* to turn up your nose at them, things that give pleasure to millions of ordinary people everywhere."

"But you said yourself that Mr. Gardiner wasn't very ordinary."

Kate paused. She realized she was overreacting. She'd scarcely thought of anything else since yesterday. She could see his face now, so good-looking, laughing, laughing, the scorn, the superiority. A warm flush of humiliation ran up her neck and into her cheeks at the memory.

"If I didn't know better I'd say that you liked him," said Frankie, stating the obvious.

"You'd say *what?!*" Kate sat up straight.

Frankie lay back against the cushions. She knew her friend so well. Kate was see-through. Steve Gardiner had got her going, then jammed her into neutral and revved her engine until it had seized. "Just an idea," she said with a knowing smile.

"OK, I *did* think he was really attractive. He *is* really attractive, physically. But it takes more than that, doesn't it? I mean, if you are deeply and meaningfully psychologically flawed, then you are a great big zero, aren't you?"

"Are you?"

"Well, *aren't* you?"

"Listen, sweetheart, they're emotions. You know best, but does not liking the idea of designing balls for Christmas trees mean that he is 'deeply psychologically flawed'? Might that not be diagnostic overkill? What about 'artistically proud' or even 'an art snob'? I don't know, I'm just playing devil's advocate."

"Yes, but to mock me. *That's* what I'm complaining about. How dare he!"

Kate splayed out her hands in supplication and Frankie had to laugh at the display of emotional vulnerability from a person who, most of the time, made Teflon look leaky.

"If he had *not* mocked you, been thrilled to make balls for the White House tree, asked you for a cup of coffee, what then?"

"Hypothetical," said Kate dismissively. She waved away the impossibility with both hands, one more than was strictly necessary.

"Humor me. Play 'what if.'"

"Well, he is not without charm. He is not unattractive. I suppose if you like glass, he is not untalented."

"I was just thinking," said Frankie, "a man committed to his art, high standards, focused, a recluse, no reputation for womanizing, rumors of an ancient divorce, rich, famous, good-looking, *nearby* . . ."

"Nearby? Nearby! God, Franks. Is that the stage of life we've got to?"

Kate and Frankie dissolved into laughter, just as they had done at school so many years ago. Frankie could get her like this. Nobody else could. Her friend was right, of course. Steve Gardiner was a dream, a dream that would never come true. The very fact that he so obviously despised such a lofty thing as a presidential commission was somehow in his favor. Kate knew herself well. She would do almost anything for the greater glory of herself and her company. That made him far more special than she . . . and yet, despite all that, she was still furious with him. And if she ever met him again, which she wouldn't, which *he* wouldn't, she would tell him to his face that—

Her train of thought was interrupted by the telephone. Kate scooped it up.

"Who?" she said. Her voice was full of incredulity, her expression scrunched up in a look of total disbelief.

"Steve Gardiner," said Steve Gardiner a second time.

"Oh. Oh," said Kate. "Ah, look, can I take you on another line? I'm in a meeting here."

Frankie was looking up, smiling. How did she *know* these things?

"I'll hang up for you," Frankie said, her smile deepening.

Kate knew that her face had gone red as she hurried into her office. She picked up the extension.

"Hello," she said. There was a click. Frankie had put down the other phone.

"I'm calling to say sorry," said Steve Gardiner. He went right to it, very direct. His apology would not be flowery.

She managed to say nothing. God, why was she so glad he'd called?

"I'm afraid I've lived alone too long," he said. "Forgotten the social graces. But I was rude and insensitive, and it's been on my mind. I wanted to call you up and apologize."

"No. It was my fault. It was stupid of me. I thought it would be a compliment. I didn't really know the sort of work you did . . . or didn't do." She managed to sound a little distant, but not very. Excitement hovered in the air.

He paused, seeming to wonder whether to sign off, the apology having been made, the wrong to some extent righted.

"The fact is . . . I enjoyed meeting you," he said, with apparent difficulty.

He paused again. The ball was back in Kate's court. She didn't know what to say. "I enjoyed meeting you, too," would sound incredibly lame. So she said nothing.

"Look, we're neighbors, and I'm glad we met. Your daughter probably told you about our book discussions. I'd hate there to be a misunderstanding . . ."

He was finding this difficult, but something was coming. Something good.

"The fact is, I wondered if you would like to be my guest for dinner one evening at my place. I don't go out much, and of course I'm not in your league, but I like to cook." He laughed as he added, "and all Christmas things definitely off the menu." It was a warm and wonderful sound, managing to convey that it was not often heard.

"I'd love to," said Kate.

35

Kate parked the Range Rover in his cobbled driveway. To the left was his house, to the right, across the field, was the barn, where she had first met him. There was a pathway through the gently falling snow, and bordering it, burning torches cast flickering shadows into the darkness. He personally had lit those lights for her. Somehow, she knew that. It was clear that he intended her to go to his studio, and not the main house. Kate wrapped the big leather coat with its fur collar tight around her. She would arrive with snow in her hair, but that was nice. What would he look like? Not the Zeus-like thunderbolt maker, sweat-stained and elemental, who had greeted her that first time. Steve would have made some attempt to smarten himself up, a suit possibly, maybe just clean clothes. She was aware that she was almost certainly overdressed, but she didn't mind. She minded nothing as she flew along the straight pathway like an arrow to a heart.

At the door, she paused and took a deep breath. Had she got her clothes right? Her Valentino was well cut, and thank God she was on top of her weight this week. The Duchess of

Windsor's earrings, coral and emeralds, were understated but interesting, and the dark blue pumps beautifully complemented the midnight blue silk of the dress. She felt the excitement. She was looking forward to seeing him again. It would be different this time. She sensed it. She rang the bell. In seconds he opened the door to her. He must have been pacing around inside waiting for her arrival. Kate had not expected what she now saw. He had dressed all right, and there had been no half measures. He wore a tuxedo, double-breasted, its cut classic, probably three decades old, maybe more. Beneath it, he wore a plain cream silk shirt. A black bow tie, large and floppy, was tied, not clipped on, and was matched by a black cummerbund. On his feet were black velvet slippers.

"You have snow in your hair," he said.

Kate laughed, reaching up to touch it. Having planned it, she now pretended it was accidental.

"Come in." He stood back a little, gesturing for her to enter, but still he took up much of the doorway. She passed close to him as she entered the barn.

He smelled of a sophisticated but reassuring cologne that he would have worn for years, lemony, masculine, with a hint of sandalwood. Kate was not sure what she had expected, but as she stepped into the vastness of the barn, the scene that confronted her took her breath away. Despite his debonair appearance, he was a man who lived alone. She had therefore imagined he would not have mastered the art of putting a guest at her ease, cooking, catering, and conversing all at the same time, graces that were second nature to Kate. Now she saw that she had stooped to condescend, and that it had been premature. The appearance of the barn showed that Steve Gardiner had a supreme command of theater and style.

"God, what a magnificent atmosphere," she said, both from the heart where the vision touched her, and from the head where the connoisseur was busy at work. In the middle of the room the furnace glowed calmly, radiating warmth into the far corners of the barn. At a judicious distance from it was a refectory table, maybe six feet long, with a simple white tablecloth hanging down to the floorboards. A fine Georgian candelabra was set on the table, bearing tall wax candles whose light danced across the room, casting shadows that probed the darkness. The table was covered with glass, six or seven different types for each of the two place settings. There were two decanters of great beauty, full of dark wine. Water pitchers and plates were of glass, also, and it was clear from the similarities that lurked in the disparate styles that every object on the glistening table had been made by the hand of Steve Gardiner. The word "romantic" was dying to be used. It hung unspoken in the warm, dry air. It danced unsaid in the flickering shadows of the candles.

"I hope you don't mind that it's just us," he said as he took her coat. "And somehow I find it more comfortable here . . . where I work." He paused, as if not sure what to say next. "I don't see a lot of people," he added.

"I see far too many," said Kate. The magical atmosphere he had created said all sorts of things about this man, things that on another level she had known the first time she had set eyes on him. There was a thrilling unreality about everything. His hand had accidentally brushed her shoulder as he removed her coat. Normally she wouldn't have noticed, but she was sensitized to everything.

"Something to drink?" he said. "Some champagne? I drink sherry before dinner, a rather fine amontillado, but you'd probably be safer with the champagne."

"Who wants to be safe?" thought Kate. "I want to be in deadly danger." The feeling of recklessness was intense. She couldn't remember ever feeling like this before. But you read about it in books, and wondered what the writer was going on about.

He walked them to a long sideboard, and Kate's practiced eye admired the layout. A bottle of pink champagne, already opened, lay in a bed of ice in a large glass bucket whose rose-colored hue offset to perfection the shade of the Pol Roger wine. Two slim champagne glasses melded with the colors, their rims splaying out interestingly like the petals of an orchid. There were flowers in shades of white and cream tied in bunches and placed strategically to frame the corner of the sideboard from which the wine was dispensed. A chunky decanter contained the nut-brown sherry, and two small sturdy goblets stood before it. Kate felt a pang of jealousy. This was superb styling, but more than that, it was good style. There was a difference.

"Steve, this is the most beautiful table setting I have ever seen. It's exquisite."

"Praise indeed from Kate Haywood," he said in a tone totally devoid of irony. "I'm sure people find it daunting to give you dinner."

"I don't see you as easily daunted," said Kate. "I'd like to try the sherry," she added before he could answer.

He poured the sherry into the Irish Waterford sherry glasses. Then he took his own glass and turned it in the light of a flickering candle, letting the fortified wine from Jerez de la Frontera cling to the side of the crystal. The Spanish Armada had met its end on the coast of Ireland, and its survivors had left their genes on the harsh rocklands of the Irish west coast. It had always seemed ironic to Steve that the grapes of Andalusia washed most frequently against the crystal of Waterford in an England that had been the perennial enemy of both Ireland and Spain.

Kate sipped the wine, feeling the brandy with which it was fortified burning deliciously at the back of her throat. She was acutely aware that they were complete strangers, but at the same time she felt she knew him. The way to approach him would be through his work.

"I don't know as much about your glass as I should," she said. "Although my daughter Samantha has made herself something of an expert on it. She said you came quite close to doing a book for us. She was very enthusiastic about it."

"Come and have a look at some," he said. "There's not a lot here. They're giving me a big exhibition at the Tate in London and most of the best work is in transit. The glasses, decanters, the bottles and things, are from the early days, the Murano tradition. Then, since Paris and the Royal College and coming back to America, I moved into abstract sculptures. I still do glasses, bowls and jugs, but mainly for myself."

He was looking out to the periphery of the room as he spoke, to the shadows. Kate had a vision of herself and him as actor and actress on a brightly lit stage. And out there, watching them from the twilight zone, was an audience more powerful and interesting than they. She could make out shapes, big, vast even, and she sensed that he longed to be among them. Here, where she was, he was, were the distractions of life . . . drink, food, small talk, mere people dancing to time's music. *There* was the stuff that would endure.

He didn't take her hand, but for a second she felt that he would. The tall rectangular block of glass loomed in the shadows. It bore the face of a cubist seraphim, or cherubim, etched in dark lines with a sharp instrument, like the swirls of a fingerprint. Up close, the face was difficult to make out. Standing back, the seraphim could be seen clearly. Another creature confronted it, a strange mythological beast of uncertain ancestry.

"This is just back from the Met for cleaning," Steve said. "Each line has to be done by hand. Occupational therapy for the end of the day." For the loneliness. For the quiet that would exist now, if Kate were not here.

Kate suddenly felt sympathy for this man's life and his solitary struggle against the devil creativity. The blank canvas. The empty page. The sounds unheard in mind or on instrument.

How did you begin with glass? She didn't know, and she wanted to. But it was more than that. The atmosphere was working on her. His charisma was. There was a lostness about him. There was pain, if not anger. There wasn't a hostess in the Hamptons who would not have traded fingers to have him at her parties. He could be married a thousand times over in the time it took a clock to tick, yet here he was, locked away with his compulsion, at war with what ghosts? She wanted to know everything about him at once. She had not the patience for normal-speed getting-to-know-you. She wanted every aspect of him, every particle of his mind and memory, downloaded into her brain by some fancy computer of the constantly promised cyber-future.

"I want to know about your world," she said, aware that it was a strange thing to say. But he didn't seem to find it odd.

"Struggle, I think. That comes first. Compulsion to create. Anxiety that it can't be done. That happens every day, believe it or not. I make glass every day, and yet I wake each morning doubting that I can do it. Each piece is the last piece. It's crazy, but at the beginning of every day there is nothing but panic. And the only antidote is the work that terrifies you in the first place. I expect you feel like that sometimes too."

He looked hard at her. He wanted her to understand him. If she knew what he was talking about, then she, too, was a creator. If, however, she came out with some line about jumping out of bed with joy in her heart just longing for the day and its "challenges," then his world and hers could never touch.

"Of course," she said. She was pleased that he had included her form of art in the same category as his. "The fact that you have done something a thousand times counts for nothing. Every blank sheet of paper strikes terror. Each time is the first time. My people sit around the table and look at me and say, 'washing dogs' or 'breakfast-table flowers.' And then they sit back, pens poised, and expect me to come up with ten brand-new ideas on each topic in a minute flat, in areas in which billions of people have been beavering away for light-years doing things the same old way."

He threw back his head and laughed. He laughed with her, not at her. "God, and I thought I had problems. Washing dogs! OK. Let's do it." He held up his hand as if timing a race. "One. Two. Three. Go!"

Kate could never resist a challenge.

"One. Use your own shampoo. The expensive one. Why should a dog be treated like a dog when you love him more than all the humans you know? Two. Don't forget the conditioner. Don't you want his hair to be soft and lustrous like yours? Three. Take his collar off first. Would you like to have a band of wet leather around your neck for the rest of the day? Four. Do him twice. It's the second shampoo that really shifts the dirt. Five. Make sure you have his favorite biscuit on hand for afterward. You want to Pavlov-condition him into liking his baths. Six. Give him his own towel. Dogs and humans like continuity. Seven. No metal combs. The trichologist says they rip out your hair, so they will rip out his. Eight. Let him shake. It's only water, and if you've followed the steps above, it's clean water. Nine. Have bath days. Children do, and both children and dogs love routine. Ten. Don't get someone else to do it for you. If he's your dog, he wants you to bathe him."

She rattled them off like a machine gun. They flew from the top of her mind, bypassing the places where serious thought occurred.

Steve was impressed. "That was under a minute. Surely you've just done washing dogs in your magazine, since you remembered the list."

"No way," said Kate, laughing. "I just thought up that topic a minute ago. And I never bathe my dogs. Haven't bathed one for years. Wouldn't have a clue."

"But it sounds so real, so practical. I mean, you couldn't make all that up. Not so quickly."

"And you couldn't possibly have created that magnificent champagne glass on the table over there, with the rim floating out like the petals of a flower, so delicate, so incredibly fine, like an orchid by O'Keeffe. It's feminine, sensual, almost sexual . . ."

"Well," he said, smiling. "Let's see how it works."

They walked back to the sideboard and he poured the champagne, before leading her to the table itself. Two plates were already laid out with smoked salmon, thick, juicy, and of a nongarish pink that said this was the genuine article . . . Scots, not Norwegian, Irish, or Canadian. Lemons were piled high, cut into no-nonsense halves devoid of the pretentious muslin, on two strategically placed plates. There were none of the chopped onions, chives, or eggs that inferior salmon, or the dreaded gravlax, needed for camouflage. It looked enormously appetizing. Each place setting had its own glass pepper mill, filled with giant black whole grains. The lemony velvet of the salmon would be perfectly offset by the gritty fire of the pepper. Kate could tell by the way it had been cut that the salmon came from a side. It had not been "bought."

Steve held back the chair for her at one end of the table, then he replenished her glass before sitting down opposite her. They were separated from each other by six feet of glittering glass, but paradoxically, the distance was irrelevant. The table and its beautiful artifacts seemed to connect them. The setting seemed almost pagan in its mixing of the ornate and the simple. The wine was so sophisticated, the glass so beautiful, and yet here they were, their feet on the dusty floor of a barn that was half studio, half foundry, warmed by an ever-burning furnace and lit by the innocent light of candles.

She bit into the salmon, savoring its lemony flavor, the crunch of a peppercorn, the soft, slippery texture of the fish. It was divine, melting in her mouth succulently. Bubbles still rose from the deep stem of her champagne glass, like a spring of eternal life, and the candlelight caught the pink of the wine and made it sparkle.

"You were married once," she said. She couldn't help it.

"Yes," he said. "To an amazing woman. We met in Venice when we were very young. She's a surgeon in London. One of the best. At least she was. There was a tragic accident, and she called me to say she was leaving London for a while."

He seemed to have difficulty with the subject. The "amazing woman" didn't go together with the lack of contact. There was more.

"She had an accident?"

"No. One of her patients died. Apparently she thought she was to blame."

Kate ate for a while in silence. Then, "So it just didn't work . . . you and her," she said, steeling herself. She was on the edge of inquisitiveness, especially with this man who kept to himself. But Kate sensed he was somehow secure in her company. He was talking about deeper things than his work, revealing his feelings.

"The fact is," he said, as if deciding suddenly to leap from the highest board. "We had a son. He died when he was left with an unqualified young girl. Neither of us was at home, and the accident wouldn't have happened if we had been. I suppose I never forgave myself for that. And I never forgave Donna, my wife, either."

He didn't give her a chance to say the inadequate words that were all that could be said in response to his.

"I never recovered from that. Never. My marriage didn't. I didn't. I haven't, even as I sit here now. I go through the motions, but part of me is dead. The rest is a cover-up." He took a deep breath and then seemed to shudder, as if shaking off the memories.

There it was. The heart of the man, exposed to her, for her. This complex soul was unlocked by a single key. He was racked by ancient grief. The loss of his son had made him who he was. He had withdrawn from the world into his work because he could not bear to show his sadness.

Kate was touched deeply. Across the flickering candles, watched by the glass sculptures that had helped him survive, she felt herself fall in love with him.

36

Kate felt the snow crunch beneath the outsize Wellingtons she wore. She hunched her shoulders against the cold and wrapped Steve's thick sheepskin coat tightly about her. Above, the moon was full, sending shafts of light down among the maples, illuminating the path ahead. She let out her breath in the semidarkness, steaming, exhaling her happiness. The snow was everywhere, painting the limbs of the trees, coating the eaves of the barn, spread even across the ice on the pond.

He walked behind her, bundled up, too, against the freezing air. Beneath the warm clothes they were still dressed for dinner, Kate in her silk, Steve in his dinner jacket, but a walk had seemed an inspired idea after such a delicious meal.

"That," said Kate, "was one of the most magnificent meals I have ever eaten."

"Praise, indeed, coming from you. I was quite nervous, you know. A bit like dashing off a few brush strokes for Leonardo, trying a homegrown sonnet on Shakespeare."

She laughed. "Come on, Steve, I'm not a cook, I'm a cookbook. I'm an industry, an illusion, a facilitator of dreams."

Kate spoke from the heart. In her moments of doubt she worried that that was all she was. She put things together, but how creative was she? Her critics called her a borrower and a rearranger of ideas, a packager, a person who sold the *concept* of cooking, entertaining, and lifestyle.

"Isn't the messenger as vital as the message? Surely a perfect meal untasted is like the sound in the forest unheard. You bring the joy of cooking to others. I think that's pretty vital."

He looked at her quickly, and she smiled back at him. He was trying to boost her. Yet, probably, he did not think very much of what she did.

"But you're reticent about your work being put in books for its beauty to be shared. For you, the creation is what's important. The thing itself. You would be totally happy for your glass to exist unseen, undiscussed, unadmired by the faceless audience," said Kate.

They walked on in silence. From somewhere nearby a horse whinnied from its stall. A bird took flight, its wings flapping noisily in the stillness of the night.

"That's true," he said. "That's my way. But for you, what you do is right. We're allowed to be different. In fact, we must be different."

"But I admire you."

Kate waited as she walked. Was it fishing? Was it true? Did she admire Steve's ascetic values, his disdain for the world and its thoughts and opinions, or did she think that arrogance? Or, again, was it the arrogance she admired? She liked him more and more. She liked the way he had produced the perfect candlelit dinner for two. She liked the danger of him. With him, there was the strong possibility that one thoughtless comment could ruin everything. She admired the depths of his sorrow, the sensitivity that had allowed him to suffer so long and so deeply from the death of his son.

"Do you really, Kate?" he said. "Or do you just admire my

propaganda? Maybe, inside, I'm not so proud. Maybe I doubt myself. And perhaps it's all a front to keep me from revealing myself, to keep me from being judged."

"I don't think so," she said, amazed by the revelation of his self-doubt, and touched by it. "You are not afraid of the Tate, or the critics, or what I think of your rabbit stew. Some people would have been a little put off by that, you know. Rabbit stew!"

He threw back his head and laughed.

"OK, so maybe I'm not *enormously* concerned with the opinions of others. And you perhaps are not totally unhappy to be an industry, an illusionist, a facilitator of dreams. That's very good by the way, facilitator of dreams. I can't think of anything more valuable on the planet than that. The one thing people are genuinely hungry for is decent dreams."

She laughed. "It's true, isn't it? We need dreams to steer by, like ships at sea need stars. That's why we need romance. It's why we need love."

"So, Kate Haywood, what are your dreams? By your dreams shall ye be known."

He turned to watch her closely as she replied. She looked down at the ground. There was a chance here, a chance for them. She felt it, and she sensed that he felt it, too.

"I want . . . ," she said. Her tone was playful, to mask the seriousness of the moment. "I want, well, this maybe sounds funny coming from someone like me. . . . OK, I want to fall in love. That's my dream."

She leaned back and looked up at him, defiantly, in the moonlight.

He avoided her gaze, and spoke slowly. "Such dreams can be midsummer night ones. You fall in love with the first person you see after you have the dream."

"So it becomes important when I dreamed my dream first," she said.

"It might," he allowed. He was almost smiling.

"I think I first dreamed my dream when . . ."

They walked on. The wind was picking up. A woodshed loomed from the darkness.

". . . . when we had dinner tonight."

He laughed, and then he stopped laughing. Then he stopped walking. The moon painted the snow with strokes of phosphorescent light.

"You're joking with me," he said.

"I don't think I am," she said, and there was a break in her voice as she spoke. Her heart broke into a gallop. Her mouth was dry.

It wasn't a time for words anymore. He stepped toward her, into her space. She did not move back. She looked at him, into his eyes. And still he advanced. She closed her eyes. It was up to him. Everything was his to decide. She had done as much as she could, more than she had ever intended.

And then he touched her. His body was against her, hard, warm. His arms reached around her and she opened her eyes then, to watch him as it happened. His head was haloed by the moon, backlit by moonlight, the delicious darkness of him enhanced by the silver shadows he cast. He drew her into him, and she went willingly, letting her body mold to the contours of his, soft and pliant as he was firm and unyielding. She turned up her face toward him, waiting deliciously for what would happen now, here at the beginning of intimacy. The air rushed from her lungs in surrender, and he held her tight as he lowered his lips to hers. He was so tender. That was the surprise—his gentleness. He brushed his lips against hers, painting them delicately with his warm breath, hot against her cold cheeks. She was passive in his arms, enjoying the alien helplessness. This was not hers to do. It was his. The wonder of her femininity filled her up, fulfilling her. But now passion was untied within him. The touch and the taste of her had unleashed the feelings in him and in her. His lips were harder, more urgent, as he fought for the togetherness they would share. She kissed him back, opening her mouth and drawing him into her, and her arms rushed out to join his in the knot of bodies that would not be untied. And together, at the start of this conspiracy of hearts, they backed toward the shed that was just a few feet away.

37

The sun was without mercy, boiling the dripping air into a steamy stew. It was a hundred degrees, but it felt like more because of the humidity. Only the flies and the apathetic half-humans they crawled over didn't seem to mind. Donna stood in the doorway of the hospital and drew her hand across her dripping brow. She looked down at her wrist, skinny now but still strong. She didn't know how much weight she had lost, but it was too much. Partly it was the dehydration, but it was difficult to eat when starvation was killing people. Each mouthful felt like a death sentence being passed on a nearby baby. It did nothing at all for the appetite.

But this morning she had much more than the heat, the flies, and the dying to worry about. They were normality. The news was not. It came from nowhere and everywhere, muttered from person to person. It seemed to flow on the feckless breeze. It rustled through the sparse scrub until everyone had a version of the new truth that would mean life for some . . . and death for others.

Donna didn't know what to do. There were smiles on the

faces of half her patients, but from the others came a new and more immediate smell than the ones she had grown used to. It was the smell of fear. There were few people that Donna could talk to. The sick took her help, but they had nothing to give back, no gratitude, no warmth, no information.

She called to one of the orderlies, a smiling one. "Is there news from Bujumbura?" She knew there was, and she could guess its nature, because the Hutus wore the happy expressions; the Tutsis, the masks of terror.

"Defense Force take town. Army defeated. Buyoya . . ." He smiled hideously, showing rows of broken teeth, and drew his finger with its filthy nail across his own throat to signal Buyoya's fate. "Soon our soldiers come," he said. He spoke matter-of-fact then, and his smile disappeared. "For many, bad news," he said simply.

Donna looked around, her and the fear touched her, not for herself but for the others. She tried to think. Should she evacuate the hospital? But to where? To the bush? Should she try to push these dying people out into the bright sunshine, the awful heat? There was nowhere to hide out there. It was hopeless. There was nothing to do but wait. Wasn't that what most of them were doing anyway? Waiting for death? She sat down on the rickety chair by her desk and buried her head in her hands. Nothing had happened yet, she tried to tell herself. Maybe things would change. Maybe there would be restraint in victory. Maybe . . . It was useless. There would be killing soon. The process of dying would be speeded up for some. For the others, dying too, there would be the grim satisfaction of watching as the neighbors they so uselessly hated stole a lead on them to the heaven that would be a release from this hell. It was difficult to know, in the bloodbath that would surely follow, if the survivors or the murdered would be the lucky ones.

As if on cue, she heard the sound of a car. Her heart beat faster with fear. The others had heard it too. They looked toward the door of the hospital, turning their heads in slow motion. Fate could not be hurried. Children moved nearer to their parents, but such was the slough of despond into which all had sunk that there was little room left for normal emotions like love. Those were for some other place, some different time before blood had washed away the real world and left only this illusion behind.

Donna stood up and walked to the door, her head held high. She didn't know what she would do. It was all so weird. She was a spectator at the edge of a tragedy. She felt oddly like an actor in a scripted scene, one that had already been written by a God whose ways seemed strange to the created. A Jeep was bumping along the dirt track, past the line of people who stared at it, cheered, or stood silent as it went by. A flag flew from its back, the Hutu Defense Union flag, and there were four soldiers in it. Behind, by about half a mile, came a truck, its back covered. It was impossible to know what it contained but it was possible to guess. These would be the foot soldiers, the victors—the danger.

The Jeep came to a halt in front of the hospital. A man, a leader apparently, but not in uniform, approached her. He wore a green wool beret, dirty shorts, and a filthy sweatshirt. He held an AK-47 in his arms as if it were a stick. He had a pistol in his belt.

"Who you are?" he said rudely. He looked up. The flag of the defeated Tutsi army still flew above the hospital.

"I'm Donna Gardiner. I'm in charge of this hospital. We have many sick people. I will need your help."

"Siiick people," he drawled, drawing out the word "sick." His eyes burned with a slow flame. His mouth was full of gold teeth. Donna's flesh crept. He turned toward his three comrades. "Siiick people," he repeated. They laughed together, in a way that made Donna feel cold in the hundred-degree heat. Never had she heard such ominous laughter. Never again would she associate laughter with humor. In the future—but she stopped herself short. What future? Would there be one?

He turned back to her and pulled the rifle up slowly so that it pointed not directly at her but at the ground in front of her feet. For one stupid moment, Donna wondered if he were going to play the mad game that they played in bad Westerns. The guy in the black hat would get the village idiot to dance by firing at his feet, until John Wayne . . . but there would be no John Wayne. In this hideous corner of this horrible country there were no John Waynes.

"This Tutsi hospital," he said. It sounded like a bottom line.

"It's a hospital," said Donna. "With people who need help. Tutsi and Hutu. We treat Hutus here, too."

He nodded mock gravely, like one might to a small child who was trying to tell you that monsters came at night. He swung the gun up slowly, so that its barrel crawled up her body, to her neck, to her head, and then on it went, above her, to the flag.

"Tutsi flag," he said, and he smiled again, leering at her. Life was so simple in his simple mind. Black and white. Hutu and Tutsi. The quick and the dead.

The truck rumbled up and stopped behind the Jeep. The back was thrown open, and the soldiers dismounted. They were ominously quiet. Some were bandaged, walking wounded. They all looked tired. Their eyes were bloodshot. They were easy around death. Death was their friend and neighbor. It was life that was suspect. Life was guilty until proved innocent.

The Hutu leader didn't have to say what he was going to say. Everyone knew what was going to happen. But he said it anyway. "Kill all the Tutsis. All the siiick Tutsis . . . and all the not sick Tutsis." He turned and looked at Donna as he spoke. The AK-47 was back from the flag now, and aiming at the pit of her stomach.

"You can't kill anyone," said Donna. "That would be a crime, a crime against humanity. It's not . . . it's nothing to do with Burundi law . . . the International Court of Justice at The Hague . . . Nuremberg . . ." She petered out. Despair overwhelmed her. Would she die here? They didn't care about her silly words. They were not of the world of laws. They had slipped their moorings to civilization, and they sailed on an alien sea whose morality was not her morality. A second-in-command barked orders, and the group of tired executioners split in two. Half the group made their way toward the door of the hospital, and half turned back to deal with the line of people on the road. They moved so slowly. They were exhausted. Murder was such very hard work, and they were underpaid. It was boring stuff, this kind of killing. Nobody shot back, nobody resisted. And afterward, they would set the whole place on fire. But the people on the road would have to be pulled a long way to be deposited in the flames. It was something to do with infection, they had been told.

"No!" Donna shouted. She took a step forward, nearer to her own end. "I won't allow it!"

But they hardly heard her. They didn't care about her. They were unslinging their rifles and machetes.

The commander took a step toward Donna. He put both hands on his rifle and then took another step. "You Tutsi friend," he said simply. He walked another step toward her, and he placed the barrel of the gun against her forehead.

Over his shoulder, down the road, Donna could see another Jeep approaching. Behind her, in the hospital a shot rang out. Somebody screamed. It was a tired, low-pitched scream. Another shot was fired, then others, several quite quickly. Donna closed her eyes. Nausea gripped her. Would it hurt? Had it hurt Gerald? Was this God's reward for her behavior? Her mind raced, here at the edge of death. She hadn't groveled, she hadn't begged. The gun barrel was hot against her clammy skin. It was dark now and the guns were going off, cries of children mixed with them. There were shouts of protest, or resignation, as the dance of horror went on.

"Oh God, help me," said Donna, and He did, because the faintness that Gerald Templer must have felt at the end welled up inside her. And so she passed peacefully into the quietness, because you never heard the shot that killed you.

38

Steve woke slowly. He lay there and the feelings rushed through him like an electrical surge. He didn't open his eyes, because he didn't want to interfere with the thoughts . . . or were they emotions? It was strange to feel like this, uncomfortably wonderful and very disturbing. Kate had done this. It was all her. She was there in his mind. The vision lingered of her vital beauty in the midnight blue dress, of the life in her eyes that had made him feel truly alive for the first time in years. He knew when he had last felt like this. It had been on the lakefront in Murano, walking the narrow streets of Venice with Donna, seeing a white bouquet fly through the air outside an age-old church. So he knew what it was. It was an ancient and influential friend whom he had lost track of and never expected to see again. He went over every moment of the evening in his mind, freezing bits of it, reversing, fast-forwarding, playing back the moments in memory.

He lay quite still, but more awake than he had been in years. She had wakened him with her kisses. He knew that he had changed and that she had changed him. He had woken on both a brand-new day and a brand-new life. He was "out there" again, no longer in self-imposed exile from the world. It felt almost unbelievably good.

He was amazed at the difference an evening could make. But there *were* turning points in life, Shakespeare's times and tides that if taken at their ebb led to great things. He was full of gratitude and warmth toward her. But what could he do for her? What did she want from him? She should not have to ask in order to receive. In an instant, it came to him. He would do Samantha Haywood's book for Kate's company. It would be his gift to both of them. He had been approached by more prestigious publishers—Abrams, Knopf, Rizzoli—but he had always recoiled from the complexities and complications of publishing, from the compromises, the contracts, and the loss of control. But now, in the context of this brave new morning, these considerations melted away. He was a man of action, and he jumped from his bed and grabbed his bathrobe, noting that it was 6:30 A.M.

He walked across to the open window and closed it. His breath was visible in the cold of the room, but inside he was warm. In the yard below, he could see the tracks in the snow that were their footprints. It had been no dream. The book idea seemed better and better. Samantha had had all the enthusiasm that he once had. He wanted to give her a chance. Daniel, had he lived, might have needed a chance like that. In giving her the book, he would be doing something for his son, too, not just for Sam, and for Kate, who had given him this extraordinary experience of rebirth.

He wanted to act now. He thought quickly of the logistics. He was going to London in a couple of days. Probably, he wouldn't have time to meet up with Samantha before that. And she might have cooled on the idea. He walked into his office and sat down at the typewriter, aware that he hadn't had his sacred cup of coffee. Something was clearly very seriously adrift. Two-fingered, he typed fast and accurately.

Dear Samantha,

    I have had second thoughts about the book project we discussed in the summer, on the beach and at breakfast when Elvis and J. D. Salinger were at the corner table in Bean's.

    I have to go to England for the Tate thing very soon, but if you are still interested, I would like to go ahead. I will leave word at my studio that you are to have access to my office here. There is far too much paper in it, photographs, catalogues, God knows what. Anyway, I have told my helpers that you are to be shown anything you want to see. If you have doubts, the material should help solidify or dispel them. I will call you before I go, or when I get back, so that we can discuss dull contracts, etc. I am sorry to seem so capricious. It is not like me to be so. But then life is strange, although you are too young to realize that yet.

Best wishes,
Steve Gardner

He found the fax number at her office and sent the letter off. He looked at his watch again—it was nearly quarter to seven. Kate had said she was an early riser. He reached for the telephone. As he did so, it rang. He didn't believe in telepathy, but somehow he knew it would be Kate. "Steve Gardiner," he said, his voice warm.

"Thank God I've got you," said a British voice, a man's. He spoke fast, urgently. "Look, I'm sorry to disturb you. I know it's early in the States. You don't know me. My name is Brian Gough, I'm a doctor, and I'm phoning from England. I've been in Africa, working with your . . . well, working with Donna."

Steve tried to get his mind straight. "Donna! Do you know where she is?"

"Did. It's why I'm ringing. I'm very worried about her. She gave me your number in the States."

"What do you mean, worried? What's the matter with her? She's not ill, is she? Where is she?" The words tumbled out of Steve. Donna spent a lot of time in his mind, but it was a shock to hear somebody say her name. Somebody from England who knew her. Now something seemed to be wrong. Africa? What the hell was she doing working in Africa?

"I don't know whether you know anything about the war that's going on in Burundi, but that's where we were. Running an army hospital. I got out of there three days ago on an American military transport. I've just got to London from Nairobi and . . . Sorry to be so untogether, but I'm knackered. I haven't slept for . . . Anyway, do you know anything about Burundi and Rwanda and what's been going on there?"

Steve tried to make sense of it. Burundi, Rwanda. Yes, vaguely. Africans killing each other. Poverty and coups. Corruption. Change and decay. It sounded like Bosnia in the sun from the pieces he had read in the *New York Times*.

"I tried to get Donna to come with me, because things were getting pretty hairy, but she insisted on staying. As far as I know she's still there, outside a dreadful place called Bujumbura, which passes for the capital. Anyway, when I got to Nairobi, things had got worse. There are two tribes, the Hutus and the Tutsis, who do nothing but kill each other. The Tutsis control the army, but the Hutu guerrillas have just defeated the army. The thing is, the Hutus are on a killing rampage. The Americans are in the clear because they'd given the Hutu president, who was thrown out in the coup, diplomatic asylum. But the Brits were neutral. I think any Brits will be targets."

"Good God! What can we do? What can I do?"

"I don't know. I've spent all day at the Foreign Office. They say that we shouldn't have been there in the first place because there was some advisory against travel to Burundi. Not such a stupid idea, as it turns out. You know the British. They take the old-fashioned view that if you do something bloody silly, then you have to take the bloody blame. But you're an American, and the Americans are the good guys for once, because they backed the right horse and stuck Ntibantunganya in a nice room in their embassy so that he didn't get chopped up. And now he's president again, and it's the Tutsis who are being hunted down."

"But Donna's English, and I'm not married to her. America couldn't give a shit about foreigners."

"Well, I don't know. I've just got to get some sleep, and when I wake up I can try again. Right now I'm a zombie. I just thought you could be working on it while I climbed back into the land of the living. And, well, I don't want to be alarmist, but she said if anything bad happened . . . to tell you that she loved you."

There was silence on both ends of the line.

"How was she, I mean, otherwise?" said Steve at last, swallowing hard.

"She's probably the bravest woman I've ever met, and the kindest," said Brian. The expressing of such feelings didn't come easily to a North Country man.

Again, silence. Steve was adrift in an alien world of feeling. "Let me get your number." He scribbled it down on the bedside pad. Sadness and fear fought for his mind. Why had he allowed them to drift apart? Why hadn't he been there for her when she needed him? He tried to think clearly.

"What was the name of the place you last saw her?"

"The locals called it Minaniville. It's about twenty miles south of Bujumbura. No telephone, no fax, no electricity, no water. Not very much life, actually."

Steve wrote frantically.

"A Burundi army hospital?"

"A 'Forces for the Defense of Democracy' hospital as of a day or two ago."

"That's all you know?"

"Everything."

Steve began to sweat in the cold room. What could he do? He knew no one in England except the effete aesthetes at the Tate. Come to that, he didn't know many people in America either. He made a point of avoiding his collectors, and his relationships with his dealer and the museum people were politely distant. He had always despised people who collected artists who "mattered." Here was the downside of being a recluse. There were people all over his homeland with Filofaxes and portable PCs positively bulging with painstakingly networked acquaintances, who existed for moments like this. Those people had IOUs as long as your arm, congressmen who would take their calls. Shit. Why hadn't Donna come to America, been a doctor here and become a citizen, for whom help would be only a Special Forces parachute drop away? Being English might have been all right in Victorian gunship days, but it sure as hell didn't help in today's Africa, where the former colonials were always looking for a chance to get even.

"Well, thank you, Dr. Gough. Get some sleep. I'll call you later."

He put the telephone down in a daze. He had to do something. But what? He didn't think more about it. He needed to talk to Kate. So he picked up the telephone he had just put down, and he called her.

39

Kate hesitated briefly before dialing the number. It was difficult to know just how close a friend the First Lady was.
Certainly, she was a million miles from Frankie close. So perhaps she was more of an acquaintance, a business friend. They
had met several times, and so far it was Kate who had done the
favors: designing the White House tree that was one of Faith
Kimble's pet projects; inviting the First Lady to appear on a
prime time ABC Kate Haywood special in which Faith was
seen baking cookies to counteract her image as an abrasive,
fiercely competent first wife. Kate had even campaigned for the
President. In marginal areas, Kate wannabes had probably delivered swing votes. But this time it was Kate who wanted the
favor, and wanted it badly. The trouble was, it was more life-
and-death than lifestyle. Kate wasn't quite sure how her request
would be received, but she was sure as hell going to make it
anyway. When asking for favors you couldn't go much higher
than Faith Kimble. There were those who thought the President
occupied a slightly lower place in the pecking order.

The number was the private one that Faith had given her.

Kate would bypass the White House switchboard and the army of no-sayers whose job it was to make access difficult to the high and the mighty.

She punched the numbers and thought of Steve. Reality had a way of chopping up the magic of dreams. The night before had been one of the happiest in her life so far, and it had seemed to be for him too. Then, this. He had been distraught on the telephone as he had told her about his ex-wife, caught up in some nightmare in Africa. As he apologized for bothering her with his problems, she had felt waves of tenderness break over her. She had immediately thought, in her practical way, of what she could do for him. Her mind had bypassed the fact that he seemed so very concerned about Donna, absentee mother whom a part of him blamed for the death of his son.

The secretary's voice was glacially efficient. She merely repeated the telephone number that Kate had dialed. The privacy of this line would be closely guarded. When Faith had given it to her there had been only the slightest hint that this was "for your eyes only." But Faith Kimble's hints had sledgehammer force.

"This is Kate Haywood. Could I speak to Faith?"

The venerable "She may be in a meeting. I'll check" was an old standby that Kate's own secretaries used.

But the First Lady wasn't "in a meeting" to Kate. She was on the line in seconds.

"Kate. Hi. How are you? You're on my telephone list. I wanted to talk to you about the White House tree. How's it going? Can't turn on the television without seeing you. You get more air time than we do." She laughed warmly.

"Things are good . . . if busy is good," said Kate. Luckily, the First Lady liked to steer conversations.

"Any more news about that great idea of yours, getting artists to do Christmas tree decorations? I thought that was brilliant."

"I'm still working on it," said Kate, relentlessly upbeat. "But you know what artists are like. Prima donnas. Just leave it to me. I can deliver."

"God, you wouldn't come and work at the White House, would you? 'Leave it to me. I can deliver.' I haven't heard those phrases around here for months." She paused. The pleasantries were over. Kate wanted something. What?

Kate launched into the story and told it quickly. "I just didn't know what to do. Whom to approach. Then I thought of you."

Faith Kimble liked what she had heard. She didn't see it as being asked a favor. She saw it as an exercise of power mixed with the exchange of some political IOUs. The former was the whole point of being who and where she was. The latter was what you did when you got there.

When Kate had finished talking, Faith summarized it neatly. "So we have a British doctor, British passport, last seen in Minaniville, twenty miles south of Bujumbura in Burundi. About three days ago. And we want her out of there. Like yesterday."

"That's it," said Kate, impressed. Faith hadn't even asked for any of the names to be spelled.

"How old?"

"Forties," said Kate, guessing. She hadn't asked Steve.

"I think she might have picked a lucky country to get lost in," said Faith Kimble. "There's just been a coup, more a successful revolution. I was reading some cables about it a couple of days ago from State. Our candidate, a guy beginning with *N*, is the new president. For once the people at Foggy Bottom picked the right horse. We should have influence there."

"Is there anything you can do?"

"Leave it to me. I can deliver," said Faith Kimble with the famous laugh, borrowing Kate's lines. Then her voice grew serious. "Look, Kate. It's Africa. I can't promise you anything. Burundi's a mess. Zaire. Rwanda. I'm going to have the

Secretary of State call the president of Burundi and lean on him. There'll be one hell of a search. I can guarantee that. If she's alive, they'll find her. But it's an 'if.'"

"God, Faith, I am so grateful."

"Hang on, darling. . . . Susan, get me Fred Seagrave at State. Take him out of his breakfast meeting if necessary. What's the name of the new president of Burundi? *N* something. Ntibantunganya? Jeez! Kate, yeah, that's about it. We have your numbers, don't we? Leave them with Susan if not. Somebody will be back to you with progress reports. Fingers crossed, OK? Talk to you soon, darling. 'Bye."

Kate put the telephone down and clapped her hands together. So that was what power was all about. The real stuff. The Secretary of State of the United States of America was about to lean on the president of Burundi because the First Lady was about to lean on him. And on whom would the president of Burundi lean, and where would the leaning end? It was a fascinating thought. The whole process had been started by one call from Kate. For a single second, she felt she owned all the missiles and aircraft carriers of the world's only superpower, all its trillions and its influence. But the next second she was thinking of how soon she could get to Steve's house to tell him the news.

40

Donna didn't know where she was and she didn't know how she'd got there. She was, however, pretty sure that she was alive. Just. Her head hurt like hell. When she reached up to the source of the pain, there was a lump on her temple and a track of dried blood down her cheek. She opened her eyes, but she could barely see in the gloom of what must be a cell. It was like the black hole of Calcutta, hot and humid. She was thirsty. Her throat was as dry as the Gobi. But she wasn't dead, which had to be good news of sorts. She tried to remember, but all she could recall was the sound of shots and screams. At once, the satisfaction of being alive floated away from her, and nausea welled up in her stomach. She tried to catch her thoughts as they floated around in the weightless atmosphere of her mind. There had been a gun against her forehead as the massacre had begun. That was all she could remember.

She looked down at herself. Her shirt had been removed. And her skirt, but not her sneakers. She was in her underwear. The question whether she had been raped or not seemed almost academic to someone who was surprised that she was not dead.

But she didn't feel as if she had been raped. Then why had she been stripped? For the clothes? It was possible. Anything was possible in this corner of hell. She was sitting on a dirt floor, and she was alone. She tried to stand. The cell danced around her, and she grabbed the wall to steady herself. She thought about calling out, but to whom? One thing was certain: the person who answered her call would not be a friend.

Donna tried to think. Someone had hit her, but they hadn't killed her. She was a prisoner. And nobody knew where she was, least of all herself. She had been moved from the hospital. That, she was sure of. Brian, who had known she was there, would not know where she was now, wherever "where" was. So she was alone, lost, and at the mercy of people for whom life was cheaper than a cigarette. The only advantage of her situation was that it was preferable to the alternative.

In the gloom, Donna could see the bars now, and a door with a big lock. She heard footsteps in the corridor leading to her cell, and she braced herself.

Then a soldier in a filthy uniform was unlocking the door. "Major," he said.

Donna didn't know how to answer his simple statement. She guessed that she was to be taken to see an officer. *Thank God!* A major might be a little more formal in his attitude to death than the guerillas who had so casually slaughtered her patients. She followed the soldier down the corridor on unsteady feet. She had no thoughts of escape. Survival would be enough.

They climbed some stairs into a bright neon-lit hallway. People milled about. Nobody seemed to notice her seminaked-ness. Apparently, no one thought her appearance odd. There was a hum of activity. Everyone . . . the soldiers, the girls who looked like secretaries . . . was clearly exhausted, but running on the adrenaline of victory. Donna stared longingly at a soft drink machine. Even in the devil's den, Coke was there, refreshing you better, or whatever the latest jingle was. A door with panes of frosted glass bore the sign "Major Somaba." This, presumably, would be the major. The soldier knocked on the door. Donna could both see and smell the sweat on him. Beneath his uniform he was scrawny and malnourished, but the pistol at his side and the machete stuck in his belt made him deadly.

"Enter." A deep voice boomed through the glass door, and Donna's head flicked back with shock. It was not a word she had expected to hear.

The room was small. Behind a cluttered desk sat a man of enormous size. His uniform was clean, and he smelled strongly of cheap eau de cologne. He wore dark glasses to protect himself from the glare of the bright overhead lights. On his desk, amidst scattered papers, was a tray holding a teapot and two cups. At his side and behind the desk, kneeling, or rather squatting, was a boy of about sixteen. The boy's eyes were bright, and he smiled, showing perfect white teeth. He wore shorts and a white T-shirt, both very clean. It was immediately clear to Donna that this catamite doubled as servant and lover to Major Somaba.

"Sit ye down," said the major. He seemed very cheerful. "Would you join me in a cup of tea?" His accent was the caricature of British speech that Indians and some Africans could mimic so well.

Donna was vaguely aware of the surreality of the situation. She was in her underwear, in deadly peril, yet this man was behaving as if they were about to partake of cucumber sandwiches on the riverside lawns at Henley.

"I can offer you a McVitie's digestive biscuit," he said. "A suggestive biscuit." He laughed loudly at his poor joke. So did the boy hovering at his side. He reached into a drawer on the left side of his desk and pulled out a packet of biscuits.

Donna sat down. Behind her, the door closed. The soldier who had brought her to this weird Mad Hatter's tea party had left her alone with Major Somaba and his underage lover.

"I wish to lodge a formal complaint about the cowardly murder of my patients—"

He held up his hand to stop her. "Very regrettable. Very. Very.

A very poor show, I am afraid, by renegade soldiers who are not typical of our forces. I stopped it myself. Nipped it in the bud. Lucky I arrived in the nick of time, madam. I was able to save your life."

Donna lapsed into silence. Was *gratitude* in order? She didn't feel any. This Hutu sadist was almost certainly lying. But she *was* alive. And there had been a Jeep coming down the track at the very moment she had lost consciousness. She remembered that now.

"I should say that the men responsible have been dealt with most severely, as they deserved. But of course you have to realize that we are at war here. Most of those men had lost family members at the hands of Tutsis. Wars are not pretty. Terrible things happen. And now, a cup of tea?"

Donna looked longingly at the teapot. Her thirst screamed at her to accept. She simply nodded. The young boy jumped up to pour it. He laid a couple of McVitie's "suggestive" biscuits on a plate, still smiling at his master's joke.

"I don't usually take tea in my underwear in the presence of males," said Donna.

"Good Lord," said Major Somaba. "I hadn't noticed." It seemed almost possible that he was speaking the truth. "Rala, fetch a towel from the bathroom for Dr. Gardiner."

"How did you know my name?" said Donna.

"We are not totally without intelligence, you know," said the major. "That British attitude was always a problem for me at Sandhurst. It was one of the reasons they threw me out. You British have not dealt fairly with us Africans. Not then, not now.

He apparently decided to forgive Donna's "British attitude," because he smiled again. "But anyway, you have brought me luck, Dr. Gardiner. Great Britain has finally produced something of a greater value to me than afternoon tea. No good deed goes unpunished in this life. I learned that from you English. Then, lo and behold, I save your life and instead of punishment I get a reward. Maybe God isn't hiding in His heaven after all."

He laughed mightily at all this, and stuffed a biscuit into his mouth. He seemed, for some reason, in an unshakable good mood. Rala returned with a towel, and Donna wrapped it around her. She reached forward for the tea and drank it gratefully.

Now she looked around her. To her right was a bulletin board. Messages and some color photographs were stuck on it with pushpins. She focused on the photographs. At once, her stomach began to churn. There were pictures of Major Somaba doing what, presumably, was his job, and his job, it appeared, was executing large numbers of people with a machine gun. There were bodies everywhere. The photographs showed before-and-after shots of the terrified victims. The after shots of blood-stained corpses were a horrible contrast to the before images in which the fear was clearly visible on the faces of those about to die as the affable major strode among them bearing his weapon of destruction.

"Terrible things have to be done in war. The wicked eliminated, crimes avenged. Justice, that's my business. A bit like your Old Bailey, but not a lot of time for the wordy preliminaries."

Donna couldn't see his eyes behind the glasses, and Donna didn't want to. Her blood ran cold. This buffoon was not merely a foolish follower of colonial practices and attitudes, he was an evil killer like all the others in this godforsaken corner of the globe. At any moment, any second, he could turn from the former into the latter. The photographs said so.

"Anyway, Dr. Gardiner. You are apparently a very valuable person. A very valuable person, indeed. A person, apparently, with friends in high places."

In all her life so far, Donna had never been described as that. "I am?" she said quietly.

"Oh, yes, you are. We have a circular here, by fax from our new government, from the president's office, actually. It says that you must be found at all costs and protected, treated with all consideration, that anybody who harms you will be in very hot water, et cetera, et cetera. The moment I saw it, I thought, 'I wonder if that is our Dr. Gardiner.' And by Jove, it was. It is. And so I called the interior minister, and he is very pleased with me. He is beside himself with joy. It seems the Americans have interested themselves in you. And, in this day and age, when the Americans say 'jump,' we all ask 'how high?' don't we? Otherwise, no more goodies, no more Coke, no more . . ." He paused and looked quickly over to the bulletin board. "No more machine guns." Again he paused, chuckling now. "And if we don't take the carrot we get the stick—don't we?—now that the Americans are the only superpower." He shook his head. "We can run but we can't hide from Uncle Sam, can we, Dr. Gardiner?"

Donna tried to make sense of it. "But I'm not American, I'm British," she said.

"Precisely," said the major, letting out a huge guffaw. "And nobody—excuse my French—gives a two-penny shit about the British anymore. I dared to ask the minister about that. Why all this fuss for a limey? I said. Since when did the Americans get their knickers in a twist about foreigners, I asked him, very politely of course. And you know what he said? 'Oh, her husband is an American with influence.' So it sounds as if you have Mr. Gardiner to thank for the fact that you are not . . ." He paused. He seemed to realize that he was about to go too far. He shot a wistful glance at the bulletin board.

Donna's blood ran cold. Had there been no American intervention, she knew, now, what her fate would have been. She would have become a Polaroid on Major Somaba's board. There would have been a picture of her blood running on some dirt floor, Major Somaba, gun in hand, standing over her. He would have had his revenge at last for whatever cruelties he had suffered all those years ago at the Royal Military Academy, Sandhurst.

"So the job at hand is to get you sorted out clothes-wise, and get you on a plane to Nairobi. Then, and then . . . well, they're going to make me a colonel."

He looked at her closely. Did this disgusting man want to be *congratulated?*

Donna closed her eyes. Already, she could feel the plane taking off, the plane to freedom. She was beginning to understand, too, what had happened. Somehow, in some incredible way, she had been saved. She even knew the name of her savior. Tears of relief and gratitude trickled down her cheeks.

41

For these last three days, which had been a subtle mixture of heaven and hell, Kate had decided to work from home. She had never been far from the fax machine. True to her word, the First Lady had come through with mildly encouraging progress reports. The search had been instigated. The Burundi government was bending over backward to help. If Donna Gardiner was still alive, she would be found. If. Kate had seen Steve only a couple of times, but she had talked to him constantly on the telephone. Their relationship had deepened, although not in the light, joyful way that Kate had hoped it would after the evening when it had all begun.

Now the fax line was ringing once again. Kate hurried from the conservatory, where she had been commanding an assault on the aphids that were attacking her prize tomatoes. As she rushed into the office, she was excited to see that it was her private fax that was whirring out paper. The head sheet was from the office of the First Lady. The body of the fax, tantalizingly, seemed to emerge more slowly than usual. Kate bent down, trying to read each line as it appeared. And then she had it in her hands at last.

She could not call him. She must go to him. This second.

Kate screeched to a halt outside Steve's house, throwing a wall of snow into the air like a skier at the end of a run. The Range Rover entered into the spirit of the arrival, turning sideways in a skidding christie stop. She cut the engine and leaped out, the fax in her hand like a banner of victory. She wanted to see Steve's face when he read it. She wanted to feel his relief, and yes, she wanted to experience his gratitude.

It had just arrived from the office of Faith Hargreave Kimble, and it had been brief and to the point.

> *Dearest Kate,*
>
> *Success! Dr. Donna Gardiner has been found. She is safe and unharmed and in the U.S. embassy in the Burundi capital. She will be flown out tomorrow on an Air Force plane to Nairobi in Kenya. See you at the State dinner for the Germans next month, but let's talk about the tree next week. Glad to have been able to help.*
>
> *Love and best wishes,*
> *Faith*

Kate banged on the door of the house. Would he be there, or in the barn? Steve had been sick with worry since the call about Donna, too distracted to work. Kate had even felt a bit of jealousy, although that was not one of her usual sins. It would be ironic if in saving the wife she had engineered a dramatic reconciliation . . . Donna Gardiner, glowing with gratitude, reclaiming her long-lost husband. But Kate hadn't dwelt on that. He had wanted Donna safe, and Kate wanted what he wanted. If it meant losing him, so be it. Kate was a doer not a thinker, and now the fax in her hand was evidence that she was an achiever, too. It was just a damned shame that this whole thing couldn't have been a smooth path rather than a rough one. But the road through middle age was full of pot-holes, and the dogs of reality were constantly snapping at your heels.

He opened the door, and his face instantly reflected the excitement of hers. She could see the burden fall from his shoulders. He seemed to straighten visibly in front of her.

"They've found her!" said Kate, waving the fax in his face. "She's safe. In our embassy. The Air Force is flying her to Kenya tomorrow."

"Thank God. Thank God," he said, shaking with relief.

"Isn't that great?" said Kate. "I can hardly believe how it works. One phone call. It's like magic."

"Oh Kate." He moved forward and reached out to her, hugging her to him. Kate let herself go in his arms, like the rag doll she had never expected to be or feel like. Since this had started, she had felt the fear. To love, you had to trust. To love, you had to let go. That meant you gave up some control over your life and put yourself partly in the power of another. Peter was still so fresh. It was dangerous, this thing called love. But paradoxically, without danger and the fear of it, love couldn't exist. It was like belief in God. You had first to trust. First there was the leap of faith with no safety net. Only then could come the peace. Now, in his arms, she felt certain that she had found it, or would find it. She tilted back her head to look at him.

"You miracle worker," he said, smiling down at her.

"Safe and unharmed and in the embassy," said Kate triumphantly. "Not bad in three days."

He led her into his sitting room, an untidy, masculine place piled high with books on art and philosophy, several open, heavily annotated and flagged.

"I expect she'll call you, or you could call her," said Kate. Her voice had changed.

Donna was alive and that was wonderful, but Steve, through Kate and Faith Kimble, had probably saved her life. Did that mean that Donna Gardiner, who for some reason had never given up the Gardiner name, was back in Steve's world? Kate's remark had been a gentle probe of his intentions toward his ex-wife.

He turned toward her. It was clear from his expression that he could read her thoughts. "I expect she's very tired and very relieved. She'll want to catch that Air Force plane to Nairobi and rest up. I think telephone calls can wait," he said.

Kate fought back the smile that his "right answer" had summoned up.

"She's out of my life, Kate," he said gently. "I couldn't bear to think of her in danger, and I wanted to help. But not because I still love her. You understand that?"

"Of course I do, " said Kate bravely. Love seemed to go with uncertainty. She remembered that from the last time. Why did every coin have two sides? Why was life so perverse?

"Look," he said, as if deciding suddenly to confront something. He sat down on the edge of a frayed couch that Kate was already redecorating in her mind with an Osborne & Little patterned fabric. "I have to go to London tomorrow for my exhibition. I want you to come with me."

"To London? With you? Tomorrow?" Kate caught her breath. Steve was full of surprises, wonderful, magical surprises. In the woodshed. Now. Of course it was totally and completely impossible. Her calendar, black with appointments, flashed before her mind. Sam. The speed of the whole amazing thing. To go to London with Steve Gardiner as his, as his . . . it couldn't be done.

"Yes," he replied simply to her question.

"Yes," she replied simply to his.

42

Kate felt the warm champagne buzz. The big plane surged forward, propelling them with the power of a million horses into their thrilling future. She held on tight and looked straight ahead. She was aware that Steve was looking at her.

"An adventure," he said. And he reached out and touched her hand briefly.

She felt the burst of electricity. She dared to think back to the snow-covered field outside his barn and the walk they had shared after the dreamlike dinner. She could smell the wood-shed, feel the body memories. She remembered the sensation of his lips on hers, so powerful, yet so strangely gentle.

"Happening fast," she said, smiling at him. They were no longer home, already abroad. Their feet were no longer on firm ground.

"Yes," he said, smiling too. "I feel a little out of my depth."

"Some more champagne?" asked the stewardess.

Kate usually didn't drink on transatlantic flights. It intensified jet lag. But now she wanted to do all the things she didn't usually do, because, in a sense, she was no longer the person she usually was.

"I'd love some," she said. Then, turning to Steve, "Champagne was where it began."

"Was it? I think it began earlier. That first time you came to see me. I think it began then," said Steve.

"You had a funny way of showing it."

"Possibly I have a funny way of showing most things. A lot of people find me rather odd." He laughed a bemused kind of laugh, hinting that people were almost certainly right, but that he seemed reasonably normal to himself.

"Singular. Different. Unpredictable. Not odd as in 'peculiar.' Perhaps difficult. Rather wonderful."

"Thank you . . . I think."

"It was a compliment. What about me?"

"Mmm. Vibrant. Energetic. Intelligent. Moral. Very strong. Very beautiful."

"The last will do," said Kate.

Sparks were flying again. She wanted to kiss him, or rather for him to kiss her. But she knew he wouldn't. They were out in public and Steve was deliciously private

He breathed in deeply, as if savoring the sweet smell of flowers. He was relaxing, and for him relaxation was not easy. It was strange. For someone so energetic and vibrant, Kate had a calming effect on him. Perhaps it was the feeling that control could safely be surrendered to someone who was used to handling it.

"So," he said at last. "What is your London, Kate Haywood?"

It was not a presumptuous remark. She had told him she had been there many times before.

"Oh, God, let me think. Well, Claridge's. The string quartet at tea time. The parks, the theater, walking everywhere, the total absence of political correctness. The whole scene, really. The new restaurants—that's a vast change. When I went there first as a teenager, the food was a disaster."

Steve laughed. "It was, wasn't it. That's a pretty good list. I always used to think that America was the land of free speech, until I got to London and realized just how many things we are not really allowed to discuss, like race, and religion, and gender, financial difficulties, depression, anything remorselessly downbeat. We pride ourselves on our ability to feel and emote, but then all the less worthy emotions, like hate and envy, jealousy and self-pity, are swept under the carpet as if they don't exist. Ask an Englishman how he is and he says, 'oh, mustn't complain,' or 'struggling along,' and yet every American is 'never better' or 'fantastic,' even when they're tying the knot in the rope they're going to hang themselves with. Anyway, lots of walking and theater and food. We can agree on that."

"I'm looking forward to meeting Donna," said Kate. She was quite unable to avoid confronting the only existing problem for a second longer. "Does she know we're coming?"

"She won't be there. She left a message saying she's staying in Nairobi for a few days to rest."

"Oh. So will I ever get to meet her?"

"One day, if you want to. I think you'd like her."

"Because you do?" said Kate. *Oh, stop it, Kate,* she thought. *For God's sake stop it.* But the words had just come tumbling out. She simply hadn't been able to help it.

"Yes, because I do. And because she is likable, admirable."

He wasn't holding back. She'd walked right into it. She had only herself to blame.

"If a little impetuous." Kate couldn't resist. Donna's endless list of pros demanded one tiny con. Anyway, "impetuous" was far more polite than "foolhardy."

"Impetuousness in defense of the defenseless might be deemed by some to be no vice," he said.

But the other damned doctor had had the sense to get out. Wasn't discretion supposed to be the better part of valor? If it hadn't been for Kate, the "likable, admirable" ex-wife would have ended up as fly food, not the subject of a pompous, Goldwateresque defense by the husband.

The romantic mood was rent. Storm clouds were already gathering, and Kate was the one and only rainmaker. Were they programmed to fight, as Donna and Steve had apparently been? Was this the pattern of events that doomed all relationships to repeat themselves throughout eternity, battered wives seeking men to abuse them; the strong searching for the weak and then complaining about weakness; the faithful drawn like moths to the flame? *Damn it.* It was simply too soon for jealousy. But jealousy had a lousy sense of timing.

"Pointless suicide isn't much of a virtue," she said, despite biting her lip in an attempt to remain silent.

"Look, Kate," he said. "I know Donna is an issue for you. But she shouldn't be. Do you think I would have asked you to London if I still loved her. Do you, really?"

"How can I know what you think?" said Kate. "I hardly know you." She was vaguely aware that in this life there were two sorts of relationship problems: knowing people not enough, and knowing them too well.

"It works both ways," he said.

"What do you mean?"

"Your ex-husband."

"Peter?"

"I didn't know his name," said Steve.

"Oh." Peter's ghost had a way of stopping conversations in their tracks. It was the equivalent of a slap in the face. Kate had been running on her own paranoid jealousy jag, completely failing to recognize that others might have problems in that direction too. "But Peter's ancient history," she said at last. "Everyone knows that." But even as she spoke, there was a part of her that didn't think of Peter as "ancient history." Peter had gone, but he had never really left. He was a part of her life. He was Sam's dad. He was memories, mostly wonderful ones. Now that time had passed, those memories survived, unmolested by the terrible thing he had done at the end. Peter had wondered if he had ever loved Kate—he'd said that—but he had, he *had*. And she had worshiped him, for so long and so deeply. It counted for something, like childhood, parents, home, happiness. You couldn't obliterate such things to order. You couldn't phase out your past. Otherwise, who was she? The past was who you were.

"Ancient history?" he said, pulling at his ear. "Well, when did you see him last? I haven't seen Donna for years."

There were answers to that. Jealousy could always find answers, as it could always find questions. For years, Steve and Donna had built mighty dams to contain the pent-up torrents of their emotions. What would happen when they met again? Steve still admired and respected the woman he had once adored. What had changed? All the years of separation sounded more like a threat than a reassurance.

"I saw Peter over a year ago," said Kate.

It had been a month or two after the divorce, and she had been walking down Madison Avenue. It was during the period of numbness, of shock, but before the terrible depression had set in. She had walked for miles, walked and found herself in strange places, hardly aware of how she had got there, or why. Then, on Madison, she had seen him coming toward her. In the fog of unreality that had wrapped itself around her in those days, she had found room for the thought that there was a good-looking man up ahead, so well dressed, with such good posture. It had been Peter. She had kept on walking, and so had he, and then he had recognized her, just as they were about to pass. He had stopped. He was wearing his overcoat, the camel one from Savile Row, and the last shirt and tie she had given him from Turnbull and Asser.

Kate couldn't remember the conversation well. Even the feelings she had felt were a bit of a mystery. Sam had been mentioned. And the weather, that trusty standby of those in conversational trouble. And Kate had even managed to ask about Ruth. It had been like one of those conversations you had with grandparents who were losing their marbles, the talk stylized and loaded with clichés designed to paper over the fact that they didn't really know whether it was Christmas or Easter. But Kate recalled the misty facts of it now, because the strange truth was that Peter was still the most important thing that had happened in her life so far, including Steve Gardiner. One day, this brand-new, exciting man might replace him, but here, now, the brutal fact was that Peter in some sad way loomed larger in her world than Steve.

"Well," he said, amplifying his point gently, cutting away at the damaged emotional tissue, probing the scars, "some might say that 'over a year' is not ancient history. Others might say that ancient history is all we have, all we are."

He was reading her thoughts. They were on the same wavelength. Perhaps he wondered how he would react to Donna, as Kate herself wondered right now how she would react if Peter were discovered sitting in the seat behind her. She flicked a look over her shoulder, quite unable not to. Peter was not there. Two businessmen were, and one of them smiled encouragingly at her.

"I think you might have a point," she said. "I'm sorry."

"Don't be. It isn't easy, this, you know. Nothing is. Even the things that are also wonderful."

He threaded his hand into hers, and she squeezed it back. She took a deep breath and let out a sigh of anticipation and anxiety. She resembled the great plane that was wrapped around them, hurtling through space into the unknown. It was scary and exciting, invigorating and nerve-racking. It was called living. Kate thought then of the remark her mother always used to make when she was a child. It was as true now as it had been then. "It's a great life if you don't weaken." That was the key. She had to be strong. She had to be brave. Then, and only then, would happiness be given to her. For the cruel truth was the biblical one. Unto them that hath, it shall be given. And to them that hath not, it shall be taken away . . . even that which they hath. It wasn't fair, of course. But then God in His wisdom had made a world in which not much seemed to be.

43

"Suggesting I go to a play called *Art!* Some people might think that was living dangerously," said Steve with a laugh.

The box looked out over the stage. It was not the best view in the house, but it was close to the action. More important, it was deliciously private. Steve had paid for three seats so that they would not be disturbed.

"I think just being here with you is living dangerously," said Kate.

It was wonderfully true. The unknown was a stimulating place. They had both had the same attitude toward jet lag. The early morning arrival at Heathrow had been night for them, but they had kept going till lunchtime, unpacking at Blakes Hotel in the gorgeous suite with its two bathrooms, lunching late in the beautifully designed restaurant, catnapping in the afternoon.

All the time, intimacy had hovered in the background. Kate had forgotten what this process was like. It was a strange and magical experience. Life was superreal—smells, tastes, sounds, visions, all were amplified. Here was meaning, and everything made sense.

"Isn't London *great?*" said Steve.

It was, and especially in an English theater about to present Tom Courtenay and Albert Finney. Both were icons of the age when last London had "swung." Now both were back on the merry-go-round as it swung once more. The lights dimmed. The curtain went up. The play was brilliant, funny in a peculiarly adult way. It dealt with two major questions: What was art? And what was friendship? Misunderstandings and disagreements about the former undermined the latter, as a dermatologist spent a fortune on a plain white painting that his friend thought was "a piece of shit." Would the friendship survive? Would prejudices be changed by argument, or indeed by the artistic validity (if any) of the stark canvas? By the intermission, it hung in the balance.

In the bar, a particularly British charade was being played out. Two people worked behind it. Around a hundred were packed tight in front of it. The interval lasted ten minutes, and everyone wanted a drink. Many of the British were quite obviously desperate for one. Those who had thought ahead had ordered and paid for their drinks before the play started. These clusters of drinks lined a shelf along one wall, with bits of paper attached bearing numbers the purchasers would have memorized in order to find their drinks without delay. The drinks were warm, and the ice in them had melted, watering down the already tiny measures of alcohol.

The bartenders worked quickly, but their task was daunting. The British, good in queues, held back as they halfheartedly waved ten-pound notes. The tourists, on the other hand, bayed and shouted, thrusting themselves forward into the spaces left in the front row as the victorious retreated, bearing, and spilling, their precious drinks. It was these high-profile go-getters who were served first. Each customer was asked if he wanted ice. Most did. One semimelted cube was then unceremoniously grabbed by tongs from a small plastic bucket and deposited in each glass. The request for more ice scored a second cube, no more.

Steve and Kate, neither of them accustomed to lines, especially lines as nasty and claustrophobic as this one, held back. This was the cunning thing to do. In true British fashion the job got done in the time available, despite all indications to the contrary. The crowd at the bar melted away like the cubes of ice. A few minutes before the bell, Steve and Kate were transporting, surreptitiously and illegally, his whisky and soda and her gin and tonic back to the safety and comfort of their box.

"God, what a crush," said Kate. "Why didn't they put on more bartenders? They could have done double the business."

"They've done it like this for years. That's the argument that has the most force over here," said Steve. "It's like the play. Finney can't believe that Courtenay can *change* so much. It's the *newness* of Serge's fascination with modern art that he finds so threatening. If he can turn into somebody so different so quickly, then he must be a bit suspect as a loyal friend. In America, change is thought to be good for its own sake. Over here, change is the enemy. At the very least it is guilty until proved innocent."

"You know, there *is* something a little threatening about people's loving art, isn't there?" said Kate. "Art is really the only respectable nonliving thing to love. It's a rival, but an acceptable rival. I mean, if somebody loves money more than his wife, or friend, it just means he is, well, not very admirable. But art . . . art is strong karma. If art is the significant other, then you have problems. Maybe Donna found that out." Donna had a way of slipping out of the woodwork.

Steve smiled at her, not seeming to mind her preoccupation with Donna, perhaps even a little flattered by it.

"If you think art is a rival with impeccable moral credentials, then what about medicine? You certainly qualify for 'small-minded' when you complain about your wife spending too much time curing the sick," he said.

"But you could complain about your . . . your . . . your what-ever spending too much time on her magazine, or her lifestyle TV program, or her business empire. You'd be allowed to complain about that, wouldn't you?" Kate couldn't help bringing it back to herself.

"Yes, I suppose you would," he said with a laugh. "You would have carte blanche to complain about that if you wanted to."

"So what I do is less . . . oh, less crucial than what you do and what Donna does?"

"Kate, are you quite good at picking fights?"

"I'm not picking fights, I'm just asking a simple question."

"Well, perhaps you're asking the wrong question."

"And what would the right one be?"

"You could ask 'Do you think I'm beautiful?' The answer would be 'yes.' You could ask 'Are you having one of the most enjoyable days you've ever had?' and the answer would be 'yes.' You could ask 'Is it because you find me fascinating and exciting and fun?' and the answer would be 'yes.' I just think that those questions have better answers than 'Do you think what I do is less crucial than what Donna does?'"

"OK," said Kate, laughing. "Consider those questions asked and answered," and a warm glow suffused her as she threaded her hand into his and the curtain went up on the second half of the play.

44

They didn't feel tired when the play was over. If they did, it was the sort of tiredness that didn't want to go to bed, at least didn't want to sleep. They had eaten earlier in St. Martin's Court, next to the theater, at Sheekey's—potted shrimps and toast, and plain grilled Dover sole on the bone—and they were already feeling like honorary English. What would an English couple like them do now, a couple finding their own delicious way into a relationship, picking their way through flowers and barbed wire to something uniquely theirs?

"Would you like to go to Annabel's?" he said.

"Yes, of course, but don't you have to be a member?"

"The guy who owns it, Mark Birley, collects my glass. He said I would be welcome whenever I wanted to go."

"Well, I'd love a drink, and to people-watch. Annabel's! I wouldn't have put you and Annabel's together in a million years."

He laughed. "Me neither! I never expected to be out on a London street with a beautiful woman, and going for a drink there, although I imagine it's a bit early for them." Steve, too, had surprised himself. Kate had changed him quicker than he had imagined possible. Before he met her, this whole trip would have been little but an ugly rush of necessity. He would have stayed somewhere sensible like the Savoy, met the minimum of people required by his dealer and the Tate people, eaten room service, been to celebrate the opening of the exhibition, and hurried back to New England on the first flight afterward. He would have carried around with him a mood as overcast as the gray London skies, and resented every minute the trip kept him away from the work. Now he felt like a tourist in that most welcoming of cities, but a tourist who knew about Blakes and Annabel's and was at ease at both. Kate had made the difference, and he marveled at the metamorphosis she had brought about in him.

As the post-theater crowds thronged about them, he tried to analyze his responses. What had led to the surge of feeling that night over dinner in the barn, and in the snow-swept field outside? It couldn't be explained. But lack of an explanation didn't stop the mind searching for one, and he searched now on the cold, bracing pavement as he watched the woman who had brought about such a change in his life.

It was Steve's way to focus inward on the struggle to find the elusive art, until the rest of the world became but an irritating distraction from the main event. To Kate, however, the world was a sandbox of infinite interest. She was out there, her hands dirty, where the real people lived. She was honest and vulnerable beneath her exterior of fierce competence. She was involved, and her involvement blew away the misty aura of melancholy that shrouded him, like a fresh wind might blow away a fog at sea. To stand by her side was to belong to the world. To stand alone was to be banished from it. But these were rationalizations. The real thing was more complex, but also simpler. It was the emotion of wanting her.

He remembered her lips on his. He knew it would happen.

He knew she knew. But when? Where? How? There was a delicious ambivalence. The longer it was put off, the more glorious would be the moment. Each second they were together amplified their feelings. Each misunderstanding, each almost-argument, each tiny clash of wills, threatened the joy to come. But the resolution of the tiny conflicts made the outcome more tantalizingly certain. To be here was perfect. In the bracing waters of a revitalized London, both had escaped their old selves.

He hailed a cab, and said, "Annabel's." To a London cabbie it was enough. They were on their way to Berkeley Square.

The dark green liveried doorman hurried forward to open the door for them. Then they were walking down the stairs to the most famous and long-lived nightclub of them all. Annabel's had been alive and well for over thirty years, but it was still very far from middle-aged.

The ancient retainer who greeted them in the narrow corridor beyond the swing doors was every day of seventy. He stood quite still, but his eyes, behind thick horn-rimmed glasses, were very much alive. Steve gave his name, and a list was consulted. "Welcome to Annabel's, Mr. Gardiner," said the man.

Inside, the bar was to the left. A crowd milled around it, although not so deep or so desperate as the one at the theater. To the right was a room in which the walls could hardly be seen for pictures, mostly of dogs, cats, horses, and the other sorts of four-legged things that the English preferred to people. There were overstuffed armchairs and comfortable banquettes at which pretty girls and not-so-pretty men perched in animated conversation. Everywhere were bottles of drink, and ice buckets of champagne. If Europe was depressed, this minuscule area of it had not heard the news. On the sophisticated sound system, Tina Turner bridged the gap between ancient and modern with a dance factor that transcended trendy. More swing doors separated the bar area from the darker part of the nightclub proper.

"Let's get one of the tables inside, along the wall," said Steve. "Away from the crush." The cruising crowd by the bar were enjoying more fluid relationships than the patrons ensconced in the club's interior. Kate threaded her way through the stylish gloom, her eyes accustoming themselves to the darkness. Eventually they were ushered to a cozy banquette behind a table in an alcove. It was formidably comfortable. When Kate sat down, the cushions seemed to eat her up. The alcove had a view of the small dance floor. At the same time, there was the feeling of privacy. You could see, but not be seen, and that was what Annabel's was all about.

Kate's practiced eye took in the details. Nina Campbell, the designer and a Mark Birley protégée, had perfected the sharper edge of the English country house style. There was a raffish air to the good taste, the pictures sporting, the tableware more Hermès than Crown Derby. It could only *just* have been somebody's house, although that was the overall impression that the décor managed to convey. The dance floor, small but packed, had flashing lights underfoot, a concession perhaps to the conspicuous Arab clientele.

She leaned back against the cushions and sipped her drink. "It's strange, tonight, isn't it, the whole business of relaxing? I so seldom do it, and yet I don't feel guilty. I don't want to call anyone and check in, check up on things, check, period. I just want to sit here and waste time, let it just drift away from me. Then, tomorrow, I can wake whenever, and get up whenever, and call lunch breakfast, or breakfast lunch. God, is this how the idle rich live?"

"I guess the idle don't get to be very rich, and the very rich haven't time to be idle. God has been good at evening the playing field. When you've finished at the factory, the evening and the six-pack belong to you. But if you're some billionaire hedge-fund guru, there's always something going on that you should know about when you're asleep. Do you find that with your company? It must be an open-ended commitment?"

"Usually, my mind has to have something to worry about. The worry comes first, then I find something to attach it to. The business is good in that way. It provides an inexhaustible supply of problems. But right now the only thing I'm worried about is that sooner or later, this evening is going to end."

"Maybe it doesn't have to. If we feel the same tomorrow, and next week, and next month, it won't matter that the evening is technically over."

"You know," said Kate dreamily, "I don't really know anything about you, and you don't really know anything about me. Yet here we are, sharing a suite, tucked away in this little corner, abroad together. I mean, if it were my daughter sitting here, I'd want to know much more about you."

"All right for you, but not for Sam," he said.

"Not for Sam," Kate repeated with a small smile.

"So, what sorts of things would you like to know about me? And how will you know that I tell you the truth?"

"Oh, you'd tell the truth, all right, however uncomfortable. I know that much about you. I guess that's a pretty big thing to know."

"What makes you think I'm truthful?"

"Because you tell the truth in your art. Because you leave nothing out and put everything in, and because that process is painful to you."

"Mmm. I like that. I think it's even true. Not much that's worthwhile comes without pain."

"OK, did you have a dog? And what was your first car? And what did your parents do? Were they nice to you, or did they beat you, or insist that you be seen and not heard? Brothers and sisters, wives, lovers, friends, favorite places, music, food, God, hobbies, health, wealth, help . . . stop!" said Kate sitting up at the banquette, her eyes suddenly wide with the enormity of the number of things she didn't know.

"From a dog to wealth, with God in between," Steve summarized with a laugh. "On the principle that God is in the detail, I did have a dog, a little Peke called Dinky. I had him for fifteen years and I cried like a baby when he died."

"A Peke! I love them, but I would never, ever have imagined you with a Pekingese. A German shepherd, a Labrador maybe, a terrier at a push, but never a Peke. That is extraordinary. Dinky! Not Vulcan or Bernard. Not Midnight or . . . or . . . Crystal. There you are. I don't know you at all. I'm falling for a total stranger. It was one of those things in kindergarten they told you never to do."

"Are you falling for me? Is that what you're doing?"

"I thought we were talking about Dinky," she teased, pleased that he had picked up on her veiled declaration. "Yes. Yes, I am. Believe it or not, I do not travel to England with someone and stay in a suite in a hotel with him, and walk in the snow with him, and . . . and . . . if I am not failing for him. If I *had* not fallen for him, to be more precise, to be more truthful."

"Would you like to dance?" he said suddenly. His voice was lower, not quite husky.

He looked at her with great intensity, a look that said more than mere words could. "Ditto," Patrick Swayze's character had said in *Ghost*. "Ditto," said Steve's expression now. Kate felt the bounce in her heart as she stood up. She twined her hand into his. Then she knew that there would be more than enough time to work through the list of things she didn't know about him. *I wonder how you dance,* she thought.

Well. She melted in toward him on the dance floor. He held her strongly, tightly, to "Lady in Red." He moved slowly but lightly to the rhythm, and she felt the warmth of him, the closeness. Her cheek was almost, but not quite, on his. The masculine scent of him was in her nostrils. All around them, the English cavorted with their careless upper-class abandon, paying no attention to the music and little enough to each other, although much to themselves. Kate and Steve were an island of togetherness, totally alone in the crowd, existing only for each other. How did he know how to do this? Where had he learned? Who had taught him? It was ceasing to matter. There was magic in the air again, amidst the scent of Joy and Opium, fine Cuban cigars, and the romantic music. She moved her hand in his, delighting at the warm touch of his skin on hers, playing surreptitiously with his fingers until he squeezed back with his. This was how life should be, focusing on the wonder of simple sensations, taking them one at a time, not hurrying. They swayed in unison, joined together actually and symbolically. It had happened so fast, but now it was slowing, as it should. There should be this peace, this comfort, after the storm of the beginning.

She relaxed her head onto his cheek, and nestled into him. She felt protected and safe in his lee. He was so certain, even now as he moved to the music, leading her and yet doing so in a way that made following him as natural as leaning against the wind. And now a delicious tiredness began at last to envelop her. It wrapped her in a cotton ball of softness, and she knew what she wanted now. She reached up, and her fingers found the nape of his neck.

"Take me home," she whispered in his ear.

45

It was time. They both knew that. They didn't speak as he unlocked the door to their suite. The door closed behind them, and he turned toward her. She took a step toward him and smiled. Close to him, she laid her cheek against his chest, and he moved his hand up to her hair and caressed it gently. She twined her arms around his waist, not nervous now, but very certain of what they both wanted. Then she looked up at him and he down at her, his eyes clouded with desire.

Slowly he bent toward her, and she reached up to him and their lips met. It had not been a lifetime since the first time, but the hunger had grown in that short interval. There was reverence at first, the tender touch of a brush stroke, so soft, yet able to fire the senses more strongly than any firmer contact. Their mouths played with each other, flirting, withdrawing, returning again. He held her tightly as he kissed her, and she loved it, being locked in his arms. She was a prisoner to the passion that would come, but also as willing as he. She reached upward now, to his broad shoulders, and she pulled him toward her, wanting even more closeness.

Then, with the impatience of lovers, the kiss grew more insistent. No longer were lips enough. She felt his tongue slip between her lips and she met it with her own as her heart pounded against his. Now there was the taste of him, so well remembered, wet and warm as she melted into him. Kate felt the madness begin, that delicious escape from the world of reality made possible by the touch of bodies, a drug more potent and more addictive than any chemical. God, how she had longed for this. She hadn't realized how much until this moment. She was greedy for him, hungry to have it all, to own his body, and more important, for him to take hers. But there the paradox began, for it must be slow. It must take so very long. And so they hovered in the nervous no-man's land of lovers, undecided whether to be connoisseurs of love, savoring the sweet preciousness of it for hours of clever passion, or whether to plunge headlong into the storm, glorying in the soaking rain, taking the moment and not heeding the future.

She moaned her pleasure and her dilemma as they fought to become one in the meeting that was the kiss. He was losing the battle of self-control, and his loss encouraged her to abandon herself to him. Slowly, they slipped away from their humanity. They were still dressed, humans with human dignity, but control had gone. The conductor of the orchestra of passion was no longer the suave ego. It was the inescapable urgency of the id that ruled them now.

His mouth roamed across her, his tongue a weapon of conquest and hers a fluttering flag of acquiescence. She wanted him to have all that he wanted. That was her goal, to make his pagan dream come true. So, with his aggression came her descent into the lewdness of lust. She was a thing now, a receptacle for him, because his pleasure had become the object of her passion. It was all that mattered. So she reached down and touched him where he reared against her, hard and mysterious, and she laid the flat of her hand against him and she moaned again, a sound low with love and longing.

He threw back his head, his lips moist with her wetness, and his eyes were hooded as he, too, murmured a soft sound of sur-render. He moved against her hand, growing, thrusting, and she could feel the heat of him through the cloth that so soon would be a barrier no more. He threw his head from side to side, aban-doning himself to ecstasy. His lips were parted and his breath came fast, breaking across her face, bathing her deliciously with its warmth.

Across the drawing room, thirty feet away, was the door to his bedroom. Opposite, the door to hers. They were so near, yet they were so very far. And there was no more precious time to lose in the urgency of the moment.

Their eyes sealed the contract. They didn't need language. They were speaking to each other in a tongue more fundamen-tal, in the dialect of desire, in the conversation of bodies. He sank to the floor, and she with him, and they knelt together, fac-ing each other on the carpet.

Kate felt the love explode within her. Her mouth was moist with him, but her whole body was wet with her own passion. She was primed for him, as ready as she would ever be, more ready than she had ever been.

"I love you," she whispered.

"I love you," he replied.

46

Jim Sinnecock looked out of the window at the falling darkness, his hands deep in his brown leather overalls. He would be glad when today was over, and he seldom thought like that. It wasn't the same when Steve was away. Life went on, but there was little enough life in it. He missed the moody energy of the brilliant master, and so he buried himself in work. There was time at last to do the routine maintenance that sometimes got overlooked when Steve was in full creative flow.

He turned back to the vast room. It was quiet now, at the end of the day, but the light from the furnace flickered and flared, fingering the surrounding gloom. He had had a new kiln fitted that morning and he was testing it, heating it to maximum strength and then letting it cool. When Steve returned, it would be dependable. The work could proceed with no mechanical interference. The air was full of the sulphurous aroma of new fire-clay. It was an acrid, unpleasant smell that irritated his nostrils and made his eyes water. He didn't like it. He would be glad when this business was over.

He walked over to the furnace and peered into its depths,

shading his eyes with his hands against the brightness of the flames. He listened carefully for the sound that would warn of cracks. But all was silent except for the muted roar of the extractor fans. The flames were even and a rich orange-red. He checked the temperature gauge. It was nearly there. In another couple of hours it would be well above 2,000 degrees. Then he would allow it to cool. In the morning, he would check for cracks. In their absence, the kiln would be ready for the vital business of creation.

He walked back to the area of the studio that served as an office. He felt a strange unease. Anxiety floated around him like a mist, and yet he had nothing to be anxious about. He went to the fridge and took out a beer. He usually had one around this time. Today his throat was dry and ticklish from the fumes of the new kiln. He opened the beer and sat down behind the desk, wondering whether to make a start on the urgent bills that needed paying. What the hell was the matter with him? He was the very opposite of the superstitious type, but there was an unmistakable feeling that something, somewhere was wrong.

He looked at his watch. The editor from New York, the young lady called Samantha, would be here soon. Steve had told him to show her everything, the glass, the transparencies, catalogs of old exhibitions, anything and everything she wanted to see. Maybe that was what was making him nervous. He wasn't very good with strangers. He pulled at his ear and then stretched in the chair. It was getting dark outside. He hoped she wouldn't be late.

The icy rain slammed against the windshield of Sam's Bronco as she tore into the village. After the long drive from Manhattan she was tired but excited. A lot had happened in five days. Out of the blue, she had the book she wanted, and she couldn't help feeling that her mother had had something to do with it. In all the excitement of lost ex-wives, White House interventions in Africa, and spur-of-the-moment decisions to go to London together, there had been time for some red hot dates. Sam smiled at the thought of the potent mix that would be her mother and Steve. She reached forward and turned up the radio, banging her hands on the wheel in time to the music.

It had all worked out perfectly for her. She'd had been told she'd have the run of the Gardiner studio, and Jim, Steve's assistant, was expecting her. By the time Steve and her mother returned from London she would have had time to see everything and get the outline of the book planned in her mind. It would be far easier to work with Steve if she was prepared. She was beginning to feel that she knew him pretty well.

There was the wall of his house now. It was strange. She had passed this wall so many times without knowing or caring who lived there. Now it was a different wall, somehow full of different meanings, like the driveway to a house you had once lived in before selling and moving away. She turned in at the gate and parked carefully on the cobblestones. She didn't intend to stay long, she just wanted to touch base with Jim, who would be in charge of the place. Sam wanted to get the feel of it and find out where everything was. Then, with a bit of luck, Jim would give her a key or something. She would be able to browse at her leisure, taking the whole weekend if need be. It was incredibly convenient. She could stay at home on nobody's agenda but her own. She was looking forward to it. Her mother was terrific, but when she was home it was more boot camp than health spa.

Sam opened the car door and a gust of wind took it, the freezing rain coming at her sideways. *Damn!* She wasn't really dressed for this. She hadn't brought her coat. Still, it wasn't far to the front door. She ran fast, reached the porch, and pressed the doorbell.

The sound was that of a single loud gunshot. Jim jumped up. He knew instantly what had happened. The kiln had cracked.

He was vaguely aware that the chair had fallen over, but didn't stop to pick it up. It clattered on the wooden boards behind him as he ran to the kiln, his heart pumping fast. Now he knew what had caused his free-floating anxiety. Something in his bones had told him that this was going to happen, the same way it warned him of snow and the arctic cold snaps that dipped down on the jet stream from Canada.

Damn! Damn! From the sound, it was a big one. Little cracks made little gunshots. This one had been of magnum force. What worried him was what would happen next. It might be the end of the story. His bones told him otherwise.

He felt completely helpless. The furnace could not be switched off like an electric light, and the fire would take hours to cool—hours of anxiety for Jim. A broken kiln was a disaster waiting to happen. Although he had never experienced it personally, kilns could explode. When that happened, red hot fire-clay would spray out across the room. In seconds, the whole place could become a maelstrom, a flaming firestorm that would consume everything within.

He felt the unaccustomed panic. On the surface, all was as it had been. The bright fire burned, the fan hummed, and the shadows played over the shelves of brightly colored glass. Jim looked over his shoulder at the telephone. He should call for help. It would be prudent to alert the fire brigade. He should mobilize Steve's team of employees so that they could get back to the studio to prepare for potential disaster. Then he looked at Steve's glass. A telephone call, several, would take precious minutes. That time could be used to save irreplaceable works of art. He made the decision. He hurried to the display shelves. Working as fast yet as carefully as he could, he began to move the smaller objects from their exposed positions to a safer corner of the studio.

Dear God, let that be the only crack, he prayed silently.

Jim Sinnecock's prayer was not answered. The second report was louder than the first. The kiln was going to explode.

Jim stood, frozen solid in the warmth of the barn. The second crack reverberated in his ears . . . and was joined by the ringing of the doorbell. He turned toward the door as if in slow motion. His whole world had all but stopped, and he had an age to take in his surroundings . . . the message pinned to the back of the fridge, the one about ordering less milk; the mauve and black mask on the totem column he had just moved to a safe corner; the remains of the packing case that had contained the new kiln. . . .

The ringing stopped. Then, almost immediately, it started again. Who was it? It must be the editor lady from Manhattan. Was the door locked or unlocked? He looked at the furnace. He had to get out, had to get away. It could blow at any moment. But it might not blow for five minutes, ten, sometime, even never. He should save the glass. And himself. And the girl was at the door, unaware of the impending disaster just inside. His eyes focused on the door's lock. Oh God, the knob was in the upright position. She was turning the handle. "For God's sake, don't come in!" he yelled at the top of his lungs.

47

The kiln exploded as Jim's warning shout faded away into a millisecond of silence. It exploded as Samantha walked through the door and saw the horror-struck expression on the face of Steve's assistant. He opened his mouth to shout again, and his hand was raised in a helpless expression of warning. Sam's face had time to register her lack of understanding, and then the wall of bright burning clay wiped everything away. In the weird way of explosions, it chose its own path, and the path it chose was toward Samantha.

Sam's hair flared in the gust of wind and fire unleashed by the fractured furnace. Her clothes smoked and flamed. The fire danced a mad tango of destruction as it consumed her, and in its intensity it consumed itself. It took only seconds.

The sound of the explosion reverberated through the barn, and the bits of smoking clay smoldering on the floor were beginning even now to turn gray as they cooled. But Sam was not heat-resistant, and she burned brighter than the fiery furnace had burned. She took a step to the side, and her hands went up to where her face had been. She stumbled, but she did not fall. Through the fire, what was left of her mouth formed the round *O* of a soundless scream.

48

Kate shifted in the downy softness of the four-poster bed. The suite at Blakes Hotel was known as the De Niro, because the actor liked to stay there. Even in the middle of the dark night, Kate could visualize the suite's black-and-gold Roman splendor. It was a tour de force of imperial style, of the type that Valentino and Versace had popularized in clothes. She reached out in the blackness and touched Steve's back, not wanting to wake him. She wanted to reassure herself that he was there and that this was not a dream. She couldn't remember when she had been so happy. It was their second night together, and already she could hardly imagine spending a night apart from him.

Her body still tingled from the love they had made, and the memory gave way to an instant longing for it to be repeated. Sometime in the early morning he would awake, and she knew that they would make love again then. But that was hours away. And she wanted him now. Her fingers at the nape of his neck became just a little more insistent. Making sure that he was still there was merging into a tiny effort to wake him up. She sighed and breathed in deeply. This was so new. It was so beautiful.

The telephone rang by the bedside, startling her. She felt
Steve stir beneath her fingers. Oh, God, the timing! She reached
out into the darkness. Steve was awake. Her fumbling hands
brushed the carafe of water, nearly knocking it over.

"What?" he said sleepily, trying to sit up.

"Goddamn telephone," she muttered half to him and half to
herself.

"Yes?" she said.

The night porter was apologetic. Blakes was one of the most
discreet hotels in the world. Kate could tell by the porter's
voice that he was still wondering if he had done the right thing
by putting the call through. Life-and-death situations had on
previous occasions turned into resilient and resourceful women
tracking down their errant husbands.

"I am so sorry, Ms. Haywood, but I have a Frankie Donovan
on the telephone from the United States."

"Put her through," said Kate. She felt a rush of fear. Frankie
would know the time in England, and would only call about
something urgent.

"Frankie?" she said. Kate's voice was small with alarm. Was
Frankie all right? What had happened?

"Kate? Kate, darling, oh, God . . . look, there's been a terrible accident. In East Hampton. There was an explosion. Sam
has . . ."

"Sam? Oh God! Is Sam . . . is she . . ." Kate shook her head
in the darkness. Her mind had almost stopped. She would remember this dreadful moment forever. She felt the wrench in
her gut, and with unmistakable certainty she knew that nothing
would be the same again. Her so very recent happiness was
gone as if it had never been.

"Listen, Kate, she's . . . she's alive. But she's been badly
burned. She's in good hands. In New York, at Columbia.
They've got her in intensive care."

Kate was aware that Steve was sitting up in bed beside her.

She hardly knew who he was. Her whole being revolved only around her daughter. She took a deep breath. She was already cold with the numbness of shock.

"Is she very badly hurt?" she managed to ask. Her mouth was dry, her tongue hardly able to move. From Frankie's careful platitudes she could tell that the truthful answer was yes, she was burned so severely that she would never look like her beloved Sam again. And then the words and feelings seemed to run away from her in chaos, and she began to sob quietly in the darkness.

"Let me speak to her," said Steve gently. Kate handed him the phone, as, so capriciously and oddly, she had handed him her life.

At once he took charge. "We'll catch a plane now, the first one. There are some early flights. Columbia. Yes, I know. Burns unit. Yes. We'll be there. Are the doctors OK? Craig Foster. Yes, OK. I understand. I'll get her permission. Yes, of course. Next of kin. What happened?"

Kate didn't know what was going on. Not anymore. She knew nothing. She didn't even know herself. She didn't know the silly adolescent she had become, obsessed with herself and her "growth," her pleasure, her entitlement to good times. That nonsense had resulted in this tragedy. Her mind was shutting down as Steve talked urgently to Frankie. But paradoxically, as it did so she began to speak.

"So we'll soon be together, won't we? All together." She spoke in a distant voice. It seemed like some kind of summary. Sam and Kate, and Steve, and Peter of course. In a few hours, they would all be together. But there would be a difference. The things that had mattered so much before . . . love, passion, betrayal, desertion . . . were all meaningless. Sam was the only person that mattered now. Sam. Sam. Poor little Sam.

Kate's heart heaved. Oh, God, what had she done? What was all this idiocy? Why was she lying in this bed with this man?

This kind of life should have died with Peter. Romance should, then and there, have been given a decent burial. Its place should have been taken by hard work, the love of family, duty, and sacrifice. Instead, she had indulged herself. She had grabbed at passion. She had fallen for all the seductive lies in the self-help books, that one was owed a good time, that happiness was a birthright, free for the citizens of the anything-is-possible age. Now the price had to be paid, and it was exorbitant. Peter! Peter had been the beginning and the end. His name sucked her from the whirlpool of thought. She had to contact Peter. Sam had not spoken to him since he had left them, but Kate knew he still adored her.

She was dimly aware of Steve's finishing the conversation with Frankie.

"Yes, she is. Yes, OK. All right. I'll call as soon as I know when we can get there. Thanks, Frankie. Thank you! Goodbye." He put down the telephone and turned on the bedside light.

"I have to tell Peter," said Kate. She knew she was in shock. The numbness clung to her.

Steve, too, was pale. Thoughts of Daniel were rushing into his mind across the years.

"Do you know how to get hold of him?" said Steve. He put out his hand and held hers.

Kate's mind wandered slowly, bumping into dead ends, stopping and then starting again with little reference to previous thoughts. She could see Sam's toy box. She could see her in the pool of the villa they had always taken in Tuscany. She had been impossibly blond and blue-eyed at two, so beautiful, so strong even then, too strong for the nannies. Photographs flashed into Kate's mind: Sam at four with great big glasses and a peaked cap. Sam in bed sick. Sam stamping her little feet. Sam's wide-eyed joy after she had decorated her very first Christmas tree. Peter had been there in all those memory pictures, and she must find him now, despite what he had done. She needed him. Paradoxically, she needed him far more than she did Steve, who sat there beside her so serious and so upset.

"How bad is she?" she said.

He looked away, then back at her, in the gesture of someone who was unwilling to give bad news.

"How did it happen . . . ?" said Kate. The silly desire for details was simply a forlorn attempt to fill the sandwich of grief. How could it matter? Who could say on the telephone how badly Sam had been hurt, and who would tell the truth about it to a distraught mother thousands of miles away? But sometime, sooner or later, there would be other emotions besides the shock and the disbelief, the denial and the numbness. There would be the search for scapegoats. Blame would have to be apportioned, and even now Kate knew who would receive its largest share. She would. But there would be enough left over for Steve. He would not escape unscathed from the tragedy, not through any fault of his own but because of her passion for him.

"I'll call the airport," said Steve.

He reached out to hold her, and she allowed herself to be swallowed up in his arms.

"It's going to be all right," he said, but a desperation in the strength of his embrace implied that he did not believe the words he spoke. She lay there passive in his arms, astounded that she could feel so suddenly indifferent to him. That she was naked seemed a strange coincidence. That he held her so tenderly and yet so vehemently seemed but an odd irrelevance.

And then she began to pray. She didn't know where to begin. It was so difficult to talk to God. You didn't want to impose on Him and ask for too much. She was dimly aware of Steve's releasing her. She lay back on the pillows and closed her eyes. She heard him calling the airport, making inquiries about flights.

"Dear God, Jesus, just let her live. Let her be there when I get there. Let her talk to me again, Lord. Let me hold her in my arms." She felt the tears squeeze from behind her closed eyes. "I haven't been good. I haven't believed in you, Lord, as I should. But please help me now. Have mercy on me. Have mercy on my little girl."

49

"Are you doing a Four Seasons lunch today, or the bank?" said Peter. "You look dressed to kill."

Peter was right. Ruth had never looked so demure, or so deadly. She was all dressed up and everywhere to go, but in fact she was going to see her lawyer. Julius Patowski was not a corporate attorney, or a criminal specialist. He didn't do taxes except his own, and he for sure was no ambulance-chaser. What he was, was the most successful, vicious, take-no-prisoners attorney in Manhattan, where there was some competition in that direction. His specialty was divorce.

Ruth laughed a nice little laugh and moved to the window of the Fifth Avenue co-op that was soon to be sold. She adjusted the freesias in the vase on the table.

"No. Can't afford the Four Seasons, and the bank is too depressing these days. It's funny how they know things, isn't it? They know without knowing. Reduced checking activity, home equity lines creeping upward. But it's more than that, I think. It's in one's aura, or your body language, the apologetic laugh replacing the self-confident smile."

Peter braced himself. It sounded as if another attack was forming in the rarefied air of the three-million-dollar co-op they had bought with the money Peter had got when he sold his shares in Kate's company.

"Listen," he said brightly, "it won't be so bad. The co-op market is hot at the upper end. We'll get our price in no time. Then we'll find something smaller in the city, a pied-à-terre, and maybe move to Vermont or Maine. Buy a little farm, a couple hundred acres. I mean, *that's* living. People would die for that, and we'll be able to afford it. Dogs, some horses, Christmas with real snow not dirty slush. Summers fly-fishing, winters skiing. God, I can't think why we've been cooped up here for so long."

"If I'd wanted to be a country housewife, I would have married a farmer," said Ruth. Her tone was still friendly, but it was on the verge of turning. From long experience Peter knew how these conversations had a way of developing.

He poured himself a glass of Chardonnay, looking at his watch as a reflex action before he did so. The rule was that it had to be noon. It was. Two minutes past. He put down the bottle, walked over to his wife, and made as if to put his spare arm around her waist, to embrace their future in the quietness of Maine/Vermont. But she moved away from him. He was left with his arm dangling in the air, until it dropped of its own weight to his side.

"I'm sorry things haven't turned out the way we planned," he said.

"So am I." It wasn't just an "I think what you think" remark. The implication lingered that Ruth was far sorrier than Peter, and that somehow, some way, Peter was not only to blame but would pay dearly for his deficiencies.

He walked away from her and sat down in his favorite chair. He took a deep breath. Heartache was coming. It would form in the conversation they always had. There were only about four arguments. Possibly there was only one, its facets highlighted in turn on each occasion they fought. For the hundredth time he went over it in his mind, trying to sort out the rights from the wrongs, the genuine complaints from the bogus ones. It was so difficult to know what had really happened in their life. The so-called facts had been obscured by both time and proximity, and their interpretation was nearly impossible. He tried to think of it all from the perspective of a stranger, a person not bogged down by the detail and the emotions. How would a newspaper reporter tell the story? . . . Someone with no ax to grind, just the purpose of telling the truth with enough feeling and human drama to make it interesting?

Peter had fallen for his wife's vibrant, *young* assistant. It was a middle-aged thing perhaps, that biological sea-change that sent men scurrying for fertile ground, to plant the seed that would be their only hope of immortality. Death was in the equation now, and if you couldn't afford to leave behind Carnegie Hall or a university somewhere, you could leave a few more kids. The reporter might indeed take the neo-Darwinian tack, that Peter was a vain older man with selfish genes, doing the dirty on his wife for the excitement, drama, and offspring that a young woman might bring.

But it hadn't been like that. Ruth had *been* Kate, but the old Kate, or rather the young Kate. It was to that excitement that he had been drawn like a moth to a flame. In the early days, he had been Kate's mentor. He had guided her creative genius, steering her clear of the business pitfalls, leading her like a Svengali with the Midas touch. Then, slowly but surely, she had no longer needed him. He had invented a self-reliant business superstar, and, as thanks, he had been put out to pasture. Oh, he had had everything he wanted, luxuries, respect, her love, but he had had nothing for himself. He had become Mr. Kate Haywood. Somewhere along the line, Peter had lost his identity.

Then along had come Ruth. The Kate clone had needed the
mentor he had once been, and Peter had discovered his old zest
for life. The past had become a future of possibility. It had been
but a simple step to fall in love—you fall in love with people
who recognize what you consider to be the real you and help
you to become it.

Ruth sat down on the edge of the couch and looked at her
watch. She had a quarter hour before she had to leave for her
meeting. She looked at Peter and smiled slightly. He looked as
if he had grown into the chair. It was difficult to tell where the
tweed became the chintz and vice versa. He was superfluous
now. In fact, he was a definite liability, no longer on the asset
side of the balance sheet at all. So, he would have to go, as lia-
bilities must. It was nothing *very* personal, but it was not
strictly business either.

Peter had been an integral part of Ruth's dream, and the
dream had gone bad. Their business had died before it had
lived, and now they were left with enough money to live a life
of genteel comfort. For some, that would have been far more
than enough. For a ghetto child, a school teacher, a miner, an
accountant, it would have been paradise found. But Ruth was
none of those, and so it was paradise lost. There was nothing
complicated about it. It was simply about who you were and
what you wanted. If you wanted success, public acclaim, and
never-ending upward mobility, then anything less was failure.
And failure, as Bob Dylan so rightly pointed out, was no success at all.

Peter looked across the room at his wife. He sensed what she
was thinking. It wasn't fair, of course. Ruth had bypassed the
issue of her role in the failure of their business plans. But it was
she who had been the Kate clone. If Ruth's ideas for their new
magazine had been more compelling, might the investors have
run with it? If her charisma had not been just a mite lacking,
might the cable programs have committed? If . . . No. Ruth's

answer to those points would be a simple "No," because, in the strange, precarious, paranoid world of Ruth, it was just too threatening to be wrong. Somebody else, therefore, had to be. If Peter had made brilliant financial investments and he himself had succeeded in getting the business off the ground, he would have received little or no credit. Instead, he would have been consigned to the back seat, much as he had been in his first wife's heyday. The glory would have been Ruth's, but the failures were all his, and therefore, as with a cancerous growth, the failure had to be surgically and speedily removed.

"I was thinking," said Peter, trying to sound perky, "that if we, well, when we get out of here and go somewhere quieter, the thing to do would be to get into some sort of desktop publishing business. You know, the Internet. Do with computers what we tried to do in . . . in . . ."

Ruth threw back her head and laughed at him.

He looked up sharply, balancing his wine glass on the armrest of the chair he loved. It was such a strange laugh, one he hadn't heard before.

"The Internet! Desktop publishing! Peter, are you stark raving mad or are you just going senile?"

He tried to smile it off, then laugh it off. It was unlike Ruth to talk like this. She always argued like a small-town lawyer. Her points were always meticulously made, her mouth tight, her words carefully chosen. This was a new Ruth.

"Just an idea," he said mildly.

"Peter," she said, and the expression on her face was frankly incredulous. "You do know, don't you, that you have totally and completely and one hundred percent blown our life to smithereens? You, personally, have screwed up everything. The whole damn thing. Sometimes I think you don't realize that."

This was more familiar ground. It was her tone of voice that was different. There was a stock reply to this attack in the memory files.

"We were a partnership, Ruth. We discussed everything together, even the hedge fund."

"I never knew anything about the damn hedge fund. That was your business. You read the financial journals all day long and spent a fortune talking to all those brokers."

"You thought the yen would get stronger, don't you remember? You said the Japanese were a people who cared about their currency, and we Americans didn't, because only ten percent of us had passports and the rest of the world hardly existed for us."

"Bull*shit!*" snapped Ruth. "And anyway, if I did say that, it was because I was talking long-term, and your hideous hedge fund thinks a commercial break is long-term."

"It is nowadays, at least on the nightly news." Peter immediately regretted the joke.

"You blew that meeting with Somers. That was the closest we ever came. I wanted to go head to head with Kate. *He* did. You didn't. We were inches from a deal and you screwed it up!"

Peter felt a pinch of guilt. "Listen, Ruth, people don't make decisions *solely* on things like that. Maybe the content of the prototype wasn't quite right for his marketing people. I'm not saying that I wasn't half responsible for what went wrong that day, maybe I was even more responsible than that. I just don't think I was *totally* responsible."

Peter's sense of déjà was overpoweringly vu. They had had this conversation a hundred times before, if they had it once. It always turned out the same way—never well.

It was Ruth's maddening trick to speak very slowly, as if to the mentally deficient, when she was angry. Anger was an emotion so secret and dangerous for her that it was only ever shown to Peter, and then in private. "Somers loved the prototype. He said so. Don't you remember? He said it was very impressive. Do you remember him saying that or don't you?" She leaned forward in irritation.

Peter looked at her and tried to analyze what he saw. He still had some feelings for her, but she was no longer the Ruth he had fallen in love with. The truth was that she was not so much a Kate clone as a Kate fake. She could turn out great ideas, but they did not wear well. They were derivative, spins on other people's creations, lacking that originality at the core of all great concepts. She looked great, and young and vibrant, and she projected energy and enthusiasm, but somehow it was like the fake bonhomie of a game show host. Her personality tended to fade halfway through meetings. Everybody would be left wondering where the electricity had gone; wondering why what had sounded such fun minutes before now seemed so much less exciting. The plain facts were these: He now realized that he had made the mistake of trying to have it all, and he had failed. Dynamic young girls turned into ambitious, mature women with no time for the vanities, insecurities, and needs of superfluous husbands.

Ruth stood up. Her face wore a strange expression. It was not at all the sort of look she usually had at this stage of the time-honored dance that was the argument.

"You're not listening to me, are you? You just don't get it, do you? You never did and you never will. You blew that deal. Somers was going to say yes that day. You know it, and I know it. And once he'd said yes, and the deal was signed, we'd have been in business and I would have buried Kate, believe it. But now we're ruined. Well, I'm not going to let you drag me down again. I have other plans."

"What do you mean?" said Peter. He felt the stirring of a pre-monition. "Where are you going?" he added. He sat up straight in the chair.

"I'm going to see my lawyer." There was triumph in her voice. She was smiling now, openly.

"What lawyer?"

"My divorce lawyer, who else?"

That explained her outfit. Smart but demure, designed to win sympathy. Rich enough to pay the bill, not rich enough not to need a mouth-watering settlement. Poor little Ruth. That was the look and that was the attitude. If there was a Manhattan divorce attorney who knew what feeling was, he might be able to dredge up some sympathy for Ruth. The role of victim was a specialty of hers.

Peter stood up. He wasn't ready for this.

"You want a *divorce?* This is ridiculous. We haven't even discussed it."

"There's nothing to discuss." She was so matter-of-fact. She was as matter-of-fact as he had been not so very long ago when he had done this to Kate.

Peter felt strangely calm. He would never have predicted that he would feel like this in response to a request for divorce. "Is there somebody else?" he said carefully. He felt oddly detached, like a spectator at a marginally serious traffic accident.

"There's always somebody else," said Ruth cheerfully. She said it with confidence because of course there was. Sinking ships were only for deserting when other ships were handy to pick you up. The attorney at French, Stanbury had been a pushover. Ruth had seen him eyeing her during some business negotiations they had had, right under poor old Peter's nose. It had taken her a bit of time to get him to agree to dump the wife and kids, but he was game for it now. He had had a friend, Patowski, who specialized in contested divorces. She felt no more guilty about it than a man would feel when disposing of a poorly performing company for its tax loss. If Peter had delivered the goods, she would have stayed with him. But he had broken their I'm-going-to-make-you-a-star-and-a-rich-star contract.

So she was free to leave. She even had a right to feel bitter about it, because he had let her down. He had failed; he had betrayed her trust and wasted her time. The only truly amazing thing was that he had failed to see this coming. A farm in

Vermont! A pied-à-terre in Manhattan! Two hundred thousand peanuts per year to live on for the rest of their miserable lives. Whom did he think he was kidding? The attorney at French, Stanbury who had fallen in love with Ruth billed at $450 an hour and would take a slice of his rich wife's assets in the divorce. He wasn't ideal, but he would see Ruth through this lean period.

"So it would be quite convenient if you could move out of here," she said. "After the divorce, I don't think you'll be able to afford the farm in Vermont, more of a homestead, I should think. And the pied-à-terre will be more of a walk-up than something swanky. I'm sorry, Peter, but you should have listened to me. Your ego got in your way. That's a male thing, isn't it? Anyway, you only have yourself to blame."

She turned to go.

Now the shock was beginning to filter through . . . disruption, mess, fights, the failure of another marriage. He felt a numbness creeping over him. Kate must have felt like this. But Kate had had the balls to throw the vase. All he could do was stand there.

As if reading his thoughts, Ruth turned and said over her shoulder, "Hey, look on the bright side. Kate never remarried. Maybe she'll take you back."

He took a step forward then. He wasn't sure what he wanted to do but he knew that he wanted to do something.

But she smiled again and slipped out of the door. It banged shut behind her before he could take more than a couple of steps toward her. The silence engulfed him. Divorce. No! He couldn't take it. He couldn't cope with it. He couldn't face the battles and the horrible things that would have to be said and felt, and then, afterward, the loneliness.

A telephone was ringing somewhere at the edges of his confused mind . . . Ruth was going to divorce him . . . in the process, she would probably ruin him. She had not just gotten the wrong end of the stick about what had happened and who was responsible, she had become the stick . . . the stick that would beat him.

He walked to the telephone in a trance. Dazed, he picked it up. "Hello," he said.

"Peter?" said Kate.

"Yes. Kate?" He recognized her voice immediately, but Ruth's words were still ringing in his ears. It was hard not to believe that what had just happened was not in some way connected to Kate's voice on the telephone.

"Sam's had an accident," said Kate. Her voice broke on the telephone.

"Sam?" said Peter. For a moment of total blankness he almost wondered who Sam was.

"It's possible she's going to die," sobbed Kate.

50

Frankie was waiting for them at the airport. She ran forward and threw her arms around Kate's neck. Kate burst into tears at the sight and touch of her friend. Frankie *was* home.

Kate was aware that Steve was standing next to her. Formal introductions were needed, through the tears, the sorrow, and yes, the relief. "This is Steve," said Kate. She tried to wipe the tears away, but they kept coming.

They nodded at each other and shook hands quickly, aware of the distance between them. Frankie was Kate's very best friend, and between friends and lovers there was a natural coldness.

"I talked to the hospital a few minutes ago," said Frankie, her own eyes misty with tears. She guided her friend away as she talked. "Darling, it's awful, but it could have been worse. They think she's going to be all right. If she can get through the next twenty-four hours . . ."

Frankie spoke quickly. Sam wasn't "all right." She was still not out of the woods, although the odds were now strongly in favor of her survival. But her face was a mess. No amount of plastic surgery would save her beauty. Frankie squeezed Kate close to her. She could see that her friend was in shock and exhausted from the sleepless flight.

"Oh Frankie. Franks. What did I do? What have I done?" Kate couldn't escape the guilt. Logical or not, it shrouded her.

"Darling, it wasn't your fault. It was nothing to do with you."

"Do you have a car?" asked Steve.

"Yes," said Frankie, "I have a driver waiting."

Kate had so much to ask. Whom had Frankie talked to? How good were the doctors? And what about Craig Foster, the plastic surgeon? Had there been predictions about prognosis? But most of all she just wanted to be there. She wanted to see Sam, to touch her.

Now she turned to Steve. They had talked on the long flight, but they had not really communicated. The whole subject of "them" had somehow become emotionally incorrect. Kate was aware that this weird attitude had come exclusively from her. Steve had been desperate to climb inside her sorrow, to help her fight it, to reassure her that he was there for her. But, perversely, she couldn't help blaming him . . . for taking her away from home, from Sam; for the explosion that had happened in his studio. She knew it was nonsense, but feelings so often were. And they were so strong, effortlessly overriding the silly dictates of the intellect. Steve had done nothing but love her. Such a very short time before, he had transformed her life.

But one single event could change everything, and it had. So she had allowed her hand to be stiff and unyielding in his when he had held it through the long flight. She felt herself pulling away from him emotionally, this man who had, a few short hours before, been the center of her brand-new world. Kate had never found it true that there was enough love in one's heart for everyone. Love was a demanding emotion, requiring total accuracy of focus. And now all her love was lasered in on Sam. There was hardly any left for Steve.

Here at the airport, as she leaned on her best friend, Kate realized that they faced a watershed, and Steve seemed to sense it. He drew himself up and took a deep breath. He loved Kate now, more than ever. Her pain was his pain, and it hurt him desperately that she couldn't allow him to comfort her. But he had to face reality.

"Kate. Listen. I would love to come with you to the hospital. You know that. I want to be there for you. But I think you might find this easier to face with Frankie, without me."

Kate and Frankie looked at each other.

Kate tried to find the right thing to say. There was so much, so many complex things. "Will you be able to get . . . wherever you're going?"

He waved away the irrelevant logistical problem, but she saw hurt in his deep, dark eyes and wished she hadn't caused it. He moved toward her then, and she allowed herself to be comforted in his embrace; but then, again, tears began to flow. That damned book. If only Sam hadn't been at his studio. She pulled back from his arms. She saw the sadness in his expression as he realized he had lost her, at least for now, and perhaps forever.

"Wherever you're going," Kate had said. Now she wondered where he would go. East Hampton to survey the damage to his studio and try to find out what had gone wrong? To Manhattan? To a hotel somewhere, so that he could be near her, ready to help, ready with support, ready with his love if she should rediscover the need for it? Or back to England to the opening of the exhibition? All were possible. But in Kate's mind at this moment there was no room for these speculations. They were Steve's problems. All Kate's problems now were to do with Samantha.

Frankie's driver had managed to park by the curb outside the terminal. He hurried from the car when he saw them and supervised loading the luggage. Steve oversaw sorting his from Kate's. His two bags lay there on the sidewalk, somehow emphasizing more clearly than any words that this was a parting. Frankie climbed into the car with a perfunctory farewell. Kate tried to smile through the stubborn film of tears.

Steve stood there, strong and silent as he had always been. Before, it had been a wonderful challenge, almost a privilege, to bridge that gap. Now it seemed not only a hopeless task but, in the circumstances, an impossible one. Both realized it. The future seemed a dim and distant place.

Mundane remarks lined up in Kate's stricken mind: *Thanks for a wonderful trip. . . . We'll always have London. . . . I'll see you when this is all over.* Each was more ridiculous than the last. So she just said, "Good-bye, Steve," and he just nodded as she got into the car.

But she did look back, through the rear window. He stood on the sidewalk, deep in thought, head bowed. Her tragedy had become his tragedy, and she wondered if they would ever be lovers again.

Steve looked up and watched her go, catching sight of her face in the window, turned to him. His whole life had been lived to avoid another moment like this. When he had lost Donna and Daniel the pain had been too great to bear twice. But Kate had slipped beneath his carefully constructed defenses. His heart had opened once again, and now destiny had another chance to break it. He was helpless. Time must pass. Kate needed that. And later, perhaps, who knew? But now the family would gather around the bed of the injured daughter. Peter . . . and Kate . . . and their child. If only he had had longer. But it had been just a week. He had sown deep the roots of his love for her, but there had been no time for them to grow. So he turned away, alone in the crowd, and he picked up his suitcases, and they were not as heavy as his heart.

51

Kate sat beside her daughter in the intensive care unit and watched her. It was Sam, but at the same time it wasn't Sam. Her face was a horrible mess of red, misshapen rawness. Clearly in terrible pain, she was wired to a central console where a specialist ICU nurse sat on twenty-four-hour-a-day vigil lest Sam's heart should stop and the graphs go straight with their high-pitched beep. Intravenous lines dripped replacement fluids and antibiotics into veins on the backs of both her hands.

From time to time Kate tried to pray, but she found it hard to concentrate. So she sat there, because there wasn't anything else she could do. Sam was heavily sedated, and full to the brim with painkillers. In the movies, at times like this, you talked to the patient. The idea was that they could hear you, could relate to the familiarity of your voice. Then, of course, they woke and made some joke about what you had just said, and you knew that everything would be all right. Kate's mind ran on. The movies! It was almost unbelievable how unlike life they were. And if that was so, did that mean that nobody liked life, because everybody liked the movies?

Once again she looked around, a little guiltily. She didn't want anyone to hear this. She whispered Sam's name. "Sam, darling. You probably can't hear me, but if you can, I'm here, darling. Mom is here and I'm going to stay here until you're well, and I'm not going to leave you until you get completely sick of me." She paused. That would have been a good moment for the movie joke. But Sam did not say "I'm sick of you already" or some such remark. She just lay there, still as the dead, like them in every way except for her destroyed face and the green traces on the EKG monitor screens.

"I'm so sorry, darling. It was my fault, all this. It wouldn't have happened if I hadn't gone away. It was unforgivable. I will never forgive myself for that. I was thinking only about me, and I should have been thinking only about you." Kate paused. She felt as if she were in a confessional without the priest.

"Daddy's coming," she continued. "I know you're still furious with him, darling, but he's your daddy, and he loves you so much. You were always his little girl. It used to make me jealous, but then you knew that. He brought you up, you know. I was away so much because I wanted us all to be rich and successful, and I was a rotten mom, darling. I'm so sorry. I'm so sorry. I just hope you can forgive me."

She began to cry gently, wiping away the tears with the back of her hand. She had always prided herself that she had no regrets in life, but she had them now. Whole chapters had surfaced from nowhere, until it seemed that hardly an act had not been the wrong one, hardly an attitude had not been inappropriate. She had thought that she had known where she was going, but in the end she had become totally lost.

She thought of Peter, and of when they had been a family . . . the time she and Peter had gone to Sam's school to do battle with the idiot teachers who wanted her to go to the counselor or the psychologist because she had been caught kissing one of the gardeners in the greenhouse; the times when she had totaled the car; brought home the drug addict; graduated from Brown. They were far more meaningful now than Kate's nights of passion such a very short time ago. *That* was the aberration. That was the silly mistake of a woman's reaching for stars that not only were out of reach but *should be* out of reach. God allowed you one love. It was the point of the vows. It was the point of family, the very foundation of the morality that the world was in danger of forgetting and which she, Kate, had all but forgotten.

"Sam, darling, when you wake up Dad will be here. Try to forgive him, won't you? I've forgiven him. Do you remember when he used to push you on the swing and sing 'Swing Low Sweet Chariot'? Do you remember that, darling? And the way you used to buy him chocolate all the time because he loved it so much?"

As she talked of it, the warmth came back in drafts amidst the overriding emotional chill of the bedside vigil. And then quite suddenly Kate realized that she wanted to see Peter again, wanted very badly to see him.

Kate took a deep breath. There was too much to think and feel. "When Dad comes, he can be a member of the family again, can't he, Sam? If he wants to be . . . if you'll let him . . "

"He wants to be. He wants to be."

Kate felt him almost before she heard him. His hand was on her shoulder. He stood there in the gloom, and the nurse who had brought him melted away. He looked tired, his face drained, his brow furrowed with worry as he stared down at the two women who had once been the only women in his life.

"Kate, I'm so sorry," he said, and tears filled his eyes. He winced once when he saw his daughter's face and hands, but he took a deep breath and kept himself under control. "How is she?"

Kate looked up at him. She put up a hand and covered his as it rested on her shoulder. It was a gesture of reconciliation, of pained and still-reproachful forgiveness. But he was here for them, now, when they needed him. She felt a burst of the old confidence. Peter was here. Peter was in control.

"She's in a drug-induced coma. Nobody knows for certain what happens next. We just have to wait. The face and hands are the worst. She has to have many operations, if . . . if . . ." Kate tried to pull herself together. Peter's presence made it easier. "She's got what they call full thickness burns over fifty percent of her body. She was within an inch of . . . not making it." Kate paused.

Peter walked to the bedside, staring down at the daughter he adored. Was this God's unknowable purpose? Had God sacrificed Sam's health, maybe her life, to bring them all back together again? He lowered his head in silence and reached out toward the plastic tent that separated him from his daughter. He had not touched her for so long, and he wanted to so badly, but the barrier prevented him, as the barrier of his behavior, and Sam's fury at it, had prevented him before.

"I talked to the doctor. He seems to think she's going to be all right," he said.

"They think she's going to make it, but she's not out of danger. And the plastic surgeons can only do their best . . ." Kate stared in despair at Sam's terrible injuries.

"I'm so sorry, Kate . . . about everything," he said at last. Kate's question followed naturally from that. "How's Ruth?"

"Gone."

"Gone?"

"Divorce," he said simply. "It didn't work. It was never going to. I never knew her."

Kate was silent. There was no triumph here. That was interesting. But in life you could never predict how you were going to feel. Revenge seldom felt good, yet you dreamed of how good it would be. So Ruth had gone, had she? She hadn't lasted long after the failure of their business schemes and dreams.

Kate, of course, had been kept well-informed about those. The same people who had considered dumping her for Ruth had been happy to dish the dirt on Ruth when it was clear that Kate was going to survive.

"Divorce?" said Kate.

"She just asked me for one. Minutes before you called, in fact."

"Oh, so it was just a fight." Kate dismissed it. Divorces only happened when papers were signed.

"She went to see Julius Patowski."

"Ah." That was different. Nobody who passed through that shark's door ever changed their minds about ending a marriage. The only bits of their minds they changed concerned the amount of cash they demanded in the settlement. Ruth and Patowski. They were bedfellows consigned in heaven . . . or was it hell? Peter would be bled dry, and it was rumored he didn't have much financial blood left.

"I'm sorry," said Kate.

"Thanks for saying it," said Peter with a wry expression.

They turned back to Sam. Once again the enormity of life and death overshadowed everything. There was nothing on earth that death didn't render irrelevant.

"I let her down," said Peter. The sorrow was heavy in his voice. "And you. And myself."

Kate said nothing. He didn't need her "yes." Sam didn't either. And it was Sam that mattered now. They both felt that, and each could sense the other felt it. It was a bond that bridged very nearly everything.

A voice cut into their thoughts.

"Dad?" said Sam, and she opened her eyes. "Dad!" she said again.

52

"I'll take it."

Donna stood in the middle of the small, dusty room and thought that it looked like paradise. The big twenties-style picture window had a view of a white tiled wall that was strongly reminiscent of a public lavatory. The gas fire was fifties, standard issue to the ancient Viennese psychoanalyst who had preceded her. Donna could picture him, stooped and decrepit as he bent over it constantly adjusting the gas flow in pursuit of some ideal but elusive temperature. It was not a large room for Harley Street, but it was perfectly formed and there was a separate bathroom with art deco tiles of the kind associated with Regal and Odeon movie theaters of the period. She looked down at the wooden floor. To carpet or not to carpet, that would be the question. She smiled. Such a short time before, the question had been Hamlet's "to be or not to be." Death, not interior design, had been the question then, a death not at her own hand but at another's.

"You'll take it?" said the nice young man from Jeremy James, who did all the Harley Street leases for the Howard de Walden estate. He wasn't used to such decisiveness, even from surgeons who used decision as a blunt instrument.

"Yes, I like it. Service charge and rates another two thousand pounds."

"Approximately," said the estate agent carefully. "Where were your last rooms?" he tried.

Again, Donna smiled. Her last rooms were not so nice. The reception room was small for Harley Street, but it would not have held a tiny percentage of the walking corpses who had so recently been her patients. There was no way of explaining her "last rooms" to this civilized Englishman. He would think her mad, perhaps, and recommend to the estate that they turn down her offer even if it was the asking price.

"I've been abroad," she said in massive understatement.

"The States?"

"Africa, actually."

"Ah," he said. Africa was a conversational dead end in this situation. "We will need two professional references apart from the financial ones." It wasn't hard to follow the drift of his thought processes. Africa scored no points at all as a location of previous work, as a location of previous "rooms."

She mentioned the name of the Queen's physician, an old friend, and that of a surgeon who had recently been knighted. The estate agent straightened himself up. The new affability was instant. "I'm sure you will be very comfortable here," he said.

"Look," said Donna, "would you mind awfully if you left me here for a bit? I'd just like to be alone and get the feel of the rooms. Then I could walk over to your office and get the paper-work under way."

He looked doubtful, but Sir Richard Bayliss's name was still ringing in his ears and so was Sir George Pinker's. Despite Africa, this woman did not look as if she would spray graffiti on the walls. Apart from the telephone in the middle of the dirty floor, there was nothing to steal.

"Certainly," he said. Then, "See you later." And he was gone.

Donna walked to the window. Window boxes would make

the difference, and a big Philippe Starck blind that she could get custom-made. In her mind, she placed the examination couch along one wall, and the screen she had in storage in front of it. Her mother's partners' desk would go across the corner. Two chairs, and some paintings, and that would be it. She took a deep breath and sighed. Get back into the saddle was what you did when you'd fallen off a horse. All Englishmen agreed on that. She hadn't realized how easy it would be. Someone on the *Daily Mail* had got hold of her story, how she had been rescued from the jungle, her patients murdered, how the Americans had intervened while the British had done nothing. There had been purple passages about doctors who worked in the middle of evil and suffering for no reward. In fact Donna, within a few days of her return, had been exposed to her fifteen minutes of Warhol fame.

The General Medical Council had been quick to remind her that she had withdrawn her name from the Register at her own request. She had only to say the word and she would be reinstated. As her own lawyers had predicted, the committee had found that she had not been guilty of professional negligence. So she had rejoined the profession in which she had once been a star. Now she was setting herself up in private practice, because she wanted the luxury of a different kind of medicine, medicine in the land of plenty, excellent medicine surrounded by PET scanners and MRIs, pathology departments, and wall-to-wall second opinions. In Harley Street, she was at the center of the medical world. It was what she needed after Burundi.

She shivered at the memories. Even now she could hear the shots and the pathetic screams of her half-dead patients. It sickened her, but she had been in Africa a long time. Luckily or unluckily she had become to some extent desensitized to pain and misery. She walked to the telephone and picked it up. There was a dial tone. Someone had forgotten to switch it off. Her fingers dialed the number, her mind only an accomplice to the event.

He answered almost immediately.

"It's Donna."

"How *are* you?"

She knelt down, then sat, not minding the dust on her Prada skirt. "I'm sitting on the floor of my new consulting rooms in Harley Street, and there's this telephone here and it's connected for some reason. I thought that was a sign that I should call you."

"Ah, a woman's logic." Then, "I'm glad you did."

"Why are you glad?" Suddenly, Donna felt playful. She had forgotten how serious Steve could be. What fun it was to wind him up, even when she sometimes went too far and made him angry. They had spoken a couple of times on the telephone since her deliverance from the evil in Africa. She had called from Nairobi to thank him, and then again on her return to England . . . the second time to stay in touch.

"I'm glad because you're safe."

"Not just glad to hear my voice?"

"Donna, I've got glass on the go."

"Oh, of *course,* the glass. How silly of me. I'd forgotten about the damn glass."

"Presumably, you are having a day off from scalpels, otherwise you wouldn't have the time to call me."

"And waste your time."

"I didn't say that, Donna."

Damn! There it was. They were already having a row. Glass versus the patients. Art versus sickness. Career versus sweet harmony. It was almost unbelievable. Every road led to this. They were programmed to fight. Who had started it? Did it matter? The dreadful thing was that the moment this conversation ended, they would both regret it. The warm feelings would come flooding back . . . until they started on each other all over again. It was why they had not spoken in all these years, and yet at some other level had remained as close as they had been on their wedding day. Not for the first time, Donna wondered if some shrink could explain it. But getting Steve to one of those would be the equivalent of getting him to dress up for a fancy dress ball. It was simply unthinkable. So, for that matter, was it for her, too.

"Steve, don't let's fight. I just wanted to talk to you. I just wanted to say I'm back, in my world, the old me, that's all. I can't say that to anyone else. I haven't *got* anyone else."

"I'm happy for you, Donna. It's just that—"

She heard him shout something to one of his helpers. The glass was on the go. The bloody glass was always on the bloody go. "OK, I'll call another time. When I'm in the middle of an operation, perhaps, and you're asleep. I'll call sometime really convenient to both of us. Perhaps we can have a really meaningful conversation about something really meaningful, like our divorce."

Donna slammed down the phone. It was the traditional ending to their conversations. The last months of their marriage had been like this. Why on earth had she never been able to wash the man right out of her hair? It was impossible. *He* was impossible. *She* was impossible. They were impossible. She stood up and brushed herself off. Had the old Viennese analyst paid for their call? Maybe *he* would have had some answers. Maybe, in the dim distant past, both Steve and she were entitled to blame it all on their parents.

She circled the telephone like an Indian a wagon train. Already, she felt like a return match. She was addicted to him, the bastard. She wanted to take him away from his beastly glass once again. She wanted to irritate him. She wanted to make love to him. Round and round she went, staring at the telephone balefully. Round and round in her head ran the ideas. This man had been her husband. He had just saved her life. He had persuaded one of his friends in high places to intercede on her behalf at the highest levels of the American government. She stopped. Who was this woman, this "friend" of her ex-husband's? She was Kate Haywood, the style guru. Donna knew that much. But what was she to Steve? And he to her? The question required an answer of some sort. How could it be answered?

She walked to the window and sat down. Uh-oh. Jet lag, tiredness, relief at her escape, excitement at her new beginning, were fading now. There was room for other thoughts. Why had Kate Haywood intervened on her behalf, and at the request of Steve Gardiner, artist, recluse, and supposedly single man. It was not so very hard to guess. Ms. Haywood liked him. That meant that Steve had, at the very least, given her the chance to do so. Now, presumably, there was gratitude floating about in the equation, gratitude owed to Ms. Haywood, gratitude that might be used as an open sesame to the closed cave that Donna had always imagined was Steve's heart.

She stood up and walked over to the phone again.

"Steve. It's me again. Look, I'm sorry for being difficult, and I know you're busy . . ." She paused. This was hard to say, but it had to be said. She had always prided herself on her ability to confront things.

"That's all right, Donna." He didn't sound impatient. He sounded pleased that she had called back to make things right. But he also sounded wary that this conversation might end up like the last one.

"I was wondering, just wondering . . . well, I've got a little time off. There's a film festival in Venice, and it would be so great to see the place again. All the memories . . ." She took a deep breath. "Would you come with me?"

The wait until he replied seemed almost as long as the time that had passed since she last saw him.

"I can't, Donna," he said at last. What he meant was "I won't."

"Oh," she said. This had to be cleared up once and for all. She had to get on with her life. With or without him. "Is it to do with Kate Haywood and the accident to her daughter? I read all about it in the paper."

Again, there was a pause.

"With Kate, yes."

She heard him sigh.

"If we had had this conversation a month ago . . ."

"Are you in love with her?" said Donna. She took a deep breath.

"Yes," he said simply.

Donna exhaled. Was it better to know? "So are you both . . . ?"

He didn't answer her half-asked question directly, or perhaps he did. "There's no room for anyone else right now," he said.

Donna bit her lip. But she could stand it. She could bear anything now, because she had borne and seen everything. She had seen their baby die, their love, their marriage. She had seen hundreds face slow, lingering death, and she had lived her own last moment. The damage she had suffered had made her strong, but she had paid for that strength with large chunks of her soul.

"I'll let you go then," she said. She didn't cheapen her remark with a Parthian shot . . . "back to your work" or "I hope you two are very happy." She was letting go, letting him go. She never had until this moment.

"Good-bye, Donna," he said.

"Good-bye, Steve."

But there were tears in her eyes as she put down the telephone, and then, though she thought she had forgotten how, she wept.

53

They sat there side by side, joined by Sam, who had regained consciousness several times now, each occasion lasting longer and longer. They had removed the plastic tent. Any day now she would be moved to a ward. She was stable and out of danger, but it was only the end of the beginning. She would be in bed for months, and there were series of complex reconstructive surgeries planned for her face and hands.

"It makes it so much easier, you being here," said Kate. She was genuinely grateful. Sam had always been Peter's little girl, but since their divorce and Sam's disowning him, it would have been easy for him to cut her out of his life and his heart. New wives tended not to get on with old children, especially when the new wife was a woman like Ruth.

He didn't respond directly. Instead he leaned forward, in that way he did when he wanted to say something rather serious. He didn't look at her as he spoke, which, again, was part of his manner in such situations. "Kate. There's been something very much on my mind that I wanted to say to you." He paused. "The night of the award, I said something I didn't mean. It's been weighing on me ever since. I said that I'd never loved you. Perhaps you've forgotten I said that, but I never forgot."

"No," said Kate quietly. "I didn't forget either."

'Well, it simply wasn't true. I adored you. I was always totally in love with you. I don't know why I said that. I suppose I wanted to make the break and I hadn't the courage to do it properly, and so I said something like that to make it easier. I don't know. I'm no psychologist. But anyway, it just wasn't true."

He looked at her carefully, to see how his remark had landed. That was a thing he did. It was strangely endearing to know someone so well and to find that they had not changed. And how had it landed? It had landed well. It was as if a cloud had lifted. Kate had her life back, or a part of it. She believed him, because there was a sense in which she had always known that all that love couldn't be lies. Now he had said it. So the memories were safe. All those early days had been real and valuable, not fake.

"Part of me thought you weren't telling the truth. Part of me believed you. I wasn't easy to love, and I took you so much for granted. I realize that now."

"I've thought so much about it all, and why I did what I did, and why it was the worst thing I ever did. It was because I loved you that I was taken with Ruth. She tried to be you, the early you, the you that I fell in love with in those early days. In a way, she succeeded, at least in my stupid eyes. You used to look up to me as a sort of mentor, and I was part of everything you did and planned. My God, I missed that as the years went by. Oh, I know that there was a logic to everything that happened. It all made such damned good sense, bringing in the professionals, you concentrating on building the business, me standing aside and keeping the ball rolling at home. We colluded in all that. It wasn't just you going off and cutting me out. It was the right thing to do for everybody and everything, except me. Perhaps it was right for me, too. I wanted the excitement back, the way it was in the beginning. Then along came Ruth, who promised just that. You made my life secure and comfortable and predictable; she offered excitement and difficulty and the re-creation of my self-respect. But at the end of the day she wasn't you. She just *wanted* to be you, and I was part of the process. She never loved me. But you loved me. You shut me out of the business, but you loved me. I just didn't realize it. You, Sam, me . . . we were a family. People who give that up are the stupidest people on earth."

"We're still a family in a way," said Kate. "Around this bedside we are, anyway."

"Yes, yes, I suppose we are," he said, and Kate could see tears of regret in his eyes as he spoke.

"You don't have to stay, you know," she said. As she spoke, she wanted him to, but his sadness had touched her. He should be released from mere obligation. "I mean, it must be a difficult time for you . . . and Ruth. People talk of divorce all the time, like suicide. Often, they don't mean it. If you spend some time with her, you could sort things out before they go too far."

"I'm staying," he said. "This is where I belong. Ruth knows what's happened. She knows where I am. She hasn't got in touch. She hasn't even called to find out about Sam. I'm not sure I want her to." He paused. "But what about you? I mean, God knows, the business can't run without you. Can't I stay and hold the fort, and give you a chance at least to get back to the office and make some arrangements pro tem? They must be running around like headless chickens by now. Do you remember that time we went off skiing and didn't tell anyone where we'd gone for forty-eight hours? The police found us at the top of that mountain in Aspen. They'd put out an APB on us. Do you remember that?"

Kate laughed, thrilled to be able to do so in the middle of so much agony. She remembered. They had run away like lovers,

although they had been married for years, and the business had
reacted like an overprotective mother. Already, it was happening again: the barrages of flowers, the handwritten letters, the
reassuring telephone calls, had been replaced by a stream of
faxes and increasingly desperate telephone calls begging almost hysterically for guidance in everything ranging from the
color of the new office stationery to the refinancing of the bank
loans.

Memories were fresh in the minds of her employees of the
last time Kate had been "away." During her depression she had
been there only in physical presence. The business had almost
collapsed. Now, because everyone knew that her daughter was
badly injured, they feared a repeat performance. The management was sensitized to the horrors that befell the business when
Kate's hands were no longer on the reins. Peter had it right: they
were running around like headless chickens, worried silly about
their twenty percent of the shares and their job security . . . and
they were right to do so.

"Right now I can't think about the business. It's a bit like
you, perhaps, not being able to get too excited about your divorce."

He smiled. "Yes, it's funny, isn't it? Sam is number one and
everything else is down the line. In fact, you're probably more
worried about my divorce than your business, and I'm more
worried about your business than my divorce. Priorities are all
over the place, but actually in the right place."

He was right, thought Kate. They were beginning to worry
about each other as they once they had. The Ruth who could so
callously steal a husband and then desert him when he failed to
provide fame and fortune would not be an ideal divorce mate.
The grapevine said that Peter had not invested his money
wisely. Patowski would take him to the cleaners. Peter's patri-
cian WASP equivalent wouldn't have a prayer against the street
fighter that Ruth had hired.

Peter's worries about her business were well founded, too. He knew everything about Kate Haywood Enterprises. He knew better than anyone the dangers that it could face a few short months from now. And Ruth was the catalyst that joined the two stories together, the divorce and the business. Kate's decline and recovery had been the mirror image to Ruth's fortunes. Now that process could repeat itself, but in the opposite direction. If the company stumbled, investors once again might look to Ruth as an alternative, albeit a Ruth divorced from Peter's valuable business experience.

"Both here?" said Sam.

They turned to her in excitement.

"Yes, darling," said Kate, leaning in close and holding Sam's arm. "Daddy is here with me. We're both here, and we're both going to stay with you."

"Want that," whispered Sam. "Dad? Dad?"

"I'm here, baby. I'm right here." He took her other arm, leaning in toward her, wanting absolution, thrilled by the fact that she was talking . . . that she was talking to him.

"I'm sorry, Daddy. I'm sorry."

"Don't be sorry, Sam. It's me that's sorry. I've been such a fool. I love you, darling. I love you so much."

"My face . . . everything . . . hurts," Sam whispered. "What happened?"

They tried to explain, but she slipped away from them and the pain. There was almost an expression on her tortured face. It was a look of peace.

Later, Sam woke again and tried to smile, and she said, "Stay together . . . for me . . . right now I need that."

54

Ruth sat on the vast couch and surveyed what Patowski had promised would soon be her domain. She picked up the telephone and made her tenth call of the morning. The secretary answered, and it was the secretary, not the boss, she wanted to speak to.

"Carrie, it's Ruth. How are you? What gives?" Ruth had learned the value of networking early on. She was the godmother of favors done against IOUs received. This particular girl, bright and shrewd, owed Ruth her job. Ruth had picked up on the street savvy of the girl at the interview. In turn, the prospective employee had recognized the real Ruth behind the facade. Nothing had been spelled out, but a protégée-mentor relationship had been offered and accepted, and from that moment on Ruth had been owed loyalty. Now she was cashing in a few of the chips even though Ruth was no longer Carrie's boss. Carrie had, through her own abilities, moved up the hierarchy of Kate Haywood Enterprises and was now secretary, personal assistant, and on occasion just a bit more to the chairman of the board.

"Ruth. Hi. Long time no hear. How are you? Are things good?"

The friendliness was deferential. Carrie was wise enough to know that good things didn't last forever. She might need Ruth again.

"Can you talk?" Ruth was earnest. She wanted information, or rather confirmation of the rumors that had been filtering through to her all morning.

"Yes. Big Brother is out on one of his mammoth lunches."

"I hear there's a bit of a panic going on," said Ruth carefully.

"Panic? That isn't the word for it. You can smell the fear. There was a board meeting this morning. Margaret said some of the directors are hysterical. You know, not hysterical as in 'funny' but hysterical as in 'desperate.' "

"Are sales down?"

"It's not so much that. It's just that everyone is terrified they will be. They remember the last time Kate fell apart. After Mr. Haywood . . ."

"So Kate is spending all her time with the daughter?"

"You bet. Word is she's delegating everything. The trouble is, nobody can do the job except Kate. And Kate is basically off the job. The advertisers have got the message and are skittish. The TV stations are pulling out their contracts and going over the small print with magnifying glasses. It's like a run on the bank: nothing has actually happened yet, but the worry that it will is making things happen anyway."

"So, what have they decided to do about it?"

"My guy tells me pretty much everything, especially after dinner when he's wasted. The directors have got twenty percent of the company, you know. If they could find a buyer, I think they'd sell in a flash."

"But Kate has eighty percent. No buyer would invest when she controls everything, especially when she's part of the problem," said Ruth, thinking out loud.

"That's what my boss says. He says that in fact Kate has forty percent, and the daughter has the other forty, but of course they vote as a block, so it comes to the same thing."

"What?" said Ruth.

"What, what? They vote as a block?"

"No, you said that Samantha has forty percent. When did that happen? I didn't know about that."

"Oh, I don't know. After Kate's breakdown, I think. My guy said that Kate had put the forty percent of the shares into an irrevocable trust for Samantha."

"Are they still using the same lawyers over there?"

"Yes, I think so."

Ruth was thinking fast. An irrevocable trust. That meant that there would be a trustee, maybe two or more. But maybe only one. Kate couldn't have anything to do with the trust or it would lose its irrevocable status. Neither could Sam, even if she weren't comatose at Columbia. A lawyer, maybe just a single lawyer, would in effect control forty percent of Kate Haywood Enterprises. What had been the name of the guy that Kate and Peter had always used for their personal stuff? Phil somebody or other. It had never been a particularly close relationship, Ruth remembered. He had been one of those lawyers who got told what to do and was always more than happy to do it.

"Carrie, thanks a lot. I owe you one. Nothing to anyone about this, of course. Just between the two of us."

"For sure, Ruth. And if it hits the fan around here and I'm out on the street, I'll give you a ring. Perhaps you'd fix me up again." The girl laughed nervously, wondering if she had pushed too hard.

"You can count on me. You know that," said Ruth absentmindedly.

"How's Mr. Haywood?" said Carrie, trying to notch up the intimacy thermostat. She could feel Ruth's coldness. It was something she could sense in people. It had always amazed her that nobody else seemed able to.

"Fine," said Ruth, who had long ago learned to give nothing away. "Listen, got to rush, Carrie. Remember, we never had this conversation."

"It's forgotten. 'Bye, Ruth."

Ruth pushed the telephone cut-off switch with one hand and immediately started dialing with the other. Joseph Somers emerged through a hierarchy of assistants after about three minutes. That was fast.

"Ruth," he said. "How nice to hear from you. I heard you had some bad luck in your personal life. Well, one man's bad luck is another man's good luck. You ought to go out with me and we could relax a bit. Talk business." He laughed.

God, thought Ruth, how she hated men. But God, Somers was sharp. No wonder he had so much bloody money.

"I thought only myself and my lawyer knew about that," said Ruth. Her laugh was her pretense that she appreciated the old lecher's scarcely veiled insinuations.

"I didn't get it from Patowski," he said. "So don't go suing him . . . not that anyone in their right mind would."

It was pointless to ask where he had got it. He would only lie. He certainly seemed to know about Patowski.

"So," said Somers. He sounded unusually boisterous. "Poor old Kate is under the gun again. Bad business. The word is the daughter is pretty badly messed up."

"Yes," said Ruth carefully. "Sounds like she'll be out of circulation for quite some time . . . Kate, I mean."

"And your husband, too, word is," said Somers quickly.

"Yes. The whole bedside vigil bit."

She didn't need to disguise herself for Somers. He liked her the way she really was. Ruth could sense it.

"I can tell you are deeply and meaningfully upset by this tragedy," said Somers with an appreciative laugh.

"I never really knew Sam, but I always felt sorry for her. You know, a trust fund kid neglected by her mother. But of course it's awful what's happened to her."

"Sure it is," said Somers. He let his cynicism hang out. "Not like our childhoods, eh, Ruth? Not that we've discussed them, but not like them, eh?"

Ruth felt the familiar feeling when the word "childhood" came up. Nausea. Bile. The hot and cold feelings that came and went as the fingers ran up and down her spine. She went silent. Somers had a second turn.

"So, if you aren't ringing up to beg for my body, what can I do for you, Ruth?"

"I just remembered that you were interested in doing something with us, with me, when Kate was in trouble last time. I have it on pretty good authority that her directors are spooked by her being effectively off the job, because of Samantha's accident. They might want out of their twenty percent."

"So what?" scoffed Somers. "Who wants to have twenty percent to Kate's eighty percent? Doormats aren't my thing." He laughed loudly at his "doormat" joke.

"Who said anything about eighty percent? More like forty."

"What? What do you mean? It was eighty last time. Who did she sell to? Are you telling me she sold?" He was no longer in the driver's seat. Suddenly he was hungry for information.

"I'm telling you that somebody other than Kate owns forty percent of the company," said Ruth. There was triumph in her voice as she felt him biting at her bait. "And," she added sweetly, "when I was in school, forty plus the director's twenty equaled sixty—and sixty outvotes forty any day of the week."

"Who has the forty, Ruth?" His voice had gone hard now. There was both carrot and stick in it.

"It sounds like information you'd like to have," she said quietly.

There was a silence. Somers was cursing himself for relaxing his guard. He had flirted with the demure little hustler because he wanted her. He wanted to have her at least once or twice, to knock the silly frills off her and get down to the tough, tasty nut beneath. But she was good at the game. Very, very good. She had information, and information was money. He had spent his life learning that. Kate Haywood Enterprises was a private company. Information about share ownership would not be a matter of public record.

"It may be information you would like to give," he said, picking up the pieces of his shrewdness. "After all, you're the one making the call."

"OK, let's just say this," said Ruth. "If, for argument's sake, you could get your hands on the forty percent and persuade the directors to let you have their twenty percent, and let's say that Kate is out of circulation for a long, long time . . ." She paused.

"OK, on you go," he prompted. He could smell the deal. Already, he knew what it was. He knew he could live with it, like it, even learn to love it.

"Bottom line," said Ruth. "Out goes Kate, in comes me. I run the company, you own it."

"For a wage?" He laughed.

"For twenty percent *and* a wage," she said quickly.

He didn't have to think for long. This was mere negotiating. Words were not bonds, they were just words. If it was true and he could buy sixty percent of her company, he could sack Kate with no problem at all. And the brilliant Ruth was probably the only woman in America who could replace her. Kate would be mortified, if not destroyed, by Ruth's usurping her position. Her own forty percent would be on the auction block the next day. There would be more than enough shares to give Ruth twenty percent. The deal Ruth was offering was cheap at the price. She should have asked, like Oliver Twist, for more. Now she needed to be beat down a few pegs from her opening demand. He felt the excitement rise within him. Who the *hell* had

the forty percent? Why on earth had Kate sold? It was so unlike
her to surrender control. She was the ultimate control freak.

"Are you sure about this forty percent being out there?" said
Somers.

"I'm sure," said Ruth.

She sounded sure. He believed her. "We have to discuss this
face to face," said Somers.

"Oh yes, we do," said Ruth with enthusiasm. She had read
him accurately. Right from the beginning.

"Can you get over here now?"

"What about your morning's schedule?" said Ruth shrewdly.

"I can clear it. There was nothing much anyway." He added
the last bit quickly, but he could feel himself being outmaneu-
vered in the deal at every step of its way. It was a weird feeling
for him. With a man, it would be an unspeakable. With Ruth it
was strangely pleasurable, much, perhaps, as masochism might
be pleasurable.

"Well, it's impossible for me," said Ruth. "I have my hairdresser coming, and then I have to go and see a picture I'm
thinking of buying."

She played her cards into the silence that now ensued. It was
game, set, and match. Somers's laugh of defeat conceded that
much. She had him well and truly hooked. Now she was just
jerking him around.

"OK," he said. "You choose the time and place and fix it with
my girls. But Ruth, one thing I should say . . ."

Ruth sensed the attempted comeback.

"The last time we met, and discussed my backing your magazine, I came close. I was close on that, I admit it. But this time,
if I get control, and if I put you in to run things . . . well, how
shall I say it?" He paused. "OK, let me put it bluntly—that's always the best way. Frankly, I wonder if you can run things
without Peter. I mean, he started Kate off. He gave you credi-
bility. You and Peter as a team are more than twice as valuable

as you alone. But you and Peter are mixed up in a Patowski legal nasty, or are about to be. That might make a difference. I want you to think about that."

Ruth laughed lightly. "Don't you worry about Peter," she said.

55

Peter was anxious. At the bar in Mortimer's, nobody else was. Only the tourists, of whom there were few, deemed New York's trendy energy "nervous." He toyed with the remains of his Bloody Mary and wondered if it would be wise to have another one. Better not. His mind should be as clear as possible for Ruth. Hers would be.

For the umpteenth time, he went over the events that had brought him to this place. It was almost impossible to make sense of them. After weeks of silence, Ruth had suddenly called him at the Lowell. The conversation was indelibly etched in his memory because it had been so unexpected. On the day of the accident he had received a curt fax from Patowski telling him to vacate the apartment and not contact his wife. All necessary correspondence and communication was to be routed through Patowski's office. It had been the set-piece beginning to a ding-dong New York divorce. He had made no attempt to get in touch because his mind had been full of Sam and Kate.

Then, early that morning, he had picked up the telephone to find Ruth at the other end. It had been far from the Ruth he had expected.

"Hello, wise one. It's me."

"Wise one" was what she'd called him. It was a term of endearment he had never expected to hear again.

"How's Sam?" she had said before he had a chance to recover.

He had told her, all the while searching for her angle. His guard had been way up. Obviously she had had instructions from Patowski to call him. The conversation would almost certainly be on tape. Yet, despite his wariness, it had been good to hear her, to hear the Ruth that he had loved, to hear her talking to him in the tones that she had used before the music died.

The small talk had ended with a bang. "I miss you," she had said.

"You miss me?" It had to be confirmed.

"Yes, I miss you, wise one."

Surely the lawyer hadn't told her to say that. What if *he*, Peter, were taping the call?

"You're divorcing me," he had said simply. "It wasn't my idea, remember?"

"I was upset." The tense had been the past one.

"You didn't sound upset, you sounded calm and calculating, and you were on your way to see Patowski. Anyway, I didn't upset you. I didn't do a thing."

He had spoken from the heart. He had suspected a trick, but he had already been examining alternative explanations. Could Ruth really have had second thoughts? And if so, where did that leave him? He had answered her remark about being upset in a way designed specifically to start up a timeworn argument. It had been a traditional response. If Ruth had been lying about having second thoughts, she would have embarked on the traditional counterargument: "No, you didn't do a thing. That was the problem. You just sat there and let it all slip away. You promised me everything and you delivered nothing, and now you wonder why I'm upset."

But Ruth hadn't said anything like that. Instead, she had said "I'm sorry" in the sort of winning, childlike way that suggested there was a cherry on the top of the apology. If she was genuinely upset, why hadn't she said something like "I'm sorry I put you through the meat grinder of a divorce at the moment when your daughter was burned and dying" or "I'm sorry I didn't have the decency to send flowers; a letter; to put things on hold at least until 'critical' changed to 'stable' and Sam was off life support"? So Ruth was sorry for her cold silence, was she? What else was she sorry for?

Peter had been unable to find anything to say to his wife's apology. So much had happened over the last weeks. Kate had come back into his life. And Sam. He had lost a wife and rediscovered a family, and the trade had been a good one.

"Listen, Peter. I was just sitting here thinking about you, and us. Well, for some time now I've been having second thoughts."

"About the divorce?" Peter had felt the pull of ambivalence.

"Yes, about the beastly divorce."

"I bet Patowski told you not to call like this, ever, without consulting him first."

"Yes, he did," she had said with a charming laugh, "but I'm being a naughty girl. Disobedient. Talking to my wise one because I'm missing him."

"Ruth, I don't know—"

"How's Kate?" she had said like a shot.

Peter had followed her thought process. "Kate's fine. She's been incredibly worried, of course, but she's pulling out of it."

Silence.

"Well, I'm so glad," Ruth had lied. Peter had known instinctively it was a lie.

"Ruth, why are you calling me? Really."

"I have to see you, Peter." She had been deadly serious then.

"What about?"

"About everything. About us, our future, about what's going to happen. I mean, right now I'm having second thoughts, but you don't seem to be. If the divorce does go through, I want to be fair to you. More than fair. Frankly, Patowski won't let me be, and I know you were never very good in confrontations. We have to talk, face to face, soon. Like, immediately."

Peter's mind had been in overdrive. All of a sudden she wanted him back. But his life was changing. He had Sam in his life again, and Kate. Then there was the business of business. Ruth was right: in a contested divorce, Patowski would take him to the financial cleaners. Ruth's wise one had never had much stomach for fights. Wise people seldom did, because fights cost everyone dearly. It would be immature of him not to hear her out. "Of course we could meet," he had said.

He caught the eye of the barman. The hell with clear minds. "Can you bring me another Bloody Mary?" he said.

"And a glass of champagne for me."

He stood up in a reflex action, as a gentleman would, as a husband ought to. "Ruth!" he said. They had arranged to meet, and she was on time, but the shock of actually seeing her was a surprise. He had expected to catch sight of her across the crowded restaurant, size her up as she approached, be *ready* for her.

She looked radiant. She was in a canary-yellow suit by Nicole Miller, looking more attractive and more assertive than she usually did. Peter reached up and loosened his tie.

"You look marvelous," he said, sitting down again. The whole business of to-kiss-or-not-to-kiss seemed, by mutual consent, to have been sidestepped.

"You look pretty good yourself for someone who's been holding hot hands in hospitals."

She smiled to defuse the surface callousness of her words. Peter stiffened. Despite outward appearances, this was not quite the old Ruth. The new hardness was only just below the surface, hardly below it at all.

She suddenly reached out across the bar and took his hand. "I've really missed you, wise one. I don't want to talk small talk."

Peter laughed. "What have you come to talk about, Ruth? Why do I somehow feel that it isn't exclusively us?"

"It *is* us. It's about our dream, the dream we always had. The dream that escaped us. It's about what we both wanted, Peter. It's about what drew us together in the first place." She squeezed his hand to emphasize her words.

Peter was bemused. He had rarely seen her react with such intensity.

"Ruth, you'll have to—"

She was so excited she couldn't pussyfoot around the idea any longer. "Listen, Peter. We can have it all. All the things we ever wanted are right here." She withdrew her hand from his, and held it in a clenched fist over the bar. There was fire in her eyes. He had never seen her so animated.

"Look," she said. "There are some things you don't know. First, Kate's business is in trouble again. It's a one-woman show. We knew that. It's déjà vu all over again. The magazine is slipping. The directors are panicking. Kate is out of the loop."

"She's looking after Sam, Ruth. We both are."

Ruth waved it away with her hand. "And last time, she was mourning the loss of you. Next time . . . well, the point is there won't be a next time."

"What do you mean?"

"The directors have had it up to here." Ruth drew a theatrical line across her throat with her finger. "They want out. They have twenty percent of the company."

Peter started patiently to explain. "But Kate will always have control. She has eighty—"

"Will you *listen* to me?" snapped Ruth. Then her voice softened. "Sorry, darling, it's just that I'm so excited."

He lapsed into silence. The punch line was coming.

"She doesn't have eighty percent. She gave forty percent to an irrevocable trust of which Samantha is the sole beneficiary."

Peter was still on the surface. What difference whether it was

Kate's or Sam's trust? Mother and daughter would vote the same through thick and thin.

"I don't have to tell you, Peter, that an irrevocable trust has a trustee, and that trustee is not Kate and it is not Sam. And that trustee has a fiduciary duty to administer that trust within the framework of the trust deed to maximize the assets of the trust for the eventual benefit of the beneficiary. Now, Kate can have no control over it, because otherwise it wouldn't be a gift and there would be inheritance tax implications. Sam can't touch it or influence it in any way until she reaches the age in the trust deed. Twenty-eight, to be precise."

Peter was getting there. The penny, as the English said, was dropping.

"Who is the trustee?" he said.

"At *last,* Peter," said Ruth, a smile of satisfaction on her face, "you have asked the right question. The answer is Phil Seeley. You remember Phil. Phil with the wife, the mistress, the mortgage, and the debt. Well, wise one. Guess what? Phil and I have had a little talk."

"What do you mean, a little talk? He's worked with Kate for years."

"Trust me when I tell you that Seeley has already agreed to sign over Sam's shares to old Joe Somers for a hefty lump of money, and the directors have done the same for their twenty percent. When this deal goes through, Somers will have sixty percent of Kate's company."

Peter's mouth dropped open slowly. He had the picture now, or most of it. "And then Somers votes Kate out and you in," he said. His mind was in turmoil. "How did you get Seeley to go along with that?"

"Ask his Swiss bankers," said Ruth simply. "He was fed up with being moderately rich. He wanted to join the big league."

"And what do you get out of it, Ruth? What for you? Surely not a salary?"

"Not just me. We, Peter. You *and* me, doing what we tried and failed to do. But instead of having to fight Kate, we have her whole organization, lock, stock, and barrel, delivered to us on a plate like John the Baptist's head. We take over the whole thing as a going concern. You're the managing director and chief executive officer, and I'm, well, I'm just me doing what I do and making the wheels go around."

He tried to speak, but she held up a hand to silence him.

"We get twenty percent. Somers will give us that, and we split it down the middle. Kate won't want anything to do with being a minority shareholder. Sooner or later she'll sell, and because nobody else will want to be minority shareholders, we'll be able to buy her out dirt cheap, or Somers will. There! Isn't it brilliant? I've set the whole thing up. It's ready to go. Somers has his checkbook on the table. The deal is as good as done. I've already signed a nonbinding deal memorandum."

Peter was ice cold in the warm room. Ruth was right. It was a deal from heaven. At a stroke he would have everything he had always dreamed of. He would be running things again, he would have the respect of others, and he would have respect for himself, the respect that Kate, with her vast competency and brilliance, had always denied him. He would have Ruth back, because Ruth would have what she had always wanted, the very thing he had always tried but failed to give her. Sam would have a load of money. And Kate?

Kate. He swallowed hard. Kate would be rich too. Her forty percent would be worth a small fraction of Sam's forty percent because Sam's stock was vital for Somers's control, but she would pocket a lot of money. And lose her soul. It was as simple as that. Ruth, his wife, would be buying Kate's essence, chewing it up and spitting it out in her face.

He took a sip of his drink, and his hand was shaking as he put it back down on the bar. There was still one aspect of the amazing, seductively wicked plot that he didn't understand. He was beginning to think that, in Ruth's mouth, wanting him really meant needing him.

"Why do you need me, Ruth? You've set this up all by yourself. It's your deal. You've got what you want. Why the hell do you need me?"

Ruth paused. She opened her mouth to speak and then she closed it again. Peter could see it all happen in her eyes. She had been about to tell him a lie, then she had changed her mind. Now, he was going to hear the truth.

"OK," she said. "Somers wants you. He isn't sure I can make the business work on my own. I could persuade him otherwise, but it's far easier with you onboard. So, I give you ten percent of my twenty percent. The way things are valued right now, that's worth about twenty million bucks. Plus you get to be the man at the top of the table, and you get to be the man with the wife in your bed." She smiled as she threw down the devil's gauntlet.

Peter smiled too. They wanted him. They needed him. They recognized the value of Peter Haywood. The deal was worth twenty million bucks. He would head the board. Everyone would know that all along Peter Haywood had been the Svengali who could make or break the front-women who pocketed all the fame and the fortune.

"Peter, Peter," he heard Ruth whispering across the bar like a siren voice from the rocks. She wanted his answer. He would give it.

"Eleven percent for me. Nine for you," he said.

"Done," said Ruth.

56

Time in its wisdom had eased some of the pain by its passage. Sam was better now, but, as Frankie was fond of saying in response to any better-or-worse question: "Compared to what?" The long, painful series of Sam's reconstructive surgeries had begun, and, as predicted, the improvement in her physical appearance had been desperately disappointing. But again it was all relative. Churchill had said, "Democracy is the worst form of government . . . until you consider the alternatives." Sam's alternative had been death, and there was no fate worse than that, despite what people said.

Kate breathed in the clean, crisp Hamptons air. The leaves were gone; the trees were bleak, but with a simplicity that was a metaphor for Kate's life, which had been shorn of its adornments and reduced to a more primal state. She was in storage, like the trees, but growing within for some later spring, some more glorious future summer. Little worries had been replaced by one great big worthy one, and that made life more straightforward even if it made it harder. She no longer cared about balance sheets and publicity. She cared instead about her daughter and the future that Kate could help build for her.

She rang the bell of the little captain's house that Frankie had bought the year before.

"Oh God, it's good to have you back, even if it's just for a day and night," bubbled Frankie as she opened the door.

Kate walked in, shedding her coat.

"She's better, Frankie. Foster is a miracle worker, and he keeps everything in perspective. And Peter's been wonderful."

The house was stuffed with objects. You had to move carefully to avoid knocking down piles of papers and photographs . . . original prints of Ansel Adams, Robert Mapplethorpe, and Kertész. The kitchen was its nerve center and they both headed toward it.

"Have you finished in the darkroom for the day?"

"Yes, thank God. And tomorrow I've got a day from hell at the studio, and then on Tuesday I'm on location in the islands for Calvin."

"I've almost forgotten what it's like to be busy," said Kate. She sat down at the kitchen table as Frankie put the kettle on.

"Is Peter at the hospital today?" said Frankie over her shoulder.

"Yup. He has been so wonderful. Far more than a shoulder to lean on."

"Old, well-known shoulders often are," said Frankie with a little laugh. "It's familiarity one needs in shoulders."

"It's funny," said Kate, gazing into space. "Peter has been so comforting."

Slowly, as the days had become weeks and then months, Peter by his caring behavior and support had somehow chipped away at the fact of his betrayal until it had lost its sharp definition and become merely a lump of angst, a formless nightmare, whose shapes and specters had lost much of their reality and power to terrify. It was much more the old Peter she saw now, the one she had once loved.

"And Sam has forgiven him, too," said Frankie.

Kate was vaguely aware that Frankie was making some sort

of subtle point. Her friend was not as forgiving as she. "You're giving him the benefit of the doubt because of Sam. Peter blew up once in your face; he might do so again" was Frankie's subterranean message. It had scarcely even been hinted at in words, but good friends could speak to each other on many levels. You didn't need mere conversation.

"I haven't really taken him back into my heart," said Kate, cutting in deeper.

"I, suppose I did say 'too,' " said Frankie. She poured the tea into a couple of big mugs.

"But you're right that I want to do everything for Sam, and that Sam wants us to be together, at least for the moment."

It was true. Kate had seen that the change in Sam's attitude toward her father had been vast. It seemed as if the accident had wiped the slate clean. Sam had woken to find her parents together at her bedside, Ruth gone, her father contrite. Kate knew that, deep down it was what Sam had wanted, what all children wanted, and that she had not shrunk from using her position as victim to bring them closer together. And, of course, she had succeeded. But it wasn't just Sam, it was Peter, too. And it was Kate herself.

Kate had heard the hooves of the apocalyptic Horsemen, and what she was beginning to see as the trivialities of her former life were fading in importance, despite the avalanche of faxes, messengers, and telephone calls from her increasingly frantic directors.

"Dare I bring up the question of our neighbor across the pond?" Frankie plunked herself down and passed a mug of hot tea to Kate.

Kate looked at her friend, a resigned smile on her face. She didn't come here for woolly bedroom-slippered coziness. Frankie was a friend not frightened of reality. "Dare away," she said.

"I didn't tell you, but I saw him in the village. He was filling his car with gas," said Frankie.

"You forgot to mention that?" said Kate, smiling slowly. "And?"

"You mean, did I talk to him? Yes, I did. Wasn't I brave?"

"And?"

"And he talked back," said Frankie, teasing her friend and easing her back into the cut-and-thrust world where people could make jokes and poke fun and be normal.

"OK. I give up," said Kate laughing. "I'm dying to know *exactly* what he said, and what he was wearing, and what you said and what you thought. There, is that enough declaration of interest?"

"Overkill," said Frankie with a rueful smile. "Sorry. I just thought you needed an antidote to Peter at this particular moment in time."

"Meaning you don't approve of me making up with Peter, of Sam making up with him?"

"Meaning only that if a man is capable of doing a terrible thing once, he is capable of doing it twice. I mean, if you'd been an apostle, would you ever have lent money to Judas Iscariot, even if he was working for nothing in a leper colony?"

"Can we please do Steve?" said Kate patiently.

"OK, OK. He looked good. A little tired. He was wearing a parka. Filled the car with premium. A Volvo, I think it was. Needed a wash. The car, I mean. You did want detail, didn't you?"

"Go *on*," said Kate.

'Well, he asked if I'd seen you, and I said yes. Then he asked how you were and how Sam was, in that order, I think. And I said Sam was better and you were distraught, and then he said, 'But her husband's there to help, isn't he?' And I said 'ex-husband.' And he said nothing. Then we both watched the meter ticking away the money and the gallons in total silence."

"Was that it?" Kate's heart was thumping. It was. Definitely.

"Not quite."

"Oh Frankie, please, *do* get on with it."

"Oh, yes. Interest, all right. Well, then I said, 'Have you seen Kate?' knowing he hadn't. And he said, 'No. She doesn't seem to want to talk to me right now.' And I said, 'I think she's still in shock. And maybe she feels guilty about being away when it happened,' and he nodded. Didn't say anything. More watching of the meter. I hung in there, but felt a bit pushy. But I sensed he didn't want me to go. He knew I was a messenger. Not a fool, Steve Gardiner. Not a very great conversationalist, either."

"He is when you know him," said Kate quickly.

"Well, he doesn't know me."

"Was that it?"

Kate tried to make sense of her feelings. She was coming out of something, shock, sadness, numbness . . . whatever. Her mind was beginning to work again. A little while ago there had been no room for any emotions except sorrow, sadness, and remorse. Passion and thoughts of passion had simply not been possible as Sam filled her thoughts. Steve seemed to understand the reasons she had withdrawn from him. But at the same time, he would have been hurt by it. He would have been wounded by his exclusion from her life.

She thought of Steve now in a way that she had not been able to during the hell of the last weeks. Fate had not been with them, but Fate could change sides. Was it changing sides now?

57

Kate seldom took a Tylenol PM, but she had taken one in the middle of the night to escape the thoughts that kept thudding into her brain like incoming rounds into a marine perimeter. It had become a pattern lately. Incredible tiredness at six and seven in the evening would be followed by a struggle to stay awake until a decent hour to go to bed. She had been losing the battle lately at around nine. Then, at two A.M., the demons would come. She would lie there wide awake in the darkness in some odd, listless state in which the world seemed half real, half illusion. Her heart would thump and the dread would course through her . . . nameless fears that grabbed on to anything they could until even the most mundane thought would take on the aspect of terror. Last night she had had enough and popped an antihistamine that had the same effect on her as a hammer to the brain. She had woken, drugged and drowsy, to the insistent ringing of the doorbell of her New York apartment.

It was daylight outside, not the early, dawning luminescence that she usually woke to, fresh and ready to take on the day. She looked at her watch. God, it was ten o'clock. Usually, she was with Sam by now. She reached for the telephone. But the door-bell had other ideas. Somebody was leaning on it.

She got up, grabbed her bathrobe, and staggered to the door like a drunk with a hangover. A man from Federal Express stood cockily outside in the corridor, escorted by one of the uniformed porters from the building. " 'Morning, Miss," he said cheerfully. "Sign, please."

Kate signed.

She wiped her eyes. The return address said that it was some-thing from the lawyer. God, she was tired. She wobbled back to bed, threw the courier package on the floor, and fell back on the pillows, closing her eyes. She felt awful. Sloth engulfed her. She could sleep for years. She could feel sleep creeping up on her again, but the telephone had other ideas. It was beside the bed, and like the doorbell, it rang and went on ringing. For a time she let it do just that. Then she thought, "Oh my God, it may be the hospital."

She snatched it up.

"Kate? It's Gale."

"Gale. Gale, hi," said Kate. "Sorry, I just woke up. I took a sleeping pill. It worked."

Gale, Sam's boss in the publishing division, called regularly for reports on Sam's progress.

"Have you heard?" said Gale simply.

"Heard what?" didn't seem to be a reasonable reply. Gale's voice was breathless with urgency. She hadn't even asked about Sam, which was usually the first thing she'd say.

Kate's silence was enough.

"The directors are selling their stake to Somers." Gale blurted it out, the bare fact.

"So what?" said Kate, trying to collect the thoughts in her fuzzy mind. "Sam and I control eighty percent. Who cares who has the directors' twenty? Somers won't even get a seat on the board. At a push we'll let him use the men's room." She was rather proud of the joke. Still, it was news she should hear. When the cat was away the mice were clearly playing. The directors had lost their nerve, but then they had never had much to lose.

"There's a rumor going around that Somers has got hold of Sam's shares. That can't be possible, can it?"

No, was the short answer. The shares were tied up tight in an irrevocable trust with the family law firm. There was no way on God's earth. Out of the corner of her eye, Kate caught sight of the Fedex package on the floor where she had thrown it. Her stomach was on the move before her mind was.

"Hold on just one sec, Gale."

She reached down to the floor, having hooked the receiver between her shoulder and jaw. She tore open the package. There were some papers and a covering letter.

Dear Kate,

In my capacity as trustee of the Kate Haywood irrevocable trust of which your daughter Samantha will become the beneficiary on attainment of her twenty-eighth birthday, I thought it polite to inform you that I have had an offer for the forty percent holding in Kate Haywood Enterprises owned by the trust. This offer is an all cash offer of $40 million from Mr. Joseph Somers, who will be known to you. It is my opinion as trustee that such an offer is an excellent one, and I have decided to sell these shares to Mr. Somers. The proceeds will be invested on a conservative basis in stocks and bonds to be managed by investment bankers Morgan Stanley under my supervision.

Of course, you realize that such a decision is mine alone to make under the terms of the trust deed, and I have sought to discharge my fiduciary duty to the trust by maximizing its assets as I see fit. However, in the circum-

stances, I thought it courteous to inform you of my deci-
sion.

I trust that Samantha is continuing to make good progress.

> *Best wishes,*
> *Phil*

Kate said, "Gale, thanks a bunch. Look. Can I get back to you. I have to make a call quickly."

She put down the telephone, picked it up again, and called Peter's hotel. There was no answer from his room. She called the ward at the hospital. The nurse in charge told her that Peter was not there. Once again, she called his hotel. The adrenaline was beginning to pump. Something dreadful was going on. Could it be the worst scenario of all? It was surprising how often in life it was. This time she spoke to reception.

"Mr. Haywood checked out this morning."

"Did he leave a forwarding address?"

"Yes, he did, ma'am. He said he was going back home. That's Nine-Three-Oh Fifth Avenue."

Kate took a deep breath. Peter had moved back in with Ruth. The jigsaw puzzle had perfect fit. Somers owned sixty percent of her company. She was outvoted. She had lost control. But Somers had not done this alone. Oh no. Behind the orchestra was a conductor. A conductress. Ruth. And she had not been content to steal a mere company, as she had tried and so nearly succeeded in doing once before. She had stolen the husband and the father a second time. Or perhaps there had never been the possibility of a divorce at all.

Kate felt a wave of nausea break over her. Dear God, it was happening all over again.

58

The boardroom table of the Somers Group was a cheerfully nervous place. At the head of it sat Joseph, flanked by two almost pretty personal assistants, both English. Behind him, in tweeds on some Scottish moor, was his angry-looking ancestor, painted by James Gunn; a Purdey shotgun was stuffed beneath his arm, a cowed dog was at his feet, and the expression on his face said that he wanted only one thing: to kill something innocent and then eat it. In the chairman's chair, his great-grandson had something of the same expression. It was more genteel, less obvious, camouflaged by the expensive clothes and sweet-smelling eau de cologne, but hungry and rapacious nonetheless.

Two seats away from him sat Ruth. On the outside she seemed calm and quiet. On the inside, a fire was raging that would and could consume anyone in its way.

Next to her was Phil Seeley, the attorney Ruth had bought for cash on the Zurich Bahnhofstrasse. He alone in the room looked nervous. In fact, he looked openly terrified, in the way that only those with a thoroughly guilty conscience can display fear. He knew that he was about to confront the person he had robbed of her life's work. Narrow legal arguments might be on his side. As trustee he had enriched the trust. Forty million dollars was way over the top for the shares. But the law was not always on the side of morality, and sometimes it was an ass. Phil moved his own posterior to find an elusive comfort. The bottom line was that he had metamorphosed from a cheerful fool into a cringing heel, and two million dollars in Swiss francs hardly made up for it, because he was now owned by Ruth for life. He shifted the files in front of him, arranging them with geometrical precision, as if by the neatness of his paperwork he could hide what everyone in the room knew . . . that of all the forms of life in it, he was the lowest of the low.

Peter sat across the table. He, like Ruth, seemed relaxed. By his side sat his attorney, and they talked together in low tones, sometimes smiling up the table at Somers, sometimes across it at Ruth. Once again, Peter had effortlessly won the sartorial war with Somers, and the great tycoon obviously felt the loss. Somers frowned briefly, but then he smiled broadly. He had pulled off a brilliant coup. He had won. It would then be merely a question of discovering a better tailor.

Two down from Peter was Tarrance, the ex-senator and chairman of the board of Kate Haywood Enterprises. He was flanked by Margaret Court, the chief financial officer, and by another director. Farther down the table on the same side was a trio of their lawyers. Tarrance was looking like God on a bad day. He was not relishing the arrival of the person for whom they were all waiting. He was not looking forward to confronting Kate.

Somers cleared his throat. Silence descended around the polished wood table. "Strictly speaking," he said, "we do not need Ms. Kate Haywood to be present in order to conduct the business at hand." He paused for dissent. There was none. Only Ruth seemed marginally discomforted that Kate might not be there to witness the totality of her triumph. Seeley nodded enthusiastically. Tarrance and the board members smiled their encouragement. If it were done when 'tis done, then 'twere well it were done quickly. The line from the murderous Lady Macbeth was peculiarly apposite for the moment.

"The shares of the trust, that's forty percent, have been transferred to me," continued Somers. "That transaction is completed. And in a separate transaction I have deeded nine percent of those shares to Ruth and eleven percent to Peter. I think I am also right in saying that the sale has been completed of the directors' twenty percent to me. Can I ask formally of my attorney that I am right in making these assumptions?"

Way down the table, a small bespectacled man stood up. "That is correct, sir. As of this moment, you control forty percent of Kate Haywood Enterprises and Mr. and Ms. Haywood control twenty percent between them. Ms. Kate Haywood is the minority shareholder, with forty percent. It is not, therefore, strictly necessary that she be here at this meeting of Kate Haywood Enterprises if she has been alerted—which she has—to the existence of this meeting." He sat down with a small, tight smile, which did not survive the opening of the door and the arrival of Kate.

Kate's expression, as she entered, was already a mask of anger and disdain.

"You *bastards,*" she hissed, striding into the room like Vengeance itself. She wore a black cape that billowed around her. Her blond hair was swept back from her face, and her skin was flushed with fury.

They swiveled around to look at her. A force field of electric anticipation filled the room. She came alone into the lion's den. She was without the protection of an attorney—perhaps because attorneys had provided her so very little protection in the past.

Somers rose like an oil slick to greet her. He ignored her global insult. "Kate," he said. "I'm so glad you could be here.

We had just established that as the minority shareholder you have the right to be present."

There was a lone seat for Kate at the end of the table. She did not take it. She made first for Ruth.

Ruth sat quite still as she watched the approach of the woman she had so comprehensively destroyed. It was possible that Kate would physically attack her, which might be momentarily uncomfortable but of course would be advantageous. The men would pull her off before she could do too much damage, and then all the attorneys would be witness to the assault. With a couple of bent doctors' reports, it might even qualify as a felonious assault. Kate would be arrested. They would take her mug shot and fingerprints. It would be a bonus.

But Kate did not attack Ruth. She stopped when she reached her, and stood over her.

"What did I ever do to you, Ruth . . . that you had to do this to me?" Kate wanted to know. She really, genuinely, wanted to know.

"Why don't you sit down, Kate," said Ruth with a tight smile. "You look tired. Have a glass of water."

"I am tired, Ruth," said Kate slowly. "I am tired of you and your hatred, and your wickedness. I am tired of fighting to keep what I have. My daughter is terribly injured and you use that against me to steal my company as once you stole my husband."

Kate shot a withering look at Peter. He was staring at her across the table, and there was the strangest look in his eye.

"Well, you needn't be tired anymore, Kate, because you'll have all the time in the world to sleep from now on. And you won't have to fight to keep what you have, because you don't have it anymore. Any of it." Now it was Ruth's turn to stare at her husband. She did so proudly, as at a possession, a knick-knack, but a valuable one . . . a trinket that had been essential to the dramatic success of all her plans.

This was it. The peak experience. In front of her, exhausted from the tension of the last months, weeks, and days, was her defeated rival. Ruth had always wanted to be Kate Haywood, and now she was. But in philosophy there was something called the law of excluded middle. No two things could actually be the same thing in the same place at the same time. In order to *be* Kate, Kate would have to be destroyed, not literally but figuratively. This was as near to Kate's destruction as Ruth would ever get. She had stolen her company and the man she adored. There wasn't much else that was Kate Haywood, at least as far as Ruth could see.

"I suppose what Ruth is saying, Kate, is basically true, if somewhat indelicately phrased," said Somers. "The truth of the matter is that you are outvoted, and it is the intention of the majority shareholders to dispense with your services and remove you from the board of the company. Of course, we have to put the matter to the vote, but that will be the merest formality."

Kate turned toward him. There wasn't anything left to say, or anything very much to do. Once again she looked at Peter, who was sitting so calmly in the camp of the enemy. He was smiling. He was actually smiling. If anything could have made this dreadful moment worse, that was it.

"Look on the bright side, Kate. Your daughter got fancy money for her shares. The bad news is that nobody will want to pay much for yours, you being the minority interest." Ruth did not try to suppress the little laugh that went with her remark.

Kate turned around again, lost in the sea of enemies.

"I move that we vote on the motion to unseat Kate Haywood from the board of Kate Haywood Enterprises," said Peter into the frigid silence.

"Seconded," said Somers. "I vote my forty percent to dismiss Kate Haywood from the board. Ruth?"

"I vote my nine percent share to dismiss Kate Haywood from the board," said Ruth, her voice quivering in triumph.

"Peter?"

"I vote against the motion," said Peter. "That would be my eleven percent."

"What?" said Somers.

"You've got it wrong, you fool," snapped Ruth. Trust Peter to make a hash of the simplest things. "The motion is to *dismiss* Kate, not elect her!"

All down the table there was a titter of laughter that someone, at this most dramatic moment, had made such a fundamental mistake.

"Oh, I don't know," said Peter. "I don't think I have it wrong at all. My eleven percent is *against* the motion." He snapped out the last three words. Everyone came to attention.

In the stunned silence, Kate, still standing, looked at him. She didn't understand, and then, slowly, understanding dawned. Peter was leaning forward in his chair, amused no more. A strange fire was burning in his eyes.

"My eleven percent votes to keep Kate on the board. And it also votes to sack every one of the other directors. And it also votes to pass a motion preventing Ruth Haywood or Joseph Somers from entering the business premises, or attempting to interfere in any way with the running of the company from this moment on. And now, unless I am very much mistaken, we are awaiting one more vote on this motion. How do you vote, Kate? How do you vote your forty percent of the shares in your company?"

And Kate smiled, because now she did understand. She understood so completely that her whole world was quite suddenly full of sunshine.

"I vote my forty percent against the motion and in favor of the subsidiary motions moved by Peter Haywood," she said.

They didn't have to do the math. Everyone knew it. Forty plus eleven was fifty-one. Somers and Ruth had forty-nine.

Kate turned to watch Ruth. She was red and quivering like

some small but malevolent reptile deprived at the last moment of its prey. She looked around for help, at Somers, at Tarrance, and then at the small army of attorneys who were busy looking at each other.

Then Kate's smile broadened, and laughter came up fast from her gut. Peter was *with* her. He began to chuckle, and the two of them were an island duet of humor in a room turned sour with bile and venom.

"Oh, Joe Somers, you poor bloody fool," laughed Kate. "You paid forty million bucks for Samantha's share in a company that you won't even be allowed to visit. Way, way over the top for or a minority shareholding—don't you think? Anyway, you'll soon find out how much over the top when you try to get rid of your shares."

There was method in her revenge. Somers had lost the deal, but he had done far worse than that: he had lost a mountain of money. For Somers that was the ultimate, the only, defeat. He would have to try to get it back. From where? From Ruth.

"Ruth!" he exploded. "You made representations to me when I gave you your shares, that all those shares, including those given to your husband, would vote with me. You signed a letter of intent to that effect. Isn't that right, lawyer?" He couldn't even remember the attorney's name.

From somewhere down the table came a definite "Yes, sir."

"Sue the ass off her! Do you hear? Sue her to kingdom come! I want lawyers crawling all over her for the next ten years. Breach of contract, damages, exemplary damages, punitive damages. Millions of dollars. Millions. Millions. Millions." He banged his hand on the table each time he said "millions," and each time, he banged louder. "I don't care how much it costs. I just want her to have NO . . . MORE . . . MONEY! None. Zip. Zilch. Zero. DO YOU UNDERSTAND?"

Again from down the table . . . "Yes, sir."

"It sounds, Ruth, as if you have been playing with fire and

got yourself burned, my dear," said Peter, serious now. He stood up and walked around the table toward Kate, past an apoplectic Somers.

She walked toward him.

"I had to pretend to go along with them," he said. "It was the only way out. They might have gone ahead without me."

He held out his arms to her, and she walked into them. The years fell away and he was the man she had married. He was the man who had given her dear, brave Samantha, and who was human, but who would be forgiven as humans should be if they were ever loved enough. He hugged her tight, and she hugged him back, and they once again had their world. And all around them, broken and bickering, were the enemies they had finally confounded.

"It's over. It's over," said Kate.

"No, it isn't," said Peter, rocking her gently from side to side. "It's a brand-new beginning."

59

It was snowing. Big flakes the size of quarters floated down on the Hamptons. As Kate drove toward the village, her mind could hardly keep track of her thoughts, nor her heart keep pace with her shifting emotions. Her publishing division people were already penciling in a new book by Kate Haywood, its provisional title *The Art of the Comeback*. She had left her Manhattan office in a blizzard of servile faxes, flowers, and congratulatory telephone calls from the fence-sitters who had been waiting to see who won before backing their horse. But Kate didn't mind. It was the game. She had shown she was the ultimate winner, a person who had not only second acts, but a whole string of them.

Peter was waiting for her at the house. He was spending the weekend. Back in the business that he had rescued for her, he was in his element once again, busy hiring a whole new team of top management, full of excitement and shrewd energy as he taught the company to hum like the finely tuned engine it had once been. She sighed as she pulled out to overtake the truck. That moment in the boardroom had opened her eyes. She had doubted him, but saw with hindsight that he had behaved brilliantly. The company would have been lost if Peter had not seemed to go along with Ruth's plan. Somers had already obtained Sam's and the director's shares, sixty percent of the votes. Only by pretending to fall in with their scheme had Peter been able to get hold of the vital eleven percent that had swung the voting Kate's way. Then, in the middle of the great victory, he had spoken of a new beginning.

Kate gripped the wheel tightly. The snow was thickening. Peter would be at home, as familiar as the trees that surrounded the house, protecting it, their trunks solid in the hard ground. Maybe this was what God intended. Life taught the lesson that you couldn't have it all. Enough was sufficient. You had to grab at happiness where it could be found, making no conditions, believing in no binding contracts.

A new life with Peter might work. It might not. But there would be moments. They would be a family. Sam would be home soon, and she would need them both. Youth, of course, in its boundless optimism, demanded more. Youth was fussy in its pursuit of perfection. The young wanted the moon and would not settle for the moonlight. Yes, Bob Dylan had been right when he had talked about his back pages. They had been so much older then. They were so much younger now. There was a sense in which the young were old, and the old, tired of the bureaucracy of life, yearned for the freedom that had been youth's dowry. But sadly, and heedlessly, it had been spent during the journey through the years.

Soon she would be home. It was only a mile or two now, and the snow was thickening. Peter and she would dine together, and talk of the distant past and of the future. And in a few weeks, Sam, too, would be sitting down at the family table. Wounded, but not broken, they would have survived.

One day, perhaps, who knew, they would get married again and the world would turn out for the ceremony. The guests would mutter about Ruth's suicide and the wages of sin. Kate bit her lip. There had been no pleasure in Ruth's death, just surprise. Suicide by hanging. It was incredible. Ruth's quiet hatred, for so long turned outward, had turned inward at the last. Her anger, for so long directed at Kate, had finally aimed itself at its owner. So now Ruth was gone, but her legacy remained . . . battered dreams like the cracked cities of war, intact but never the same. Evil, like good, left its mark on those it touched, and Kate could feel its scars still raw in her soul as she drove through the falling snow.

And then there was another voice, with a different message. From somewhere beautiful came the epiphany. Beyond the frozen lake was the familiar clump of stark, snow-covered trees. And beyond the trees would be the lane, fairy-tale white and hardly touched by the meager traffic. At the end of the lane was the fork in the road.

Kate's heart beat faster. Her heart beat stronger. One turning would take her home, to Peter, to safe familiarity, to security, to the memories, to Sam's family. But the other road led to Steve. His name seared across her heart, like the whip of a lash. Suddenly she was full of excitement, yes, and fear of the unknown. She felt life hurry through her, sensed resignation fade, found the rush of courage to question the cozy complacency of a Peter Haywood future. What was there but this one life? What rule decreed that it should be lived for others? Whose lie was it that one should fade gracefully, not ride triumphantly, into the sunset?

And then Kate was there, and she knew she must stop. She knew she must stop at the fork in the road.

Steve had not gone away. As guilt, and shock, and the chaos of Sam's accident subsided, the memories of him had returned to the spotlit center of her heart. He would be there now, waiting perhaps as Peter was waiting, although not expecting her as Peter was. Her body was on fire again as she dared to remember the passion. They had found the borders of a great love. They had not had time to cross them. As the adrenaline rushed through her, Kate hurtled toward the fork in the road, and she reached out with her foot for the brake.

What would she do? Which way would she go? Kate did not know.

60

He opened the door. She knew she was dusted with snow, and that her expression was of anticipation and doubt. She looked up at him as if she would find the answer to her dilemma in his face.

"Kate," he said simply. That familiar voice, that so well known inflection.

"I . . . I . . . have something to say," she said. But she didn't know what it was. She only knew that something had to be said. Something had to be done. She was torn in two at the most crucial moment of her life.

She could see the concern in his eyes. He did not know what she was going to say any more than she did. His future hung in the balance like hers.

"Come in," he said.

"Oh, Steve," she said, and she fell into his arms. He held her tight, as if shoring up a dam that might burst and shower him with sorrow. It was a hug of love and of helplessness. Had she come to say yes? Or had she come to say no?

"Kate. Kate. I've missed you so much. I've thought about you. Every minute. Every . . ."

"I know. I know," she said. Her eyes glistened with tears as she looked up at him.

"I didn't forget you," she whispered. "You were always there."

He looked down at her with the desperation of the damned. Which way would it go?

"I love you. You know that, don't you? I love you so much, Steve." A tear squeezed from her eye and she trembled on the edge of her future.

"Sam," she said, ". . . and Peter. They need me. I promised . . . so long ago." Her tears ran free and his arms tightened around her.

And so, as they do, the decision made itself. Kate hardly knew that she was making it. "I have to stay with them, my darling." She reached up and touched his cheek.

She felt him release her. He was too proud to argue, too strong to beg. He would let her go, as once before he had let Donna go, and perhaps he would remember her in the way that he had never forgotten his wife. . . .

"You're a part of me," he said. "You always will be."

She nodded in his arms, trying to smile through the tears. "It's so unfair," she said, shaking her head. "So unfair."

She backed toward the still-open door. He did not follow her, and she turned and walked away from him into the cold whiteness.

More Women's Fiction From Kensington